An Amish
Market

OTHER NOVELS BY THE AUTHORS

AMY CLIPSTON

THE AMISH HEIRLOOM SERIES

The Forgotten Recipe

The Courtship Basket
(Available July 2016)

THE HEARTS OF THE LANCASTER GRAND HOTEL SERIES

A Hopeful Heart

A Mother's Secret

A Dream of Home

A Simple Prayer

THE KAUFFMAN AMISH BAKERY SERIES

A Gift of Grace

A Promise of Hope

A Place of Peace

A Life of Joy

A Season of Love

A Plain and Simple Christmas

Naomi's Gift

NOVELLAS

A Spoonful of Love included in An Amish Kitchen

A Son for Always included in An Amish Cradle

Naomi's Gift included in An Amish Christmas Gift

YOUNG ADULT

Roadside Assistance

Destination Unknown

Miles from Nowhere

Reckless Heart

NONFICTION

A Gift of Love

KATHLEEN FULLER

THE AMISH OF BIRCH CREEK

A Reluctant Bride

An Unbroken Heart
(Available March 2016)

THE MIDDLEFIELD AMISH NOVELS

A Faith of Her Own

THE MIDDLEFIELD FAMILY NOVELS

Treasuring Emma

Faithful to Laura

Letters to Katie

An Amish Market

Four Novellas

Amy Clipston, Kathleen Fuller, Kelly Irvin, and Vannetta Chapman

THOMAS NELSON
Since 1798

Published in Nashville, Tennessee, by Thomas Nelson. Thomas Nelson is a registered trademark of HarperCollins Christian Publishing, Inc.

Thomas Nelson titles may be purchased in bulk for educational, business, fund-raising, or sales promotional use. For information, please e-mail SpecialMarkets@ThomasNelson.com.

Scripture quotations are taken from the King James Bible, Holy Bible, New International Version®, NIV®. Copyright © 1973, 1978, 1984, 2011 by Biblica, Inc.™ Used by permission of Zondervan. All rights reserved worldwide. www.zondervan.com. The "NIV" and "New International Version" are trademarks registered in the United States Patent and Trademark Office by Biblica, Inc.™ and the New King James Version®. © 1982 by Thomas Nelson. Used by permission. All rights reserved.

Publisher's Note: This novel is a work of fiction. Names, characters, places, and incidents are either products of the author's imagination or used fictitiously. All characters are fictional, and any similarity to people living or dead is purely coincidental.

Library of Congress Cataloging-in-Publication Data

An Amish market : four novellas / Amy Clipston, Kathleen Fuller, Kelly Irvin, Vannetta Chapman.
pages cm
ISBN 978-0-529-11868-4 (paperback)
 1. Amish--Fiction. 2. Christian fiction, American. I. Clipston, Amy. Lovebirds. II. Fuller, Kathleen. A bid for love. III. Irvin, Kelly. Sweeter than honey. IV. Chapman, Vannetta. Love in store.
PS648.A45A43 2016
813'.01083823--dc23
2015032144

Printed in the United States of America

16 17 18 19 20 RRD 6 5 4 3 2 1

CONTENTS

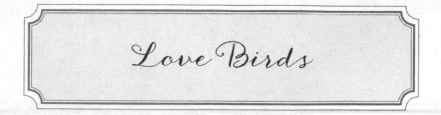

Love Birds

AMY CLIPSTON

For my awesome sons, Zac and Matt, with love

GLOSSARY

ach—oh

appeditlich—delicious

bedauerlich—sad

bruder—brother

daadi—granddad

danki—thank you

dat—dad

Dummle!—Hurry!

friend/freinden—friend/friends

froh—happy

gern gschehne—you're welcome

gut—good

gut nacht—good night

haus—house

Hoi!—Get back here!

kaffi—coffee

kind/kinner—child/children

liewe—love, a term of endearment

maed/maedel—young women, girls/young woman

mamm—mom

mammi—grandma

mei—my

mutter—mother

onkel—uncle

schee—pretty

schmaert—smart

schweschder/schweschdere—sister/sisters

Was iss letz?—What's wrong?

Wie geht's—How do you do? *or* Good day!

wunderbaar—wonderful

ya—yes

*The German dialect spoken by the Amish is not a written language and varies depending on the location and origin of the settlement. These spellings are approximations. Most Amish children learn English after they start school. They also learn High German, which is used in their Sunday services.

AMISH HEIRLOOM FAMILY TREES

Martha "Mattie" m. Leroy Fisher

Veronica Rachel Emily

Annie m. Elam Huyard

Jason Stephen

Tillie m. Henry (Hank) Ebersol

Margaret m. Abner *(Deceased)* Lapp

Seth (Deceased) Ellie

Fannie Mae m. Titus Dienner *(Bishop)*

Lindann

Susannah m. Timothy Beiler

David Irma Rose Beiler Smucker

Irma Rose m. Melvin Smucker

Sarah

CHAPTER 1

Ellie Lapp hummed to herself as she hung her freshly washed laundry on the line that stretched from the back porch to the barn. The warm May afternoon air filled her lungs and the sun kissed her cheeks as she clipped her and her mother's dresses onto the line to dry.

It was still so strange not to see Seth's trousers and shirts among the clothes she had laundered in the wringer washer earlier. She had to remind herself that she no longer had to care for his laundry, not since he'd died a month ago in an accident at the shed company where he worked.

One month ago. She shivered despite the warm spring breeze. How could it have been that long already?

It seemed like only yesterday that her big brother was talking and chuckling at the dinner table, sharing a joke or funny stories from his day spent building sheds. As though it was only yesterday that he called her "Squirt" instead of Ellie. Only yesterday that she was working in her garden when he threatened to drench her with water from her watering can if she didn't laugh at one of his silly jokes.

But now Seth was gone, and since her father had died fourteen years ago when she was only five, Ellie and her mother were left alone in the too-big and too-quiet house on their small farm.

"Ellie!" Her mother, Margaret, sounded urgent as she appeared in the doorway behind her. "Daisy escaped the pasture fence again. *Dummle!*"

Ellie turned her head toward the gate leading to the small pasture and saw it was wide open. And Daisy the cow was trotting toward the road.

"*Ach*, no!" she muttered under her breath. Then she took off running after the cow, shouting, "*Hoi! Hoi!*" On several occasions she and Seth had retrieved wandering cows with the help of the neighbor's dog, Spike, and she longed for both Seth and Spike's help now. Corralling a cow was not easy when it was a one-person job.

Ellie dodged puddles from last night's rain as she closed in on Daisy.

"Daisy!" she shouted. "Daisy! *Hoi! Hoi!*"

She tried to mimic Seth's method of catching disobedient cows. She rushed closer, determined to get ahead of the animal and direct her back to the pasture.

As Ellie closed in on Daisy, her feet began to slide. She realized too late that she'd run right into a puddle. And, much to her dismay, her feet flew out from under her. She landed on her bottom in a puddle with a loud *splat*. When she looked down, she saw her purple dress, apron, stockings, and shoes were covered in dark brown mud.

"Ellie!" a male voice called behind her.

Ellie looked over her shoulder and saw Lloyd Blank, one of Seth's best friends from school, loping toward her.

Members of the community, along with Seth's friends, had been taking turns coming over to help Ellie and her mother with the animals since Seth's death. Seth's friends were pleasant to Ellie, but Lloyd was the only one who had always taken the time to acknowledge her. And Ellie had had a secret crush on him since she was a preteen. She'd never told anyone, not even her closest friends, especially not Lloyd's sister Rebecca, that she liked him. It was a far-fetched dream to believe Lloyd would ever consider her more than an acquaintance since she was the same age as Rebecca.

Now here she sat in a puddle as his lean, six-foot-two frame, brown hair, and powder-blue eyes that reminded her of the brilliant sky in springtime raced toward her. The sleeves on his blue button-down shirt were rolled up on his arms to just above his elbows, revealing the muscles he'd developed from working on the Blank farm.

Ellie fought the urge to cover her face with her hands as humiliation rained down on her. The boy she'd liked for years had managed to see her at her absolute worst. *Could this day get any worse?*

When he reached her, Lloyd's lip twitched as if he were holding back a smile. "Are you all right?"

"*Ya*, I'm okay." Ellie's cheeks heated with embarrassment. "I didn't see the puddle."

"Need help?" A smile spread across Lloyd's face as he held out his hand. At least her hands were still free of mud.

"*Ya,*" Ellie muttered, taking the outstretched hand. "*Danki.*"

He gently lifted her to her feet as if she weighed only a few pounds. She longed to find someplace to hide away from his sparkling eyes. But instead she glided her hands down her apron, making mud splatter to the ground, then craned her neck to peer past him. "Daisy is getting away!"

"I'll get her before she reaches the road," Lloyd said. "You stand ready at the gate." Lloyd followed the cow and Ellie ran to the fence. Her apron and dress felt heavier with the mud weighing them down, to say nothing of her shoes.

She turned to see Lloyd had caught up with Daisy and was waving his arms wildly, yelling "*Hoi! Hoi!*" as he herded her back toward the pasture. Ellie silently marveled at his skill as he commanded the cow. He was an expert, just as Seth had been.

Daisy trotted into the pasture, and Lloyd helped Ellie shut the heavy gate before turning to look at her.

"You have some mud on your cheek," he said with a grin. He looked like he was about to touch her face, but instead he pointed. "It's right there."

Ellie brushed her hand across her cheek. "Did I get it?"

Lloyd shook his head. "You smeared it."

Ellie swiped her hand over her cheek again, but knew she'd probably only made it worse.

"This lock needs to be repaired," Lloyd said, now studying the latch. "I'll work on that today."

"*Danki.*" Ellie gnawed her lower lip. She wanted to thank him for helping with Daisy, too, but she didn't want to gush. "I'm glad you came along when you did. I clearly wasn't going to be able to persuade her to come back. Seth was the expert when it came to herding cows."

Lloyd looked up from the latch. "You were doing fine until the mud got the best of you." His blue eyes sparkled with amusement. "I'm *froh* I could help."

"*Mamm* and I appreciate all you're doing for the farm," she said as she rested a hand on the fence. "You're a tremendous help."

"I haven't done much." Lloyd fiddled with the latch again. "I wish I could do more, but I'm busy with my chores at home too."

"I understand." Ellie searched for another subject to prolong the interaction. "I heard the youth gathering is at your parents' *haus* Sunday night."

"*Ya.*" Lloyd leaned against the fence. "Rebecca and Marie are excited. They've been cleaning like crazy."

"It will be fun." When he responded with an unenthusiastic shrug, she was alarmed. "You'll be there, right?" She wanted to kick herself as the words spilled from her lips. Why did she have to sound so immature and eager?

"I suppose I'll be around somewhere since I live there." He lifted his straw hat and raked his hand through his dark hair. "I don't know if I'll mingle since I'll be the oldest person there—other than my folks, of course. Twenty-four is too old for that."

"That's not true," she insisted. "You're not too old to be a part of the youth group. You can still be an active member."

He smiled. "I'd make a better chaperone, but thanks for the encouragement."

"Seth used to go," Ellie continued, hoping to change his mind. "He and Veronica would stop by sometimes."

"That's true. He mentioned that a few times." He seemed to agree with her only to avoid further discussion. "So maybe I'll see you there."

"Okay." Ellie hoped he would.

"I guess I'd better work on this latch." Lloyd gestured toward the largest barn. "Are Seth's tools still in there?"

"*Ya*, they are."

"I'll fix this so Daisy doesn't try to escape again." His eyes moved to her dress. "You probably want to get cleaned up."

"Oh, right." She'd almost forgotten about the mud while they were talking, and she found herself feeling self-conscious once again.

"I'll see you later, Squirt." Lloyd grinned at her.

Ellie pursed her lips. Why did he have to ruin the moment?

"My name is Ellie. I'm too grown up to be called Squirt." She squared her shoulders and started toward the house as tears threatened her eyes. Ellie was still just a child in his eyes. Why couldn't Lloyd see her as one of his peers? After washing some of the mud off at the outdoor pump, she rushed up the back steps and into the mudroom with renewed humiliation.

She blew out a deep sigh as she sat on a bench to take off her shoes. She was being silly. After all, Squirt was the nickname Seth liked to call her. Lloyd knew that.

Mamm came into the mudroom. "Ellie! You're a mess! What happened?"

"I fell in a puddle," Ellie said, her voice quaking. "But Lloyd was able to stop Daisy. She's back in the pasture, and he's going to fix the latch on the gate."

"Oh, good." *Mamm* clicked her tongue. "I suppose we'll need to get the wringer washer going again for your clothes."

"*Ya*, you're right." Ellie pulled off her apron as her mother disappeared into the kitchen. She looked out the window to the pasture fence where Lloyd was already working on the gate.

Disappointment stole over her. She'd managed to look immature in front of Lloyd, the only boy she'd ever cared about.

"Why aren't you going to get changed?" *Mamm* called from the kitchen.

"I am. I'll be right back."

Ellie walked to the stairs and climbed to the second floor. As she reached the landing, her glance fell on the closed door leading to Seth's room, and she stopped. She took a shaky breath as she stared at the door, her hands trembling.

The familiar sadness crept in. She hadn't seen the inside of her brother's room since the day of the accident, and the door called to her, inviting her to step inside and see the only tangible things he'd left behind.

She turned the knob and slowly opened the door. Both the stale air and her grief nearly overcame her as she stepped into the room. Her eyes filled with tears as she imagined Seth grinning at her as he stood near the window. His smile always lit up a room. Six years her senior, Seth had been tall and lean, towering over her by four inches. He'd become her protector and surrogate father after their father had died from a massive heart attack.

But now Seth, with the same seafoam-green eyes and sandy blond hair their mother had passed on to Ellie, was gone too. Her lower lip trembled and tears spilled onto her cheeks.

Ellie scanned the room, taking in all of Seth's things. Nothing had been disturbed since the accident. Her mother had avoided this room too. Seth's dresser stood in the corner with his favorite trinkets lined up on top of it, including the wooden sign that said *Love*. Veronica, his fiancée, had given it to him on

Valentine's Day. The pegs on the wall held his jackets, and with the closet door cracked open, she spotted his trousers hanging there.

Her thoughts turned to Veronica, and a lump filled her throat as the events of the day of the accident assaulted her mind. Ellie had been baking when she'd heard a knock on the door and left the kitchen to see who it was. The bishop was on the front porch, telling her mother there had been a terrible accident. Her blood ran cold as he explained that Seth's boss had called him. Seth had fallen from the rafters of a shed. Ellie moved closer to her mother as the bishop explained that EMTs had come to the shop, but there was nothing they could do for Seth; he was already gone. They called the coroner, and Seth's body was going to be brought to their house. Her mother had dissolved into tears in Ellie's arms, and all Ellie could think about was how to tell Veronica.

Ellie called Veronica and managed to tell her to come to their house as soon as she could, but when Veronica and her father had arrived, and she asked Ellie what had happened, the reality of the situation flooded Ellie's soul. Her voice broke on a sob as she told Seth's fiancée he was dead.

In an instant, all their lives had been changed forever because their precious Seth was gone.

Ellie and her mother moved in a fog during the next couple of weeks. Before Ellie knew it, Seth was buried, and she and her mother were going through the motions of each day, doing their best to keep their little farm running without Seth to help with the animals. She was thankful for his friends and their family members who came by to assist with the chores, and for all the meals their community provided as they grieved. But how would they continue to pay for their household expenses without Seth's paycheck from the shed company? Her mother hadn't talked about that yet, but it wouldn't be long before they'd have to. Ellie knew her mother was downplaying their financial need when people asked if they needed help. Her mother didn't want to burden anyone, but Ellie suspected the time would come soon when they would have to face reality.

She stood and crossed the room to the window. After raising the green shade, she unlocked and lifted the window, sending a stream of warm, sweet air bursting into the stagnant room. She pushed away memories of her brother and then hurried to her own room to change clothes.

◦◦◦

"Let's figure out what we want to have for supper." Ellie crossed the small kitchen to the propane-powered refrigerator later that afternoon. "What sounds *gut* to you, *Mamm*? I think we still have some—"

A knock sounded on the back door.

"I'll get that." Ellie hurried through the mudroom and found their neighbor, Sadie Esh, standing on the back porch, holding a covered dish. "Sadie," she said, opening the door wider to let Sadie step in. "*Wie geht's?*"

Sadie was a few inches taller than Ellie, so Ellie had to look up at the plump woman with graying brown hair and brown eyes.

"Hi, Ellie." Sadie followed Ellie into the kitchen. A delicious aroma filled the room.

"How are you, Margaret?"

"I'm doing all right." *Mamm* gave her a sad smile. "How have you been?"

"Fine, fine." Sadie placed the covered dish on the table. "I brought you supper."

"Oh, Sadie." *Mamm* lifted the lid and examined the chicken and dumplings. "It looks and smells *appeditlich*."

"*Danki*, Sadie." Ellie moved to the stove. "Would you like a cup of tea?"

"Oh, no, thank you." Sadie gestured toward the back door. "I can't stay. I have to help Katie pack."

"Pack?" Ellie asked. "Where is she going?"

"She decided to go to Ohio to spend time with my niece, Clara." Sadie rested her hand on the back of one of the wooden dinette chairs. "Just last week, Clara had her third baby in less than four years, so she's looking for some help. Katie is eager to get out there and spend some time with her cousins. I'm going to miss her, but she'll have fun."

"Oh my," Margaret said with a smile. "It sounds like Clara has her hands full, *ya*?"

"*Ya*, that's true." Sadie shook her head. "So now her boss, Gene Rider, is scrambling to find a replacement for Katie at his gift shop in town. Katie was working there part time up until yesterday. If you know anyone who is looking for a part-time job, let me know. He asked me to check around."

"What shop is that?" Ellie asked as she leaned against the kitchen counter beside her.

"The Bird-in-Hand Gifts and Treasures shop up on Old Philadelphia Pike, across from the Farmers' Market," Sadie said.

"That's the shop that has the *schee* ornaments made out of metal, right?" Ellie asked.

"*Ya*, that's right." Sadie nodded.

"That's a busy place," *Mamm* chimed in. "Whenever I'm in town, I see lots of tourists going in and out of there."

"Katie really liked working there," Sadie continued. "She said Gene is very nice, and he has always been flexible with her schedule."

An idea ignited in Ellie's mind. She needed to find a place to work as a way to contribute at least a fraction of what Seth used to earn. Maybe Bird-in-Hand Gifts and Treasures would give her the flexibility to work while still helping out at home.

"That sounds *wunderbaar*," Ellie said, contemplating the opportunity. Would *Mamm* permit her to take the job?

"Well, I have to get going," Sadie said, starting back through the mudroom. "I'll stop by to visit again soon."

Ellie and *Mamm* followed Sadie to the door and thanked her again as she left.

"Wasn't that nice of Sadie to bring us a meal? Our neighbors have been so kind." *Mamm* opened the cabinets and fetched two plates. "It smells fantastic."

"*Ya*." Ellie lifted utensils from a drawer and brought them to the table. "I can't wait to try it."

They sat at the table and, after silent prayer, scooped the chicken and dumplings onto their plates.

"This is *wunderbaar*," *Mamm* said. "Sadie is a very *gut* cook."

"She is." But Ellie only moved a dumpling around on her plate as she considered asking *Mamm* about the job.

"Is something on your mind, *mei liewe*?" *Mamm* asked.

Ellie placed her fork on the corner of her plate and wished her expression wasn't so transparent. "I want to ask you something."

"What's that?" *Mamm* said, then dabbed her mouth with a paper napkin.

"I was thinking about Katie's former job at Bird-in-Hand Gifts and Treasures. I think I may want to look into it." When her mother's expression clouded with confusion, Ellie pressed on. "I need to find a part-time job, and it sounds like working there would be ideal."

"You want to get a job?" *Mamm's* fork paused in midair as she studied Ellie.

"*Ya.*" Ellie fingered her own napkin. "I need to contribute more now that Seth is gone."

Mamm put her fork on the table and her expression warmed. "Ellie, you know my brothers have been paying the mortgage since your *dat* passed away."

"I know that, but Seth took care of everything else." Ellie's stomach tightened. "You don't have to protect me from the truth. I'm an adult, and I understand the situation we're in. I don't know what you've been thinking we'd do about our other expenses, *Mamm*, but my getting a job only makes sense."

Her mother's eyes misted, and a lump swelled in Ellie's throat. *Please don't cry*, Mamm. *Please don't cry.*

"I'll just work a couple of days each week," Ellie pressed on. "It will be enough to help with groceries, and probably anything else we need. We'll be frugal. But now that Seth is gone, I need to take care of you."

"But you've never worked in a store. And besides, it's not your responsibility to take care of me," *Mamm* said softly as she touched Ellie's shoulder. "We will be fine, and we'll take care of each other."

"How? What are we going to do when people stop bringing us meals?" Ellie asked. "We won't even have money to buy food without Seth's income—unless we have money I don't know about. Do we?"

Mamm shook her head. "No. At least not enough to last. You're right. But I haven't wanted to burden you with it. I thought God would provide somehow."

"Please, *Mamm*." Ellie's voice quavered. "I really want to do this. I want to do this for *us*. Maybe this *is* how God is providing. If it doesn't work out, if some other option comes up, then I'll quit." She held her breath as she waited for her mother's approval.

Mamm sighed, and then smiled. "All right. If it will make you *froh* to get this job, then I give you my blessing."

Ellie smiled, excited. "*Danki, Mamm*. I know this will be *gut* for us both."

CHAPTER 2

Lloyd Blank closed the barn door later that evening and started toward the large, white farmhouse where he'd lived since he was born. He yawned, and every muscle in his body ached from the work he'd accomplished since he'd risen at dawn. After completing his morning chores at his father's farm, he'd headed to the Lapp place. Although he was worn out from the extra work, he was thankful that his father allowed him the time to help Margaret Lapp.

When Seth died, Lloyd and several of Seth's friends promised Margaret they would all help with chores, and Lloyd had kept his promise. In honor of Seth, he longed to spend more than a couple of afternoons a week helping Margaret. But he had too much responsibility at home. Since he was the only son, Lloyd was expected to keep the dairy farm running alongside his father. He would also eventually inherit it.

Lloyd climbed the back porch steps and lowered himself onto his mother's favorite glider. As he moved the glider back and forth and looked at his father's line of four barns and vast pastures, his thoughts stayed on Seth. It still seemed surreal that Seth was gone. Lloyd had grown up with him, both in their church district and at school. They were instant friends beginning in first grade. Although they had taken different, busy paths after school—Lloyd becoming a dairy farmer and Seth going into construction—they still kept in touch, talking at church services and other gatherings.

But now Seth was gone. Lloyd sighed and rubbed his chin as grief hit him once again. He missed his friend. They had enjoyed long discussions about everything from farming to their personal lives. While Seth had been engaged to Veronica and was preparing for marriage, Lloyd still hadn't found the right *maedel*. But even though Seth talked nonstop about Veronica, Lloyd had been happy for them.

The sadness he saw in Veronica's eyes at church haunted him. His heart broke for both her and Seth's family.

As he continued to rock back and forth, his thoughts turned to Ellie. When he'd arrived at the Lapp farm today, he'd planned to muck out the stalls. Instead, he was surprised to find Ellie running after Daisy, their misbehaving cow. He'd heard Seth's hilarious stories about that rogue cow. She frequently found a way to open the latch on the pasture fence and take a leisurely walk around the farm or, like today, head for the road. Today was the first day he'd seen Daisy in action.

Lloyd was rushing after Ellie to help her catch the cow when she slipped and fell in the mud. His first reaction was to help her up. When Lloyd reached her, he had to fight back his amusement because she looked so adorable. He felt terrible that she had fallen, but she had the cutest expression on her face. Her clothes and shoes were all splattered with mud. She even had a smudge of mud on her face.

Lloyd had to swallow a bark of laughter when he lifted Ellie to her feet. He could tell she was embarrassed. He was certain that would have embarrassed his sisters too. He hoped someday they could look back on that and laugh together. He was just thankful he was there to help her corral Daisy and then fix that latch for Seth. He recalled that Seth said he repaired it more than once. Daisy was one smart cow.

He had spent the rest of the afternoon mucking the stalls and feeding the animals. When he spotted Ellie clad in a clean blue dress as she hung out the muddy clothes now washed, he hoped she wasn't still humiliated by her fall.

Lloyd crossed his arms over his chest as he contemplated Seth's little sister. He was old enough to remember when Ellie was a newborn. Ellie and his sister Rebecca were the same age, and he recalled their playing together at church services. The two girls became close friends at school and remained best friends after they'd finished eighth grade. Ellie was always a sweet girl, and she was attached to Seth, especially after they'd lost their father.

The back door opened and then clicked shut, interrupting Lloyd's thoughts. Lloyd sat up straight and nodded a greeting as his father took a seat in the rocker beside the glider. Lloyd's father was about thirty pounds heavier than him, and Lloyd heard the rocker creak a little as his dad settled in.

"The animals are set for the night," Lloyd said as he leaned back in the glider and crossed his long legs. "I was just enjoying the warm night."

"*Danki* for taking care of everything." *Dat* turned toward him. His father was a few inches shorter than Lloyd, but sitting they looked at each other eye to eye. Unlike Lloyd's blue eyes, however, his father's were brown, the same color as their hair.

"How was Margaret today?"

Lloyd folded his arms over his chest. "I guess she was okay. She got emotional when she thanked me for helping."

"I can't imagine losing a *kind*." *Dat*'s voice was wistful, causing Lloyd to feel a pang of emotion too. He rarely saw his father's emotional side. "I admire you for making time to help the Lapp family. You're generous with your time."

"Well, that's what we do, right?" Lloyd didn't want to make it a big deal, but he was glad his father felt that way. He not only enjoyed helping the Lapp family, but he was sure Seth would have done the same for him if he had been the one killed in an accident—especially if Lloyd's father wasn't around. The Lapp family had had only one son, just like Lloyd's family. If anything happened to his father, Lloyd knew he would be the one responsible for his mother and his sisters, Rebecca and Marie, who were only nineteen and sixteen. The burden of supporting family fell to the sons, and he wanted to do all he could for the Lapp family in place of his friend.

"I was surprised to see you out here," *Dat* said, interrupting Lloyd's thoughts. "I expected to find you in your woodshop."

"Not tonight." Lloyd wiped his hands down his trouser legs, knocking dust and hay onto the porch. He wasn't in the mood for one of his father's lectures about his woodworking hobby, so he quickly changed the subject. "I'm pretty worn out from all the chores I did today."

"I imagine you are." After a few moments of silence, *Dat* stood. "Well, we'd better head inside. Work comes early in the morning."

"I'll be there in a minute." His thoughts were stuck on the Lapp family and their loss. He hoped his weekly visits were helpful. But for some inexplicable reason, he realized, he also couldn't wait to return to their farm and do more.

❦

Ellie took a deep breath and ran her hand over her blue dress as she approached the Bird-in-Hand Gifts and Treasures shop the next morning. The glass in the large front window of the brick building was etched with the shop's name in script. A variety of detailed metal ornaments, keepsake boxes, photograph frames, decorative plates, mirrors, trays, dishes, and figurines adorned the window display that was garnished with potted plants and wooden furniture.

She had walked by the place dozens of times while shopping in town, but she had never ventured inside. Her hands trembled with a mixture of excitement and anxiety as she pulled the door open. A bell sounded above her, announcing her entry.

She passed shelves filled with more beautiful metal decorations on her way to the desk in the center of the store. A young woman there, clad in jeans and a gray blouse, smiled at her.

"Good morning. How may I help you?"

"Hi. I heard Gene Rider is looking for someone to help since Katie Esh no longer works here."

"Oh, wonderful!" The young lady motioned for Ellie to follow her toward the back of the store. "I'm Phoebe. My uncle Gene owns this shop. I can only work here part time due to my school schedule, so he needs someone else a couple of days a week."

"That would be perfect for me." Ellie hoped Gene would decide she was the best person for the job. She followed Phoebe into the back room, which was a large workshop cluttered with benches, tools, and machines.

A tall man with graying brown hair and a matching full beard looked up from a bench where he was working on a small metal ornament. He smiled as he stood.

Phoebe made a sweeping gesture toward Ellie. "Uncle Gene, this is Ellie Lapp. She's here about the job."

"Hi. Katie Esh's mother told me you're looking for someone to work part time. I'd like to apply." Ellie fingered her apron and her stomach tightened with apprehension. Was she ready to work in a busy store? She needed to be brave. She was counting on this job to keep her and her mother afloat. Despite her doubts, she forced herself to stand up straight.

"It's so nice to meet you." Gene shook her hand. "Have you worked in a shop before?"

"No, but I've helped out at my friend's vegetable stand." Ellie rattled off her experience working with a calculator and counting change. "I'm good with numbers, and I'm a fast learner. I know I'll do a good job for you."

Gene nodded and crossed his arms over his blue button-down shirt. "I'm looking for someone who can work Mondays and Fridays. Phoebe handles all the other days I'm open, which is every day but Sunday."

"That schedule would work well for me." Ellie grinned. *This will be perfect! I can still help* Mamm *at home!*

"Great. I'll need you to handle the front while I work back here to keep up inventory. That means helping customers, running the register, and keeping the showroom floor tidy. Let me show you around."

Gene gave her a tour of the shop and explained that each area was categorized by the type of item for sale, including home and accessories, jewelry, cities and sports memorabilia, and gifts for certain occasions.

"All these items are lovely," Ellie said as she examined an ornament featuring a horse and buggy in front of a farm scene. "You do incredible work."

"Thank you. That's one of our most popular items. The tourists love anything with a horse and buggy on it."

"That's the truth." Phoebe pointed toward the back of the showroom. "I'm trying to convince Uncle Gene to allow me to find some more Amish-made gifts to sell over in that corner. We have the typical quilts, cloth dolls, potholders, key chains, and homemade jellies made by the Amish, but I think it would bring in even more business if we had some unique Amish-made things to sell. The tourists will go crazy for that."

Gene looked skeptical. "I don't want to sell more quilts and potholders, even if they are unique patterns. Plenty of other shops sell those items."

"That's not what I meant." Phoebe sighed. "I'm talking about something completely different, unique." She turned to Ellie. "Can you think of something we could sell that would be different from what the other shops around here have?"

Ellie shrugged. "No, I really can't."

"I promise I'll find something, Uncle Gene." Phoebe smiled. "Just trust me."

Gene rubbed his beard. "Keep thinking about it. We've been losing sales since that new gift shop opened up the road in Gordonville. Maybe offering some unique Amish-made item is the way to go."

Phoebe leaned against the end of a set of shelves. "I'm sure we can figure something out."

"So, Ellie," Gene began, turning his eyes back to her, "what do you think? Do you want the job?"

"Absolutely," Ellie said, rubbing her hands together. "When would you like me to start?"

~⚬~

Ellie burst through the back door and into the kitchen. She was so excited she thought she might explode as she started walking through the downstairs in search of her mother.

"*Mamm*?" she called. "Where are you?"

"I'm in the sewing room," *Mamm* responded.

Ellie rushed there to find her mother pinning a new apron. "*Mamm*! I got the job!" She clapped her hands together, but then her smile faded as her mother frowned. "*Was iss letz?*"

"I didn't really want you to get the job." *Mamm* placed the apron on the table next to her treadle sewing machine.

Ellie sank into the chair beside the table. "*Mamm*, we talked about this. We need the money." She rested her hand on the surface of the table. "It won't be as much as Seth made, but I'll make enough money for groceries. We'll still need to cut back on other things."

"*Ach*, Ellie." *Mamm* shook her head, her green eyes full of concern. "You shouldn't worry about things like that."

"*Mamm*, you're wrong," Ellie said gently. "I should be worrying about things because it's just us now." She took her mother's hands in hers. "Like you said, we'll take care of each other. I'm only working Mondays and Fridays, so I'll still be here to help with the *haus* and the farm. I'm not leaving you to take care of everything. I'll help with the cooking and baking and gardening and laundry just like I do now."

Mamm gave a reluctant nod. "All right."

Ellie hugged her mother as her excitement swelled again. She couldn't wait to get started at her new job. This was the best way for her to take care of her mother, and she was certain Seth would be proud of her.

CHAPTER 3

L loyd sat on a stool in front of a long workbench in his wood-shop at the back of the barn. The soft yellow glow of two Coleman lanterns lit the room, and the aroma of pine filled his senses as he whittled the small block of wood in his hand. While his fingers and tools shaped the wood, the stress from the day left his body and his mind cleared.

Woodworking was the only way he truly found peace after a long day of farm work. While his hands shaped a plain piece of wood, his mind found a perfect peace through relaxation and prayer.

The workbench was cluttered with woodworking tools and a table was covered with his creations—small, detailed birds whittled intricately by his hand. The hobby was a surprise even to Lloyd. When he was fifteen he found whittling tools in the back of his grandfather's barn and asked what they were. His grandfather showed him how to turn a plain block of wood into something beautiful. Not only did Lloyd enjoy the time with his grandfather, but he found a new passion—whittling.

His grandfather passed away when Lloyd was eighteen, and his grandmother gave him the tools. Now Lloyd whittled not only to keep his grandfather's memory alive, but also to enjoy the relaxation of the hobby.

The shop door opened with a *whoosh*, interrupting his thoughts. He glanced back over his shoulder and spotted his father in the doorway, an unreadable expression on his face.

"Hi, *Dat*." Lloyd spun on the stool to face him. "Is everything all right?"

"I was wondering where you were." *Dat* leaned against the doorway. "It's late, and I thought you would be heading to bed by now."

"I just wanted to get started on another bird." Lloyd nodded toward the block of wood in his hand. "You know I like to come in here and unwind at night."

"*Ya*, I know that, but you need your rest." *Dat's* expression hardened. "This farm is your obligation, Lloyd. The farm will go to you since you're the only *bu*. It's your responsibility."

Lloyd's stomach tightened with resentment. "I know that." *Especially since you remind me all the time.* "All my chores are done. I love this farm, and I will take *gut* care of it when it's mine. I just needed some time to myself, and this is how I relax. You enjoy reading the *Budget* before you go to sleep, and I like to whittle. That's all it is, *Dat*. It's just a hobby."

His father crossed the shop and peered down at the wooden birds. "I hope you realize this hobby is prideful." He lifted a cardinal, regarded it as if it were pernicious, and placed it back on the table.

"It's prideful?" Lloyd crinkled his nose with confusion. "How is this hobby prideful?" And why hadn't his father ever said this is what he thought?

Dat met his expression with a frown. "You're simply showing off your skill."

"I don't understand how I'm showing it off if the birds don't leave this shop." Lloyd pointed toward the table. "I create the birds and then leave them here. It's just something that makes me *froh*. *Daadi* did the same thing, and no one ever criticized him."

"You're more skilled than your *daadi* ever was." *Dat* started toward the door. "You need to get to bed, Lloyd. It's late." With a quick nod, he disappeared.

Lloyd examined the piece of wood in his hand as frustration surged through him. When would his father ever accept that his whittling was a hobby and nothing more? How could a hobby that made him happy be a sin? He wasn't hurting anyone and he wasn't bragging. After all, Lloyd wasn't a skilled woodworker. But he was a responsible adult who should be able to decide how to spend his free time.

He set the wood and the whittling knife on the workbench and switched off one of the lanterns. As he lifted the other lantern, he started toward the door, still chafing at his father's pronouncement. His father would never understand, but his grandfather had. Lloyd missed his grandfather more than ever on days like this.

✧

Ellie stood at the cash register at Bird-in-Hand Gifts and Treasures on Friday morning and smiled as a woman dressed in blue jeans and a white shirt decorated with a sparkling butterfly design approached.

"Hi," the woman said. "I was wondering if you had any other Amish gifts." The woman pointed toward the back corner. "I see the quilts and dolls, but I'm looking for something I can't find in every other store in Lancaster County."

"Oh." Ellie pressed her finger to her chin while contemplating the question. "Did you see the metal ornament over there with the horse and buggy on it? That's one of our popular sellers."

The woman frowned. "I was looking for something more . . . rare. I always take a gift home for my sister-in-law when I visit here, and she doesn't like the run-of-the-mill gifts. She's not interested in quilts or straw hats."

"I'm sorry." Ellie forced a smile. "All we have are the metal ornaments over there and also the Amish items in the back corner."

"Oh well." The woman was still frowning. "Thanks for your help." She walked toward the exit without buying anything.

Ellie was dusting shelves in the back corner of the store later that afternoon when another woman came up to her.

"Excuse me, miss." The woman with short, graying hair and a round face gestured toward a display of cloth dolls. "Do you have any other Amish-made crafts?" She held up a doll. "These are cute, but I'm looking for something my grandson would like."

"We have the straw hats," Ellie offered, but when this woman frowned, too, Ellie glanced across the store. "We have metal trucks over by the sports items. Does he like trucks?"

The woman shrugged. "I suppose he might, but I was hoping to buy something Amish for him. I've been telling him about the Amish culture."

"Does he like quilts?"

The woman shook her head. "No, he doesn't." She smiled. "Well, I tried. Thank you for your help."

As Ellie watched the woman walk away, she thought about the conversation she'd had with Phoebe. Maybe she did need to help her and Gene find something special to sell.

❧

After work, Ellie paid her driver and rushed up the rock driveway to the front door of her house.

"*Mamm*! Where are you?"

"I'm on the back porch," her mother responded through the open windows.

Ellie dropped her tote bag on a chair in the kitchen and hurried out to the back porch. Her mother was sitting on the glider and snapping string beans.

"How was your first day on the job?" *Mamm* asked.

"It was fantastic." Ellie sank onto the glider beside her and picked up a bean. "Gene trained me to use the electric cash register in the morning, and I quickly learned how to use it. I was ringing up customers before noon. He also gave me another tour of the showroom, this time more thorough to ensure I knew where the different types of gifts are located. He has the store set up by categories of gifts. For example, I had to know where to find treasure boxes if someone came in looking for one."

Mamm nodded. "That makes sense."

"*Ya*, it does." Ellie considered some of the customers. "A few people asked for more Amish-made crafts. Gene's niece thinks we need to add more unique items to the Amish section, and I think she's right. I just need to figure out what we can sell. Can you think of something unique that we don't see in many tourist shops?"

Mamm shook her head. "No, I can't. I'll have to think about that. So you liked the job?"

"Oh, *ya*. By the afternoon, I was running the showroom by myself, and I loved it." Ellie grinned as she snapped another bean and placed the snapped-off end and extra fibers into the discard bowl. She put the trimmed bean into the larger bowl with the others. "It's a lot of fun, and Gene said he'll pay me every other week. Do you need me to do anything now that you didn't get to finish today? Do I need to weed the garden again?"

"It's fine, Ellie." *Mamm* touched her shoulder. "I handled the garden today. You're helping me plenty now. I'm *froh* that you like the job."

Ellie glanced toward the pasture. "Have any animals tried to escape today?"

Mamm chuckled. "No, Daisy has been safely nestled in the pasture today. And Seth's friend Jason Huyard from work came by and took care of the animals earlier."

"Has Lloyd been by today?" Her stomach trembled a little when she said his name. She longed to keep her feelings for him tucked away, but her emotions always got the best of her. Why did she bother thinking about him? He'd never be more than a friend to her. The age difference would always come between them.

"Lloyd?" *Mamm* asked, shaking her head. "No, I haven't seen him, but I think he did a great job fixing the latch on the gate."

"That's *gut*." As Ellie snapped more beans, she wondered when she'd see Lloyd again. She hoped he'd decide to mingle during the youth gathering at his parents' farm Sunday night. In fact, hadn't he promised he would?

~⊚~

Ellie sat between Rebecca and Marie Blank at the youth gathering Sunday evening. Although the sisters were three years apart, they could nearly pass for twins since they were the same five foot five and had matching brown hair and eyes. Lloyd was the only child who had inherited their mother's blue eyes.

Three volleyball nets were assembled in the grassy lot adjacent to the Blank family's large white, two-story clapboard house. Teams of young people played at each homemade court, leaping, jumping, and laughing as the volleyballs sailed through the air. Small groups of young people sat nearby, some cheering on the teams and others oblivious of the games while they talked among themselves.

Ellie ripped out blades of grass while the sisters talked and the noisy games continued. Memories of playing volleyball with Seth and his friends took over Ellie's mind. She recalled the day Seth patiently taught her how to serve the ball. He showed her over and over again until she served it correctly, and his girlfriend, Veronica, returned it to her, bumping it gracefully over the net.

Why had Ellie thought coming to the youth gathering would be fun when the memories dampened her mood? She knew the answer to that question. She'd hoped to see Lloyd, but she hadn't caught a glimpse of him all afternoon.

"Ellie?" Rebecca's voice broke through Ellie's thoughts. "Are you all right?"

"*Ya.*" Ellie swiped her hands together to brush away the blades of grass and then leaned back on her palms.

Rebecca and Marie exchanged skeptical looks.

"Do you want to play volleyball?" Marie jammed her thumb toward the nets. "They're getting ready to change up the teams."

Rebecca's brown eyes brightened. "We could play together on the same team."

"*Ya!*" Marie agreed with excitement.

"No, but thank you." Ellie tried to force a smile, but she was sure it looked like a grimace instead.

"*Was iss letz?*" Rebecca's expression clouded with concern.

"You seem upset," Marie chimed in.

"I'm fine." Ellie feigned a yawn. "Just tired." She pointed toward the volleyball courts. "You can go play if you'd like. I'll be happy to root for you."

Another expression passed between the sisters, this time one of suspicion. Did they think Ellie wouldn't notice?

"Really, it's okay," Ellie insisted. "I know you both love to play. Don't let me hold you back."

Rebecca and Marie stood, wiped off their dresses, and headed toward the nets. Ellie watched them play for a few minutes, but she soon grew tired of sitting alone and decided to take a walk. She stood and started toward the house, nodding and greeting friends as she passed them.

As she ambled past one of the smaller barns, she noticed the door was open. She stepped inside and the scent of earth filled her nostrils. Her shoes crunched on hay as she moved past rows of shovels, saws, racks, and other tools toward a small room at the back, where another door was open to a smaller room.

Ellie hesitated in the doorway, but then stepped inside what looked like a small woodworking shop. She examined a workbench cluttered with whittling tools and then touched one of the knives, wondering whose shop she'd discovered. Seth had never mentioned that Lloyd liked to work with wood, so she doubted it was Lloyd's.

She moved to a table and found the most beautiful wooden birds she'd ever seen. She lifted one and nearly gasped as she examined the detailed work that had gone into this creation. The bird was small enough to fit into her hand, but it looked as if she were holding a real bird.

Ellie ran her fingers over the smooth wood, taking in the wings, the beak, and the eyes. Whoever had created this bird clearly loved it.

She placed the bird back in its original spot on the table and then examined another bird. She scanned the table and surmised there had to be at least two dozen birds there representing different species. A few she recognized as seagulls, cardinals, and bluebirds. Others were familiar, but she didn't know the bird names.

Ellie gingerly picked up one of the birds whose name she didn't know and took in its intricacies. She suddenly remembered Phoebe Rider's comment about trying to find some unique, Amish-made item for the gift shop. What if Gene sold these beautiful birds? She hadn't seen anything like them in any of the shops in town.

This would be perfect! She excitedly held up another bird. Yes, it would be perfect. She just needed to find out who had made these birds and ask permission to show one to Gene and Phoebe.

"May I help you?"

Startled, Ellie spun around, nearly dropping the bird when she found Lloyd watching her from the doorway.

CHAPTER 4

L loyd." Ellie righted herself as embarrassment burned the tips of her ears. She shouldn't have barged into this shop uninvited. Where were her manners? "I didn't hear you walk up behind me."

"Hi, Ellie." He stepped inside. "What are you doing in here?"

"Oh, well, I saw the barn door was open, and then I was curious to see what was back here." She spoke quickly, stumbling over her words. "I didn't mean to snoop."

"I didn't realize I had left the door open." He moved to the workbench and leaned his hip against it as he faced her.

"This is your shop?" Her eyes widened with surprise. Why hadn't Seth told her Lloyd did woodworking? Did Seth even know about this secret talent?

"*Ya.*" Lloyd shrugged. Ellie noticed the sunbeam coming through the window made his eyes seem a lighter shade of blue and gave his hair golden highlights.

"Where did you learn how to make these *schee* birds?" She

held up the one in her hand and suddenly felt ashamed for touching his private things.

"*Mei daadi* taught me a long time ago. We used to make little projects together for fun." He looked down at the bench. "*Mei mammi* gave me his tools when he passed away, and *mei dat* let me set up a little shop back here. I just play around with the tools sometimes. It's a hobby really."

"Seth never told me about these birds. Did he know about them?"

"No." He shook his head, and he seemed self-conscious. "Only my family knows about them."

She took a step toward him and breathed in his scent, earth and wood mixed with soap. "This is the most *schee* carving I've ever seen in my life."

"*Danki.*" Lloyd shook his head. "But you're just being nice."

"No, I'm not. It's incredible." She turned the bird over in her hand. "What kind of bird is this?"

He took the bird from her hand, and she almost shivered when their fingers brushed together. He held the wooden creature up to the window and examined it in the sunlight. "It's a yellow warbler." He motioned for her to stand beside him. "See there?" He pointed to letters carved in the bottom of the bird. "I put the names of the species on the bottom."

Ellie shook her head with surprise. "How do you know so much about birds?"

Lloyd gave her an embarrassed smile. "I'm not really that smart." He pulled a thick book from one of the drawers in the workbench. "I use this to look up the birds. See?" He flipped to a page and pointed to a photo of a bird. "I model the carvings after the photos. I'm really not some sort of genius. I just like working with wood."

"You have a real special talent." She smiled while imagining the birds in Bird-in-Hand Gifts and Treasures. "You need to sell these."

"No." He waved off the suggestion. "This is just something I do to relax after a long day."

"I'm serious, Lloyd." Ellie held up the carved bird again. "I just started working at Bird-in-Hand Gifts and Treasures in town. The owner is Gene Rider, and he makes beautiful metal items as gifts."

Lloyd folded his arms over his chest and nodded. "I've heard about that store, looked in the front window a time or two."

"Well, he's looking for something unique made by a local Amish person to sell there. He thinks it will help boost his sales because that's what customers have been requesting lately." She spoke quickly, hoping to use the right words to convince him. "Your birds are just what he's looking for. He could sell these birds for you, and you would make some extra money."

"No." Lloyd took the bird from her and placed it back on the table. "I already told you that it's just a hobby."

"You are so talented, Lloyd," she insisted.

"No one would want to buy them."

"You're wrong," she said, pleading with him. "I'm certain they will sell."

Lloyd's expression softened and he gestured toward the door. "Would you like to go for a walk?"

She blinked, stunned by his suggestion. Did he want to spend time with her or was he simply trying to distract her from talking about selling his carved birds? *"Ya,* I would."

"Gut." Lloyd gestured toward the door, and they made their way out of the barn by the light still coming through the windows.

They started toward the pasture, but then Lloyd stopped and turned to her.

"Wait. Did you want to play volleyball?"

"No, not really." She gave him a shy smile.

"I thought you liked volleyball," he said, looking surprised. The volleyball games were still going strong on the other side of the house.

"I used to." Ellie ran her fingers along the pasture fence as they walked. "It's not the same anymore."

"It reminds you of Seth." His words were gentle.

Her eyes met his and she found sympathy there. "That's exactly right. Rebecca and Marie invited me to play with them, but I couldn't do it. I kept thinking about the day Seth and Veronica taught me how to serve and bump the ball. It was too painful."

Lloyd stopped walking. "I know what you mean. A lot of things remind me of Seth too."

"Some days are worse than others." She kept one hand on the fence. "I can't stand it when my *mamm* cries. It tears me apart inside."

"I imagine it does." Lloyd looked past her toward the youth group, and she wondered if she was holding him back from having fun.

"Am I stopping you from playing volleyball?" she asked.

"Who, me?" He smiled and shook his head. She enjoyed seeing

his handsome smile. "No, I don't belong out there with those young people."

"You're not old, Lloyd." She wagged a finger at him. "You were going to hide in your woodshop until I found you. You weren't going to keep your promise to mingle at the youth gathering."

He rubbed his chin. "I never promised you I would do that."

"*Ya*, you did."

"I said I would be around since I live here, but I never said I'd take part." He turned toward the house. "Are you thirsty? *Mamm* made her famous iced tea. Let's get a glass. We can sit on the porch and watch everyone play volleyball."

"That sounds perfect." A smile spread across her lips as Ellie followed Lloyd to the house. She'd never dreamt of spending so much time with Lloyd. She prayed he'd soon see her as more than a friend.

❦

Lloyd stepped into the mudroom later that night and set his lantern down on the bench. He'd spent the entire evening with Ellie, and he was surprised that he'd had a good time with her. After they gathered glasses of iced tea and a plate of snacks, they sat on the porch together. They ate and talked until it was time for Ellie to head back home. They discussed everything from the weather to her brother and some of their mutual friends. She'd been sweet and funny, and for some inexplicable reason, he felt himself growing attached to her.

He mentally shook himself. But how could that be possible? Ellie was the same age as his sister Rebecca. Any feelings for her would be inappropriate. In fact, he'd be furious if one of his friends wanted to date Rebecca. He pushed the thoughts away as he sat on the bench and shucked his work boots. This was just craziness. Ellie was his friend, and that was all she'd ever be to him—a special friend.

"There you are, Lloyd." Rebecca appeared in the doorway. "I was wondering where you'd gone."

"I made sure the last of your friends got off safely and then checked on the animals." He set his boots under the bench and noticed she was lingering. "Do you need something?"

"No. I want to ask you something, though."

"What is it?" He leaned back on the bench, waiting for her response.

"I saw you talking to Ellie earlier. How was she?" Her expression was filled with concern.

Lloyd shrugged. "She seemed okay. Why are you asking about her?"

"She seemed really *bedauerlich* earlier." Rebecca rested one hand on the back of a chair as she talked. "Marie and I tried to convince her to play volleyball with us, but she didn't want to. I had a feeling it reminded her of Seth."

"Yeah, she told me that." Lloyd rested his ankle on his opposite knee. "We talked about Seth a little bit, but we also talked about other things. She was fine. I think it helped her to get away from the volleyball nets and think about something else."

"Oh." Rebecca grimaced and rubbed her forehead. "I'm such a bad friend. I didn't even think about that."

"It's not your fault." Lloyd shook his head. "Don't blame yourself. I think grief is unpredictable sometimes."

"*Ya.*" Rebecca's expression softened. "I suppose you're right. I'll try to be more attentive the next time I see her."

"She wasn't upset with you," Lloyd insisted. "You don't have anything to worry about."

"Oh good. I'm glad you could cheer her up. You two looked like you were enjoying each other's company." Rebecca tapped the back of the chair. "I'm going to head upstairs."

Lloyd nodded as she left. He stood, went into the kitchen, and crossed to the sink. As he filled a glass with water, his thoughts turned back to Ellie and their conversation in the woodshop. She'd seemed determined to convince him to sell his carved birds, and the excitement in her eyes surprised him. He'd never imagined anyone would show such an interest in his work.

For a split second, he had considered taking her up on her offer, but he couldn't allow himself to entertain the idea of selling his creations, especially after his father called his hobby prideful. He wouldn't dare disrespect his father, and besides, who would want his silly birds? Just because Ellie thought they would sell well at Bird-in-Hand Gifts and Treasures didn't mean anyone would actually buy them. It was a ridiculous notion, but he was still amused by her interest. Ellie was a sweet *maedel.*

He drank the water and set the glass in the sink before heading toward the stairs. He tried to push away thoughts of Ellie, but her pretty smile filled his mind. What was wrong with him? She was only nineteen.

Lloyd climbed the stairs to his bedroom and tried to shake off all his thoughts of Ellie. He'd enjoyed spending time with her tonight, but they were just two friends sharing conversation and pretzels and iced tea on the porch, and nothing more.

〜◎〜

Ellie was still smiling when she arrived at Bird-in-Hand Gifts and Treasures Monday morning. She hadn't stopped smiling since she'd left the youth gathering last night. She had never in her wildest dreams imagined that she'd have the opportunity to spend an evening talking to Lloyd. It had been wonderful. She'd felt a strong connection with him while they talked. It was as if they really understood each other. Could he possibly like her as more than a friend? The possibility sent a shiver of excitement through her as she stepped into the showroom and set to work.

Ellie's thoughts lingered on Lloyd throughout the morning as she helped customers and kept the showroom tidy. When she wasn't busy with customers, her eyes frequently drifted to the back of the store where Phoebe suggested they add unique Amish-made goods. Maybe she'd been right when she'd told Lloyd the birds were an example of what those customers said they wanted in the Amish section of the store. Ellie found herself mentally designing a display for Lloyd's beautifully carved work. She would set up special shelves and arrange the birds by size, giving each one a good amount of space on the shelf so customers could appreciate the intricate detail.

She recalled the feel of the carved birds she'd held in her hands. She'd been overwhelmed by Lloyd's craftsmanship. How could he not appreciate his own talent? Why had he kept his creations a secret? Those birds deserved to be shared and loved by others. Why didn't he want to sell them? After all, God had blessed Lloyd with that talent, and they were called to share their talents with the world.

Ellie continued to contemplate the birds all morning. When it came time to break for lunch, she peeked into the workshop. Gene was sitting at his bench, polishing a metal treasure box.

"Gene?" she said, leaning into the room from the doorway.

"Hi, Ellie." Gene smiled over at her. "How are things going?"

"Everything is going fine. I thought I'd take lunch in the break room now." She pointed toward the small room next to his workshop.

"Sure thing." He stood and wiped his hands on a red shop rag. "I'll take care of the front while you're gone."

"Thank you." Ellie started toward the break room and then stopped. She felt compelled to tell Gene about Lloyd's carvings even though Lloyd had insisted he would never sell them. She lingered in the doorway and ran her finger over the woodwork while considering whether or not she should tell him about the birds.

"Is everything all right?" Gene asked as he tossed his shop rag onto the workbench.

"I think I found something unique," she said, now fingering the hem of her apron. "It's something I've never seen sold at the shops around here."

"Really?" Gene raised his eyebrows with interest. "What did you find?"

"Last night I was at my friend's house," Ellie began, "and I found out he whittles carved birds. They aren't just ordinary carvings. They're incredible." She cupped her hand. "I held a couple of them, and it was like holding real birds."

"Interesting." Gene rubbed his beard. "Do you think customers would buy them?"

"*Ya*, I do," Ellie said. "Last week a couple of customers asked for something more unique that was Amish-made. Another one asked me today. They all said they're tired of seeing the same gifts in every store, or at least they've already bought everything that appeals to them."

Gene frowned. "I can understand that. As I mentioned that Phoebe brought this up with both of us, I have to admit that sales have been down for a while. I'm concerned that I may have to cut back somehow if the sales drop much lower."

Worry seized Ellie's heart. She needed this job so she could help support herself and her mother. What if Gene meant he'd have to cut her hours—or her job altogether? "I think the birds might be perfect for the store. The detail is so real. He has all different birds, some I hadn't even heard of. He uses a bird manual as a guide and writes the species on the bottom of each carving. I think people would love to own them. As I said, they're different from anything I've ever seen at another shop."

"They sound great." Gene's expression brightened. "I'd love to see one of his carvings. Do you think you could get me one?"

"I can try." Hope swelled inside of Ellie. "I'll talk to him about it the next time I see him. Thank you so much for considering them."

"You're welcome." Gene nodded toward the door. "Enjoy your break."

Ellie spent the remainder of the day thinking about Gene's offer to look at one of Lloyd's carvings. Now she just had to find a way to convince Lloyd to let her show one of his precious birds to Gene. Maybe his carvings would be the key to keeping her job as it was.

~⊙~

Ellie scrubbed a pot later that evening as her mother wiped off the table. "Did you know Lloyd whittles beautiful carved birds as a hobby?"

"Lloyd Blank?" *Mamm* asked with surprise.

"*Ya.*" Ellie dried her hands and faced her, leaning back against the counter. "I found out last night at the youth gathering. I accidentally found his woodworking shop." She described the carvings in detail, and her mother's eyes widened. "He's never told anyone about his hidden talent."

"Oh my." *Mamm* shook her head. "Lydia never mentioned it to me either. That's really *wunderbaar* that he can make those."

"Apparently he never even told Seth. He's kept it a secret for years." Ellie shared the story of how Lloyd's grandfather taught him how to whittle and how he'd inherited the tools. "Remember when I told you Gene is looking for something unique that's Amish-made to sell at the store?"

"*Ya,* you said some customers were looking for something different to buy."

"Exactly," Ellie said. "I told Gene about the birds, and he wants to see one."

"That's great," *Mamm* said. "I'm sure Lloyd will be thankful that you shared the information about his birds with Gene. Maybe he can sell them and help his family."

Mamm returned to wiping the table and guilt nipped at Ellie. She had to tell her mother the whole truth.

"Actually, Lloyd already told me he doesn't want to sell the birds," Ellie admitted as she gripped her dish towel. "When I told him about the possibility of selling the birds at the store, he said it's just a hobby and refused to talk about it further."

Mamm tilted her head. "Are you saying Lloyd told you no, but you talked to Gene about the birds anyway, against Lloyd's wishes?"

Ellie sighed. "*Ya,* I did. Gene said sales are down and he may have to make some cut backs. I was hoping maybe Lloyd's birds could help."

Mamm's expression was one of disapproval. "You really need to respect his wishes. There may be some special reason why he doesn't want to sell them. If you push the issue, you could lose Lloyd's friendship."

The thought worried Ellie, but she held on to her belief that the birds needed to be shared with others, whether or not their sale made a difference in her job. "I don't think he realizes how special those carvings are, *Mamm.* He probably could make a lot of money for his family as well as make tourists *froh.*"

Mamm's expression softened as she moved to stand beside Ellie. "Your intentions are pure, but it's Lloyd's decision. They're his carvings. The best thing you can do is respect his feelings about his work."

"*Ya, Mamm.*" Ellie nodded as she returned to the dishes in the sink. But deep in her soul, she was certain she could convince Lloyd to sell the carvings. She just had to find the right words.

She also knew the fear of losing her job made her intentions a little less pure than her mother thought, but she was going to try to think only of Lloyd's best interests.

Ellie pulled a weed from the garden and dropped it into the bucket at her feet. The afternoon sun warmed her neck and her back as she squatted down and tugged at a robust, green weed that seemed to have a root system as healthy as a hundred-year-old oak tree.

"Need some help?" a voice behind her asked.

As Ellie looked up, her sweaty hands slipped from the weed, and she fell backward, landing on her bottom at Lloyd's feet. Heat crept up her neck and into her cheeks. Why did she have to fall like a klutz in front of him again?

"I seem to keep finding you in the dirt." Lloyd held out his hand and chuckled. "Let me help you up."

Ellie reluctantly took his hand, and he again lifted her to her feet as if she were nearly weightless. "I'm really not a clumsy oaf." She wiped her hands down her apron.

"I know that." Lloyd continued to smile, and her heart thumped despite her humiliation. "It was that pesky weed. Let me help." He gave the weed a couple of yanks before it exploded from the ground in a tangled mess of roots and dirt. He dropped it into the bucket and then swiped his hands together.

"*Danki.*" She glanced down at her apron, thankful she wasn't covered in mud this time. "I didn't realize you were here. Have you been working in the barn?"

"No." He shook his head. "I just got here. I've been trying to get over here to help since Monday, but unexpected projects kept coming up at the farm. I guess Thursday is better than never, right? I wanted to say hello before I got started on the stalls."

A smile spread across her lips and she forgot her embarrassment. *He came to see me before he started on his work?*

"How's your week going?" he asked.

"Fine." She recalled her conversation with Gene on Monday, and despite her mother's warning, she decided it was the perfect opportunity to ask him again about his carved birds. She took a deep breath and plowed forward. "I told my boss Gene about your carvings on Monday. I explained how amazing they are."

Lloyd's smile faded. "Why did you do that?"

"I really believe they would be a great addition to the store," she continued. "Gene is interested in seeing one. I'm working all day tomorrow. You should stop by and bring that yellow warbler."

"Wait, Ellie. Slow down." Lloyd held his hands up to stop her from speaking. "Why did you tell him about the birds? I already said I don't want to sell them."

"I truly believe your birds will bring joy and happiness into the lives of the people who buy them, Lloyd." She folded her hands to plead with him. "Please reconsider."

He shook his head, and his frown deflated all her hope like a punctured balloon. "No, I can't sell them." He gestured toward the barn. "I need to get to work. I'll see you later."

As he loped off toward the barn, Ellie wondered why he couldn't see the beauty in his own work.

～✦～

Lloyd moved the knife over the dove he'd been working on all evening. His thoughts had been stuck on his conversation with Ellie earlier that afternoon. He couldn't stop his laughter when she fell backward in the dirt. Even though it wasn't funny to see her fall, her expression was priceless. She looked both bewildered and embarrassed, and she was adorable.

Ellie never ceased to surprise him. He couldn't fathom why she had talked to Gene when Lloyd had asked her not to. Why was she so insistent on selling his birds? Seth wasn't as stubborn as his little sister. He had been even-tempered and patient.

Lloyd's fingers moved over the wooden dove in his hand, and he thought of Seth. He wanted to do something special in memory of him. This dove would be a humble memorial, but it seemed to be a fitting one. He would finish the dove in memory of Seth.

As Lloyd continued to work, he couldn't get the image of Ellie telling him about her conversation with Gene out of his mind. Although he was disappointed that Ellie had talked to her boss about the birds, he had enjoyed the sparkle in her light-green eyes as she gushed about his creations. He couldn't explain this sudden awareness of Ellie. What was wrong with him? He'd seen her grow up. It wasn't right for him to think of her as anything other than a friend.

A tap on the doorframe interrupted his thoughts.

He looked over his shoulder and found Rebecca standing in the doorway. "Hi, Becca."

"It's late," she said, crossing her arms over her blue dress. "*Mamm* asked me to come and get you."

"I was just finishing up." He placed the knife on the table.

"What are you making now?" Rebecca closed the distance between them and took the bird from his hand. "This is *schee*, Lloyd."

"*Danki*," he said as she turned it over in her hand. "It's going to be a dove."

"This is fantastic, Lloyd." Her eyes were wide as they met his. "You are so talented."

"Do you really think so?" The question leapt from his lips before he could stop it. He couldn't stand sounding so vulnerable. Why did it matter that someone liked his work? It was just something he did for relaxation.

"*Ya*, of course I do." She sank onto the stool beside him.

"Ellie thinks I should sell the carvings at Bird-in-Hand Gifts and Treasures in town. I don't think I can, though. *Dat* would never permit it."

A knowing smile spread across Rebecca's lips. "Do you like Ellie?"

He was speechless for a moment. "Why would I like Ellie?"

"You hesitated." Rebecca's smile transformed into a sly grin. "You do like Ellie. I had a feeling you two liked each other when I saw you talking at the youth gathering, but I didn't want to say anything."

"We don't like each other," Lloyd said quickly. "I couldn't possibly like her."

"Why not?" As she set the bird on the table beside her, she looked bewildered. "Ellie is *schee*, smart, and funny. What don't you like about her?"

"It's not that." Lloyd shoved his hand through his hair. "It wouldn't be right for me to like her that way. She's Seth's little *schweschder*."

Rebecca chuckled. "Lloyd, in this community, we're all someone's *bruder* or *schweschder*."

He blinked, speechless. He hadn't expected that response.

She stood. "Let's go before *Dat* comes looking for you."

Lloyd flipped off one lantern, then lifted the other one and used it to guide their way back to the house. As they walked in silence, his thoughts were consumed with Ellie. Was Rebecca right when she said Ellie liked him? These feelings were brand new and confusing. He tried to push the thoughts away, but they lingered in the back of his mind.

❧

Lloyd sat between two of his friends during the church service the following Sunday. Rebecca's words from Thursday evening echoed again through his mind as the hour-long main sermon played like background noise to his deep thoughts.

His sister had simply stated that everyone in the community was someone's sibling, but he understood the deeper meaning. Rebecca had given him permission to like Ellie as more than a friend. The idea still didn't sit right with him, though. He still felt as if he would break an unwritten code between Seth and him.

He could never imagine one of his friends dating Marie or even Rebecca, so how could he entertain the notion of asking Ellie to be his girlfriend?

Still, Rebecca's words lingered in his mind, overshadowing his other thoughts.

As the minister continued to talk, Lloyd's eyes moved to the unmarried women sitting on a section of benches across from the unmarried men. Ellie was sitting between Rebecca and another friend. She was dressed in a light-green dress that complemented her eyes, and her golden hair peeked out from under her white prayer covering. She was beautiful, and he watched her as she leaned over to Rebecca and whispered something. Both of the young women grinned and then looked down toward the barn floor as if trying to hide their amusement at whatever Ellie had whispered.

Lloyd glanced down at the hymnal in his hand and tried to make sense of the confusing feelings swirling inside of him. Ellie was sweet and beautiful, but no, she was too young.

After the service was over, Lloyd helped the other men convert the benches into tables for the noon meal, then sat with his friends while they waited for lunch. They were all discussing the rising price of diesel needed to run milking machines when he felt a gentle bump on his shoulder. He turned and found Ellie smiling at him.

"*Kaffi?*" She lifted her coffeepot.

"Oh, *ya. Danki.*" Lloyd handed her his cup. "How are you?"

"I'm fine. You?" Ellie smiled. Oh, how he loved that beautiful smile.

The thought caught him off guard for a moment. "I'm fine too," he said quickly.

"*Gut*. I'll see you later." She moved on to the next person at the table, and he realized he didn't want her to go.

Lloyd tried to think of a reason to see her again and an idea struck him when she reached the end of the table. As she exited the barn to return to the kitchen, he stood and followed her outside.

"Ellie," he called. "Wait a minute."

She spun to face him and raised an eyebrow with concern. "Is something wrong?"

"No, no." He closed the distance between them. "I want to ask you a question."

"Oh?" She held the coffeepot close to her chest. "What did you want to ask me?"

"Are you going to the youth gathering tonight?" Suddenly self-conscious, Lloyd stuffed his hands in the pockets of his trousers.

"*Ya*, I am." Ellie nodded.

"I am too," he said. "Would it be all right if I picked you up?" he asked.

Her eyes widened with shock. "That would be fine."

"Great," Lloyd said. "Rebecca, Marie, and I will get you on our way out there." He turned to head back to the barn.

"Lloyd," she called after him, and he whirled around. "I thought you said you were too old for the youth gathering." Amusement twinkled in her eyes.

He shrugged with a grin. "I guess one of my *freinden* changed my mind. She said people of all ages go to the gatherings."

Ellie grinned. "You have a very *schmaert* friend." With that she turned to go.

Lloyd chuckled as she walked toward the house. He couldn't wait to see her later.

⌒❧⌒

As her pulse pounded with excitement, Ellie rushed from her room and down the stairs. She was still flying high with anticipation after Lloyd had offered to pick her up for the youth gathering this evening. Did the invitation mean he planned to ask her to be his girlfriend? The notion caused her insides to warm. She'd dreamt of being his girlfriend since she was twelve, and now she was almost certain it could actually happen.

She walked into the family room, where her mother was reading a Christian novel. "I'm ready to go." She crossed to her mother's chair and kissed her on the cheek. With suspicious eyes, *Mamm* peered at her over her half glasses. "Why are you so eager, Ellie?"

"I'm just looking forward to seeing my *freinden.*" Ellie grinned. "Lloyd, Rebecca, and Marie are picking me up in a few minutes." She started for the door. "See you later."

"Be safe," *Mamm* called.

As Ellie stepped outside, she heard the *clip-clop* of Lloyd's horse making its way up the rock driveway to her house. Her stomach fluttered as the buggy drew near. She found his sisters were in the back, so she climbed into the front. She greeted Rebecca and Marie as she settled into the seat beside Lloyd.

"*Danki* for picking me up," Ellie said.

"We're glad you could join us," Lloyd said. When he smiled at her, her pulse quickened again.

Lloyd guided the horse back down the driveway toward the main road. During the ride, Marie and Rebecca discussed the boys they hoped to see at the youth gathering. Ellie chimed in now and again, giving her thoughts on the boys they liked while Lloyd mostly shot Ellie sideways glances with rolled eyes.

When they arrived at the farm hosting the event, Ellie climbed down from the buggy and Rebecca and Marie jumped out after her. The sisters immediately started toward the volleyball courts, where the majority of the youth were already gathered.

Ellie lingered behind while Lloyd took care of the horse. She'd hoped to get some time to talk to him alone.

Rebecca stopped walking and looked back at Ellie. "Aren't you coming with us?"

Ellie hesitated, and Rebecca gave her a knowing smile. She winked, then ambled on.

Ellie swallowed a gasp. How did Rebecca know she liked Lloyd? Had she been too obvious with her feelings even though she'd tried to keep them to herself? Panic surged through her. Did all their friends know she liked Lloyd?

"Ellie," Lloyd said, interrupting her thoughts as he appeared behind her.

She spun toward him and hoped her cheeks weren't as red as they felt. *"Ya?"*

He gestured toward the volleyball courts. "Do you want to play volleyball this time?" His easy smile relieved her worry.

Ellie shrugged. "I don't know. Do you?"

Lloyd shook his head. "Not really, but we could sit near the volleyball courts and talk."

"I'd like that." Ellie was glad he wanted to spend time with her, and a smile teased the corner of her mouth as she followed him toward the makeshift courts.

When they reached a flat patch of lush green grass, he pointed down.

"Would you like to sit here?" he asked.

"*Ya.*" She sat on the ground and smoothed the skirt of her green dress over her legs. "It's a *schee* night, *ya*?"

Lloyd sank down beside her. "It sure is." He stared off toward the volleyball games, where the young men and women bounced the ball over the nets as they laughed and shouted.

Ellie searched his expression. She hoped she wasn't holding him back from enjoying the games with other friends and he'd been too polite to go off without her. "You can go if you want. You don't have to sit here with me."

He glanced at her. "No, I really don't want to play. I was just thinking back to when I used to play with my *freinden* when I was younger."

Ellie shook her head and grinned. "You talk like you're forty."

He gave a bark of laughter. "You're funny, Ellie."

"*Ya?*" Her smile widened. "I will take that as a compliment."

"I meant it as a compliment." He studied her for a moment. "Do you remember any of the jokes your *bruder* used to tell?"

"Of course I do." She picked a blade of grass from her dress. "I remember the last one he told me. It was the morning of the accident."

"What was it?" Lloyd rested his elbow on his bent knee.

"Seth came into the kitchen that morning and said, 'Hey, Squirt! What nails do carpenters hate to hit?' I played along and

said, 'I don't know, Seth. What nails do carpenters hate to hit?'"
She paused. "Do you know what the answer is?"

Lloyd shrugged. "No, I can't say that I do."

"Fingernails!" she announced, then laughed.

He groaned and then laughed too. "That sounds like Seth, all right." He rocked back on his hands.

"He was still chuckling about that when he left for work." Her eyes misted as she recalled the details of the morning. "That was the last time I saw him alive. I still remember the warm sound of his laugh. I dream about him some nights. A couple of times I've woken up in the middle of the night and thought I heard him laughing." She turned toward Lloyd and found him studying her. "You're the only person I've ever told that to."

"Really?" He looked surprised.

She nodded. "I hadn't told anyone the last joke he shared with me. And I hadn't told anyone about the dreams." She knew now that she longed to share all her secrets with Lloyd.

"I'm honored that you told me." His expression was full of empathy. "I miss Seth's jokes."

"I remember another one," she blurted out. "What did the green grape say to the purple grape?"

Lloyd grinned. "I don't know."

"Breathe, stupid!" A belly laugh bubbled up from her toes, and some of the pent-up sadness evaporated from deep in her soul.

Lloyd laughed, too, and for a moment she wondered if he was laughing at the joke or at her ridiculous reaction to such a corny joke. But somehow she knew Lloyd was laughing with her, not at her.

"I miss those jokes," Ellie admitted with a sigh. "I miss our talks too. Seth and I used to talk about everything. I never had to worry about what he might say or think if I shared my feelings with him."

"He was a *gut* listener." He leaned back on his hands again and was quiet for a moment. "Tell me about your new job."

"I really like it. The shop is so *schee*. Have you ever been in it?" she asked as she pulled at a dandelion.

He shook his head. "I don't think I've ever been in it, but I have checked out the window display. Gene does great work."

"He does. It's beautiful. It stays busy there too."

"How many days are you working?"

"Two." She tossed the dandelion. "I work Mondays and Fridays. You'll have to stop by."

He nodded. "Maybe I will sometime. You can give me a tour."

Ellie's stomach quivered with the possibility. "That would be nice." She hoped he would.

When Lloyd smiled over at her, she knew she was falling in love with him. She also hoped he wouldn't break her heart, continuing to think of her only as Seth's little sister.

CHAPTER 6

L loyd stepped out of the hardware store and glanced down at the bag he gripped in his hand. Although he had bought everything listed on the crumpled paper he'd jammed into his trouser pocket, he was certain he'd forgotten something. He was distracted, and the trip to the hardware store wasn't in the forefront of his mind. Instead, he was thinking of Ellie's radiant smile. She'd been on his mind ever since he'd dropped her off at her house last night.

He'd spent the entire time at the youth gathering talking to her, and he hadn't regretted a single moment. In fact, it was the most fun he'd had at a youth gathering in years. He'd hung on every word of their conversation. They'd talked about Seth and shared some of their favorite memories of him. Then they talked about friends, her new job, and his work on the farm. The hours had flown by, and too soon it was time for him to take her home.

This morning Lloyd had awoken thinking about her, and he couldn't wait to see her again. He made a quick list for the hardware store during breakfast, called for a driver, and after his morning chores were complete, headed to town.

Now standing in front of the hardware store, Lloyd glanced down the block and spotted the sign for Bird-in-Hand Gifts and Treasures. If he were honest with himself, he would admit why he'd truly come to town. The reason lay only half a block away. Ellie had told him she worked on Mondays, and he was eager to see her again.

Lloyd walked up the block and went inside the shop. He stood by the door and watched Ellie while she helped a customer at the cash register. She was beautiful clad in a dusty-rose-colored dress. She smiled, and her face seemed to glow as she spoke with the woman. After wrapping up the items and placing them into a bag, she took the customer's money and thanked her for coming in. Then she looked toward the front of the store and gasped when she saw him.

"Lloyd!" She rushed over to him. "I'm so surprised to see you here."

He lifted the bag from the hardware store. "I was in the neighborhood, so I thought I'd stop by to see you. You said I should see the shop sometime."

"I'm so glad you came by today." She motioned for him to follow her toward the front window display. "Since no customers are here, I can give you a quick tour."

Lloyd followed her around the store as she explained the theme of each display. He stood close to her and breathed in the scent of her shampoo, some kind of flower mixed with cinnamon. She explained Gene's process for creating the elaborate metal ornaments, pointing out which items were the most popular with the tourists.

When they reached the back of the shop, Ellie gestured toward the Amish items. "This is where we keep the Amish gifts. Gene's niece, Phoebe, would like to add more unique, locally made items to the collection."

Lloyd's shoulders stiffened. He didn't want to discuss selling his birds again, and he hoped she wouldn't pressure him. He didn't want that subject to ruin the mood. She paused for a quick moment, and he was thankful when she didn't mention the birds.

"Would you like to meet Gene?" she offered.

"Sure," he said.

"He's in the workshop, which is in the back." She led him to a doorway.

"Hi, Gene," she said as they stepped into the large shop cluttered with tools. "This is my friend Lloyd Blank."

"Hi, Lloyd." Gene stood and shook Lloyd's hand. "How are you?"

"I'm fine." Lloyd gestured back toward the showroom. "You have a really nice store and your metal work is just amazing."

"Thank you." Gene glanced at his watch.

Lloyd looked at the clock on the wall and an idea sprang into his head. "It's almost noon. Could I possibly take Ellie out for lunch?"

Ellie looked surprised, and she gave him a questioning look.

"I promise I won't have her out too long," Lloyd continued. "We'll just go across the street to the Bird-in-Hand Restaurant and get something quick."

Gene smiled at Ellie. "That sounds like a great idea. I'll run the front until you get back. You can take your time too."

"Thank you," Ellie said. "I just need to grab my purse from the break room."

Lloyd said good-bye to Gene and headed to the front door. He examined a few decorative metal dishes until Ellie emerged with a black purse dangling from her shoulder. They walked together to the Bird-in-Hand Restaurant, where they were seated at a booth.

"Gene is nice, isn't he?" Ellie asked after the waitress had taken their orders.

"*Ya*, he is." Lloyd ran his fingers down the condensation on his glass of water. "The shop is really *schee*, just like you said it was."

She tilted her head and her light-green eyes twinkled with anticipation. "You know, you could talk to him about your birds if you want to. I've already told him about them, and I know he'd love to find out more."

Lloyd shook his head, but instead of being frustrated with her as he expected to be, he was flattered. She was determined for him to sell his birds, but it felt like a compliment instead of harassment. "I'm really not interested in selling them, but *danki* for offering to help. They're sort of a stress reliever for me. Designing and making the birds helps me clear my head after a long day of farm work. While I'm whittling, I sometimes pray or just think about my day and what I have to do the following day. It helps me unwind."

Her expression became bemused. "I just don't understand why you don't want to sell them. You have so many of them, and they just stay in your shop where no one can enjoy them. God gave you that talent, and He wants us to share our talents with others to celebrate His glory. Why do you want to hide that talent when there are so many people who could cherish those birds?"

He contemplated her words as he continued to run his fingers over the glass. Although he understood her point, his father's admonition echoed loud and clear in his mind. "Selling them would be prideful. If I charged money for them, then I would be bragging about my talent."

Ellie shook her head. "I disagree."

He had to change the subject. "I can see why you like working for Gene. It really is a nice store. It didn't seem like it was too busy this morning, though."

"No, it really hasn't been busy today." Ellie smiled, and he was certain it lit up the room. "I'm glad you stopped by on a day when it wasn't. I'm not certain I could've left to have lunch with you if there had been a store full of customers."

The waitress appeared with their lunch orders. She placed a turkey sandwich in front of Ellie and an Angus burger in front of Lloyd. After a silent prayer, Lloyd lifted a fry.

"Ellie, I've been wondering something," he began.

"What's that?" She took a bite of the sandwich and then blotted her mouth with her napkin.

"I was a little surprised when you told me you took this job. You hadn't worked outside of the home much, except for helping out at Lizzie Ann King's vegetable stand, right?" He bit into the juicy burger.

"*Ya*, that's right." She examined her plate as if avoiding his stare. "I felt it was time for me to do something to help out."

"Is everything all right at home?" he asked as worry filled him. "Are you and your *mamm* financially okay without Seth?"

"We're doing okay." Ellie's smile faded. "My uncles have taken care of the mortgage since my *dat* passed away, but Seth managed everything else." She met his gaze, and he saw a hint of sadness in her beautiful eyes. "I feel a responsibility to do my part since I'm the only one left to take care of *Mamm*. It's not like my *onkels* can do any more than they are."

Lloyd placed the burger on his plate. "I understand. Since I'm the only *bu*, I'll inherit the dairy farm. I feel a lot of pressure to make sure the farm is run well and the family is financially stable. If my *schweschdere* don't marry, I'll have to take care of them too."

"I never realized how much pressure Seth was under until he was gone." Ellie's eyes shimmered with tears, and he hoped she wouldn't cry. "Now that he's gone, I need to try to take care of *Mamm* just as well as he did."

She wiped away a stray tear, and he started to reach for her hand. He stopped with his hand in the air, not wanting to be too forward. He quickly pulled his hand back and lifted the burger.

"I'm certain you're a wonderful support to your *mamm*, Ellie. Don't be so hard on yourself."

Ellie nodded and her smile returned. "*Danki*." She lifted her sandwich. "This is *appeditlich*. Thank you so much for lunch."

"*Gern gschehne*," he said, grateful to see her smile again. "Thank you for the company."

They spent the rest of lunch discussing their plans for the week. After they were finished eating, Lloyd paid the check and they walked back to the store. When they reached the door, Lloyd held out his hand.

"*Danki* for joining me at lunch," he said as she shook it. "I'm sure I'll see you at your farm this week."

"*Wunderbaar*. I look forward to it." She smiled as she said good-bye and stepped inside.

Lloyd knew there was a spring in his step as he walked down the sidewalk to meet his driver. He felt a strong connection growing between Ellie and him, and once more, he couldn't wait to see her again.

❦

Ellie hummed softly as she swept the front porch and thought about Lloyd. During the last three weeks, they had fallen into a comfortable pattern. Lloyd came to the Lapp farm twice every week to help with chores. They spent time together while he was there sharing a snack or a meal. They visited at church on Sundays after the service and at youth gatherings. Lloyd even stopped by to see her at the shop again a couple of times, including the Saturday she subbed for Phoebe when she was sick.

Ellie felt their friendship growing as they learned more about each other. She couldn't squelch the notion that his feelings for her were growing, but she was afraid to truly believe that he might like her as more than a friend. She hoped someday he would see that she cared for him. Until then, she allowed herself to enjoy his company and looked forward to the days when he visited the farm.

Now on this Tuesday afternoon she swiped her hand across her forehead as the mid-July sun beat down. She heard the *clip-clop* of a horse approaching on the rock driveway, and her heart felt like it turned over in her chest when she saw it was Lloyd. She'd hoped he would come to help with chores today, and she was thankful that God answered her unspoken prayer.

She waved as he climbed down from the buggy.

"Ellie," he called as he walked to the porch. *"Wie geht's?"*

"I'm doing great." She leaned against the broom. "Are you here to help with chores?"

"That's one of the reasons I came over." He climbed the porch steps. His dark blue shirt complemented his bright eyes. "I also have something for you."

"You do?" Ellie propped the broom against the railing as curiosity consumed her.

Lloyd reached into his trouser pocket and pulled out something hidden in his hand. "I made this in memory of Seth, and I want you to have it." He opened his hand and held it out.

Ellie opened her own hand, and Lloyd placed a carved bird in it. His fingers brushed hers, lingering for a long moment. She enjoyed the warmth of his skin against hers. She examined the carving, a beautiful, delicate dove.

"Lloyd," she whispered, her voice strangled with emotion. "It's the most *schee* bird I've ever seen."

"It's a dove." His voice was equally soft and sentimental.

"It's perfect. *Danki* so much." She nodded, and her eyes stung with threatening tears. "I'll treasure it."

"I know you will."

She looked up into his eyes and something between them sparked. They studied each other, and her breath caught in her throat. Did he feel the same overwhelming force pulling them to each other? Did he care for her the same way she cared for him?

"I better get to work." Lloyd took two steps back. "I'll see you later."

Ellie held the dove close to her chest. It was the most mean-ingful and beautiful gift she'd ever received. She would cherish it forever.

~~∽⊙∽~~

Lloyd hurried toward the barn, aware of an unexpected warmth inside. He'd never experienced such a strong, overwhelming emotion for anyone. He didn't know how to handle it, and the urge to flee overtook him. What did these feelings mean? Where had they come from?

Lloyd grabbed a shovel and began mucking out the first stall he came to. As he labored, he remembered how it had felt to touch Ellie's hand. He couldn't stop thinking about the ten-derness in her eyes as she contemplated the bird. The carving had obviously meant so much to her, and the expression on her beautiful face had touched something deep in his soul.

When he had finished the dove last night, he decided to bring it over and give it to Ellie today. He had created the dove in memory of Seth, but as the bird took shape, he realized he wanted to share it with Ellie. He had never before given away one of his birds because he'd never felt they were good enough to share as gifts. Yet Ellie was the first person who had ever shown a real interest in the birds, and he was determined to share one with her. She had become his champion, his dear friend.

No, Ellie was more than a friend. She had become some-thing much more precious than only a friend.

He stopped shoveling when he realized what those deep emotions meant.

He *loved* Ellie.

Yes, he loved Ellie with his whole heart.

Rebecca was right when she'd said they were all someone's sibling in this community. Ellie may be Seth's little sister, but she was also a beautiful young woman in her own right. And Lloyd wanted to be more than her friend. After all these years he had finally figured out whom he loved, and she had been a part of his life since they were children.

Lloyd's heart pounded with a mixture of worry and excitement. Now he had to find a way to tell her how he felt, and he prayed she felt the same way.

⌘

Later that evening, Ellie knocked on her mother's bedroom door. She cradled the beautiful carved dove in one hand.

"Come in," *Mamm* called.

Ellie stepped inside and found *Mamm* propped up in bed with two pillows behind her back, reading another Christian novel. "I want to show you something." She held out the carved dove. "Lloyd gave me this today. He made it in memory of Seth."

Mamm closed her book and placed it on the nightstand. She took the dove and turned it over in her hands. "Ellie," she said with a gasp, "this is amazing. Look at the detail."

"I know." Ellie sank onto the edge of the bed beside her. "I told you he's talented."

Mamm continued to examine the bird. "I can't get over how beautifully crafted this is. Lydia never told me Lloyd is so talented."

"Lloyd has kept his talent a secret for a long time." Ellie traced her fingers over her mother's blue quilt.

Mamm handed her the bird. "You need to put this in a special place and cherish it. That was made out of love."

Ellie smiled when she heard the word, and her cheeks heated.

"Ellie?" *Mamm* gave her a knowing smile. "Is there something you want to tell me about you and Lloyd?"

Ellie's eyes widened with surprise. "What do you mean?"

"Do you have feelings for Lloyd?" *Mamm* patted the quilt next to her. "Come here and talk to me."

Ellie scooted up next to her and leaned back against the pillow. "There really isn't anything to tell."

"I've seen you and Lloyd talking and sometimes eating together when he's here. You seem to enjoy each other's company."

Ellie nodded. "We talk when he's here, and even at church and youth gatherings, but I'm not sure if he likes me the same way I like him."

"Your *dat* and I started off as friends," *Mamm* said with a smile.

"I know." Ellie fingered the stitching on the quilt. "I just don't know if he could ever consider me as more than a friend since he's older than I am. He said he was too old for youth gatherings."

"He may have said that, but he's been attending them, hasn't he?"

"*Ya*, he has." Ellie looked down at the dove again. Lloyd hadn't missed a youth gathering since he'd picked her up to attend one together weeks ago. "He seemed different today when he gave me the dove. I think this meant a lot to him, and he seemed almost nervous when he gave it to me."

"It was a gift from his heart," *Mamm* said.

Ellie turned the bird over in her hand, studying the detail. Her thoughts turned to that corner in the shop that she'd love to design for Lloyd's beautiful creations. "I know Gene would love this. He'd love to sell these in his store."

"Ellie." *Mamm*'s voice held a hint of a warning. "Lloyd told you he doesn't want to sell them. You have to respect his wishes."

Ellie nodded. *Mamm* was right, but if Gene saw the bird and loved it, maybe she could persuade Lloyd to change his mind. And maybe these beautiful carvings could boost Gene's sales and keep him from possibly taking away her job.

CHAPTER 7

E llie touched the wooden bird hidden in her dress pocket on Friday afternoon. Although her mother had warned her not to go against Lloyd's wishes, she'd carried the bird to work today with the intention of showing it to Gene. Every time she'd planned to show it to him, however, a customer had interrupted her. She hoped the perfect opportunity would present itself before she left for the day.

At five, she rang up the last customer and then flipped the sign from Open to Closed before starting to shut down the register.

"How were sales today?" Gene appeared from his workshop and approached the counter where she had been counting out money.

"It was fairly busy," Ellie said. "At least, I think it was a little busier than this time last week." She placed the cash in the moneybag and zipped it up.

Gene sighed and shook his head. "I haven't wanted to tell you this, but sales have continued to go down these last few weeks.

I was hoping they would pick up during the summer, but they haven't. I think I may have to start cutting back your hours." He leaned against the counter as his frown deepened. "I'm really sorry to do this to you, Ellie. You're a great worker, but I'm not selling enough stock to keep you here two full days. I'm going to have to cover the showroom myself on one of your days."

Ellie nodded as alarm gripped her. How was she going to buy groceries for herself and her mother only working one day a week? Friends and neighbors had stopped bringing meals over to their house weeks ago, and the cupboards would be bare without her paychecks. Where could she quickly find another job?

She suddenly remembered the carved dove in her pocket and considered showing it to Gene. Doubt filled her. Was she making a mistake by going against Lloyd's wishes? Would Lloyd understand why she did it, because she had her and her mother's livelihood in mind?

"Do you want me to drive you home tonight?" Gene offered, interrupting her thoughts. "I need to run a few errands on my way home and I could save you the cost of a driver."

"Oh." Ellie was surprised by the offer. "That would be nice."

"Why don't you call your driver, and I'll finish closing out the register."

"Thank you." Ellie dialed her driver's cell phone number and canceled the ride. Then she slipped her hand into her pocket and trailed her fingers over the dove. She was absolutely sure God would want Lloyd to share his talent, and . . .

"Gene," she said as she pulled the bird from her pocket, "do you remember when I told you about my friend who makes the carved birds as a hobby?"

"Yes, I do. I thought you were going to bring one for me to

see." Gene placed the moneybag on the counter and turned to her as she held out the bird.

"This is a dove he made in memory of my brother." She placed the bird in his hands.

"Ellie." Gene gaped. "This is gorgeous."

"Do you remember Lloyd?" Ellie asked. "He took me out to lunch a few weeks ago. He's the one who made this."

"Really." Gene turned the bird over in his hand. "He didn't sign his name, though."

"He's very humble," Ellie said. "It's our way. He only puts the species of bird on the bottom. He models them after pictures in a book he has."

"This is breathtaking." Gene looked at her. "Ellie, this could be the key to getting our sales back up to where they used to be. Tourists would go crazy for this. This would be perfect. This is exactly what Phoebe had in mind when she said she wanted to sell something unique that was Amish-made. I don't think we could keep these on the shelves."

He turned the bird over in his hands again, taking in every inch of it. "I'd love to discuss price. Of course, I'll pay him what he's worth. I'm certain he's poured plenty of time, along with his heart and soul, into creating this. Do you know how long it took him to make this?"

"I have no idea."

"Does he live near you?" Gene pulled his keys from his jeans pocket.

"*Ya*, he does." Was Gene suggesting . . .

"Could I meet him again? Do you think it would be all right if we stop there on our way to your house?"

"*Ya*," Ellie lied. "Amish are used to people just stopping in."

It was true that Amish were used to people stopping in, but Lloyd wouldn't be happy when he found out why they were visiting. Ellie shook her head as her mouth dried. What had she done? She certainly hadn't thought this through. Lloyd would be furious when she showed up with Gene asking about the birds. But she had to think of her mother.

The worry transformed to dread and pooled in her stomach. She wasn't prepared for this.

After they finished closing the store for the night, Ellie followed Gene to his vehicle and gave him directions. She wrung her hands as Gene steered his burgundy SUV through town and toward Lloyd's place. She was certain she would lose Lloyd's friendship forever when she arrived unannounced with Gene. She should've left the dove on her dresser this morning.

As the SUV's tires crunched on the rocks leading to the Blank family farm, Ellie's stomach twisted with apprehension. Not only was she about to lose Lloyd's trust, she may also lose her job when Gene found out she hadn't had Lloyd's permission to show him the carved bird. The SUV came to a stop and they climbed out. Thankfully no one else in the family opened the front door to greet them.

"He's probably doing his evening chores," Ellie said as she led Gene back to the large barn. Just as they got there, Lloyd stepped out. He met Ellie's eyes and lifted his eyebrow in question.

"Hi, Lloyd," Gene said. "Could I talk to you for a moment?"

Lloyd nodded as confusion twisted his handsome face. His father, Wilmer, stepped out of the barn behind him, and Ellie felt sick with apprehension. This would be far worse than she'd ever imagined. She should've heeded her mother's warning last night.

"Hi," Gene said to Wilmer. "I'm Gene Rider. I own Bird-in-Hand Gifts and Treasures up on Old Philadelphia Pike."

Wilmer shook his hand, his expression mirroring Lloyd's. "I'm Wilmer Blank, and this is my son, Lloyd. How may we help you?"

"Ellie has been telling me about Lloyd's talent with carving birds." Gene pulled the dove from his pocket. "She showed me this one today, and I can't get over the precision and detail."

To Ellie's horror, Lloyd's expression transformed from confusion to pure anguish. Ellie tried to tell him she was sorry with her eyes, but he just stared at her, his expression becoming more and more pained as the moments passed. Her soul filled with regret, and she longed to apologize to him. Instead, she stood cemented in place, feeling helpless as their friendship dissolved right before her eyes.

"I'd love to talk to you about selling these at my store," Gene continued, oblivious to the silent conversation passing between Ellie and Lloyd. "I've been looking for something unique to sell from the Amish community, and these birds would be perfect."

Lloyd shook his head and turned to his father, whose mouth had formed a thin line.

"I'd love to see what else you have if you have a moment," Gene continued. "I know I've shown up here unannounced, but I couldn't wait to talk to you."

"We appreciate your offer, Gene," Wilmer began. His voice was polite but had a cold edge. "Unfortunately, this isn't the best time."

"Oh, I understand," Gene said. "I can come back another time, and we can look at what you have and then discuss a fair price. Since I'm also an artist, I understand how much time and emotion you've invested in your carvings."

Lloyd's cold blue eyes locked on Ellie, sending a chill through her. She crossed her arms over her chest as if to guard her heart. How could she hurt him like this? She wanted to take it all back. If only she could start the day over again and put the bird in a safe place, locked away from the world.

Holding up the dove, Gene went on. "I'm certain tourists will be glad to pay a good amount for something this beautiful that is also Amish-made. They go crazy for anything Amish, especially if it's authentic and unique."

Wilmer gave him a curt nod. "I'll need to discuss this with Lloyd before we give you an answer."

"I understand completely. You don't want to rush into this." Gene pulled a business card from his pocket. "You and Lloyd can discuss it and then give me a call."

Wilmer took the card and regarded it with a scowl. "We will be in touch."

"Wonderful." Gene handed the carved bird to Ellie. "I'm so glad you shared this with me today. I'm certain this is going to work out well for the store and also for Lloyd and his family." He turned his attention back to Lloyd and Wilmer. "I look forward to talking with you soon. Have a nice evening." He nodded at them and started back toward the SUV, his western boots crunching on the rock pathway.

Ellie held the dove close to her chest and watched Lloyd. His frown was now a grimace. The hurt and disappointment in his sad eyes cut her to the bone. Her heart pounded so hard that she was certain he could hear it.

"Lloyd, I'm so, so sorry. I only thought that—"

"Ellie?" Gene called, interrupting her. "Are you ready to go?"

"Just a minute," she said, still staring at Lloyd.

"Just go, Ellie." Lloyd spat the words at her through gritted teeth. "You've done enough."

She hesitated, hoping he'd tell her everything would be all right.

"You should go, Ellie," Wilmer chimed in, his words full of warning.

Ellie tried to clear her throat as a lump formed. She nodded and then hurried to Gene's car, praying that somehow she could salvage her precious friendship with Lloyd.

⁓⁓

Lloyd was certain he was going to be sick. He could taste the betrayal like bile rising in his throat as Ellie walked to Gene's fancy SUV. He had given her that precious dove out of love and respect for both her and for Seth. Yet she had given it to Gene just to prove how much money Lloyd could make by selling his special creations.

He had never imagined that she would use him and then double-cross him this way. He had believed Ellie Lapp was genuine. She was the first girl he'd ever loved, and she had smashed his trust into a million pieces.

"What do you have to say for yourself, Lloyd?" His father's voice boomed over the SUV's engine as it motored toward the road. "I told you your carvings were a prideful hobby, and you went behind my back and tried to sell them."

Lloyd swiped his hand down his face and took a deep breath in an attempt to curb his flaring temper.

"Lloyd?" *Dat*'s voice grew louder. "I'm talking to you."

"I hear you, *Dat*." Lloyd turned toward him. "I didn't give the carving to Gene. I gave it to Ellie as a gift, and she works for Gene."

"You need to concentrate on your responsibilities *here*." *Dat* pointed to the ground for emphasis. "You don't have time for trivial hobbies like carving. I will not permit you to sell them, either."

"I had no intentions of selling them." Lloyd's voice rose as fury gripped him. "I just told you. I didn't give the carving to Gene. Ellie has been trying to persuade me to sell them ever since she wandered into my shop the night we hosted the youth gathering. I've told her more than once that I don't want to sell them, but she won't take no for an answer. I gave her that carving as a gift yesterday, and I guess she took it to work and showed it to Gene."

He kicked a stone with his muddy work boot. "Ellie went behind my back and tried to sell it. I never asked her to do it. I know how you feel about the carvings."

"Well, I'm going to call Gene and tell him the answer is no. We're not going to sell the carvings, no matter the price." *Dat* stuffed the business card into his pocket. "I'll call him tomorrow. It's time for supper."

Dat started toward the house, but Lloyd remained by the barn. He was frozen in place, staring off toward the driveway as he contemplated Ellie and his shattered trust.

"Are you coming inside?" *Dat* called.

"I'll be there in a minute." Lloyd pointed toward the barn. "I forgot to do something."

"Oh." *Dat* studied him and his expression softened slightly. "Fine. Don't be long." He headed up the path to the house.

Lloyd leaned back against the barn door and took deep breaths in an attempt to calm his temper. He never expected Ellie to betray him, but she had. Confusion washed over him. Why would she hurt him that way? He had believed the connection he felt with her was real. Had he been blind? Was he wrong when he assumed she loved him too?

None of this made sense, but now Lloyd had to find a way to recover quickly. He couldn't allow Ellie to hurt him again. No, he couldn't let her know how much pain she'd caused him. Instead, he would treat her like an acquaintance and never let her see how much she had meant to him.

From now on, Lloyd would regard Ellie as someone he hardly knew and never let her know how her betrayal had cut him to the core. He stood up straight and walked toward the house, hoping he could conceal his splintered soul.

⋙⟐⋘

"I made your favorite," *Mamm* said as she sat across from Ellie at the kitchen table. "It's the last of our chop meat. We'll have to go shopping after you get paid."

Ellie stared at her plate as the aroma of barbecued meat loaf, mashed potatoes, and string beans caused her stomach to sour. She couldn't get the image of Lloyd's anguished eyes out of her mind.

"Ellie?" *Mamm's* voice broke through her mental tirade. "What's wrong, *mei liewe?*"

"I did something terrible." Ellie's voice hitched on the last word. "I think I've lost Lloyd's friendship forever."

"What happened?" *Mamm* asked, putting her fork on her plate.

Ellie explained how she showed the carved bird to Gene after he gave her the news about her hours, and then described the scene at the Blank farm. *Mamm*'s eyes filled with empathy when Ellie told her how upset Lloyd looked.

"You were right, *Mamm*, and I should've taken your advice." Ellie's voice quavered. "I've made a mess of things, and now Lloyd will never trust me again. When Gene finds out I didn't get permission to show him the carved bird, he won't trust me either. I was too impulsive, but when Gene said he was going to cut my hours, I panicked." Tears sprinkled her cheeks as her emotions poured from her broken heart. "I was afraid we wouldn't be able to buy groceries if he cut my hours, and I thought selling the birds might help the store and save my job."

"Just calm down, Ellie." *Mamm* handed her a napkin. "I imagine Lloyd is upset, but you can always apologize. We all make mistakes sometimes. Explain to him that you didn't mean for this to get so blown out of proportion, but you will make things right. You'll tell Gene you didn't have permission to show him the carving and you realized it was a mistake. Both Lloyd and Gene will understand, and it will all be forgiven and forgotten."

Ellie wanted her mother to be right, but she knew it was more complicated than that. "I went against Lloyd's wishes. He won't ever trust me again."

Mamm reached across the small table and touched her hand. "Lloyd is a *gut* man. He will forgive you." Her expression brightened. "I think he cares about you. I can see it in his eyes when he looks at you. When you talk to him, speak from your heart, and he will listen."

Ellie wiped her eyes and nodded. "I hope you're right."

"I know I am. And, Ellie, I think both of us need to trust that God will care for our needs. We don't have to worry so." *Mamm* pointed her fork toward Ellie's plate. "Now, eat your supper."

Ellie forked a piece of meat loaf, and even though it normally was her favorite, it tasted like sawdust. Deep in her soul she was certain she'd lost Lloyd forever, but she prayed her instinct was wrong—and for forgiveness in letting her worry get the best of her.

CHAPTER 8

Ellie scrubbed a breakfast dish in hot, frothy water the following morning. She glanced out the window as she worked and yawned. She'd spent most of last night tossing and turning as she recalled the hurt expression on Lloyd's handsome face. She turned her mother's advice over in her mind and wondered if she could somehow find the right words to apologize to Lloyd.

A knock on the back door startled her. She dried her hands on a dish towel as she made her way to the mudroom. When she saw Lloyd scowling at her from the porch, she gasped. She tossed the dish towel onto a bench and opened the screen door.

"Lloyd?" Ellie searched his face and found hurt and anger brewing in his eyes. "How are you?"

"Can we talk?" he asked.

"*Ya*, of course." Ellie smoothed her hands over her black apron and stepped out onto the porch. She sank onto the glider as Lloyd leaned against the railing across from her. His posture was rigid and his expression was frosty as he crossed his arms over his chest. She missed his warm smile and wondered if she'd ever see it again.

"I was awake most of last night," he began. "I kept trying to figure out why you went against my wishes and tried to sell my carvings behind my back after I told you more than once that I wasn't interested in selling them."

"Lloyd, I—"

"Wait, please." He held up his hand to shush her. "Let me finish. I gave you that carving as a gift, a special gift in memory of Seth, and you used it to go behind my back and show it to Gene. You betrayed me, Ellie." His frown seemed more sad than angry, and it bore a hole in her soul.

"I didn't mean to hurt you," she began, her voice thick. "I was wrong, Lloyd. Please forgive me. I made a mistake."

Lloyd ran his hand down his face and gritted his teeth. "I just don't understand it. That dove was meant for you and only you."

"I know that." A single tear trickled down her hot cheek. "I will explain everything to Gene and tell him that I didn't have permission to show him the dove. I'll tell him you had made it clear that you didn't want to sell the carvings. Let me explain it all to him, and I'll make it right."

He shook his head. "I just don't understand what you were thinking."

"I wasn't thinking clearly." She stood and took a step toward him. "Please forgive me. I can't stand the thought of losing your trust and your friendship. Let me fix it, Lloyd. Please."

Lloyd regarded her with disappointment. "I don't think you can fix this. My father is angry with me now. He thinks I went behind his back to try to sell the carvings, and he had already made it clear that it is a wasteful and prideful hobby."

Ellie gasped. "I'm so sorry. I never meant to make things difficult between you and your *dat*." She swiped another tear. "Let me talk to him."

"No, you've done enough." His words stung, and for a moment neither of them spoke. Then as he walked toward the steps, his boots were heavy and loud, cutting through their painful silence.

"Lloyd." She started after him. "How can I make this right? There must be a way."

He shot her a glare over his shoulder. "I told you, I don't think you can fix this, Ellie."

"But I have to. I don't want to lose your friendship." She folded her hands, pleading with him.

"Unfortunately, you've already lost it." He descended the steps as tears flowed from her eyes. "Tell your *mamm* I'm working in the barn."

As Lloyd walked away, Ellie sank down on the porch steps and dissolved into sobs.

❧

Ellie sat alone at the youth gathering a week later. She had wanted to stay home, but *Mamm* insisted she get out of the house and see her friends after sulking for so long. She'd tried to talk to Lloyd when he came to the farm to help with chores, but he avoided her, saying he was too busy to talk or insisting there was nothing left to say. She had explained to Gene that she'd made a mistake when she shared the carving, and Gene told her it wasn't a problem. He and Phoebe would try to find something else to sell. Ellie was thankful that she still had her job, though it was now only one day a week and she and her mother were making every dollar stretch until God provided another solution. But she wanted to win Lloyd's friendship back. She missed him so much that her heart ached for him.

"Ellie?" Rebecca sat down beside her in the grass parallel to the volleyball games. "Are you all right?"

"*Ya*, I'm fine." Ellie tried to force a smile, but it was weak.

"What's wrong? You've been acting *strange* all evening."

"I made a mess of things with your *bruder*." Ellie's voice quavered, but she fought against her threatening tears. She explained what happened when she shared the wooden dove with Gene and then the subsequent fallout between Lloyd and her. "When Gene said he was going to cut my hours, I panicked. *Mei mamm* and I need my paycheck to buy groceries. Seth used to cover all our household expenses with his salary from the shed company. Now that he's gone, we're struggling to stay afloat." A single tear splattered on her cheek and she pushed it away.

"*Ach*, Ellie." Rebecca squeezed her hand. "I had no idea. Why didn't you tell me you and your *mamm* needed help?"

"I didn't want to burden anyone." Ellie sniffed. "I never meant to hurt Lloyd. I've tried to apologize to him, but he won't talk to me. I've lost his friendship, and it's eating away at me. I miss him, and I want to make things right. I want to fix this."

Rebecca frowned. "So that's why he's been in such a rotten mood."

"What do you mean?" Ellie brushed away another stray tear.

"He's been moping and snapping at everyone at the *haus*."

Rebecca crossed her legs under her purple dress. "I had a feeling something was bugging him, but he wouldn't talk to me. I imagine he misses you as much as you miss him. I tried to convince him to come tonight, but he refused. He said he had something to do, but I didn't believe him."

Ellie sighed. "I have been trying to figure out what I could say or do to make things right between us, but nothing seems to work. I've tried talking to him when he came to work on my farm, but he refuses to listen. Do you have any advice?"

Rebecca pulled at a blade of glass while she thought for a moment. "Why don't you let me talk to him?"

Ellie nodded with emphasis at the glimmer of hope. "That would be *wunderbaar*. Please tell him I'm sorry, and I'll do anything to make things right between us. Tell him I miss him, and I want another chance to be his friend."

"I'll do my best." Rebecca patted her arm. "Lloyd sometimes listens to me, so I'll give it a try when I get home tonight."

Ellie smiled her first genuine smile since she and Lloyd stopped speaking. "*Danki.*" She silently prayed Rebecca could make Lloyd realize how much she missed him and wanted his forgiveness.

❧

Lloyd sat on the back porch and looked up at the stars glimmering in the clear sky as cicadas sang in the distance. For over a week he'd tried to put Ellie and her beautiful smile out of his mind, but no matter what he did, his thoughts always turned to her.

This evening he found himself wondering if she had gone to

the youth gathering. Had she been disappointed that he hadn't gone, or had she found another young man to spend time with in his place? The thought of Ellie liking someone else sent jealousy coursing through him, even though he was still angry with her. How could he be angry with her but not want her to like someone else? The paradox made no sense at all.

The *clip-clop* of a horse coming up the rock driveway signaled that his sisters were home from the gathering. He met them at the barn, and after Rebecca and Marie climbed down from the buggy, he began to unhitch the horse.

"I'll help you," Rebecca offered.

"I've got it," Lloyd insisted. "You can go in the *haus*."

"No, I want to talk to you." Rebecca's voice was full of determination. "I'll help."

They unhitched the horse, and he led it into the barn. After stowing the animal in the stall, they walked together toward the house.

"I spoke with Ellie tonight," Rebecca began, and Lloyd stopped in his tracks. "She was really upset."

Lloyd stared at Rebecca, holding his breath as he waited for her to continue.

"She misses you, and she's heartbroken." Rebecca rested her hands on her hips. "She never meant to hurt you, and she can't figure out how to make things right between you. I can tell she loves you, Lloyd. You need to forgive her."

"Ellie hurt me." Lloyd finally admitted the words aloud, and a weight lifted from his shoulders. "She betrayed my trust, and I don't know how to forgive her. She went against my wishes by trying to sell my carvings."

"I know that." Rebecca's brown eyes were full of understanding. "And Ellie knows that too. Do you know why she tried to convince Gene to consider selling your carvings?"

Lloyd shrugged. "She just wanted to see them at the store."

"That's not it at all." Rebecca shook her head. "Seth's paycheck used to cover all their household expenses. Now that Seth's gone, Ellie and Margaret don't even have enough money for food. It's true that she was still considering showing him the dove because she believes so much in your talent, which is why she took it to work with her. But she was still reluctant to go against your wishes until Gene said he had to cut her hours because sales are down. When she heard that, she panicked and showed Gene the carving."

"What?" Lloyd felt as if he'd been punched in the stomach.

"Ellie had hoped that by selling your carvings she could not only help you have confidence in your work, but help Gene, and save her job. She had no idea *Dat* told you your hobby was prideful. You didn't share that with her."

"Why didn't she tell me things were that bad for her and her *mamm*?" Lloyd asked, his voice thick with emotion. "I even asked her once if they were all right."

Rebecca shook her head. "I don't know why she didn't tell you, but she didn't even tell me until now, and I've been one of her best friends since we were *kinner*. She feels terrible for going behind your back. She regrets it, and she wants to make it up to you. You have to give her a chance."

Lloyd studied his hands as her words soaked in. Why hadn't Ellie felt she could tell him she needed help? Hadn't they become close enough over the past weeks? Guilt and shame coursed through him. Why wasn't he a better friend to her?

"You're both miserable, Lloyd," Rebecca continued. "You need to talk to her. We all make mistakes, but it's also our way to forgive. So stop being so stubborn and forgive her. She loves you, and you love her too."

He nodded. "You're right."

She smiled. "I know I am. Now, tomorrow you can tell her you forgive her." She pointed toward the house. "Let's go in. It's getting late."

Lloyd followed her up the steps, and his thoughts turned to Seth. He remembered how Seth told him he would always take care of his mother since his father had passed away. When they reached the porch, he stopped at a new thought. His carvings were an opportunity to help Seth take care of Margaret and Ellie and also keep Seth's memory alive.

"Becca," he said, making her turn around. "I just had the best idea. Do you think *Mamm* and *Dat* are still awake?"

"They might be." She gave him a befuddled expression.

Lloyd hurried through the kitchen and family room to his parents' bedroom. He spotted faint light flickering under the door, and he knocked softly.

"Come in," his father's voice called.

"*Dat?*" Lloyd asked, pushing the door open. "I need to discuss something with you."

Both his parents were propped up in bed reading. They lowered their books to their laps and studied him.

"What's going on?" *Dat* asked.

"I have an idea, and I want you to hear me out." He stepped into the room and Rebecca followed him. "You have already agreed with me that we need to do what we can to help Margaret Lapp. Well, I believe that my carvings could help her."

His father shook his head. "I don't understand."

"Ellie told me she took the job at Gene's store to help support her mother. I only found out tonight how much she needs the job. Although her *onkels* make the mortgage payments on their farm, Seth used to take care of all the household expenses, including buying groceries. Now that he's gone, they have no money for food," Lloyd continued as he stood at the foot of the bed. "Gene has cut back the number of hours Ellie can work because sales have been down at his shop. Ellie thinks my birds can help boost their sales.

"I want Gene to sell my carvings at his place, and I'll give all the money I earn to Margaret and Ellie. My carvings will help support them since Seth isn't here to take care of them anymore."

"That's a great idea," Rebecca said as she sidled up to Lloyd.

His father scowled. "I don't know. It's still prideful to sell those birds."

"How is that prideful?" *Mamm* asked, placing her book on her bedside table. "Seth used to make sheds to support his family. Lloyd will be doing the same thing, except that he's making birds."

"I agree," Rebecca chimed in, grinning at Lloyd. "I think Seth would love that, and Ellie will too."

"*Dat*, please," Lloyd continued. "I really want your permission for this. God has put this in my heart. I believe my birds are supposed to help someone, and I want to use them to help Margaret and Ellie. Please give me your blessing on this."

"I think it's a *wunderbaar* idea, Wilmer." *Mamm* touched *Dat's* hand. "Other people are helping Margaret, and this is another way for us to help, giving Lloyd our blessing and supporting his efforts."

His father nodded and his expression softened. "You're right, Lydia. We need to do our part by approving this plan. You have my blessing, Lloyd."

"*Danki.*" Lloyd smiled as hope flourished in his soul. "*Gut nacht.*"

Lloyd followed Rebecca out to the kitchen. "I can't believe I didn't think of this earlier."

"Ellie will love it." Rebecca touched his arm. "This is a wonderful way to help her and her mother."

"I can't wait to tell her." He started for the back door.

"Where are you going?" Rebecca asked.

"I'm going to see Ellie," he said.

"But it's late," Rebecca called after him.

"I can't wait until morning." Lloyd sprinted out the back door and down the porch steps. As he hurried to the barn to retrieve his horse and buggy, he hoped Ellie was still awake.

⌀

Ellie was drifting off to sleep when she thought she heard the sound of horse hooves crunching up her driveway. She leapt out of bed and peeked out the window. She gasped when she saw a horse and buggy making its way to the back porch.

She pulled on her robe and rushed down the steps to the back door, pushing it open just as Lloyd climbed the steps.

"Lloyd?" she asked, clutching her robe tight to her body and hoping *Mamm* was still asleep. "What are you doing here?"

"I had to talk to you." He gestured toward the glider. "Would you please sit with me? I promise I won't take too much of your time." His expression was anxious, and his warm eyes pleaded with her to say yes.

"All right." Her pulse leapt as she sank onto the glider beside him.

"I owe you an apology," he began. "I'm so sorry for losing my temper with you. I realize now that you never meant to hurt me, and you believe my carvings should be shared."

"I was wrong." She shook her head.

"No. Actually, you were right." Lloyd smiled, and her insides swelled with hope. "I should sell them, and I want to sell them."

"You do?" Ellie regarded him with suspicion. "I don't understand."

"I decided tonight that I want to sell them at Gene's store, and my father gave me permission." Lloyd took her hands in his, and she enjoyed the security of his warm skin against hers. "I want to sell them in memory of Seth and give all the money to you and your *mamm*."

"Why would you give the money to us?"

"Rebecca told me you need to work to even be able to buy groceries." His expression clouded with concern. "Why didn't you tell me you needed help?"

A lump swelled in Ellie's throat. "I don't know." She shrugged. "I guess I didn't want to ask for help. I thought I could take care of my *mamm* myself."

"I want to help you take care of your *mamm*. I know that's what Seth would want me to do. If the sales help Gene increase your hours again, and you want to keep your job, too, that's your decision. You aren't a *kind*. But I want to help."

Ellie sniffed as tears filled her eyes. "Lloyd, that is too generous."

"It's not nearly enough to show you how much I care for you," he said. "Ellie, I love you. I've loved you since you fell in the mud while you were chasing Daisy. I'm so sorry I was upset with you for showing the dove to Gene. You're the sweetest, most thoughtful *maedel* I've ever met, and I know you would never betray me. I can't stand the thought of losing you." He touched her cheek and wiped away a tear. "I would be honored if you would be my girlfriend."

Ellie was speechless as she searched his eyes. Was she dreaming? Had Lloyd truly said he loved her? This couldn't possibly be real.

"Will you be my girlfriend?" he asked, worry filling his expression.

"*Ya*, of course I will." Her heart raced with happiness. "I love you too. I've loved you since I was twelve years old."

"You have?" His eyes widened with shock.

"*Ya*." She smiled. "I was hoping that someday you'd figure out how I felt about you and then decide to love me too."

"*Danki* for waiting for me." Lloyd leaned down and brushed his lips over hers, sending her stomach into a wild swirl. "I'm so sorry it took me this long to figure out how strongly I feel about you. I promise I will never let you go."

As he kissed her again, Ellie closed her eyes and silently

thanked God for her precious friendship with Lloyd and his wonderful carved birds. Then she chuckled at her next thought.

"You know what I think Seth would say, Lloyd? I think he'd call us the love birds."

Lloyd chuckled too. "And I think he'd be right."

DISCUSSION QUESTIONS

1. Ellie is determined to convince Lloyd to sell his special carvings despite his clear objections. While Ellie's intentions are good, she is not taking into consideration what Lloyd truly wants. Think of a time when you may have had misguided intentions for a loved one. Share this with the group.

2. At the beginning of the story, Lloyd sees Ellie only as Seth's little sister. His feelings for her change throughout the story. What do you think causes this transformation?

3. Lloyd feels Ellie betrayed him when she showed the carved dove to Gene Rider. Were you ever betrayed by a close friend or loved one? How did you come to grips with that betrayal? Were you able to forgive that person and move on? If so, where did you find the strength to forgive? Share this with the group.

4. Ellie truly regrets going behind Lloyd's back and showing the carving to Gene Rider. Did you ever lie to someone or do something behind their back and then have to ask for

forgiveness? Did that person forgive you? Why or why not? What Bible verses would help with this?

5. Which character can you identify with the most? Which character seemed to carry the most emotional stake in the story? Was it Ellie, Lloyd, Margaret, or someone else?

6. Rebecca is determined to help Lloyd and Ellie work out their differences. Have you ever found yourself as the peacemaker due to a family, social, or work situation? If so, how did you handle the conflict? Did it turn out the way you'd hoped? Share this with the group.

7. Lloyd's father calls the carvings prideful at the beginning of the story. He changes his opinion, however, near the end of the story and agrees to allow Lloyd to sell the birds after Lloyd explains that God has called him to use the carvings to help the Lapp family. Think about a time in your life when you were certain of God's will. Share this with the group.

8. What did you know about the Amish before reading this book? What did you learn?

ACKNOWLEDGMENTS

As always, I'm thankful for my loving family. Special thanks to my special Amish friends who patiently answer my endless stream of questions. You're a blessing in my life.

To my agent, Sue Brower—You are my own personal superhero! I can't thank you enough for your guidance, advice, and friendship. I'm thankful that our paths have crossed and our partnership will continue long into the future. You are a tremendous blessing in my life.

Thank you to my amazing editor, Becky Philpott, for your friendship and guidance. Thank you also to Jean Bloom, who always helps polish my stories and connect the dots between my books. You're a blessing! I'm grateful to each and every person at HarperCollins Christian Publishing who helped make this book a reality.

Thank you most of all to God—for giving me the inspiration and the words to glorify You. I'm grateful and humbled You've chosen this path for me.

DAN DAVIS PHOTOGRAPHY

Amy Clipston is the award-winning and bestselling author of the Kauffman Amish Bakery series. Her novels have hit multiple bestseller lists including CBD, CBA, and ECPA. Amy holds a degree in communications from Virginia Wesleyan College and works full-time for the City of Charlotte, NC. Amy lives in North Carolina with her husband, two sons, and four spoiled rotten cats.

Facebook: Amy Clipston
Twitter: @AmyClipston

A Bid for Love

KATHLEEN FULLER

To my husband James. Love you always.

GLOSSARY

aenti—aunt
bruder—brother
daed—dad
danki—thank you
familye—family
geh—go
grossmutter—grandmother
gut—good
haus—house
kaffee—coffee
kapp—prayer cap
kinner—children

lieb—love
maedel—girl
mamm—mom
mann—husband
mei—my
mudder—mother
nee—no
nix—nothing
schee—pretty
sohn—son
vatter—father
ya—yes

CHAPTER 1

ill he stop by today?

W Hannah Lynne Beiler tried to pull her gaze away from Ezra Yutzy, but it was impossible. Instead of staring at him, she should be focusing on selling the butter and pies at her stand inside the main building at the Middlefield Market. But once she saw him across the room, perusing a table covered with a variety of tools for sale, she couldn't stop looking at him.

Her cheeks heated as they always did when Ezra was around. So what if he was twenty-seven and she was only twenty-two? What difference did it make that he barely spoke to her every time he stopped by her stand to buy butter? Did it matter that the man of her dreams barely knew she existed? Or that everyone knew he was a *very* confirmed bachelor?

"That's a big sigh," Rachael said.

"I didn't notice I was sighing." Hannah Lynne glanced at her sister-in-law, who had joined her a few minutes earlier. Though she married Hannah Lynne's brother Gideon two years ago, and he made a good living running the family dairy farm, Rachael still grew and sold plants. Usually she had a small stand outside, but while today's weather prohibited that, setting up her stand inside the market building hadn't impeded her sales. She'd already sold all she had.

"Is something wrong?" Rachael asked.

Hannah Lynne flicked another glance in Ezra's direction, but he had disappeared. She hid her disappointment. *"Nix* is wrong."

"Gut." Rachael glanced at the dwindling crowd inside the building. The Middlefield Market was held every Monday, rain or shine. Most of the sellers marketed their wares outside, except during the winter months. But Hannah Lynne preferred indoors. She had been selling her own fresh churned butter and her mother's seasonal fruit pies for the past two years, and she rarely had to take any unsold items home. Today might be the exception.

"Not much of a crowd this morning," Rachael commented, smiling at a Yankee woman as she passed by their table.

"I think the rain kept most everyone home." Hannah Lynne tugged her navy blue sweater closer to her body, covering the light blue dress she'd put on that morning. Then she saw Ezra again, and her breath caught. He was coming toward them.

His height made him easy to spot. He wore his straw hat pushed low on his brow, but not far enough to obscure her view of his face. Brownish-black wavy hair curled over his ears, the color matching the thick brows above his blue-gray eyes. What fascinated her most was the small, dark freckle under his left eye, resting right on top of his cheekbone. She could imagine skimming the tip of her finger across it—

"Glad to see you haven't run out of butter yet." He stood in front of her table, his gaze not meeting hers, but focusing on the square packages. "Thought I might have been too late." He finally looked up, his lips curving into a smile.

She gripped the edge of the table, her pulse starting to thrum. She wondered how she could convince him to *unconfirm* his confirmed bachelorhood.

Ezra glanced at her price sign. "Five dollars, right?" He dug into the pocket of his dark blue jacket and pulled out a few bills. She watched as he unfolded the money with his work-roughened hands. A carpenter by trade, he was also renovating a Yankee house he'd bought a month ago and converting it to an Amish home for himself. Gideon had commented that it was a strange thing for Ezra to do, considering he wasn't dating a *maedel*. "Why *geh* to the trouble if he's just going to live there by himself?"

Hannah Lynne had no idea, and she wasn't sure she wanted to find out. What if he was secretly seeing someone? If he was, he was doing an excellent job hiding it.

Ezra peeled off a five-dollar bill and held it out to her. "Did you raise *yer* price?"

"Huh?" She looked at him, her face reddening.

"Actually," Rachael said, "we're offering a special deal. Five dollars will get you two packages of butter. Throw in an extra two dollars and you can have three."

He rubbed his chin. "That's a lot of butter for one person."

"It freezes," Hannah Lynne blurted. *Ugh.* Couldn't she have thought of something clever to say? Something *flirty*?

"I don't have a freezer," he said. He glanced at the butter again. "But *mei mudder* has a gas-powered one. I'm sure she'd appreciate the extra butter, and I can't resist a *gut* deal." He counted out the seven dollars and handed it to Rachael, who was already putting the butter in a paper bag.

"Did you find what you were looking for at the market today?" Rachael asked. Thank goodness her sister-in-law's customer-service habits had automatically kicked in. At least Hannah Lynne *hoped* Rachael had no idea she'd become speechless and immobile in this man's presence.

Ezra shook his head. "*Nee.* We need an extra hand planer at the shop. Thought they might have one here, but I didn't see any. Maybe next week." He took the bag from Rachael. "Appreciate it." He turned and left, and Rachael busily rearranged the remaining goods they hadn't sold.

Hannah Lynne finally smiled at him, even though he was already walking away. Carrying her butter . . . and her heart.

Then she frowned, knowing she was fooling herself. Yet a tiny spark of hope remained alive that one day the man she loved would notice her. And maybe one day, if she hoped and prayed hard enough . . . he would love her back.

～৯৫

Ezra dodged the heavy raindrops as he headed for his buggy, carrying more butter than he knew what to do with. That was the first time he'd seen Rachael Beiler at Hannah Lynne's stand. Rachael didn't know he bought a pound of butter from Hannah Lynne almost every Monday. His purchases were taking up more and more room in his mother's gas freezer, to the point that she had already transferred some of the butter blocks to a portable cooler. Still, he'd been truthful when he said he couldn't resist a good deal.

He also couldn't resist stopping by Hannah Lynne's table.

As he untied his horse, he wondered, not for the first time, why he always wènt to her table when he visited the market. Sure, he liked butter, especially slathered on a stack of hot pancakes. He also really liked the sayings she wrote inside the paper butter wrapper—a proverb, a joke, a few words of wisdom, a thought-provoking Scripture verse.

But that wasn't enough to keep him going back. There was something else, something he couldn't put his finger on. It wasn't like she talked to him when he bought the butter, which was strange. He knew Hannah Lynne Beiler wasn't afraid to talk. He'd seen her with her friends after church service, often smiling and gesturing with her hands as she spoke. He wouldn't characterize her as quiet, yet each time he visited her stand she became almost mute.

She did have a nice smile. He had to admit that—though unfortunately, he noticed she hadn't smiled today.

He shrugged, tossed the bag of butter on the bench seat next to him, and guided his horse to his parents' home. His new house, which was precisely three doors down from theirs, was barely legal to live in by both Yankee and Amish standards. For some unknown reason he'd been drawn to the house, even though it was too large for just him. Because it needed extensive renovation he'd gotten it for next to nothing. At least the barn was in decent shape. Oddly enough, he also felt a sense of peace once he purchased the property, and he was looking forward to making it his permanent home.

The rain started coming down harder, bringing a stronger breeze. The maples and pin oaks had already started to turn, their green leaves transforming into bright yellows, reds, and oranges. He turned down his street. Their cabinetry shop was behind his parents' house, and he would drop the butter off in his mother's kitchen before he went back to work.

Maybe next week he'd find that hand planer he was looking for. Or maybe not. There was one thing he knew for sure—if Hannah Lynne was there next Monday, he'd stop by her stand. He'd buy her butter. And he hoped he'd get to see her smile.

CHAPTER 2

H ow was the market today?"

Hannah Lynne set down the cardboard box hold-
ing two unsold fruit pies on the kitchen table and looked at her
mother. "Slow," she said, removing her black bonnet. It had water
spots on it from the rain that was still falling. "I brought two
pies back."

"Only two?" Her mother smiled as she stood over the cutting board on the counter, her knife slicing through a carrot with
quick precision. "You took ten. I'd say that was a *gut* day, despite
it being slow." She glanced at Hannah Lynne. "Did you sell all
yer butter?"

"*Ya.*" She stepped into the mudroom, right off the kitchen,
and hung up her bonnet and shawl. Later she would give her
mother her share of the money from the sale of the pies, plus a
little extra from the butter money. Her mother said she could
keep all her money, but Hannah Lynne didn't feel right about
that. She wanted to contribute to the household expenses. The
rest she was saving for the future . . . whatever it held. "I'll have to

make some more butter this week," she said as she stepped back into the kitchen.

"Do you plan on making anything for the auction?" *Mamm* slid the carrot slices into a pot of boiling water on the gas stove.

Hannah Lynne paused. The annual auction to benefit the DDC Clinic, a special needs care and research facility in Middlefield, was a couple of weeks away. Several years ago the Amish community had organized the auction, and this year it was being held at the Middlefield Market. Over the years it had grown, and Yankees attended as well. Many of the items, from handmade quilts to cords of firewood to simple broom-and-dustpan sets, were auctioned off, and the proceeds given to help support the clinic. Hannah Lynne's family had always made donations.

Last year she put together a basket of butter and cheeses for the pick-a-prize drawings that took place during the auction. A small paper bag was placed in front of each donated item, and participants dropped pre-purchased tickets in the bags for any items they were interested in winning. One ticket was drawn from each bag, announcing the winner of that item.

"Hannah Lynne?" Her mother turned to her, her light-brown eyebrows pushing together. "Did you hear me?"

Hannah Lynne nodded. "*Ya.* I'm not sure what I'm going to do." She didn't want to make the same donation as last year, but she'd have to figure out something soon.

Mamm put down the wooden spoon she was using to stir the vegetable soup and went to Hannah Lynne. "Sit for a minute," she said, pulling out a chair from the table and sitting down.

Giving her mother a wary look, Hannah Lynne pushed the

box with pies aside and sat down across from her. "Is something wrong?"

"You tell me." *Mamm* folded her hands and rested them on the tabletop. "You haven't been *yer* sunshiny self lately."

"I'm sorry."

"Don't apologize. I just want to know if there is anything you need to talk about." She unfolded her hands and reached for both of Hannah Lynne's. "You know I'm always here for you."

Hannah Lynne nodded and forced a smile. It was ridiculous how her feelings for Ezra were now affecting every aspect of her life. Harboring secret, unrequited love was becoming exhausting.

"Is it Gideon and Rachael?"

Hannah Lynne frowned. "I don't understand."

"There have been a lot of changes in the past two years. Like Gideon getting married, and *yer* older *bruder* moving to Indiana right after that."

"Gideon lives next door, *Mamm*. I see him all the time. Why would I be upset about that? Or about Abraham moving away? We get regular letters from him and his wife."

"I know . . . but it's not the same." Her mother withdrew her hands. "Things aren't the way they used to be."

Hannah Lynne caught a note of sadness in *Mamm*'s voice. This time she grasped her mother's hand. "I'm not going anywhere," she said firmly.

"That's what I'm worried about." She sighed and looked at Hannah Lynne, who was feeling even more confused. "You should be thinking about a life of *yer* own. A *familye* of *yer* own."

"Oh. But wouldn't that make you even sadder? If I left home too?"

"Sad?" Her mother chuckled. "*Lieb*, I'm not sad. I'm happy for *mei sohns*. They've found the perfect women for them. They're making their way in the world, and doing it while staying true to their faith." She paused. "I'll admit I don't like change very much. But I'll take it if it means *mei kinner* are happy. I want the same happiness for you."

So do I. But how could that happen when the one man she thought could make her happy was out of reach? "God's timing," she said softly. "That's what you've always told me."

"*Ya*. God's timing is best." *Mamm* glanced down at their hands, fingers entwined. "I hesitate to ask this, because I know it's not *mei* business." She was looking at Hannah Lynne now. "Is there . . . anyone?"

Hannah Lynne pressed her lips together and looked away.

"Never mind." Her mother gave her hand a squeeze and released it, then stood. "I shouldn't have pried."

"It's all right." Hannah Lynne wished she could give her mother the answer they both wanted. Maybe someday she could.

"Vegetable soup and bread okay for supper?" *Mamm* went back to the stove and stirred the soup. "I guess we'll have pie for dessert."

"Sounds delicious." Hannah Lynne rose, glad her mother was dropping the subject. And like her mother, she was happy for her brothers. She only wished she had some of that happiness for herself.

She pushed the empty chair to the table, then ran her fingers absently over the smooth pinewood. Her mother was right— being quiet and moody wasn't like her. She missed the sunshiny part of herself too. Maybe if Josiah Miller asked to take her home from the next Sunday evening singing, she wouldn't make an excuse to tell him no this time. In fact, maybe she should start paying more attention to him as soon as possible. He didn't compare to Ezra, but he was a nice guy. Unlike Ezra, he at least seemed a little interested in her.

Hannah Lynne left the kitchen, already feeling more at ease. She'd focus on making more butter to sell at the market and on figuring out a donation for the auction. She had plenty of things to keep her mind off Ezra Yutzy. After a year of pining after him, perhaps it was time to let him go.

❧

That Sunday, Hannah Lynne put Operation Pay-Attention-to-Josiah-Miller in action. After the service, she lingered outside the barn to wait for him. He was talking to a couple of his friends a few feet away, so she bided her time. She was determined to not try to spot Ezra. That's what she usually did on Sundays, even to only catch a glimpse of him.

Josiah's the one you're interested in, remember?

As if he sensed her looking at him, Josiah turned around and smiled. He gave his friends a short wave good-bye and headed toward her.

"Hi, Hannah Lynne," he said, his hazel eyes shaded by his black hat.

"Hi," she said softly.

He smiled, and she tried to convince herself he was just as striking as Ezra. He definitely wasn't bad looking. Josiah was average height, with nice blond hair and a perpetual tan from working outside as a landscaper most of the year. She returned his smile, waiting for him to say something. But he stared at her, his expression slightly . . . goofy.

Goofy. That was one thing Ezra wasn't.

She steeled her resolve, searched her mind for a topic of conversation, then asked, "Are you going to the auction?"

"Which one?"

"The one for the DDC Clinic," she said, realizing she should have clarified. Auctions were always being held in the area, but this one was special.

"*Nee*. Too crowded." He sniffed, which sounded more like a snort.

"Did you donate something, then?"

Josiah shrugged. "Hadn't really thought about it. It's not something I usually do."

"The clinic is very important to the community."

"I guess. I don't really know what they do there."

She proceeded to tell him, but his eyes started to glaze over. "Anyway," she said, a little irritated that he wasn't interested in the important research the doctors at the clinic conducted, or in how so many children benefited from the special care offered. "If you change *yer* mind, you can come with me." Her eyes widened. Had she really just asked him out?

He shook his head. "I won't be changing *mei* mind. I'll probably be working on rebuilding a lawn mower for Carl Biddle."

She feigned interest as he started explaining to her that by the time he was done with his Yankee friend's mower, he would have improved the power by 20 percent. "That's nice," she said, her gaze straying over his shoulder. She drew in a sharp breath when she saw Ezra walking to his buggy with long, even strides. He was so handsome in his church clothes. He was handsome in anything he wore.

"So would you like to?"

Josiah's question drew her attention. Realizing she was being unfair to him by looking at—and longing for—Ezra, she gave Josiah what she hoped was an innocent smile. "I'm sorry. Could you repeat the question?"

"Would you like me to take you home from the next singing?"

She cut a quick glance at Ezra as he climbed into the buggy, then nodded. "*Ya,*" she said, looking at Josiah again. "I would like that."

"*Gut.*" His grin widened, which made his expression a bit more endearing than goofy. Why couldn't she find him as appealing as Ezra? Maybe when they spent more time together she would.

"Then it's a date," he said. "I'll see you then."

As he turned and walked away, Hannah Lynne wondered if she had done the right thing. When she saw Ezra's buggy leave without him glancing her way, she knew she had.

～◎◇～

Ezra went into his mother's kitchen to grab a sandwich made from some leftover ham. As he continued to work on his own house, the realization that his current living arrangement would be coming to an end became clearer each day. He'd definitely miss his mother's cooking.

His father had left early that morning to go to the local

sawmill and haggle about wood prices. The owner of the mill always gave them a fair deal, but *Daed* enjoyed the dickering. Ezra sometimes went with him, especially on a Saturday, but he had a rush, custom-ordered sideboard to finish by the end of next week. It was part of the reason he hadn't gone to the market this past Monday, and he probably wouldn't make it this coming Monday either.

It wasn't like he'd needed more butter, anyway.

He'd seen Hannah Lynne at church, though, talking to Josiah Miller. He frowned as he cut two thick slices of bread from the loaf in the bread box. As he'd walked toward his buggy to go home, he'd been close enough to see both of their faces. They'd paid no attention to him, but it was clear from the wide-eyed way Josiah looked at Hannah Lynne that he was interested in her. It was also clear from the way Hannah Lynne peeked at Josiah from underneath what Ezra knew to be long, brown eyelashes that she was welcoming that interest.

"Ow!" He glanced down at his hand, realizing he'd slid the knife blade across the tip of a finger. The cut wasn't deep, but it stung. He shook his head and turned on the tap, running his finger underneath the cool water. Why was he even thinking about Hannah Lynne and Josiah? Yes, he thought he'd seen Hannah Lynne glance at him for a moment, but he was sure he imagined it. Her focus was all on Josiah.

Lucky guy.

Ezra jerked up his head. Where had that thought come from?

A knock sounded on the front door of the house. Ezra turned off the tap, grabbed a dish towel, and dried his finger. The bleeding had already stopped. When he opened the door he saw Sarah

Detweiler, one of his mother's closest friends, standing on the front porch.

"Hello, Ezra," Sarah said, smiling.

Ezra had known the Detweilers all his life, and had even been friendly with Sarah's son Aaron, who was a few years older than Ezra. Friendly, until Aaron was arrested for dealing drugs. When Aaron returned from jail he'd straightened up his act, landed a job as a farrier, and married Elisabeth Byler. How long ago was that now? Ezra couldn't remember. All his friends, even his most superficial ones, had either left the community or were married and busy with their own families.

Realizing he was leaving Sarah's greeting unanswered, he opened the door wider. "Hi, Sarah. Come on in."

She nodded her thanks and walked into the living room. He shut the door against the cool outside air. "*Mamm* isn't here right now. I'm not sure where she went." His mother had left shortly after his father had, and she hadn't told Ezra where she was going.

"Oh." Sarah looked puzzled, her black bonnet shading her wrinkled forehead. "She must have forgotten."

"Forgotten what?"

"I mentioned last Sunday that I would be by today to pick up the quilt for the auction. She said she wanted to donate one." She looked up at Ezra. Sarah wasn't a short woman, but Ezra's six-foot-three height made him tower over almost everyone. "You wouldn't happen to know which quilt she was planning to donate?"

He shook his head, then spied a quilt neatly folded on the chair nearest the door. He didn't recognize the blue, white, and yellow spread. Then again, he never paid attention to stuff like that. Quilts were usually in two places in the house—on a bed or draped over the couch. Not folded up on a chair. This had to be the quilt she was planning to donate. "Here," he said, snatching it off the chair. It felt soft. Old, even. For a tiny second he doubted his theory. But why else would the quilt be here? He handed it to Sarah. "I'm sure this is it."

Sarah took the quilt. "*Danki*, Ezra. Are you planning to come to the auction Friday night?"

"Wouldn't miss it." He went every year, and usually came away with some good deals. He enjoyed listening to the auctioneers, usually Amish men who took turns making the calls. A Yankee service was hired to manage the auction, but the Amish auctioneers did the bulk of the work.

Sarah smiled. "Tell *yer mamm* I'll talk to her soon."

"Will do."

After Sarah left, Ezra finished making his sandwich, his mind now turning to the cherrywood sideboard he needed to sand. He also thought about what he could donate to the auction. He gave something every year, usually a small piece of furniture or a wooden toy he'd privately worked on and donated anonymously. He gained a lot of satisfaction knowing the sale of his handcrafted items went to a good cause.

This year, though, he had nothing to give. He'd spent so much time working on his house, and there wouldn't be enough time for him to make something. He decided to take some extra money with him and make a cash donation. It wasn't a homemade item, but it was something.

CHAPTER 3

An hour before the auction started, Hannah Lynne rushed inside the building at the Middlefield Market, basket in hand. She was late, and she hoped Sarah Detweiler, who was in charge of both the pick-a-prize drawings and the quilts at the auction, would still let Hannah Lynne make her donation—a set of matching cloth napkins and a table runner. She'd made them the week before out of fancier fabric than she would have normally used. But she liked the bright primary colors—lemon yellow, royal blue, and crimson red—cut into thick strips and sewn together to make a striped pattern. Just looking at her handiwork, neatly arranged in the off-white, square-shaped wicker basket she'd purchased to contain the items, made her smile.

She waited as Sarah finished talking to another woman who was helping her set up the pick-a-prize items and the small paper bags that went in front of them. Hannah Lynne usually bought a few tickets, but she'd never won anything.

As she waited, she glanced at her basket again and smiled. She was pleased with her offering and hoped it would garner a lot of tickets. She looked up, just in time to see Ezra standing a few feet away, looking at a wringer washer that would be auctioned off later.

She clenched the handle of her basket. She hadn't seen him since church the Sunday before last. He hadn't come to the Middlefield Market for two Mondays—or if he did, he hadn't stopped by her table.

Hannah Lynne turned her back to him, reminding herself that because she had agreed to let Josiah take her home from the next singing, she had no business thinking about Ezra Yutzy anymore. Never mind that her skin was tingling from him being so close by.

"Oh, hi, Hannah Lynne," Sarah said from behind her, putting her hand on Hannah Lynne's shoulder. "Did you bring something for the auction?"

"*Ya*," she said, turning around. Disappointment shot through her when she saw Ezra was gone. Giving her head a quick shake, she focused on Sarah. "It's not too late to donate, is it?"

"*Nee*," Sarah took the basket from her. "Oh. These are very . . . bright."

Hannah Lynne smiled as she nodded. "I liked the fabric a lot."

"It should be popular with our Yankee visitors." She set the basket in an empty space on one of the long tables that were already covered with a variety of small auction items, including homemade cookbooks, candles, quilted potholders, and crocheted layettes. The layettes were made of pastel yarns, of course. Hannah Lynne's donation stood out among the others.

"Do you need any help?" Hannah Lynne asked.

"*Nee*, but *danki* for offering." Sarah smiled. "We're just about ready."

Hannah Lynne told Sarah good-bye, then walked among the tables, looking at the smaller items for the pick-a-prize drawing, making mental notes about which ones she would try to win. Then she went to look at the quilts.

Several quilts were hung over a long clothesline, carefully secured with clothespins. Slowly she walked past the first two, examining the perfect stitching. She was a decent seamstress, but she couldn't create anything as beautiful as what had been donated today. A sign was posted near the quilts, explaining how they would be auctioned off. This would be a silent auction, where each bid would be written on a sheet of paper until the bidding time ended. She didn't intend on participating in this one. She had enough quilts at home. Besides, handmade quilts like these always went for a high price.

Then she froze. Her heart skipped more than one beat and she changed her mind about not bidding. She couldn't believe she almost didn't see it. She moved closer, her heart pounding. She had to have this quilt.

‎⁓❧⁓

Ezra wandered around the interior of the market building, eventually making his way to the back where a large group of women and a few men had set up tables and stands selling all kinds of food—homemade pretzels, beefy hot dogs, freshly fried and glazed donuts, cream sticks, barbecue sandwiches, small bags of chips, and more. Right outside the building was another tent set up with just baked goods. He'd visit that one next. His stomach rumbled with hunger. Right now he was ready for a hot dog and a can of pop.

After he purchased his food, Ezra found a spot to stand along the perimeter of the room. As he ate, he observed the milling crowd. Amish, Yankees, even several groups of Mennonites had all arrived from nearby counties to enjoy the auction. There were a lot of families. He also saw a couple of young children who were probably recipients of the special needs clinic's services. One was a young Amish girl in a wheelchair. She looked to be about five years old. From the stiff posture of her limbs he could see she had cerebral palsy.

The other child was walking, but Ezra noticed the young boy's cleft lip, one that had been surgically repaired. His straw hat was tipped back on his head, revealing a hank of light blond bang across his forehead. He grinned, showing he was missing two front teeth. Ezra thanked God that the community had the resources to care for him, and any other children with special needs. Although he knew he shouldn't be prideful, he couldn't help but feel a spark of satisfaction deep inside that they were all coming together to take care of their own.

He polished off the hot dog as more people filed in, some perusing the auction items, others purchasing food, still others finding a spot in the stacks of bleachers that had been pulled out for seating. He never sat at these things, instead preferring to walk around the floor and interact with the auction.

He tipped his head back and finished his pop, threw away his can and napkin, and headed for the middle of the building where there was a thickening crowd around several of the items on display. Many of the women—Amish, Yankee, and Mennonite—were looking at the quilts. He spied the one his mother had donated. She hadn't said anything to him about it, so he assumed he'd been right in giving the quilt to Sarah that day.

Ezra squinted a bit, his gaze locking on Hannah Lynne. She was there, staring at it, her mouth partially open almost as if in a state of shock. Strange. He frowned. Was there something wrong with her? He rubbed his eyebrow as he walked over to her, noticing that her gaze never left the quilt. When he stood next to her, she still didn't move. He doubted she realized he was there.

"Hannah Lynne?" he asked, leaning over a bit so he could see her face.

She slowly turned to him and smiled.

His voice suddenly stuck in his throat. Her smile was always appealing. But for some reason her expression was different . . . and beautiful. He couldn't stop from basking in the unexpected glow of Hannah Lynne Beiler's gorgeous smile. It was as if he'd never seen her before.

She turned from him, looking at the quilt again. "It's perfect, isn't it?"

He swallowed, his mouth dry as a cotton sock. "What?"

"This quilt." She reached out and touched the fabric. "It even feels the same," she whispered.

He had no idea what she was talking about. And he didn't really care, at least not about the quilt. He was more concerned about the tickle in his belly, and the fact that he couldn't take his eyes off her—two things he'd never experienced before.

She opened her small black purse and pulled out a wallet. He saw her thumbing through the bills before snapping the wallet closed. Then she grabbed the pencil next to the piece of paper on the table in front of the quilt. She wrote on the paper, took a step back, and closed her eyes. Her lips moved as if she was saying a silent prayer. Then she opened her eyes, turned, and walked away . . . as if she'd never seen him at all.

He followed her with his gaze, pushing back his hat to scratch his suddenly itchy forehead. *What had just happened?*

"Excuse me."

Ezra turned at the sound of an older woman's voice. The gray-haired woman's bright pink-and-lime-green-striped sweater was almost blinding, and she smelled like she'd dunked herself in a vat of sickly sweet perfume. She gave him an annoyed look, and he realized he was standing in her way. He stepped aside, then turned to search for Hannah Lynne. But he couldn't see her. She had disappeared into the crowd.

He looked at the quilt again to see if he had made a mistake. No, it was the one his mother had donated. More women were admiring it now, but none of them seemed to be showing the interest or sheer joy Hannah Lynne had. She really wanted to win that quilt.

For some reason he would be hard-pressed to explain, he really wanted her to win it too.

Had she bid enough? As the main auction started and the women admiring the quilts dispersed, he had the crazy notion to check out the bids. Then he shook his head. What would happen if he found out, anyway? What would he do if she didn't have the winning bid?

How would Hannah Lynne feel if they didn't call her name?

He paused, scratching his forehead again. Why was he overly

concerned about this, when he should have been paying attention to the auction? That was his primary reason for coming. He turned his back on the quilts and went to the crowd that had gathered in front of the auctioneer's platform. Right now a young Amishman, who couldn't be more than sixteen or so, was auctioning off one of the wringer washers. He was doing a fine job of it too.

Ezra was thinking earlier that he could use a wringer washer in his new house. He should bid on it.

Instead he turned away from the auctioneer and the men helping him keep track of the bids and scanned the crowd again. Where was Hannah Lynne? Why hadn't she stayed around to see if she had the winning bid? He walked back to the quilts and saw that the papers with the bids had been removed. The winner was already decided. He frowned. Later he could try to figure out why he cared so much, but right now he needed to find her.

Because for some strange reason, he knew he had to be with her when the winner of that quilt was announced.

⚈⚈⚈

Hannah Lynne paced outside the entryway of the Middlefield Market building. She hugged her arms as the cool night air enveloped her. All around she could hear the sounds of the auction—the late Yankee arrivals pulling their cars into the huge gravel parking lot, the faint whinnies of buggy horses as they waited for their owners to return, the rapid fire of the auctioneer's voice as he auctioned off the latest items. In years past she'd been in the thick of the auction, visiting with friends, munching on sweet, sticky glazed donuts, and enjoying the bidding.

But that was before she saw the quilt. Now her nerves were tightly wound, coiled, and ready to spring at any moment. She had to win that quilt. She felt so rattled she hadn't been able to stick around to see if anyone else had bid on it. She stopped her pacing and for the tenth time closed her eyes and prayed. *Please, Lord. I bid every cent I could spare. Please let that be enough. In fact, weren't you the one who prompted me to bring more money with me than I normally do?*

"There you are."

Her body jerked at the unexpected sound. Her eyes flew open and she saw Ezra standing in front of her, barely inches away. She lifted her head to meet his gaze. He was a half foot taller than she was, so she had to crane her neck to look into his eyes, something she didn't mind. But for some reason her brain wasn't registering that Ezra Yutzy was not only standing in front of her, he was speaking to her. All she could think about was the quilt.

"I was looking for you," he said.

Her eyebrows pushed together. "You were?" she asked absently. "Why?"

"Because . . ." He shifted on his feet, not looking at her. "Well, I, uh . . ."

The fog cleared from Hannah Lynne's mind and it finally sank in how close he was to her. Not to mention he had been *looking* for her. That was a first. But why was he backing away?

"Is something wrong?" she asked, still looking up at him. Once again, she felt the zing of attraction that happened whenever he was around. Great. So much for her plan to move on. How could she do that when her heart wouldn't cooperate?

"*Nee . . . nix* is wrong." But he kept moving farther away from her, as if she had some sort of contagious illness. "It's just . . ."

"This conversation is turning weird," she said. For once she didn't have time to moon over Ezra. She was sure they would be announcing the winner of the quilt and she wanted to be there. "I have to *geh*."

She pulled her gaze away from his and started to go inside the building, fully expecting to leave him behind.

To her surprise, he did the exact opposite and fell in step beside her. She glanced up at him, trying to read his expression, but his handsome face revealed nothing.

When they entered the building, a bulky, broad man wearing a Cleveland Browns baseball cap bumped into her. "Excuse me," he said as he brushed past, but he'd caught her off guard and she lost her balance. Before she could stop herself, she was leaning against Ezra.

His hand cupped her elbow. It felt warm. Strong. She looked up at him at the same moment he abruptly released her. "Sorry," he mumbled.

"It's okay." But it wasn't. None of this was. She should be ecstatic that Ezra was by her side. That he'd touched her, even if it was accidental. Instead everything felt wrong, like he was in her presence out of some unknown sense of obligation.

She forged ahead, hoping he wouldn't follow. She grimaced when he did. She stood in front of the quilt. The bidding had closed, and the paper with the bids on it was gone. Part of her was relieved she didn't know right away who won the quilt. She still had a little while to pray that hers was the winning bid.

Ezra stood beside her, but didn't say a word. He was ignoring the rest of the auction to stay with her, which didn't make any sense. Finally unable to take the awkwardness stretching between them, she turned to him. "What's going on, Ezra?"

"*Nix.*" He shrugged, giving her a lopsided smile that under normal circumstances would have had her toes curling, but instead set her more off balance than she'd been after the Yankee man had bumped into her. "I want to see how the quilt auction turns out."

"Really," she said, arching one eyebrow in doubt. She crossed her arms over her chest. "Any particular reason why?"

"Nope." He stared at the quilt and shoved his hands into his jacket pockets.

She gave a skeptical glance at his handsome profile. Was there possibly a man more perfect than him? He even smelled good, like soap and lightly scented shaving cream. Suddenly her eyes widened as she realized her wish was coming true—Ezra had finally noticed her. Sort of. At least he was standing near her. If she reached her hand out a few inches, she could graze his fingers with hers.

She didn't dare, partly because she wasn't that bold, but mostly because he would probably think she'd lost her mind. She curled her fingers into fists and kept her arms tight across her chest.

For the next ten minutes they stood side by side, neither of them moving, neither of them saying anything. But Hannah Lynne's annoyance grew. Did he somehow find out how she felt about him? Was he teasing her by standing beside her and being silent? If so, it was the weirdest teasing she'd ever experienced. Why wasn't he bidding on the main auction items? Surely he wasn't here because he wanted the quilt.

Or did he? She could see he kept staring at the quilt, except for the few times he glanced at the auctioneer's stand to see what new item was being auctioned off. Otherwise, he seemed highly focused on the quilt.

She didn't see his name on the bidding paper when she had written her bid. What if he bid on the quilt after she did? That didn't explain why he sought her out, but at that point she didn't care. If he placed a bid after she did . . . A tiny knot formed in her stomach.

"Why do you want the quilt?" she asked, sounding sharper than she meant to.

His head snapped toward her. "What?"

She pointed at what she hoped would be her quilt . . . although that hope was disappearing quickly. "There are six other beautiful quilts here. Why do you want *that* one?"

"I—wait, you don't understand—"

Alma Yoder, one of the women helping Sarah with the auction, came up beside them. "We're ready to announce who won this lovely quilt," she said, grinning. She took down the quilt, and Hannah Lynne watched as she folded it, then walked back to Sarah and two other women standing nearby.

Hannah Lynne chewed on her bottom lip, forgetting about Ezra. She prayed again that she would win. She had to. The moment she saw the quilt, touched the soft, well-worn fabric, she knew it was meant to be hers. The resemblance was too close for it not to be. She watched as Alma took the name of the winner to the auctioneer stand.

Hannah Lynne followed Alma's every move as she hung up the quilt in front. One of the Yankee men who owned the auction business held the microphone, giving some of the Amish auctioneers a break. Alma handed him the paper.

"We have the first winner from our quilt auction. This is for the blue and white—"

"And yellow," Hannah Lynne whispered.

"—quilt hanging on the line to my right." He pushed up his small, square glasses, which had been resting on the end of his nose. "The winner is . . ."

CHAPTER 4

E zra's palms were damp as the auctioneer took the paper
from Alma. He glanced at Hannah Lynne and saw her top
teeth pressed against her bottom lip. Her *pretty* bottom lip.

He yanked away his gaze and slid his palms against his
pants. What was wrong with him tonight? He'd never been this
off-kilter.

"The winner is . . ." the auctioneer said into the microphone.

He looked at Hannah Lynne again. She seemed to be holding her breath. Then he realized he was too.

". . . Sarah Detweiler!"

His heart dropped at the announcement. But that was nothing compared to the disappointment he saw on Hannah Lynne's
face. She pressed her lips together and turned around. He followed her gaze to see Sarah smiling, happy that she now owned
the quilt.

"*Nee,*" Hannah Lynne whispered.

Ezra had the urge to put his arm around Hannah Lynne and
draw her close. His arm was actually itching to do it. He watched,

helpless, as she gave the quilt one last long look, pasted a smile on her face, and walked away.

He had to do something. His gaze followed her as she headed for the exit. She was leaving without her beloved quilt. Although he had no idea why she wanted it so much, that wasn't the point. She was unhappy. More like devastated. He couldn't stand to see her like that.

He shoved his hands in his jacket pockets as he tried to think of something he could do to cheer her up. Then his fingers grazed the top of his wallet. He remembered the extra cash he'd brought with him. Without hesitating he went to Sarah, who had just received the quilt and was commenting to Alma about the precise stitching.

"Sarah," he said, surprised at the desperation in his voice. "Can I talk to you for a minute?"

She nodded and Alma stepped away. Sarah draped the folded quilt over one arm and looked up at him.

"How much did you pay for the quilt?" At her stunned expression he added, "If you don't mind me asking." He looked around, trying to catch a glimpse of Hannah Lynne. He didn't see her.

"Sure."

When she told him the amount his eyebrows lifted. "Wow," he said. "That much?"

"*Ya*. And *mei* bid was only two dollars more than the second highest one. A lot of people wanted that quilt. I also wanted to make a *gut* donation to the clinic so I didn't mind paying that amount. It's a wonderful quilt, so *schee*. Perfectly stitched. One of the finest I've ever seen. I'm surprised *yer mamm* was willing to part with it."

Ezra nodded as Sarah spoke, but he barely heard what she was saying since he was mentally counting the money in his wallet. He pulled the brown leather billfold out of his pocket and asked, "Can I buy it from you?"

Sarah's brow wrinkled above her plain, silver-rimmed glasses. "You want to buy back *yer mamm's* quilt? I can return it to her if she changed her mind."

"She didn't change her mind." He took in a breath. "I can't really explain the reason I need to buy it from you . . . I just do. I can pay you almost twice as much as you bought it for."

Her eyes widened. "What? No. That's too much."

He opened his wallet and pulled out all the money he had. "Here," he said, thrusting it into Sarah's free hand. "Is this enough to double what you bid?"

"Ezra, I said I'd give it to you—"

"I don't want the clinic to miss out on a donation, and you shouldn't have to make one if you aren't going to get the quilt. You can give half of this to the clinic and keep the other half to buy a quilt." He glanced at the quilt in her hand, then at her again. "Please?"

Sarah nodded, taking the money from his hand and giving him the quilt. Before she could say anything, he left, taking off in the direction he'd seen Hannah Lynne go.

⟡

Hannah Lynne kept her head down as she walked out of the market building, not wanting anyone to see the disappointment she couldn't keep off her face. She'd been so sure she would win the quilt. She was willing to pay almost three months of her butter money to own it, and it would have been worth every penny.

She stopped halfway to the part of the lot where the buggies were parked and took a deep breath. She knew her mourning was misplaced. She'd had an opportunity to own a link to the past, but it had gone to someone else, which meant it wasn't God's will that she have the quilt. And here she was, pouting about it, instead of going back inside and using her butter money to bid on something else. In the end, all the money went to a great cause. Wasn't that the important thing?

Hannah Lynne sighed. Acknowledging the truth didn't make her disappointment any less real. She swallowed it, choking down the bitter emotion. She couldn't leave. There were other items to bid on, and if she didn't win any of those she would donate her money. Reminding herself of the real reason she was here, she turned around—and smacked right into a solid, warm chest.

"Oof," Ezra said, taking a step back, his jacket open, exposing one of the shirts she liked best.

Mortified, Hannah Lynne looked up at him. "I'm sorry. I didn't realize you were behind me." She averted her gaze, trying to avoid looking at his blue-gray eyes, or his strong chin, or anything else she found appealing—which was basically all of him.

"*Nee*. I should be the one to apologize. I kinda snuck up on you."

She nodded, then tried to make her way past him to the market building. Idly, she realized they had spent practically the last half hour together but had said next to nothing to each other. Which was nothing new. He couldn't have made it any plainer that he wasn't interested in her, not even enough to hold a decent conversation. Her eyes suddenly burned. The evening, which she had looked forward to earlier, was turning into an emotional disaster.

She took another step forward, only to be stopped.

"Hannah Lynne?"

She glanced at his hand resting on the fabric of her navy blue sweater, so large it looked like he could encircle her arm with his long fingers. Then she noticed he was holding something in his other hand. The quilt. She spun around. "What are you doing with that?"

"I . . . uh . . ."

"I thought Sarah had won it."

"She did."

"Then why do you have it?"

"Because . . . I bought it from her."

So she was right. He had wanted the quilt. Which was strange. His reason wasn't any of her business, but she couldn't deny a tiny bit of irritation at seeing him owning what she had wanted. Nor could she push away the idea that he was going to give it to someone. That was the only explanation that made sense. Ezra wouldn't buy a quilt for himself. But he would buy one to give as a gift.

The perfect gift for a serious girlfriend . . . or a future wife.

Ezra's staunch bachelor status was no secret, but perhaps he did have a girlfriend, or even a fiancée. It wasn't uncommon for relationships to be private until a few weeks before the wedding. Although she'd vowed to release him from her heart, thinking of him getting married made her chest tighten.

"Congratulations," she said dully, unable to think of anything else to say. She started to leave again.

This time his hand squeezed her arm. A soft, gentle squeeze that sent shivers down to the tips of her fingers.

He dropped his hand and cleared his throat. "Here," he said, thrusting the quilt at her.

"What?" She stared at his outstretched hand.

"This is for you."

Puzzled, she looked up at him and blinked. "I don't understand."

He took her hand, gently stretched out her forearm, and draped the quilt over it. "It's *yers* now."

Hannah Lynne gaped at the quilt. She couldn't believe what was happening. He had bought the quilt for her? Images flew through her head—all the times he'd stopped by her table to buy her butter, how he had sought her out earlier, the long minutes he'd stood by her side, waiting for the winner to be announced. Her pulse thrummed. Did she dare believe he had feelings for her?

She looked up at him and saw his perfect mouth curved into an engaging smile that reached right to her heart. She was powerless to not smile in return, and when she did, his grin grew wider, lifting the dark freckle on the top of his cheek.

Warmth, along with a sensation she'd never felt before, flooded her body. She did the only thing she could do—she threw her arms around his narrow waist and hugged him tight, resting her cheek on his chest, the quilt snug between her arm and his side. She could hear his heartbeat through his shirt, against her ear. She paused, enjoying his nearness, listening to his steady pulse.

She was so wrapped up in surprise and happiness that it took her a moment to realize his arms were still at his sides. *Oh, nee.* She jerked back, looked up, and felt her heart sink to her knees at the bewildered expression on his face.

"I'm—" The apology stuck in her throat, as if it were coated with a gallon of peanut butter. She stepped back, her face flaming, moving the quilt to her hands. Whatever his intention was in giving it to her, it definitely wasn't romantic.

He coughed into his fist.

She wanted to sink into the gravel parking lot. She had made a huge, embarrassing mistake, one that didn't help clear up the confusion whirling in her mind. She brought the quilt to her chest, wishing she could bury her humiliation in the cozy fabric. "*Danki,*" she said. But the word was lost as a car whizzed by Navoo Road and honked its horn.

He nodded. Shifted on his feet. Then turned to go.

"Ezra," she said suddenly, unable to let him leave until she had some answers. "Why did you give me this?"

"I saw how much you liked it." He shrugged, sticking his hands in his jacket pockets.

"That's it?"

"*Ya.* That's it."

"Then I have to pay you for it." She slipped the quilt onto one arm, opened her purse, then realized she didn't know how much she needed.

He shook his head. "You don't have to pay me back—"

"I do." She fumbled for the money out of her wallet. "How much did you pay for it?"

"Hannah Lynne—"

"How much?" Her voice was too loud and too shrill, but she couldn't help it. She'd embarrassed herself already tonight. What was a little more mortification? Besides, she wasn't going to be beholden to him.

He paused. Then told her the amount the quilt had sold for.

She tried to hide her shock as she pulled out every last dollar she'd brought to the auction. "I know it's not enough . . ." Her mind whirred with ideas for making more money—doubling her butter production and sales and . . . and . . . She scowled. Other than getting a job, she didn't know how else to make up the rest. A thought came to her. "*Yer haus.*"

"What?" he asked, sounding dumbfounded.

"I can help you with *yer haus.* Make curtains, clean the kitchen, scrub the floors—"

"Stop." He took a step forward and bent down so their eyes were on an even level. "Please . . . stop."

CHAPTER 5

E zra straightened, thankful Hannah Lynne had heeded his plea and stopped talking. He rubbed the back of his neck with one hand. Now what was he supposed to do? When he'd given her the quilt, she did what he expected her to do—light up like a Yankee Christmas tree. But then she stunned him into near paralysis when she hugged him. That was something he hadn't expected, or been prepared for. Feeling her arms around his waist, her cheek against his chest . . . his heart rate had suddenly had a mind of its own and started to race.

He couldn't have moved even if he had wanted to. Not that he'd wanted to, which gave him a moment's pause. Her warmth, combined with the prettiest smile he'd ever seen in his life, had shocked him. When she pulled away . . . he'd wanted to kick himself.

Not only had the smile disappeared, but disappointment had crept into her eyes, their true color washed away by the fluorescent lights in the parking lot. A soft, rich brown, fringed by long, thick eyelashes. The sparkle he'd seen in them a moment ago had dimmed—and he would do anything to bring it back.

She offered him money, which was bad enough. Now she was naming off chores she could do for him, as if she were his indentured servant. He'd given her the quilt to make her happy, not because he expected anything in return.

And that's where he'd made his mistake. Gifts always had strings attached, and in his haste he hadn't thought about the ones connected to this quilt.

"You don't have to help me with *mei haus*," he said, keeping his voice steady—a major challenge considering that for some bizarre reason his vocal cords were unstable. "You don't have to give me money, either."

"Then I can't take the quilt." She pushed it at him, shoving it against his chest with so much force he had to take a step back to regain his balance. "I appreciate the thought but . . ." She backed away. "I can't accept it."

Ezra glanced at the quilt. He'd just spent a huge amount of money—well-spent money, but a lot of money—for a quilt that up until recently had belonged to his mother. He didn't ponder the irony of that for very long, because all he could think about was Hannah Lynne's face. She'd gone from happy to disappointed in a split second, even though she was doing a good job of hiding how she felt.

Although he couldn't explain why, he wanted to see her happy. He needed to see her smile again.

"Okay," he said, taking a tentative step forward. "I could use some curtains in the *haus*. And the kitchen counters need a *gut* wiping." But she was not, under any circumstances, going to scrub his floors.

"I can also make you some more butter—"

"*Nee!*" he blurted, thinking of all the butter in his mother's freezer. "I mean, I think this is a *gut* arrangement." He handed her the quilt.

There was barely a hint of a smile on her lips when she took the quilt from him. Small, but he would take it. He relaxed a bit.

"I can come over tomorrow morning," she said. "Since it's Saturday."

"All right."

She told him the time she'd be there, and he made a mental note of it. Truthfully, he still wasn't comfortable with this. But he didn't want her giving the quilt back, so he nodded his agreement. "See you then," he said, ready to leave. *Very ready to leave.*

Hannah Lynne grabbed his hand and put the cash in his palm. Then she folded his fingers over it. "Don't forget this."

He looked down at her fingers touching his. He'd never noticed how small her hands were, or that she had such delicate fingers. He felt a whisper of air whoosh across his skin as she pulled away.

Ezra watched as she walked back to the market building. He waited until she was inside before he turned on his heel, crushing the gravel as he went to his buggy. He drove home in a daze, still trying to process what had happened tonight. Good thing his horse knew the way home.

Rather than spending the night at his parents' house, he had planned to sleep at his own place, getting up early in the morning to work on some roof repairs. His father had been kind enough to give him the day off from work. As he pulled into the driveway and looked at the dilapidated house, he felt a bit of embarrassment. The place was a mess, and tomorrow morning Hannah Lynne would see exactly how bad it was.

He parked his buggy, led his horse to the barn and settled him down for the night, then went inside the house. He climbed the stairs to his bedroom, not bothering to turn on a lamp. When he started to take off his jacket, he remembered the money she'd given him, pulled it out of his pocket, and put it in the top drawer of his dresser. Later he'd give it as another donation. Keeping it didn't feel right.

⚬⚬⚬

The next morning, Hannah Lynne turned her buggy into Ezra's driveway. She was more than fifteen minutes early, but she couldn't stand pacing in her bedroom another minute. Her palms were slick as she held the reins and pulled her horse to a stop.

She studied Ezra's house. She'd seen it before. It was a nice size and had a lot of potential. She could see why he bought it. What she couldn't see was her being inside it. Yet here she was, cleaning supplies in a bucket on the bench seat next to her, a tape measure in her purse, and a sandwich and an apple in a plain paper bag for her lunch later.

At least when she'd told her parents she would be gone all day helping a friend clean, they hadn't asked any questions.

If there had been any other way to pay him for the quilt, she would have. Her impulsively hugging him had weighed on her mind last night, especially as she carefully folded the quilt and put it on the top shelf of her closet. She wanted to avoid him for the rest of her life. The embarrassment was still fresh in her mind.

But the best way to get it out of her mind was to work, so she tethered her horse, grabbed her lunch and the bucket, and strode to the front door. She knocked on it. Once. Twice. When he didn't answer she turned the knob, surprised to find it completely turned and clicked.

"Hello?" she said, slowly opening the door and stepping inside. She immediately tripped on a loose board and fell forward, landing on her knees. "Ow!"

"Hannah Lynne?"

She heard thundering footsteps above her as she pushed herself to her feet. Ezra was scrambling down the stairs and at her side by the time she was upright.

"Are you all right?"

"*Ya,*" she said, spying the apple rolling on the floor toward the back of the room.

He glanced behind him. "Floor is warped." Then he looked down. "And there are a few loose boards."

"I found out the hard way."

"I'm sorry."

She looked up at him as he shoved his huge hand through his thick hair. His chin was damp, as if he'd freshly shaved. Then she saw that his short-sleeved, light-yellow shirt wasn't tucked into the waist of his broadfall pants. It was also sitting a little crooked on his shoulders, as if he'd just thrown it on.

"I got here a little early—"

"I'm running a little late—"

They both stopped talking. She tore her gaze from him and looked at her palms. They were red, but the skin was intact.

"I'll get that board fixed soon," he said, sounding a little sheepish. "I never use the front door, so I haven't worried about it. I guess I should keep it locked too."

That was the most she'd heard him speak, at least directly to her. She waved her hand and retrieved her apple. "It's fine. I should watch where I'm going." She picked up the apple, rubbed it on her dress, and held it up. "See? No harm done." She noticed his gaze wasn't on the apple. It was centered on her. But she knew better than to read anything but concern into Ezra's look. She'd learned that lesson the hard way too.

"*Gut.*" He nodded. "I wouldn't want you to get hurt."

Her heart sighed. This was one of many reasons why she'd fallen for Ezra. He was *nice*. Very nice. And even though he didn't have any romantic feelings for her, he wouldn't suddenly change his personality and become rude. That wasn't in him.

"I'd cook up some breakfast, but the stove's out of commission," he said, stepping across another askew floorboard. He was barefoot, and she was certain now that she had caught him in the middle of getting dressed, a visual she definitely couldn't think about.

"I already ate." She picked up her bucket and forced her thoughts on the reason she was here. "And I'm ready to work. Just point me in the right direction." She even managed a smile. Maybe the fall had knocked the tension out of her, but she suddenly didn't feel nervous around him. Or awkward. It was nice to be in the same room with Ezra Yutzy and feel . . . normal.

Well, not exactly normal. But at least calm enough to appear that way.

"The kitchen?" he said, sounding unsure. He was gesturing with one lanky arm to an adjoining room.

She followed, aware that he was right behind her. When she entered the kitchen her jaw dropped.

The place was a mess. Electrical wiring was scattered on the floor, not connected to anything. Dust covered the countertops. The bare kitchen window was coated with a thin film of dirt and grease. But none of that caught her attention as much as the huge jagged hole in the drywall above the stove. "What happened there?"

He moved to stand beside her. "The hole came with the house. That hole and that one." He pointed to another hole in the wall on the opposite side of the kitchen. "There are several of them all through the place. Along with some graffiti." He let out a disgusted sigh. "I think there were squatters here at one point. The house has been stripped of copper."

"Is that bad?"

"It's stealing, that's for sure. I have to replace a lot of it for the plumbing." He went to the sink and opened up the cabinet doors underneath. "I can show you what I need to replace—" Suddenly he slammed the doors shut.

"What's wrong?" she asked.

"*Nix.*" He stood in front of the cabinet and forced a smile.

"You look like you're hiding something."

He shook his head. "Nope. Not me."

But he had a nervous lilt to his voice. There was something under that sink. Now she was curious. Very curious. She went to him and tried to sneak around. "Let me see."

He shook his head and blocked her way. "*Nee.*" But his tone had changed, from unnerved to teasing. "*Nix* to see here."

"I don't believe you." She looked up at him and smiled. "You're not a *gut* liar."

His lips parted, as if he was about to say something. Yet he didn't move. Just stared at her.

A familiar pleasant shiver went through her as their eyes held. Then her mouth twisted into a grimace. Just when being around him was feeling natural, she had to read something else into his look. She backed away. "Okay. I won't look under the sink."

"You promise?" He wasn't looking at her, his gaze strangely averted. But his question held complete seriousness.

"I promise."

He nodded. "Uh, after I finish . . . upstairs, I'll be on the roof if you need me. There are a few leaks that have to be fixed. I'll just go out the front door and then around to the barn to get *mei* ladder and tools. I don't want to get in *yer* way." He flicked a quick glance at her, then hurried out of the room. She could hear loud creaks as Ezra climbed barefooted up the stairs.

Hannah Lynne sighed and went to her bucket of supplies. There was so much to do in the kitchen she didn't know where to start. As she thought a few minutes about the best plan of attack, her gaze kept dropping to the cabinet under the sink. *Hmm.* It would be impossible to work, knowing Ezra was hiding something in there. But she'd promised she wouldn't look.

Such a dilemma. She inched toward the sink, curiosity overriding her promise. She'd apologize to him later. Besides, what could possibly be under this filthy sink that he wouldn't want her to see?

Hannah Lynne crouched down and opened the cabinet doors.

✥

Ezra had barely finished dressing when he heard Hannah Lynne scream. He groaned. He should have checked under the sink before she arrived that morning. Better yet, she should have kept her promise. He headed down the stairs for the kitchen, steeling himself for what he knew was coming next: hysteria.

When he walked in she jumped in front of him. "Gotcha!"

He jerked back in surprise. "What?"

"Is this what you didn't want me to see?" She held her bucket in front of him, letting the handle swing back and forth in her grip.

He looked down. There it was, a dead mouse the size of a small rat. And here was Hannah Lynne laughing with glee as she dangled it in front of him.

"I'm not afraid of mice. Or rats. Or snakes." She grinned.

"*Mei mamm's* terrified of them."

"So is mine." She leaned forward. "And *mei daed*," she said in a loud whisper. "But he'll never admit it." She looked up at him, still smiling. "I'm the resident rodent wrangler at *mei haus*. I was even before *mei bruders* moved out."

"Really?" He found himself grinning right back at her.

"*Ya*. Don't get me wrong, I don't love them. But I'm not afraid." She fluttered her eyes with exaggeration. "I don't need a big, strong *mann* to take care of them for me."

He leaned against the doorframe, enjoying the teasing. "Is that so?"

"*Ya*." She tilted up her chin, which was already lifted due to her having to look up at him. "You don't have to protect me."

Her words unearthed an unexpected emotion inside him. No, Hannah Lynne didn't need protecting. She was independent.

He'd seen enough of that through casual observation. The fact that she could handle vermin without flinching shouldn't have surprised him. But what did was the sudden feeling that while Hannah Lynne Beiler didn't need protecting, if she ever did, he wanted to be the one to protect her.

The feeling knocked him off-kilter, and his shoulder slid against the doorjamb.

"Where should I dispose of the dearly departed?" she asked.

"The woods," he said, glad she didn't notice his fumbling. "Out back." He'd offer to do it for her, but he knew she'd refuse. Instead, he walked across the kitchen floor and opened the back door for her.

With a quick nod she scooted past him, her shoulder touching his bare forearm. He glanced down. The hairs were actually standing on end from the fleeting, light touch.

What was going on here? He was confused, but his confusion wasn't disturbing. It was . . . pleasant. He liked the teasing lilt of her voice when she spoke to him, the way she'd batted her eyes, pretending to be helpless. He enjoyed the flirting—

Flirting? Was that what was going on? Then he shook his head. Why would Hannah Lynne flirt with him? She was interested in Josiah. Plus she'd never shown any interest in him.

No, she was being nice. Funny. She had a good sense of humor. That didn't translate to flirting. He knew better than that. Putting the notion out of his mind, he left the kitchen and headed out the front door to repair the roof.

CHAPTER 6

By lunchtime, Hannah Lynne had made some headway in cleaning the countertops and cabinets, including the one under the sink. Fortunately she'd only found one more rodent, one that had been dead for a while. She quickly disposed of it, chuckling over Ezra's assuming she'd be afraid of a harmless mouse. Well, not harmless, as they could do plenty of damage if not taken care of in a swift manner. They were also a health hazard. But vermin weren't the only health hazard in this house.

She stood and arched her back. Sunbeams tried to penetrate the thick film of grease and dirt coating the window above the sink. She'd tackle that after lunch. Right now her stomach growled, and she went upstairs to wash her hands. At least that plumbing worked. She also refilled her bucket and then went downstairs to retrieve her sandwich and apple, setting the bucket on the floor.

As she pulled her wrapped sandwich out of the paper bag she'd put on one of the counters, Ezra walked into the kitchen. He'd been stomping around on the roof all morning. His shirt and pants were dirty, but his hands were clean. She noticed this as he put them on his trim waist and looked around the kitchen. *There must be a working pump outside.*

"Wow," he said, nodding his approval. "You've done a lot in here."

Hannah Lynne followed his gaze. She had worked all morning, but it suddenly seemed like she hadn't accomplished as much as he was giving her credit for. There was too much work to do in a day. Or a week, or a month, even. "Not as much as I wanted," she mumbled.

"I know what you mean." He blew out a breath. "It's going to take a long time to get this place livable." Then he shrugged. "It's all right, though. I'm not in any big hurry."

Which probably meant he didn't have a secret girlfriend in his life. If he did, he would want to get the house ready for the two of them as soon as possible. She started to smile, then realized that little tidbit of information didn't matter. Even if he didn't have someone now, someday he would find a girlfriend . . . and a wife. She was coming to understand it wouldn't be her.

However, that didn't mean she couldn't enjoy his company, which she definitely did.

"I watered *yer* horse," Ezra said as she unwrapped her sandwich.

She turned to him and smiled. "*Danki.*" Nice and thoughtful. *He's perfect.* She stifled a sigh so she wouldn't sound like a thirteen-year-old girl mooning over her latest crush—which was exactly what she was doing, minus the thirteen-year-old part.

"What's his name?" he asked.

"George Washington Junior."

His brow lifted. "Seriously?"

She nodded. "But we call him Junior."

"Okay, I'll bite." He moved closer to her. "Why did you name him after a president?"

"When I was six *mei mamm* took me to the library. We would *geh* there all the time, and one February they had a display for President's Day. There was a children's book with a young boy and a cherry tree on the cover. It was George's biography, and I read that book at least five times before *Mamm* returned it." She looked up at him. "I have *nee* idea why I was so fascinated. Neither does *Mamm*. About a month later *mei daed* bought George and said I could name him. So I did."

"And *yer daed* was okay with the name?"

"He said it was a mouthful, but kept it. He was right about it being too long, though, so I shortened it to Junior about a year later."

"Why not just George?"

"I don't know. I guess I like Junior better." She was about to bow her head to pray before eating, but she realized something was wrong. "Where's *yer* lunch?"

He took off his hat and set it on the counter. His hair was slightly molded to his head, and she wanted to reach up and fluff it out for him.

"I knew I forgot something," he said. "That's all right. I'll eat later."

"You can't *geh* the rest of the afternoon without lunch."

"Sure I can."

She carefully split her sandwich in half and offered it to

him. It was a bit messy, with peanut butter and gooseberry jam dangling over the sides. "Here."

He shook his head. "That's *yer* lunch."

"This is *mei* lunch." She held up one half. "This is *yers*." She pushed it toward him again.

He eyed it dubiously, and she couldn't blame him. It didn't look like the most appetizing sandwich. Finally, he accepted it. "Hang on," he said, dashing out of the room. She heard his footsteps upstairs, then after a few minutes he was back in the kitchen. "Here," he said, handing her a can of pop. "I have these stashed up in *mei* room."

She accepted it, grateful since she had also forgotten something—a beverage. They both paused, eyes closed, and prayed before eating.

He leaned his upper thigh against the countertop, his hip rising just above it. His legs were so long they seemed almost endless. "I can't remember the last time I had peanut butter and jelly."

"I have it all the time." She took a swig of pop. "Peanut butter is *mei* favorite. I'm not real picky about what flavor of jelly."

Since it didn't take long to eat half a sandwich, they both finished quickly. After taking a long drink of his pop, Ezra looked at her. "I'm curious about something."

"What?"

"Those sayings on the butter wrappers. What made you come up with that idea?"

Hannah Lynne lifted her shoulders, trying not to show her delight that he noticed her effort. "I thought it would be a nice little extra for *mei* customers. The regulars seem to appreciate it."

He nodded, but didn't say anything else. She looked at the

apple. There were no knives, or any other silverware, in the kitchen. Considering he was repairing the roof, he needed the nourishment more than she did. She handed him the apple, expecting him to refuse it. To her surprise, he didn't.

Even more to her surprise, he took a bite of the apple and handed it back to her, as if sharing the same piece of fruit was the most natural thing in the world. "Got to get back to work. I have a couple more holes to patch." He turned and walked out of the room.

She stared at the apple—more specifically, the bite he took out of the apple. He wasn't making it easy to forget her feelings about him.

⟿❦⟾

Ezra hammered down a piece of flashing, squinting against the sunlight glinting off the metal strip. He was primarily a carpenter, but his father and grandfather had been able to do almost anything with their hands, from building houses to plumbing, and they'd handed those skills down to Ezra.

But his mind wasn't on the roof. Or even his house. As the sun shone brightly overhead and a chilly fall breeze whirled around him, the only thing on his mind was the pretty *maedel* in his kitchen. Pretty and quirky. Who knew she not only could handle mice, she also loved peanut butter. And George Washington. Not to mention her thoughtfulness toward the customers who bought her butter. He chuckled. Hannah Lynne was definitely an interesting girl, and unlike any other female he'd ever met.

He forced himself to focus on his task, because tumbling off the roof wasn't on his to-do list today. Once all the holes in the roof were repaired, he slid down the ladder and went back to the kitchen, wondering what Hannah Lynne had accomplished this afternoon.

Who was he kidding? He just wanted to see her again—closer than when he'd seen her get clean water from the pump in the backyard.

Ezra smiled as he quietly entered the room. Her back was to him as she scrubbed out the sink, the tie of her white apron drooping a bit at her waist. She wore a light blue dress, the hem brushing against the back of her calves, which were covered in black stockings. She wasn't a thin girl, but she also wasn't stout. More like curvy . . .

He yanked his gaze from her, heat rising from his neck to his face. What was he doing, staring at Hannah Lynne like that? Yet it took every bit of internal strength not to look at her again.

She turned and dipped a sponge into her water bucket, then squeezed it out and continued to scrub. She'd been working all day, and her efforts showed. The window above the sink gleamed. The cabinet doors were no longer covered in dust, and the light honey-stained wood shone. The countertops were warped and would need to be replaced, but that hadn't stopped her from tackling the dirt in the corners.

And she was doing all this for a quilt.

He wondered why the quilt was so important to her. His curiosity almost drove him to ask, but he pulled back. Her reason wasn't his business. Today she'd done enough work to pay for the rest of the quilt—which he still wished she would have freely accepted from him.

"Hannah Lynne," he said, surprised at the low, husky tone of his voice. He cleared his throat as she turned around.

"I'm almost done with the sink," she said, wiping the back of her hand across her forehead. "I thought I'd work on the floor next."

"*Nee*," he said, going to her, recalling his vow that she wouldn't scrub his floors. "You've done enough today."

"But there's still plenty of daylight." She turned around and faced him, the back of her waist leaning against the sink. "And there's so much more to do—"

"For me to do, not you." He took the sponge from her hand. Then he reached around and squeezed it into the sink behind her. A thoughtless move, because if he had taken a moment to think before he acted he would have realized he would be very close to her. Close enough to hear her breathing, to see the sheen of perspiration on her forehead that she'd unsuccessfully tried to wipe off. He could smell her hair still tucked neatly under her *kapp*, the clean scent cutting through the mingling odors of cleaning products, dust, and stale air. If he leaned down he could easily touch his lips to hers . . . and found himself wanting to.

He dropped the sponge and took a step back, then several more as he scurried away from her.

"I'm going home," he said curtly. More curtly than he'd intended, but he couldn't help himself. He couldn't look at her for a moment, then finally got the guts to meet her eyes.

They were wide. Surprised. And so very, very beautiful.

"Okay," she said, sounding unsure. She turned to retrieve the sponge. "I'll dump the water outside—"

"I'll take care of it." He grabbed the bucket before she had a chance to, water sloshing on the sides and spattering his pants.

But he didn't care. He had to get out of that room. He had to get away from her.

When he stepped outside the air cooled off his face, but not his emotions. At twenty-seven, he'd never dated anyone. He quit going to singings years ago because of the expectation to find someone. Not a single girl had caught his eye or captured his interest, not that way. That included Hannah Lynne.

Until now. Which didn't make sense. He'd seen her all the time. At church. At the market. She was as familiar a presence to him as anything else in his life. And when she wasn't around, he had never given her a second thought.

And then I saw her looking at that quilt. Lord, what is happening here?

He heard the back door open and he quickly tossed out the water. Hoping his face didn't look as hot as it felt, he turned and handed her the empty bucket.

"*Danki*," she said, taking it from him. Her cheeks were red, too, but that was to be expected, considering the amount of work she'd done in the kitchen. "I can come back next Saturday. I'll make sure to bring a broom. Plus I didn't get a chance to measure for the curtains."

"That's okay," he said, his words coming out in a rush. "You more than made up for the quilt."

She eyed him. "I don't think so. That quilt cost you a lot of money. More than a little scrubbing and rodent wrangling is worth."

"I said we're square."

His heart pinched at the flash of hurt in her eyes. Wow, could he have been any more surly? Yet the thought of her coming back, of them spending the day together even though they were both working, unnerved him.

Even worse, it confused him . . . because a huge part of him would like for them to work together again. *And again . . .*

But that wasn't fair to her. Or Josiah, who Ezra hoped realized what a lucky *mann* he was.

"Okay." She spoke the word in a low, almost imperceptible tone. "Junior and I will be on our way." Without saying anything else she walked over and untied her horse. Soon Hannah Lynne and the equine version of the country's first president were gone.

He went back into the house, the back door slamming behind him. He leaned his forehead against a dirty wall, trying to get a grip on his emotions. It was a long time before he could.

CHAPTER 7

That evening after supper, Hannah Lynne sat on the edge of her bed and stared at the quilt still on the top shelf of her closet. She wanted to take it down, but she was afraid to. On the shelf it was safe. Nothing would happen to it there. It wouldn't be ruined.

Like her day with Ezra had been.

She didn't know how it happened. They were getting along so well. Lunch was *gut*, if not sparse, and he was in such good humor when he had last come into the kitchen. Then he had moved closer to her . . .

Her breath hitched at the memory of him standing inches from her. The scent of hard work and sunshine had permeated his clothes and skin, filling her senses. Nothing in her life had felt as right as being within inches of touching Ezra Yutzy, so close she thought she'd heard the rapid tempo of his pulse.

But that must have been her own racing heart she'd heard, because before she knew it he was practically on the other side of the room and couldn't wait to get rid of her. Had she done something wrong? Said something? Or maybe she'd let her true feelings slip out in a secret glance or quick draw of breath. Ezra wasn't stupid. And he wasn't interested in her. Why she couldn't get that to stick in her head, she didn't know.

She turned and flopped onto her bed, cupping her chin with her hands. What she did know is that she had to tell Josiah he couldn't take her home from the next singing after all. Being around Josiah didn't give her a fraction of the pleasant feelings she got from just looking at Ezra. She was hopeless, but she wasn't cruel, and stringing Josiah along was wrong.

Trying to get both men off her mind, she pulled out her book of inspirational quotes, searching to pick out a few for her next batch of butter wrappers. But the quotes reminded her of the conversation over lunch with Ezra, and she shut the book. Holding it against her chest, she closed her eyes and prayed.

Lord, what am I supposed to do? I can't completely ignore him for the rest of mei *life. How do you* unlove *somebody?*

Because after spending the day with Ezra, she knew what she felt wasn't infatuation. It had to be love. If it wasn't she wouldn't feel this intensely. She wouldn't still remember the sting of his words. *I said we're square.* That was the same as saying he didn't want her help. Didn't want to be around her anymore.

Didn't want her.

She opened her eyes and sighed.

"Did you get a lot of work done on the *haus* today, *sohn*?"

Ezra looked up from his supper of meat loaf, gravy, mashed

potatoes, and glazed carrots and nodded. "Got the holes patched in the roof."

"*Gut.*" His father drank from his glass of water. "Do you need any more time off?"

Ezra pondered the question. He'd told Hannah Lynne he wasn't in a hurry to get his house finished. At the time he'd said the words, they were true. But suddenly an overwhelming urge to finish the place came over him. He didn't know where it came from. His parents had never said anything to make him feel like he needed to be out on his own. Living here was convenient for everyone—he was close to work, he helped his parents with the chores, he contributed to paying the living expenses, and in return he had a roof over his head and food in his belly. He'd been satisfied.

Now he felt dissatisfied. More than he'd ever been in his life.

"*Ya,*" he said, swirling the potatoes around on his plate. "I could use a few more Saturdays off, if you can spare me." He turned to his mother. "As soon as I can get the plumbing going, I'll be moving out."

His mother set down her fork. "You will?"

Ezra nodded. "I know it seems sudden—"

"Not really," his father said dryly.

"—but I think it's time."

Mamm nodded slowly. "If you're sure. Just remember, you always have a place here."

"I know." He squeezed her hand. "I appreciate it."

They continued eating in silence for a few moments. Then *Mamm* said, "I talked to Sarah Detweiler today. She said the auction was a huge success." She turned to Ezra. "She also told me how you paid her to get *Grossmutter*'s quilt back."

Ezra frowned. "Huh?"

"The quilt you gave Sarah for the auction." *Mamm* speared a shiny, sweet carrot slice with her fork. "That was *Grossmutter* Keim's quilt. Now, don't pretend you didn't overhear me telling *yer daed* that. If you hadn't, why would you have bought the quilt back for me?"

He stared at his mother. "Why didn't you say anything about this before?"

"I figured it was God's will that the quilt be in the auction. It's been packed in *mei* hope chest for years. On a whim I decided to get it out and clean it. But when I found out it was in the auction, I didn't want to pull it out. I was sure it would get higher bids than the quilt I had intended to donate. And I know *yer grossmutter* wouldn't have minded since the proceeds of the sale went to a *gut* cause."

He nodded. That's why he'd never seen it before. He smiled as he remembered his *Mamm's* mother. She died when Ezra was ten, but they'd had a special bond. She'd make his favorite butter pecan cookies for him whenever he asked, and she called him by a special nickname. He never knew what it meant, but whenever she said the word it felt like he was wrapped up in a warm blanket on a freezing winter day. He still missed her.

"So where is the quilt?"

Ezra froze.

"I'd like to drape it over the back of the rocking chair. That's what I intended to do with it, but then you gave it to Sarah for the auction." She smiled at Ezra. "And that was fine. It's just nice to know it's now back in the *familye*."

His smile slipped from his face. His mother looked so

happy, as happy as Hannah Lynne had been when he'd given her the quilt. His grandmother's quilt, now he knew. His mother should have said something. Then again, this was just like her, to assume God was in the details, including little—and big—misunderstandings.

"She only made that one quilt," his mother continued. "She started several others, but she never finished them."

The meat loaf in his stomach rebelled.

"Maybe because the first one she made was so beautifully done." His mother raised an eyebrow. "Or it was because she had twelve *kinner* and very little time for quilting."

"Why were you the one to get the quilt?" Ezra asked.

"I'm not sure. I know when she made it she said she wanted me to have it. I'm the oldest, so that makes sense. I should have taken it out years ago, but . . ."

Ezra saw her swallow, and he sank lower in the chair.

"I didn't want anything to happen to it." She brightened, a carrot still poised on her fork in midair. "Later on I realized that was silly. *Mutter* would have wanted me to enjoy the quilt, not keep it boxed up."

"It's at *mei haus,*" Ezra blurted, causing even his father, who had checked out of the conversation at the mention of the word *quilt,* to give him a sidelong look. "I accidentally left it there." Great, now he was lying to his parents.

"Oh, *nee.*" *Mamm* sighed. "I'll have to wash it again after it's been over there."

"*Nee* need," Ezra said, mustering a half-grin. "It's not dirty, I promise."

"*Gut.* Bring it as soon as you can." She smiled again, and her blue-gray eyes sparkled. "I guess the quilt was meant to stay in our *familye* after all."

He stared at his nearly empty plate, dazed. What was he going to do now? He had no choice—he had to get the quilt back from Hannah Lynne. Not only did it belong to his mother, it meant a lot to her. How could he tell *Mamm* Hannah Lynne not only had it but he'd sold it to her? Never mind he wasn't going to keep the money. It still sounded greedy. Heartless.

Thoughtless. He pinched the top of his nose.

"Ezra?" his mother said. "Do you have a headache?"

"*Ya,*" he said, lying again. "Just came on."

She started to rise. "I'll fix you some peppermint tea. That will help."

He nodded, and she went to the stove to get the kettle. His mother had dozens of tea recipes, a variety of concoctions to cure almost any ailment. But tea wouldn't solve this dilemma. He'd made a mess. Now he had to clean it up.

He just hoped Hannah Lynne could forgive him.

❧

Hannah Lynne had just dozed off when she heard a knock on her bedroom door. She hadn't meant to fall asleep so early, but she'd been so tired from the day's work, and from dealing with the turmoil in her heart, that once she'd laid down on her bed, she'd conked out. She was still wearing her dress and *kapp*, although she'd taken off her stockings and shoes. Rubbing her eyes, she got up off the bed and answered the door. "*Ya, Mamm?*" she said to her mother, her voice still thick with sleep.

"Were you expecting company tonight?"

Hannah Lynne shook her head. "*Nee*. Why?"

"Ezra Yutzy is here to see you. He's waiting downstairs."

Hannah Lynne gripped the door handle. She blinked, wondering for a moment if she were sleepwalking. "Ezra?"

"*Ya*." Her mother took a step back. "He said it was important that he speak to you."

"Tell him I'll be right there." Hannah Lynne willed her pulse to slow. Ezra could be at her door for any number of reasons—she might have left something at his house, for example. Or maybe he wanted to apologize for being so short with her when she left. She could see him doing something thoughtful like that.

She smoothed out her dress, checked her *kapp* to make sure it was in place, and noticed that one thin lock of hair had escaped during her sleep. She should properly secure it, but that would mean undoing her *kapp* and redoing the bobby pins, and she didn't want to keep him waiting. She tucked the lock behind her ear, put on her stockings and shoes, and headed down the stairs.

When she reached the bottom step, she saw Ezra standing in the living room, next to her father. Or rather towering over him. They were talking, probably about cows, since that's pretty much all her father ever liked to talk about. Ezra nodded and listened politely, but she could see the strain around his mouth. Uh-oh. That wasn't a good sign.

"Hi, Ezra," she said, walking toward him. She put her hands behind her back and forced an even tone. "What brings you by?"

"We'll be in the kitchen if you need anything," *Mamm* said, her announcement as subtle as a dog howling at the moon. She tugged on *Daed*'s shirt, and he followed.

When her parents were gone, she raised her chin to look up at Ezra. Now he looked almost sick, like his stomach was upset. Her awkwardness disappeared as concern took over. She stepped forward and placed her hand on his arm. "What's wrong? Is there something I can do?"

His Adam's apple bobbed up and down, but his gaze remained steadily on hers. "*Ya*. There is something you can do."

"Anything." She moved closer to him, all sorts of tragic scenarios going through her mind. He was in pain, and she wanted to take that from him. To hug him like she had in the parking lot at the Middlefield Market. A sweet man like Ezra didn't deserve to be hurt like this. She lowered her voice. "Tell me what you need."

"I need the quilt back."

CHAPTER 8

E zra stifled a groan at the shock on Hannah Lynne's face. "Excuse me?"

"I need the quilt back." Oh, this was painful. He dug into the pocket of his jacket for the money she'd given him at the auction. He'd stopped by his house to get it, and the musty smell of the rest of the house hadn't yet overwhelmed the clean scent coming from the kitchen. Which made him feel even more like a heel. How could he put a price on the work she'd done today?

Dear Lord, how can I take the quilt from her?

His fingers touched the bills in his pocket at the same moment he looked into her eyes. He stilled. Whatever spark had started between them earlier that day—or at least on his part—was not only still there, it seemed to grow, warming his belly and his heart. Her *kapp* was a little crooked, and a strand of hair was tucked behind her ear. She still smelled as wonderful as she had in his kitchen, and her skin took on a creamy tint in the low light of the gas lamps in the room. She was so beautiful he could hardly breathe.

Then she grimaced as he brought out the money. When he held it out to her, Hannah Lynne's sweet face contorted into an angry expression he hadn't known she was capable of.

"I have to buy back the quilt," he said, holding out the money to her. "If you could get it for me—"

"Why?" She crossed her arms over her chest. "Why do you need the quilt?"

He pressed his lips together. Was it even possible to explain why? He wasn't sure he could, at least not in a way that made sense. He was standing there, holding out money that was really her money, to buy back a quilt that he'd bought for her that belonged to his mother and was made by his favorite grandmother. No matter how he looked at it, he was at fault. It was his dumb mistake.

One he didn't want to admit to Hannah Lynne.

"Does it matter why?" He thrust the money at her, more irritated with himself than with her. "I just need it back."

She looked at the money and shook her head. Her eyes narrowed. "You said we were square."

"Would you just take the money?"

"*Nee*! You want *mei* quilt."

"Technically it was *mei* quilt," he countered.

"That was before you gave it to me," she answered back hotly. "Remember? You didn't even want me to pay for it."

"That was before."

Her hands dropped to her sides as she took a step toward him. "Before what?"

Her voice was raised, and he matched his level to hers. "Before . . . never mind." He bent over until their gazes were even. "Why do you want the quilt so badly? You never told me."

"You never asked."

"I'm asking now."

She paused, her eyes never leaving his. "It's none of *yer* business."

"So it's okay for me to tell you, but you not to tell me?"

"That doesn't make any sense!"

He tossed the money on the nearby coffee table and moved closer to her. "None of this makes any sense!" He was thoroughly angry right now, and he had no idea why. He couldn't take his eyes off her. The lock of hair had escaped from behind her ear and hung against her cheek. She blew at it from the corner of her mouth, but it fell right back in its original place, drawing his attention to her cheek, then to her mouth.

Ezra could feel his pulse pounding in his ears. He couldn't take this—whatever *this* was—anymore. So he did the only thing he knew to do—he grasped her by the shoulders and kissed her.

❧

Ezra is kissing me. Ezra Yutzy is kissing me . . .

Those words were somewhere in the back of her mind, which wasn't working quite right as Ezra drew her against him and continued to kiss her. But just as soon as she started to kiss him back—at least she thought she was kissing him back, but she really didn't know since she'd never been kissed—he dropped his hands from her shoulders and pulled away.

She looked up at him, her eyes wide and her chest expanding further with each breath she took. How long had she wanted

Ezra to notice her, to like her? She'd never even dreamed of kissing him. Well, at least not that often.

It was wonderful and confusing and—

"I'm sorry," he said.

Hurtful.

He moved away until his backside hit the door. He thrust it open and darted out of her house, as if his pants and hat were on fire. The screen door bounced shut behind him, and the cool night air flowed over her heated body.

She touched her fingers to her lips. He kissed her, and he regretted it.

"Hannah Lynne?"

She turned at the sound of her mother's voice. "*Ya,*" she ground out, her voice sounding like crushed gravel.

"*Yer daed* and I thought we heard yelling." She went to Hannah Lynne. "Are you okay?"

Nee. She was *not* okay. "*Ya.* We just had a disagreement. A friendly one." The smile she gave her mother was so tight she thought her skin would crack. "Because we're . . . friends."

Her mother nodded and returned the smile. "I didn't realize you and Ezra knew each other that well."

"We don't." She was realizing she didn't know him at all.

"*Yer vatter* and I are going to bed," *Mamm* said as *Daed* entered the room. He gave Hannah Lynne a tired wave and started climbing the stairs. "See you in the morning," *Mamm* added, then followed him.

Hannah Lynne stayed in place, her lips still tingling, the front door still open. The night air sifted through the mesh screen. She could hear the crickets and cicadas starting up their nightly melodies, punctuated by the intermittent sound of a hoot owl. She shivered, but still she didn't move.

Ezra had kissed her and she had no idea why. But despite being irritated with him—and now plainly angry—she wouldn't have traded those few seconds for anything.

She shivered again, and the chill brought her to her senses. She shut the front door and started for the stairs, noticing the money on the coffee table as she passed by. Terrific. Now she had to see him again. She couldn't keep both the money and the quilt—and she definitely was not parting with the quilt. She scooped up the bills and went to her room.

After she shut her bedroom door, she put the money on her dresser. She tucked the stray hair back over her ear and went to the closet. The kiss was forgotten for a moment as she looked at the quilt. Why would a *mann* want a quilt that much? *Why won't he tell me why?*

She reached up and retrieved the quilt, then unfolded it on her bed. She kneeled in front of it, her fingers grazing over the old, soft fabric with reverence. It wasn't the same quilt. She knew that. But it was close enough. Memories came back, along with tears as she remembered a time long in the past, when she was a child of seven. A bratty child her great aunt Edna was watching while her mother was in the hospital with an attack of appendicitis.

Hannah Lynne was mad. She missed her mother, and Aenti *Edna was mean. Her brothers didn't have to stay with* Aenti, *so why did she? She wanted to be home, to play in the barn and be around the cows. Not stuck inside while her aunt made her wash dishes. When Hannah Lynne had asked for macaroni and cheese for lunch,* Aenti

Edna made her eat liverwurst. Hannah Lynne hated liverwurst. When her aenti wasn't looking, Hannah Lynne had taken her glass of grape juice and poured it all over the pretty quilt on Aenti Edna's bed. That would show her.

Hannah Lynne cringed, as she always did when she thought about that time. Her father had picked her up before her aunt had discovered the quilt. By then the grape juice had hours to seep through and stain the fabric. Which it did, ruining what Hannah Lynne later found out was an engagement gift to her aunt from her uncle, who had died in a farming accident two months earlier.

It didn't matter that Hannah Lynne was only seven when she ruined the quilt. Or that her aunt had forgiven her, and that she and Hannah Lynne had ended up very close up until her aunt's untimely death from ALS four years ago. Despite the ugly stains on the quilt, her aunt had still used it. She'd cuddled Hannah Lynne with it when she was ten and had a fever from the flu. She displayed it in the living room during the holidays, not caring that people saw the damage Hannah Lynne had caused. Whenever anyone asked what happened to the quilt, *Aenti* Edna shrugged it off, telling everyone that she wasn't as careful with it as she should have been. No one, including her mother, had known what Hannah Lynne had done. Her aunt and uncle had no children, and near the end of *Aenti's* life, when she could still talk, she told Hannah Lynne that she had loved her like a daughter.

After *Aenti* Edna was buried, Hannah Lynne had gone with her mother to pack up the house. When Hannah Lynne couldn't find the quilt, her mother admitted they had hidden it in the casket. "It was her last request," her mother had said, tears glistening in her eyes. "That quilt was always her tangible connection to Abel. She wanted it with her when she was buried."

Hannah Lynne hadn't understood how an object could hold so much emotional value. Until she saw this quilt. Tears slipped down her cheeks as she picked up the quilt and wrapped it around her shoulders, the way *Aenti* Edna had done when she was a little girl. It was like her aunt was there, sitting next to her, ready to bring her chicken soup when Hannah Lynne felt well enough to eat.

How could she part with it? How could anything replace the feeling she had right now?

She glanced down at the quilt, looking at the binding. Her aunt's quilt hadn't been so finely stitched, but the pattern, small squares of quilted yellow-and-blue baskets on a white background, was similar. Her aunt's quilt had only been yellow and white. And purple, once Hannah Lynne had finished with it.

Guilt still nagged at her, not as strong or intense since it had faded with time and maturity. But she doubted she'd ever get over what she'd done. Just like she'd never stop missing *Aenti* Edna.

Running her finger down the edge of the quilt, she felt something irregular in the stitching. She paused, and peered at it. Sure enough, the stitching at the trim of this part of the quilt was different. She moved the area closer to her lamp so she could see more clearly. Even squinting, it was hard to make out what she thought were words. Two words. One she recognized immediately. She sucked in a breath.

Ezra.

The other one next to it she didn't know, even though she could make out the letters. *Amor.* Ezra Amor? That didn't make any sense. Amor wasn't an Amish last name, and Ezra was the only Ezra she knew in her district. Surely it wasn't a coincidence that he wanted a quilt that had his name stitched on it, the letters so tiny and perfect that she doubted she would have ever seen them if she hadn't felt them first.

Her shoulders slumped. How could she keep the quilt now? And why didn't he just tell her it really belonged to him? Somehow it ended up in the auction by mistake. It would be like Ezra not to pull it from the auction, but to pay for it so the special needs clinic would still get the money.

Then why would he turn around and give it to her?

None of this made sense. It was too late to talk to him now. She'd have to see him tomorrow. But church wasn't the right place to talk, and she was sure he would avoid her anyway. Besides, she had to tell Josiah her plans to spend time with him had changed. Then she'd drive to Ezra's parents' house in the afternoon.

The memory of his kiss came to the front of her mind. While she was finding out about the quilt, she would find out why he kissed her too. She was done hiding her feelings for him and puzzling over his odd behavior. By the time they were finished talking, she would have answers—whether she liked them or not.

She turned off her lamp and lay down on the bed, the quilt still wrapped around her body. As her eyes closed, her fingers continued to touch Ezra's name.

~⊛~

On Sunday afternoon, Ezra went out to the carpentry shop. He couldn't work, but at least it was an escape from his father's loud snoring as he napped on the couch and his mother's more delicate snoozing as she leaned back in her chair. At least they had stopped asking him how he was feeling after he'd feigned a stomach upset to avoid going to the service that morning.

The scent of sawdust and fresh wood hit him as he opened the door, then closed it behind him. Outside the weather threatened rain, and gray, dull light shone through the windows, leaving the room dimly lit. He could turn on one of the gas lamps, but he didn't bother. He started to pace.

He'd left his hat in the house, and he fisted his hands through his hair. Fatigue dragged at him. Last night he'd barely slept, kept awake knowing he was caught between two women he cared about. One of them he loved and the other one . . .

The memory of Hannah Lynne's sweet mouth made him pick up the pace. His heart clenched at the thought of upsetting her. But hadn't he done exactly that yesterday? Then he took advantage of the situation by kissing her. He still didn't know why he did it, just that he had to. And because he was such a *wonderful* person, he apologized for it, when he wasn't sorry at all.

Ezra rubbed his eyes as he walked the length of the woodshop, his shoes kicking up the sawdust he and his *daed* were never able to sweep completely off the floor. Hannah Lynne obviously had some sentimental attachment to the quilt that he wasn't aware of, and that she didn't want to share. But his mother had an attachment, too, an important one. Sure, he could probably go to her, explain his blunder, and she would chalk it up to God's will. Yet that wouldn't be fair to her. This was his error, one he had to fix . . . and he had to break Hannah Lynne's heart to do it.

At the sound of the door opening he stopped his pacing,

which had him ending up in the back of the shop. *"Daed?"* he said as he turned around.

"Nee." Hannah Lynne walked into the shop. Alone, without the quilt. She continued to walk toward him, while he continued to be stuck in place. She stopped when she was a few feet from him. Her *kapp* was straight this time, her hair combed and parted neatly and mostly hidden underneath the white head covering. Her hands were clasped in front of her, but her gaze remained steady. Calm. Bold, even.

"Ezra," she said, her chin lifted. "I saw you coming back here as I drove in. We need to talk."

The first thing Hannah Lynne noticed after she spoke was Ezra's hair. It looked as if he'd used an eggbeater instead of a brush that morning. Some of the ends were standing straight up. His hair was thick and wavy, and he looked a little wild. Maybe more than a little wild, since his blue-gray eyes were wide open and wary as he looked down at her.

Then he spoke. "Hannah Lynne, about yesterday—"

She held up her hand. "I don't want to talk about yesterday. I want you to tell me about the quilt." She took a step toward him. "The truth, this time."

He ran his hand through his hair, and now she could see how it had gotten so disheveled. "The truth is, I'm an idiot." He gave her a wry smile. "And all of this is *mei* fault."

Hannah Lynne listened as Ezra told her about accidentally giving the quilt to Sarah Detweiler for the auction. "What I didn't know was that the quilt was made by *mei grossmutter*. When *mei mutter* found out from Sarah that I had bought it back, she was relieved." He sighed. "That's why I need the quilt. It belongs to *mei familye.*"

She nodded. "I know." She took another step forward, and she was glad to see he didn't move away. "What I don't understand is why you gave it to me?"

His hand went to his hair again, but he pulled it away and rubbed the back of his neck instead. "When I saw you looking at that quilt," he said, his low voice dropping even lower, "I could tell how much you liked it. It was almost as if you . . ." He glanced away.

"As if I what?"

"As if you loved it." He met her gaze again. "Because of that, I knew you had to have it. I didn't want something as unimportant as money to keep you from something you loved."

Her bottom lip trembled, and she took one more step closer to him. "Why didn't you just tell me that yesterday?"

"Because . . ." His eyes turned the color of dark slate and he seemed to search for the words. "I should say it was because of *mei* pride. It wouldn't let me admit I'd messed up." This time he took a step toward her. "But the real reason is because I didn't realize until now . . . right this minute . . ."—he bent his head closer to her, his voice lowering more than she'd thought possible—"that *yer* happiness means everything to me."

If her body had been made of ice she would be a puddle by now. His words, combined with the sincere tone of his voice and the darkening of his eyes, made her feel more wonderful than any dream she'd ever had of Ezra Yutzy. Questioning the why and the when and the how that brought them to this place, to this realization that there was an undeniable attraction and connection between them, would be a waste of time. And where Ezra was concerned, Hannah Lynne was tired of wasting time.

They moved toward each other in unison. They stopped a few seconds later, also at the same time. And at the same time, they reached for each other's hands, and held tight.

"Hannah Lynne?" Ezra said, his eyes never leaving hers. "I need to ask you something."

"Okay." Her pulse raced as it always did when she was around him, but this time the feeling was different. Relaxed. Peaceful. As if she was destined to end up here with him, his warm hands holding hers. It took a beautiful quilt to get them to this point, an heirloom that had an important, yet separate connection to them both.

He leaned closer. "May I kiss you again?"

Before she answered, she ran the tip of her index finger over the prominent freckle on his cheek.

"Why did you do that?" he asked.

"Because I've always wanted to."

He smiled. "You didn't answer *mei* question. Is it okay if I kiss you? I want to do it right this time."

She nodded . . . and the kiss she received was more than right.

<hr/>

The next morning before she went to the Middlefield Market to set up her butter stand, Hannah Lynne stopped by Ezra's parents' house. She pulled into the driveway, brought her buggy to a stop, and looked at the quilt neatly folded on the seat beside her. She sighed and ran her hand over the soft fabric one last time.

She picked up the quilt and got out of the buggy. Ezra would probably be in his workshop by now. She smiled dreamily as she remembered the kiss—and several more after that—he'd delighted her with yesterday. She'd returned home floating on fifty clouds of sheer bliss.

However, she wasn't here to see him, as much as she wanted to. She was here to give his mother back her quilt. She knocked on the door, and a few moments later *Frau* Yutzy opened it.

"Hannah Lynne, this is a surprise."

Ezra's mother smiled, and Hannah Lynne wondered if Ezra had said anything to her about what happened between them yesterday. She hoped he hadn't. She didn't mind if his mother or anyone else knew about the change in their relationship, but she did want a little private time to savor the reality that she and Ezra were now a couple. She hadn't even told her own parents yet.

Frau Yutzy opened the door wider. "*Kumme* in. Would you like some *kaffee?*"

"*Ya,*" Hannah Lynne said. Once inside, she held out the quilt to *Frau* Yutzy.

"I thought Ezra had this?" his mother said. "He told me it was at his *haus.*"

Uh-oh. Maybe she should have consulted Ezra before bringing the quilt. She thought about telling her the long convoluted story, but she quickly changed her mind. "Ezra wanted me to give it to you," she said simply. Which was true . . . she was just leaving out some details.

Frau Yutzy gave her an odd look before accepting the quilt. Then she smiled, holding it close to her body. "*Danki,*" she said softly, then started to lay it on the chair near the door, only to pause. "I'm going to put this in *mei* room," she said. "*Geh* ahead and make *yerself* at home in the kitchen. I'll be there in a minute."

Hannah Lynne walked into the Yutzys' kitchen, the strong scent of coffee hitting her right away. She looked at the table, imagining Ezra and his parents eating meals there together. Her mind wandered to the thought of her and Ezra eating at their own table in his house . . . then drew her thoughts up short. No need to ponder that possibility right now.

She glanced in the corner of the kitchen and noticed a large cooler on the floor. The lid was open . . . and naturally Hannah Lynne was curious. She glanced at the kitchen door, then crept over to the cooler. She would take only a little peek. Maybe the contents would give her some insight into what kind of food Ezra liked.

She gasped when she looked inside. The cooler was full of butter. *Her* butter.

"How do you like *yer kaffee*?"

Hannah Lynne spun around, stepping away from the cooler. "A little sugar," she said, going to the table and pretending she hadn't been snooping. She sat down as *Frau* Yutzy poured their coffee before joining her at the table.

At that moment Ezra walked into the kitchen. His eyes lit up as he met Hannah Lynne's gaze. "Hi," he said, his deep voice sounding shy.

"Hi."

They looked at each other for a long moment, long enough that she forgot *Frau* Yutzy was there.

"I forgot about the wash," Ezra's mother said suddenly, rising from the chair. "I need to get it out soon so it will dry. Ezra, would you mind keeping Hannah Lynne company until I get back?"

Ezra glanced at his mother. "I'll be glad to," he said, his gaze returning to Hannah Lynne.

When his mother left, Hannah Lynne asked, "Does she know about us?"

With a shrug Ezra went to Hannah Lynne. "Maybe. I didn't say anything to her, though." He leaned down and kissed her. "I didn't expect to see you here. Although I'm not complaining."

"I stopped by on the way to the market to give the quilt to *yer mamm*. She put it in her room."

He sat next to her. "Probably the safest place for it."

Hannah Lynne chuckled. "Probably."

"Yesterday she told me there's a story behind the quilt," he said, taking her hand. "After you left and I went inside, she was just coming down from the attic and started talking about it again." He looked down at their hands clasped together. "It's a pretty amazing story."

Hannah Lynne leaned forward, eager to hear it.

"The quilt is actually mine," he said. "*Mei grossmutter* even stitched *mei* name on it."

Nodding, Hannah Lynne took a sip of her coffee, still keeping her other hand snugly nestled in Ezra's. She already knew this, of course, but she continued to listen.

"*Mei grossmutter* also stitched another word on the quilt. *Amor.*"

"What does that mean?"

"It was her nickname for me," he said. "Her family was originally from Romania, and she married an Amish man in

Lancaster. Then they moved to Middlefield. *Mei grossmutter* had stopped speaking Romanian and spoke only English and *Dietsch*, except for one word. *Amor*. It means *love*."

She squeezed his hand. "That's so sweet."

He nodded. "Apparently *Mamm* found a letter yesterday, one that had been misplaced for years. She didn't know *mei* name was on the quilt until she read the letter." He swallowed, and looked into her eyes. "That quilt was not just an inheritance for *mei mamm*. It was *mei grossmutter*'s gift to me for *Mamm* to keep, for when I married and had *mei* own *familye*. She told *mei mamm* the secret of the names in the letter *Mamm* had somehow never read."

His gaze held hers, which made her thoughts wander again to the possibility of a permanent future with him. The love she saw in his eyes made her believe it was possible.

He released her hand. "I'm sure you have to get to the market," he said.

"*Ya.*" She didn't want to leave, but they both had to go to work. They stood at the same time, and he moved a step closer to her.

"Maybe I'll see you there later today," he said with a grin.

"Ezra, you don't have to buy any more butter." She tilted her head in the direction of the cooler. "I think you've got more than enough."

He leaned down, his lips near hers. "That's because I can't resist the *maedel* who makes it."

EPILOGUE

One Year Later

Hannah Lynne fell back on the full-sized bed, her body sinking into the soft mattress, the skirt of her dark blue wedding dress bunching up slightly around her legs. She looked up at the ceiling and smiled, content. She closed her eyes, only to open them again when Ezra landed beside her.

"Finally," he said, taking her hand. He pressed it against his chest, which was covered in a crisp white shirt and black vest that made him look absolutely gorgeous. "Alone, at last."

She turned to him, her smile widening. Their wedding had been a few hours earlier, and while tomorrow they would do the obligatory visiting of friends and family, tonight belonged to them, in Ezra's house. *Their* house. They had finished renovating it together.

She released his hand and scooted up a little, glancing at her new husband's feet as they dangled a bit over the edge. "Maybe we should get a longer bed," she said.

"Someday." He sat up next to her and grinned. "It's fine for now." He leaned over and kissed her cheek. "I have something to give you."

She watched as he scrambled off the bed and went to the hope chest at the foot of it. The chest was the engagement present he'd given to her five weeks ago. He'd made it himself, even carving a quote in the center of the lid. It was from the wrapper of one of the many, many, *many* blocks of butter he'd bought from her. *Being in love makes every morning worth getting up for.* At the time she wrote it down she had no idea how true those words were.

Her eyes widened as he pulled a quilt out of the chest. Ezra laid the folded quilt on Hannah Lynne's lap and gazed down at her. "It's back where it belongs. With both of us."

She could hardly speak. "I'd hoped . . . I didn't want to presume . . ."

"You knew it would be *yers* again." He sat down next to her on the bed and tweaked her nose.

She reached over and planted a soft kiss on his freckle, then leaned her head against his shoulder.

"There's something else," he said. He showed her the stitching on the quilt, where his name and *Amor* were. "Can you see it?" he whispered.

On the other side of *Amor* were more carefully stitched letters. She smiled as she realized what they spelled.

"*Mutter* tried to match *Grossmutter's* stitching."

"She came close." Hannah Lynne peered at her name, now a permanent part of the quilt. A tangible connection to her aunt, and now to the man she loved.

She gazed at him for a long moment. "I love you," she said, resting the palm of her hand on his cheek.

"I love you too," he said, leaning into her touch. *"Amor."*

She pressed her lips to his, and as they kissed, he pulled the quilt around them both.

DISCUSSION QUESTIONS

1. Hannah Lynne and Ezra were brought together by several misunderstandings. Sometimes God uses the unexpected to make things happen. When in your life has something unexpected happened and you could clearly see God bringing those circumstances together?

2. The DDC Clinic is a real special needs clinic in Middlefield, OH. The auction in this story is also a real auction (although I took a few fictional liberties with the actual quilt auction). Is there a cause in your life that is important to you? How do you and your community come together to support it?

3. Do you have a special heirloom that you treasure? What is it and why?

4. If the quilt mix-up hadn't happened, do you think Ezra and Hannah Lynne would have eventually revealed their feelings for each other? Why or why not?

ACKNOWLEDGMENTS

A big thank you to my editors Becky Monds and Jean Bloom and my brainstorming/critiquing partners-in-crime Eddie Columbia and Kelly Long. Once again, I couldn't have written this without you all.

Kathleen Fuller is the author of several bestselling novels, including *A Man of His Word* and *Treasuring Emma*, as well as a middle-grade Amish series, the Mysteries of Middlefield.

Visit her website at www.kathleenfuller.com.
Twitter: @TheKatJam
Facebook: Kathleen Fuller

KELLY IRVIN

To my grandbabies Brooklyn and Carson,
because you, too, are sweeter than honey.
Love always.

GLOSSARY

aenti—aunt

Ausband—Hymnal

bopli—baby

daed—father

danki—thank you

dawdy haus—grandparents'
   house

dochder—daughter

doplisch—clumsy

Englischer—English or
   non-Amish

fraa—wife

Gott—God

groossdaadi—grandpa

Guder mariye—Good morning

gut—good

jah—yes

kaffi—coffee

kapp—prayer cap

kinner—children

lieb—love

mann—husband

mudder—mother

nee—no

onkel—uncle

Ordnung—written and
   unwritten rules in an
   Amish district

rumspringa—period of running
   around

schtinkich—stink, stinky

schweschder—sister

wunderbarr—wonderful

FEATURED BEE COUNTY
AMISH FAMILIES

Mordecai and Abigail King

Rebekah · Caleb · Hazel · Esther
Samuel · Jacob · Susan · King (Mordecai's sister)

Deborah and Phineas King

Leroy (bishop) and Naomi Glick
Adam · Joseph · Simon · Sally · Mary · Elizabeth

Jesse and Leila Glick

Andrew and Sadie Glick · Will
Patty · Henry · Catherine · Nehemiah

CHAPTER 1

The piquant aroma of pickled beets—sharp with vinegar and spices—tickled Isabella Shrock's nose. She froze, staring in dismay as the purple juice pooled around her sneakers and ran willy-nilly across the dusty wood-plank floor. A spray of droplets decorated her once-pristine apron. She blew out air, her frustration tightening the skin around her eyes and mouth. Her first trip to the Combination Store at the center of her new community in Bee County, Texas, and she'd managed to drop a box filled with jars of vegetables fresh from Abigail's canning frolic.

Mudder and Abigail had trusted her with this simple task. Isabella sank to her knees. Being a part of their first canning frolic since moving to Bee County had made her feel like she would fit in here. *Mudder* and the rest of the family would be happy in their new home. Leaving Tennessee to make a fresh start had been a good idea. Now, she stood here with beet juice soaking the hem of her dress. Only one jar had broken. Still, one jar too many.

She tugged the box upright and began to replace the jars of

tomatoes, sweet corn, and nopal jam. They needed wiping down. Surely Will Glick, who worked in the store for Bishop Leroy, had an old rag she could use.

"Hey, you need some help?"

Patting the sweat on her forehead with her dress sleeve, Isabella pivoted to seek out the owner of the high voice with a soft Texas twang floating toward her.

An *Englisch* girl, dressed in a white V-necked T-shirt and tight blue jeans, strode down the aisle, her pink flip-flops making a *smack, smack* sound. Head down, long, blond hair hiding her face, she rummaged in a huge, polka-dotted canvas purse, apparently unmindful of how close she veered toward a shelf loaded with jars of honey. "I know I have something in here. Oh, here it is." She waved a packet of tissues. "Quick, start cleaning it up before sourpuss sees the mess."

Sourpuss? "Thank you."

The girl squatted alongside Isabella, her tanned face creased with a wide smile that featured perfectly aligned white teeth. "No problem. I don't want you to get in trouble with the guy who's running the place today. He's a piece of work."

Will Glick was a piece of work? Abigail's daughter Rebekah had introduced them after the church service Sunday and he seemed nice. Not much of a talker, but then neither was Isabella.

"I did make a mess."

"Accidents happen. Be careful not to cut yourself on the glass." The girl dropped a pile of tissues on top of the juice. They turned pink, then purple, and sank until they covered a pile of beets like a small, wet blanket. "I'm Maisie Lantana, by the way. You must be new around here. I thought I'd met all the Amish girls. I'm a friend of Rebekah Lantz's. She used to run around with us until she got baptized."

"Rebekah's mom and mine were best friends back home." Isabella introduced herself as she dabbed around the jagged pieces of Ball jar, trying to capture the juice, which seemed to race beyond her reach like a cat trying to escape a bath. "We're staying with them until we can do some work on our new house. We've been here about two weeks."

Exactly fourteen days in this flat, brown countryside where April felt like July in Tennessee, but who was counting or comparing, for that matter?

Nodding, Maisie snapped and popped her gum in a staccato of tiny explosions. "From Tennessee, like the others?"

"Carroll County, but we lived in McKenzie. My *daed* can't work like he used to do. Rebekah's family is helping us out."

Bee County District might be small, but they were kind and helpful. The folks had been that way in McKenzie, too, but *Mudder* said *Daed* wanted a new start. Which meant a new start for everyone.

Isabella turned at the sound of footsteps so heavy they rattled the jars. Will rounded an end cap that displayed cookbooks and homemade candles. A box filled with jars of honey in his arms, he stomped down the aisle in scarred work boots, his fair features reddened. "What happened here?"

He towered over them, tension apparent in the way he held his lean, muscled frame. His fierce gaze landed on Maisie and stayed there as if he was certain the *Englisch* girl was the source of the problem.

"I dropped the box. I guess it was too heavy or I tripped

over something." Isabella scrambled to her feet. Truth be told, she'd been gawking instead of watching where she was going. The store, with its dusky interior, had the same fascinating mishmash style of merchandise inside as the adjacent junkyard seemed to have outside. A little of this, a little of that. Straw hats, a few quilts, a beautiful handcrafted double rocking chair, farm implements, jars of jam and honey, and produce all laid out on shelves in no apparent order. "One of the jars broke."

"I see that. Stop messing with it before you cut yourself." Instead of heading off to fetch rags or a bucket of soapy water and a mop, he slid the box of jars onto the shelf and crossed his arms over his chest. His cobalt-blue shirt had been washed so many times it had acquired a soft sheen. "Don't worry about it. I'll take care of it."

"I'm Isabella Shrock. We met—"

"At church. I remember."

His gaze seemed locked on Maisie. That didn't surprise Isabella. Men rarely noticed her. Shy, that's what her *mudder* called her. Nothing wrong with that, according to *Daed*, who said no Plain man wanted a loudmouth, flighty woman for his *fraa*. Plain men wanted a good woman who knew how to reserve comment and acquiesce after a decent amount of discussion. He claimed she would come into her own, given time.

At eighteen, Isabella had begun to wonder exactly how much time would be required for such a transformation. And how would the young men notice her if she never had the nerve to speak up?

This move to Bee County, this *was* her new start, her chance to make herself anew. To find a way to be noticed by the person *Gott* intended to be her *mann*.

"I'd like to help clean up, if you don't mind. It's my mess."

"It's my job to take care of the store while Leroy is breaking a horse today, so I reckon you can go on back to Abigail and Mordecai's." His tone was kind, but something in his blue eyes seemed disapproving. "Let Abigail know she'll be one short on her count."

She'd only just met the man and he'd already seen how *doplisch* and inept she was. Isabella swallowed against the rush of heat that surged through her. "I made the mess, I'd like to clean it up."

"Not necessary." Will turned his back and headed toward the front of the store. "You probably have plans with your *Englisch* friend."

Plans? Friend?

"Don't let him bother you." Maisie stood and wiped her hands on her shorts, apparently unconcerned about the permanent nature of such stains. Her long fingernails had turned purple with beet juice. "He's had a bee in his bonnet about *Englisch* folks, as y'all call us, ever since *his* cousin rode off into the sunset with *your* friend Rebekah's sister Leila."

Isabella had heard pieces of that story, but she didn't know how Will fit in. Or what it had to do with *Englischers*. It didn't matter. She wasn't one to gossip. Especially with a stranger from outside the community. "Thank you for your help."

Picking up her skirt to avoid juice now seeping into crevices, Isabella trotted after Will. He strode along as if he had no idea she followed. He ducked around the rocking chair, with its sagging handwritten price tag. She did the same. He wove around a box of horseshoes. She wove. Still, he didn't look back.

He rounded the corner of a streaked glass counter by the front door, picked up a basket of rags, and set them on the counter next to an old battery-operated calculator, a cardboard sign handwritten with produce prices, and a metal cash box.

"If you'll give me the rags, I'll finish the job."

"It'll take a bucket of water and a scrub brush." He shook his head without looking up. "Even then, the juice will stain. I told you not to worry about it. I'll clean up your mess."

His tone was soft, but still there seemed to be an emphasis on *your*.

He was a man, after all, and she would bow to his wishes in the end, but that didn't keep her from trying to make things right. "We can do it together." She swallowed, surprised by her own audacity.

Will looked up. He seemed to see her for the first time. His eyes were blue, his nose long and narrow, his cheeks clean-shaven. Tufts of blond hair peeked from under his straw hat. If he ever smiled, he would be pleasing to the eye, no doubt. He looked a little older than her, old enough to be married, but his whiskerless face said differently. "It's not necessary. You've already stained your apron and your dress. Let me do it. It's fine. I don't mind."

"Were you not taught to clean up after yourself?"

"*Jah.*"

"Then?" The word came out in a whisper.

His lips turning up in what surely must be the start of a smile, he held out a rag. Isabella leaned forward to grasp it. She caught his fresh scent of soap. Their gazes mingled and held. Her fingers touched his. In his eyes the color of sky, she saw what surely seemed like misery he fought to shutter.

"I—"

"Don't—"

"Isabella, you have to come meet my friends. They're wait-ing in the car. They're a lot of fun." Maisie strolled to the counter. "Rebekah will tell you. She used to run around a lot—before the big scandal."

His smile gone, Will snatched the rag back, leaving Isabella with her hand grasping at air and her throat tight with an inexplicable sadness. He stared down at the *Englisch* girl, a pulse beating in his jaw. "Are you buying anything?"

"A jar of honey for my mom's tea and the beeswax lip balm." Maisie waved a ten-dollar bill at him. "I like the spearmint, and my friends think it's cool y'all make lip balm from beeswax."

He set the bag of rags on the counter, took the girl's money, and made change in a rapid-fire manner. Maisie stuffed the ones and the jar of honey in her bag and proceeded to use the lip balm in a slow trip around full lips held in an exaggerated pucker. She batted mascara-laden eyelashes at Will for a few seconds. Smiling, she turned to Isabella. "Come on, just let me introduce my friends. Don't waste any more time here."

Isabella stumbled backward toward the door, looking for some indication in Will that he wanted her to stay and finish the job.

His expression cool, he kept his head bent, gaze on the coun-ter. Whatever tenuous connection she'd felt had disappeared.

Maisie tugged the door open. The bell overhead chimed. "I'm surprised you haven't heard of the concept of forgiveness." Her grin wide, she waved toward Will. "I hear it's big with you folks."

She slammed the door before Isabella could hear his response. She found herself wanting to know what it would be.

A person so unhappy surely needed to give or receive forgiveness—maybe both.

CHAPTER 2

J ust as he figured. Will jerked away from the store window
before they saw him peering out like a little boy not allowed
to come out and play. Isabella Shrock stood there in front of
God and everyone talking to those *Englisch* teenagers as if she
couldn't wait to get into their car and drive away. That's how it
started. He should go out there and tell her so. As a member of
her community, he had a responsibility.

His knuckles on the windowsill turned white. He breathed
and forced himself to loosen his grip. He'd intervened before and
what had it gotten him? An irreparably damaged heart.

Isabella looked innocent enough with her fair skin, dark-
brown eyes, and slight body. Barely past being a child. Her
cheeks had stained the color of the tomatoes in the jars she carried into the store when she asked to clean up her mess. Her voice
quivered. Yet she stood her ground. It meant something to her.
She had the strength of her convictions, a quality that appealed
to him. He should've let her do as she asked. He still could. All he
had to do was walk out that door.

Nee. Better he should let her learn her lesson on her own.

She had displayed spunk or pluck. She might fare better than he thought.

Snorting to himself, he strode behind the counter and into the back room for the bucket and cleaning supplies. Plain women did not aspire to have spunk or pluck or whatever.

Yet there had been that moment, over a bag of rags of all things. Her gaze had been piercing. Knowing. Those deep-brown eyes the color of strong-brewed *kaffi* had peered into him past the stone walls he'd constructed around his heart. Still waters ran deep and something about his encounter with Isabella made him wonder just how deep hers were.

Her fingers were soft and tender on his. No one had touched him in a long time. Years.

Stop it.

He was past the stage of thinking he would find love. He lived alone on the farm his father had given him when his family moved back to Tennessee and he liked it. No fuss, no muss. His moment had passed when Leila Lantz chose his cousin Jesse, despite all the repercussions she would face as a result. Like never coming home. Never seeing her family again. Never seeing Will again.

Like Isabella, Leila had the strength of her convictions. She had made her choice. Now, he lived with it. *Gott* had blessed him with a new beginning when Leroy decided to let him help out in the store on a regular basis. He was blessed. Reminding himself of that fact set Will in motion.

He picked out the glass from the broken jar and tossed it into a bag on the floor next to him. Then he filled the bucket with soapy water, grabbed a scrub brush, and went to work. He scrubbed the floor until his shoulders ached. The beet juice refused to be vanquished. Still he scrubbed, taking satisfaction in the work itself.

The door banged with a vengeance, causing the bell to chime in an angry-sounding chatter. Hand on his aching back, Will stood, intent on telling the customer to take it easy on the door.

"Will, Will!" His cousin Simon sounded distraught. "Where are you?"

Will picked up the bucket and strode toward the front of the store. "Take it easy before you break the door. What's going on?"

Simon trotted around the end cap. He was the spitting image of his father before Leroy's hair had turned white and his shoulders had begun to stoop with age. "*Daed* fell at the house. Looks like it's his heart."

Will set the bucket on the counter. He strode to the door and flipped the OPEN sign on the window to CLOSED. "Where is he?"

"Adam fetched Mr. Cramer. He's driving them into town. Jerry Cummings is outside. He says he can take us if you want. Everyone is on their way."

Will grabbed the key from its nail by the door. "Let's go."

Forty minutes later, they strode into a waiting room at the medical center. Everyone had indeed converged on this point. Glicks mingled with Kings and Hostetlers and Shrocks. Will headed to Naomi first. His *aenti*'s face was as white as the sheets she dried on the clothesline every week but her expression placid.

He gripped his hands together and willed his voice to behave itself. "Any news?"

She dabbed at her cheeks with a handkerchief. "They said something about his heart." Her voice quivered. "I'm not sure, really. But he's in *Gott's* hands now." Her lips clamped shut. Putting on a strong show of faith in the face of her own more human fears.

Will nodded, searching for similar grit in himself. He turned and winded his way through the small clusters of folks talking quietly, waiting, until he reached Mordecai King. As deacon, Mordecai would step into Leroy's shoes for the moment. "How is he? What are they saying?"

"He's stable. They're taking him in for surgery to repair some blockage." Mordecai squeezed Will's shoulder. "Everyone's here. It would be a good time for a moment of prayer."

The murmuring ceased. Will closed his eyes, letting the silence envelope him. The words of the Lord's Prayer ran through his mind intoned in Leroy's sonorous voice. Followed by the words of Psalm 23. *"Yea, though I walk through the valley of the shadow of death, I will fear no evil: for thou art with me; thy rod and thy staff they comfort me."* His own words escaped him.

Thy will be done. That would be what Mordecai prayed. If Leroy's days on earth were done, so be it. Somehow that frame of mind escaped Will. He wanted his *onkel* to be around more days. Many more days. Since his own father had moved back to Tennessee, Will had grown closer to Leroy. And Leroy to him since Jesse's decision to leave the community.

Thy will be done. Will forced the words, knowing obedience came first, followed by humility. It was their way. It was hubris to think he knew better than *Gott* the Father when Leroy should go home.

A throat cleared, breaking the silence. Will opened his eyes.

Jesse stood in the doorway, a Texas Rangers ball cap clasped in his hands. Despite his khaki pants and button-down, collared white shirt, he looked the same. The same Jesse who'd been Will's catcher when he pitched in softball games. The same fellow who'd caught the twenty-pound catfish at Choke Canyon Lake. The same guy who'd bagged the first turkey for Thanksgiving Day three years in a row.

Not the same. "What are you doing here?" Will started forward, not sure what he would do when he reached the doorway and his cousin. His once best and closest friend. "You know better."

Mordecai gripped his arm. "I sent Samuel for him. He needs to be here for his *daed*. Leroy will need all his *kinner*."

"*Jah*." Will managed the word through gritted teeth. He tugged his arm free. "You're right."

Without another glance, he slipped past Jesse into the hallway, ignoring the soft sound of his name coming from his cousin, letting it float away in the frigid air of the hospital corridor. At least Jesse hadn't brought Leila. And their daughter.

Gott, *help me to forgive.*

He prayed that prayer every night. And every day he awoke with a heavy heart that told him professing to forgive was not the same as actually doing it.

He leaned against the pale-blue wall, letting his head rest against the solid construction.

"Are you all right?"

That soft voice with no hint of south Texas. Will opened his eyes.

A mixture of trepidation and concern etched on her thin

face, Isabella stood a few yards away, as if she didn't want to disturb him. Or she wanted room to escape if he exploded. Her cheeks were pink, her gaze filled with a soft concern that brought a sudden, unwanted lump to his throat.

"You're here?"

Her expression turned puzzled. "I came with Abigail and my *mudder*."

Will straightened. "I thought you were going for a ride with Maisie and her friends."

"And leave Mordecai's horse and buggy unattended in front of the store?" The concern disappeared. Her tart tone suggested he rethink his impression of her intelligence or lack thereof. "I only just met Maisie in the store today. I'm not one to run off with folks I hardly know."

Good for her. She was right to be offended. He'd painted her with the flaws of another. A bad habit when it came to women he hardly knew. "I'm sorry. It's not my place to judge."

"You seemed upset." She gestured toward the waiting room door. "Just now." Those fingers. They had such a soft touch.

Stop it.

"*Nee.*" He brushed past her and started down the hallway. "I wanted some air. Too many people in too small a room."

To his surprise, she kept pace with him. "This place gives me the willies. Cold air and false lights. How can a person heal when it's so cold? Your *onkel* would be better off with his own bed and Naomi's cooking."

"Leroy told me once that it's hard for germs to grow when it's like this. That's why hospitals keep it so cold." When *Groossdaadi* Solomon died in a room in this very hospital. "We need to do whatever is necessary to be good stewards of our health, even if that means taking advantage of *Englisch* medicine."

"Agreed." She nodded as if to put punctuation on her understanding of his position. Their district's position. "You're close to Leroy."

"*Jah.*"

"But not his son Jesse?"

"*Nee.*"

She clasped her hands behind her back as she walked. She looked so serious, yet still childlike with her purple-stained apron and flat chest. "Am I allowed to ask why?"

"Why I'm close to Leroy and not Jesse?"

She nodded, a becoming pink sweeping up from her neck to her cheeks.

"It's a long story and not one that bears repeating. Your friend Maisie was right. Forgiveness is necessary."

"So Jesse did something that needs forgiving?"

"I doubt he sees it that way."

"I saw his face." She hesitated. The pink turned scarlet. "When you passed by him, I saw a great sadness there. Almost... a longing."

Jesse had his ministry and his wife and his child. No way he missed his life as a Plain man. No way he missed Will. "What are you doing out here in the hallway? Naomi needs the women of the community around her right now. You should be in there."

"I meant to find water for her. She was coughing."

Will stopped walking. "The water fountain is just around the corner, down the hallway to the left."

She stopped, too, but didn't turn away. Her hand fluttered to her cheek and then her neck. "You could show me where it is."

Those soft fingers. She was the opposite of Leila in every way—dark to Leila's light, thin to Leila's rounded curves—yet something drew him to her. *Nee*, nothing but trouble came of such thoughts. "I'd rather stay here for a bit."

"I hate for you to be alone." The words came out in a barely audible stutter. Her gaze, so full of kindness, didn't waver from his face. "Eventually you'll have to face Jesse and put aside your differences."

She was wise too. Even if her advice couldn't be heeded. As much as he tried, he found it impossible to forgive Jesse. "I don't mind being alone."

That hadn't always been the case. Something in Isabella's face told Will she didn't believe him, anyway. She might have the look of a child, but no doubt remained that she was a smart woman who saw past his carefully constructed, stalwart defenses.

Once again their gazes locked. It was as if she beseeched him to open up to her, to pour out his misery. He couldn't. He wouldn't. No man worth his salt would. "You should get the water—"

"Hey, Will!"

This time the shout came from his cousin Adam. "Get in here. The doctor has word. Come on."

Will backed away from Isabella, turned, and loped down the hallway. He didn't look back, but somehow he felt her presence with every step, her soft, tender touch on his back long after he left her behind.

CHAPTER 3

The aroma of fresh-baked banana bread would make it impossible for the worst glass-half-empty person in the world to be in a bad mood. Isabella reveled in the scent as she arranged the baked goods in a box in the back of the buggy. Cinnamon rolls, peanut butter cookies, apple pie, sour cream spice cake—the smells mingled and made her mouth water.

She lifted her face to the sun, letting its rays seep into her pores. A beautiful April day and she wouldn't let anything ruin it, not even the prospect of seeing Will at the store. Now that Leroy was past the worst and expected to make a slow but sure recovery, Will would surely be back at work. No matter how much the thought of him made her stomach roil as if she'd eaten one fry pie too many. She couldn't put her finger on why he bothered her so much. He'd been brusque with her at the store, then lost and sad at the hospital. Neither place had he wanted her around. He'd made that obvious. Yet something in his face made him look like a lonely child. A fact that made her heart hurt in a way that was most uncomfortable.

Downright painful in fact.

"Here's the bread." Rebekah trotted around the buggy with a smaller box filled with white and wheat bread loaves, each individually wrapped in plastic. "Let's get going. We want to get these to the store before the folks come out from Beeville to stock up this morning."

"They really come all the way out from town to buy our baked goods?" Isabella moved her box over to make room for the breads. "Surely they have bakeries in town."

"That and Mordecai's honey. They have bakeries, but they don't carry Amish bread." Rebekah grinned, her dimples deepening under high cheek bones that made her look like her *mudder*. Her blue eyes sparkled as if the joke was on Isabella. "It's special. Just like honey that comes from the bees out here is special. It's made with pollen from local plants."

"I know we work extra hard to make the desserts and the breads tasty, but—"

"It's not about tasty; it's about Amish." Rebekah climbed into the buggy and grabbed the reins. "Not that it matters why *Englischers* are fascinated with Plain folks. It helps us pay for the things we need."

"I know. I ask too many questions." Isabella joined her friend on the seat. "I'm glad you could come with me to the store today."

Rebekah clucked and slapped the reins. Chocolate whinnied, a reproachful sound, and the buggy took off with a jolt. "I saw the look on your face when *Mudder* told you to go. It seemed like you didn't want to go by yourself. Still afraid of getting lost?"

"*Nee*. It's only a stone's throw . . ."

"Then what's the problem? You kept saying you'd go, but your face kept saying *don't send me, please don't send me.*"

Isabella squirmed. Rebekah would laugh at her. She seemed content, helping out Susan King at the school. If she had a special friend, no one seemed to know about him. Under Abigail's vigilant gaze, it must be difficult. "It's nothing."

"Come on, you're squirming like the *kinner* when Mordecai wants to know who dropped the egg basket. You can tell me. I'm a good listener."

"It's Will."

"Will?" Rebekah slapped her hand to her mouth, but not before a giggle escaped. Her blue eyes lit up with delight. "You have a hankering for Will?"

"A hankering? *Nee, nee.*" She should've kept her mouth shut. "I just . . . I mean . . . I broke a jar of beets in the store, and he had to clean it up. I surely made a terrible first impression. He seemed really out of sorts with Maisie Lantana, and I think he thinks I'm not a very good Plain person."

She didn't mention the connection she'd felt at the store when their hands touched or conversation in the hospital or the lost way he'd spoken.

"Child, child." Rebekah had only one year on Isabella, but she made her feel like a baby. "Will is out of sorts with himself. Not you."

"I can see that."

"I'm afraid he's let some things fester in his heart. And the Lantz women are partly responsible for that."

"Lantz women? You mean you and Leila and Deborah?"

"*Nee,* not me, although I played my little part." Rebekah

sniffed and sighed. "Believe me, I'm not laughing at you or Will. It would be lovely if you were the one for him. He meant to ask out Deborah, but she took up with Phineas before he had a chance. Then he set his sights on Leila and she chose Jesse. His cousin. Jesse chose his *Englisch* friends and their church. I reckon Will feels responsible for not being able to talk either one of them out of it. It's been almost two years and his heart is still sore."

That seemed like a good way to put it. Will's heart did indeed seem sore. "So that's why he's so bitter about *Englischers*?"

"Leila was the first woman from the district to work in Beeville. She took a job at the day care, going to and from with an *Englisch* family. Jesse convinced her to join his new church. Will tried his best to talk both of them out of it. In the end, Jesse's feeling that somehow *Gott* called him to preach was stronger than either of them."

"That's not Will's fault."

"He believes it is." Rebekah slowed the buggy and they turned onto the paved road that led to the store. "I'll never forget . . ."

"Never forget what?"

"Christmas Eve. He knocked on our window. She was already gone."

"Leila?"

"*Jah*. He had a gift for her in a box, but it was his heart he wanted to give her."

"Did he tell you that?"

"*Nee*, of course not. Courting is private. But the look on his face when I told him that she had gone to town with Jesse, I'll never forget it."

"Like his heart was broken?"

"Like he would never be hurt like that again."

"What was in the box?"

"I don't know. I told him where she was. He went to follow her. We never talked about it again."

They were silent for several minutes.

More than two years had passed since that Christmas Eve. Still, Will's heart hadn't mended. Nor had he forgiven the *Englischers* who took Jesse and Leila from him. Hanging on to that bitterness kept his hurt and brokenness alive. Isabella had never felt the kind of love Will must've felt for Leila to let it affect him to this very day. "Do you think there's only one love in the world for a person?"

Rebekah shook her head as she slapped her hand on her prayer *kapp* in a humid breeze that kicked up dust in plumes around the buggy. Strands of her dark, chestnut hair slipped from the *kapp*, giving her a windswept look. "Look at my *mudder* and Mordecai. I'm old enough to remember how sweet *Mudder* and *Daed* were together before he died. Like teenagers in love when they had five *kinner* themselves. The way they sneaked around for kisses when they thought we weren't looking. The thought they put into their Christmas and birthday gifts even after all those years and all those gifts."

"And now Abigail does the same with Mordecai."

"*Jah*. She doesn't love my *daed* any less. She has room in her heart for the two of them. Mordecai makes her happy."

It would be lovely if someone could make Will happy like that. Or even give him the hope of a love that made him feel that alive again.

"The thing is . . ." Rebekah's voice faded away. She sighed. "You're on your *rumspringa*. This is your time to find the right *mann* for you. You still have time. Have fun doing it. Then you can move on and be baptized."

"Is that what you did?"

"I suppose so." Her tone belied the words. "It was different for me. Everyone here knows what happened with Leila and Jesse. Because of my sister no one is allowed to work in town. I help Susan at the school because that's all *Mudder* will allow."

"That shouldn't keep you from finding a special friend, should it?"

Rebekah shrugged. "In case you haven't noticed, we don't have a lot of young men here who are seeking *fraas*."

"Will wasn't interested in you after Leila left?"

"*Nee*. He gave up on Lantz girls." Rebekah snorted. "Like I would want to be third choice."

True.

"There is someone out there for you." Isabella couldn't help but believe in happy endings. Life on this earth was hard, her *daed* said it often enough, but in the journey existed joy, he also said that. "And me. I think *Gott* wants us to have patience."

"I try." Rebekah rewarded Isabella with a smile that made her dimples pop. "And in the meantime, I'm having fun with my scholars. Susan's scholars, but I get them at recess! I get to play kick ball and softball and volleyball every day and I'm a grown woman!"

The rest of the ride passed in companionable silence. Rebekah was nice. Isabella was blessed to have a new friend. She would pray for a special someone for her.

A few minutes later they pulled into the store. Isabella hopped from the buggy. She smoothed her *kapp* and then her apron. Rebekah giggled as she brushed past her.

"What?"

"You look fine. Will won't find anything wrong with you."

"*Nee*. I felt a little windblown, that's all."

"Hah. You like Will."

Feeling foolish, she tugged the box from the buggy and headed to the store. The door opened just as she reached it. Simon Glick held it open for her. "*Guder mariye.*" He smiled, looking very much like his father, Leroy, with his gray eyes and wire-rimmed glasses perched low on his narrow nose. "Those cookies look mighty good. They'll sell fast."

Isabella set the box on the counter and took a quick look around. No Will.

Rebekah followed, then slid the box of honey into the spot next to the desserts. "Hey, Simon, where's Will?"

"He's visiting with Leroy this morning." Simon looked inordinately pleased at the situation. "So I'm in charge of the store until he gets back."

Simon might look like his father in the face, but he had his brother Jesse's stocky, barrel-chested build, dark hair, and burnt-caramel-colored eyes. He had a bit of a stutter, but he didn't seem the least bit concerned by it. His simple smile said he was a happy soul.

"Good for you." Isabella managed to smile back. All the anticipation fizzled inside her like a firecracker with a bad wick. "I'm sure your *daed* is comforted knowing his son is here taking care of things."

"He never let me do it before." Simon didn't sound hurt by that admission, rather pleased at this new development. "He says I'm better at farmwork. I'm not much for numbers."

And his cousin Will was.

Rebekah patted Isabella's shoulder. "You should see your face."

"What?" Abandoning her thoughts on who should run the store, Isabella turned her back on her friend and began unloading the baked goods into their spot on the shelf, next to that lovely double rocking chair just waiting for a *mudder* and *daed* to sit in it and rock their newborn baby together. "You are making this whole thing up."

Rebekah's knowing chortle made Isabella's ears and cheeks burn hot as a fireplace poker. "You're disappointed."

"Hush." Isabella sneaked a glance at Simon. He looked from her to Rebekah and back, a puzzled look on his face as he grabbed a two-pack of peanut butter cookies. "This isn't the time or place."

And it never would be. Will had no interest in her. He had no interest in love. He'd been burned.

"I'll pay for this." Simon moved behind the counter. "If that's what you're wondering."

"This has nothing to do with you." Rebekah's tone was airy. "It's girl talk."

"And I can never make heads or tails of such silliness." He sounded pleased with himself as he bit into the cookie and chewed. Crumbs deposited themselves on his smooth chin. "If it's about *lieb* and such, I don't want to know."

Neither did Isabella. Her disappointment at Will's absence

from the store could only mean one thing. She was in danger of sprouting feelings for a man who had no interest in her or any other woman. No one could live up to the life he'd created in his head—the one he wouldn't live with Leila.

Least of all a skinny, drab, quiet girl like Isabella Shrock. She sighed and sank into the rocking chair. It was roomy and solid. The rockers were tight and they didn't squeak when she rocked. Of course, it was only her weight. A double rocker was meant for two, *fraa* and *mann* with a *bopli* in the *fraa's* lap.

"You like the chair?" Simon spoke through a mouthful of cookie. "Mordecai made it."

Isabella ran her hands over the varnished oak. She couldn't explain why the chair produced a sense of longing in her, along with a lump in her throat. "It's nice."

"I hope an *Englischer* buys it soon." He brushed crumbs from his upper lip. "We could use the money."

She also couldn't tell him she hoped no one bought it. It wasn't nice to covet something so beautiful, but in her heart of hearts she could see herself nursing her baby while sitting in this chair, then rocking him—or her—to sleep.

Such silly flights of fancy. They'd all started when she came into this store with a box of fresh canned goods. Isabella pushed herself away from the chair. The back smacked the wall. "Oops, so sorry." She'd never thought of herself as clumsy before. She ran her hand over the back. No gouges. "I didn't hurt it."

"Mordecai makes a sturdy chair, don't you worry." Nothing could pry that smile from Simon's face, it seemed. What a nice quality in a person. "It shouldn't be sitting so close to the wall anyway."

The door opened and banged against the wall behind it. In

strolled Maisie Lantana. She wore a sundress the color of fresh lemons, matching sandals, and a smile that stretched across her face. "Hey, y'all. Is there still sour cream spice cake?" She whipped her long hair over her shoulder with an exaggerated flourish. "Rebekah, long time no see. Isabella! I was hoping I'd run into you."

Isabella held out a spice cake, fresh from the oven only two hours earlier. "I hope your family enjoys this cake. It's one of my favorites."

Maisie scooped up the cake with one hand and grabbed Isabella's arm with the other. "They will, I promise you that. Walk with me. I promised my mom I'd bring home another jar of honey. She's started using it in her cookie recipes. She says it's the sweetest honey ever."

Isabella threw a glance at Rebekah, who shrugged and went back to pricing the loaves of bread. Feeling like a child following the Pied Piper, she skipped to keep up with Maisie. "Why did you want to run into me?"

"We're having a get-together tonight. Some of the other Amish kids are coming." She picked up a jar of honey, held it up to the light streaming from a nearby window, frowned, and then returned it to its spot on the shelf. "We'll pick you up after dark."

"I don't know—"

"You can't say no. You're running around, right? And there's not a thing for you to do around here. *Nada.* That means 'nothing' in Spanish. I can teach you a lot of Spanish words. You'll need them when you go to the valley. When are you going to see the Gulf? Did Rebekah tell you about that? It's fabulous. Give us a chance. We'll have fun. I promise."

She grabbed another jar of honey and swished past Isabella.

"This will do. See you tonight. Be ready! You could come, too, Rebekah. It would be like old times!"

"Sorry, I can't." Rebekah waved and smiled. If she really regretted her circumstances, she did a good job of covering it up. "You have fun, though."

Isabella stood in the middle of the aisle, feeling windblown all over again. Maisie could talk. And she had a point.

Or maybe Isabella wanted to do something, anything, to take her mind off a dilemma by the name of Will Glick. He didn't approve of the *Englisch* teenagers. He didn't approve of her either.

A match made in heaven.

～◎～

The hospital room was nicer than Will expected. It smelled funny and the air felt frigid as usual, but a comfortable-looking recliner sat next to the bed and a couch provided more seating on the other side under a long window that had a pleasing view of a string of red oaks with petunias in pinks and purples planted in rings around them. A TV hung from the wall. Turned off, of course. The walls were painted a pale-green color that matched the darker evergreen tiles on the floor.

He forced his gaze to the bed. Leroy looked small under a pile of sheets, his grizzled head against a large pillow. His mane of white hair and beard seemed lost against all that white. Machines behind him kept track of information that determined if Leroy was getting better and when he would go home.

Soon. Gott, soon.

"Don't hover. Sit." Leroy's voice hadn't changed. That was a good sign. He sounded as commanding as ever. "I'm not dying. Leastways, not yet."

Exhaling for what might be the first time since he entered the room, Will tugged a straight-back chair closer and did as he was told. "Mordecai said you were asking for me."

"I did." Leroy paused, his breathing labored. His skin and lips had a faint purple tinge to them in the shine of the overhead fluorescent lights. "It's time we spoke of what happens next."

"Next?" The doctors had told Naomi that Leroy would recover. Time would be necessary for him to regain his strength. He would need to take some medicines and change his diet. Not propositions Leroy would enjoy, but necessary all the same. "Naomi says they'll discharge you in a day or two."

"I'm looking forward to that." The faint humor in his voice spoke of the understatement in his words. "I may be blessed by the good care offered to me by the doctors and nurses here, but home will be the best place to get better."

No doubt. "It won't be long before you'll be good as new."

"*Nee.* I will work hard to regain my strength." He shifted as if the words themselves caused him pain. "But it is clear to me that it is time to look to the future and those who come after me."

"What do you mean?"

"I mean that when I leave here, my *fraa* and I will move into the *dawdy haus*. My charge as bishop says that when I become old and weak, I'm to seek the ordination of another as bishop."

"You aren't old and weak. You have much left to give as bishop."

"I will do what's best for the district. No individual is more important than that."

So be it. "I understand."

What Will didn't understand was why Leroy was telling him this. A new bishop would be drawn by lot between the deacon and the minister. Mordecai and Jeremiah. Then lots would be drawn for the new vacant position. "Is there something I can do to help, in the meantime? The store is running smoothly. The produce is coming in now. We have lots of onions to sell to the grocery stores. Phineas and Mordecai sold bees to the citrus growers. We're in good shape all around."

"I'm getting to that." Leroy coughed and pointed to a plastic mug with a straw stuck in it sitting on a nearby cart. Will handed him the mug. Leroy sipped and wiped at his beard with the back of his wrinkled hand covered with brown age spots. "Adam will take over the farm and the buggy business. Jacob King will continue with the training of horses."

That left the store. It belonged to the entire community, but Leroy's father had started it and Leroy had managed it for almost twenty-five years. "And Simon?"

"Simon has a good heart. He's a special gift. He will be a helper for Adam and Jacob. Even at the store, he can help."

But not manage. "They all will work hard. They're good sons."

The unspoken words hung in the air between them. Except for Jesse. Jesse had been a good son. A good son who loved *Gott* and loved his family. Until he'd announced his calling from *Gott* to become a minister. The worldliness of those words still astounded Will. The ego.

Leroy shifted to his side and set his gaze with his brilliant gray eyes on to Will. "You're to take over the store."

Will swallowed against sudden emotion. His throat ached

with it. He ducked his head in hopes that Leroy wouldn't see the moisture in his eyes. He cleared his throat and breathed. "I'll do my best for our community."

"I know you will."

"Adam and the others won't feel that a son should do this?"

"They would not be so arrogant as to question the wisdom of this decision. Mordecai, Jeremiah, and I have talked. I have talked with my sons." Except Jesse. "This is the best use of each man's strengths."

Will leaned back in his chair. Each day he arose in the morning with a sense of purpose, a place to go, a place where he could be useful. His work at the store gave meaning to his life.

"However, there is additional direction attached to this responsibility."

"What is that?"

"You need to stop brooding and find yourself a *fraa*."

"That's not—"

"I would have to be blind not to know what happened between you, my son, and Leila. We don't speak of these things, but that doesn't mean we don't see them." Leroy's voice grew gruff. "It's been over two years. Forgive, forget, and move on. Don't let my son's choices affect yours."

"I do forgive. I try to forgive."

"Those are not the same thing. You are called to forgive just as *Gott* forgave you."

"I know that."

"It's not enough to know. You must do it. Seventy times seven."

"Forgiving is one thing. Choosing a *fraa* is another. It may be that my time has passed."

"As men in this community, we're expected to marry, to be heads of our houses, to be fathers. This district especially needs that. Our numbers are few."

Which was part of the problem. The unmarried women in this community knew all about Will's history with the Lantz sisters. First Deborah, then Leila. By some merciful blessing he hadn't added Rebekah to the list. But she knew. She knew of his love for Leila and how he'd pursued her sister into town with a Christmas gift when she'd already given the gift of her love to another.

"I don't know—"

"Pray on it. Ask *Gott* for guidance." Leroy looked tired. He looked ancient. "What I'm asking you to do is to open your heart to the possibilities. If you hold on to bitterness with one hand and anger with the other, you have no hands available to extend to a new love. No arms for embracing a life lived in love with another."

"I will try."

"Try hard." Leroy's voice faded. His eyes closed. "Now go. One of the blessings of being here is that I can take a nap whenever I like. And I like now."

Will stood. He touched the shoulder of Leroy's hospital gown. "Sweet dreams," he whispered. "I will try. Hard."

CHAPTER 4

The *schtinkich* of cigarette smoke greeted Isabella at the door of the pool hall. It burned her nose and her eyes. Pausing, she slapped her hand to her mouth and coughed. Her courage almost deserted her. She should've stayed home, ignored the headlights in her bedroom window after the others had gone to bed. She should've marched out on the porch and turned down the invitation instead of sliding into the backseat of the red car that Maisie called Pony because it was, according to her, a Mustang.

Isabella turned, but Maisie's hand with its bubblegum-pink-painted fingernails on her shoulder prodded her forward. That and curiosity. Isabella had never been in a pool hall or any place where alcohol was served.

Stumbling forward, she tried to take it all in at once. Orange, red, and yellow neon signs glowed in the dusky interior, advertising beer and cigarettes. Overhead fluorescent lights buzzed. The sound mingled with the murmured conversations of people who sat on high red-vinyl and stainless-steel stools along a bar that featured a red vinyl bumper from one end to the other.

They clutched bottles or glasses in their hands, talking and laughing as they sipped or gulped. The aromas of hamburgers, French fries, and onions frying in grease cut through the acrid smell of the smoke.

"Go on, go on, into the other room." Maisie laughed, a high sound that mingled with raucous music. "You're like a tourist on an outing in a foreign country."

The other room held the pool tables, along with two huge flat-screen TVs that screamed with more music. Tall, round tables with wood stools dotted the open spaces around half a dozen pool tables. Racks along the wood-paneled walls held pool sticks in a variety of lengths. In the muted light of round fixtures that hung low on chains, she found faces she recognized. Jacob King. Milo Plank. Sarah Hostetler. Ruth Miller. The girls seemed to divide their attention between the boys playing pool and the TV screens. Jacob and Milo handled the cues as if they knew what they were doing. The *smack, smack* of stick against balls and the rumble as they ricocheted into pockets supported their confident stances. They'd done this more than a few times.

Isabella wanted to turn and run. They would see her here in this place. The thought was ludicrous. She saw them too. Jacob and Milo wore jeans and T-shirts. Sarah and Ruth had removed their prayer *kapps*. Their long hair, blond for Sarah and brown for Ruth, lay loose down their backs. Yet they still wore their gray dresses and their aprons. Isabella's hand went to her own *kapp*. *Nee*. She let her hand drop. She couldn't.

Sarah gave a halfhearted *what-are-you-doing-here?* wave. Isabella waved back. Should she go stand with them? They'd chatted at the last singing and she'd talked to them during Abigail's canning frolic, but she didn't really know them. They looked as surprised to see her as she was to see them.

"Come on, don't be shy." Maisie tugged her along until they made it to the first pool table. "We're missing all the fun."

An *Englisch* boy leaned over to make a shot on an almost-empty table. His cue smacked against the white ball, which shot across the table and hit a black ball, then disappeared into a side pocket.

The other boy straightened from the wall he'd been holding up and twirled his cue, his expression disdainful. "Lucky shot, dude."

"You've been saying that all night." The first boy grabbed a bottle of beer from a shelf that ran along the wall and chugged it. He emitted a loud burp that made him sound like a toad, then grinned. "Yet I keep beating you."

"Yeah, yeah." Maisie intervened by slapping the loser on the chest. "Bella, this is my brother Ray. He's gonna teach you to play pool."

Ray's gaze meandered from Isabella's head to her toes in a lazy slide. He was tall, about Will's height, and had the same broad shoulders and lean but muscle-bound frame. Why was she comparing him to Will? His eyes were the same lake blue and his short hair the color of wheat. If he liked anything he saw, he didn't show it. "Maisie—"

"Don't Maisie me. This is Isabella. She's new around here. Be nice to her."

Maisie promptly trotted off, calling after someone named Nick, leaving Isabella standing there, her mind blank, her feet stuck to the floor. The winner of Ray's game wandered after Maisie, mumbling a line that began with *babe*.

"You new around here?" Ray picked up a plastic rim shaped like a triangle and slapped it down at one end of the green felt-covered table. He extracted balls of all colors from the various pockets of the table and plopped them into the triangle in some sort of pattern that seemed to make sense to him. "I don't recognize you."

"I've been here a few weeks. I'm from Tennessee."

"Dandy. Let's see what you can do with a stick." He held out the cue. "I bet you're a quick study. In more ways than one. Do you want a drink? I can get you one. I'm twenty-one."

Twenty-one. Close to Will's age. No, no thinking about Will right now. He would be horrified to see her here. Prayer *kapp* and all. *Stop it.*

"No, thank you." She took the stick. It weighed more than it looked like it should. She tried to hold it the way the others did, with their fingers just so. "I really haven't done this before."

Ray shoved the triangle back and forth on the felt. He slipped his fingers from the edge and lifted the triangle with a ginger touch. The balls kept the perfect shape of a triangle. "Of course you haven't, a good little Amish girl like you. I guess you decided to break out of that mold tonight."

Heat toasted her cheeks. "Maisie invited me."

"My sister is a force of nature." He tugged the stick from her grasp and leaned over the table at the opposite end from the balls. A second later his cue connected with the white ball, which catapulted into the neatly arranged triangle. The *smack* made Isabella jump. The balls scattered in all directions. At least two disappeared into the pockets.

A satisfied look on his face, Ray straightened. "Now that's a good break."

He stuck his hand in one of the pockets and displayed a ball. "I'm solids. That makes you stripes. You can use my stick for now. We'll pick out one of your own later."

Isabella accepted the stick. She inched closer to the table. She leaned over and propped her left hand on its edge the way she'd seen the others do.

"No, no, baby, not like that. Let me show you."

Ray slid in behind her. His arms came up as if to embrace her. His fingers touched hers, moving them a little this way, a little that way.

She could smell the beer and tobacco on his breath and the spicy scent of aftershave on his clothes. Her throat closed. Her heart pounded against her rib cage. Sweat beaded on her forehead despite the frigid air blasting from vents overhead. "You don't have to do that."

"You'll be my little pool-playing Amish protégé."

His low chuckle tickled her ear. She wanted to escape, but she was trapped between the table and his body. She straightened. Her shoulder bumped his chest. "Excuse me. Please."

"I'm just trying to help." Ray backed away, both hands in the air. His chuckle turned into a belly laugh. "It's okay, sweetie, take your shot. You're fine."

"I'd rather watch." Her voice held not the slightest quiver, which pleased her to no end. "Why don't you go ahead? This will be a . . . teaching demonstration."

"You're a shy little thing, aren't you?"

Shy had nothing to do with not letting a strange man touch

her. She gritted her teeth and took another step back, letting him see her face.

"Whatever." Ray took the stick back, bowed, and pivoted to the table. He proceeded to knock in ball after ball, pausing only to guzzle from his beer bottle, until all the solids were gone except the white one and the black one. Isabella had gathered from his steady flow of chatter that a person didn't want the white one to go in—ever—and the black one had to go in last. She suspected he made it look much easier than it actually was.

"Side pocket." He swaggered around the table and tapped the pocket with his stick. A second later the black ball disappeared. "Game."

He lunged and did a fist pump as if he'd defeated a major foe.

"Congratulations." Did one say such a thing when there was no opponent?

Ray patted the stool at the closest table. "Sit. Sit. I'll get you a beer."

"No, thank you."

"Come on." He folded his arm around her shoulder and squeezed. "Let's get to know each other."

She tried to shrug away from his touch. "I think I'm ready to go."

"It's early, early. Maisie will close the place down so you might as well relax, have a beer." His arm tightened. "They won't card you, I promise."

He surely would feel her heart hammering against her rib cage. A surge of fear turned into a lump that choked her. She swallowed. "I'm ready to go home."

His nose wrinkled as if he smelled something foul. "Think about it, babe. How will you do that without a ride?"

"We'll get her a ride." Jacob King strode toward them. His voice sounded just like Mordecai's. Such a deep voice for such a tall, lanky man. "We take care of our folks."

Ray's arm dropped. Relief flowed through Isabella like a massive waterfall. Did Mordecai know Jacob frequented a pool hall? *Rumspringa* had to be hard for parents. She ducked toward the door, following Jacob. He didn't look back. From the corner of her eye, she saw Milo heading their direction. Along with Sarah and Ruth. The girls didn't look happy.

"What's going on?" Milo strode past her and out the door. "Why are you leaving?"

"Isabella wants to go." Jacob held the door for the girls. "Ray was being a jerk."

"Nothing new about that." Milo tugged on his jacket. "You have to take him with a grain of salt."

"We just got here." Sarah rolled her hair into a bun with expert hands. "We don't want to leave."

"Stay then." Jacob let the door slam, muffling the sound of laughter from the bar. "I can come back and pick you up later."

How exactly would he do that? For the first time Isabella wondered about transportation for the four of them. Hadn't the other *Englischers* given them a ride?

"*Nee*, that will take too long." The look Ruth gave Isabella could only be described as unfriendly. "I don't know what you were expecting."

"I didn't expect anything. Maisie didn't really explain where we were going. She said a get-together."

"That's right. A get-together *here.*" Ruth motioned at the squat red-brick building with its blackened windows and a neon sign missing a *p* and an *l*. "Playing pool."

And drinking. Both girls had silly looks on their faces, and Ruth's words slurred at the end as if slippery on her tongue.

"I'm sorry. Go back in. I'll figure something out."

Like walking home. Or hitching a ride. *Nee. Mudder* and *Daed* had been adamant that the *kinner* understand about the prison near their new community and escapees and how dangerous this innocent-looking little town could be.

"Forget it. We stick together." Jacob's stride picked up. "We'll drop Isabella off. If y'all want to come back, you can. I'm done for tonight."

Isabella scurried to keep up. Something jingled in Jacob's hand. He tossed it in the air and let it land in his palm. The streetlight caught a flash of metal. "Where are we going?"

"We're here." He pointed to a rust-and-green beat-up car parked on the curb between two much nicer, newer models. "Your ride home."

CHAPTER 5

Isabella stopped in her tracks. Ruth bumped into her from behind. "Hey."

"You have a car?"

Jacob made a circle with his long index finger. "We have a car. We went in together."

"How . . . why . . . where . . . ?"

The others laughed at her faltering response.

"It's just for now." Milo tugged open a door that squeaked and groaned. It took two hands to budge it enough for him to squeeze through and push forward the front seat. "Get in the back. I've got shotgun."

"Who drives?" She hesitated. Her life seemed more at risk here than it had in the pool hall. "Does one of you have a license?"

Jacob shook his head. "No license. But I've been driving a while now. You're safe. I promise." He opened the driver's side door, slid in, rolled down the window, and stuck his head out. "It'll be an adventure. I'm thinking you never did this back in Tennessee."

He was right about that. Isabella shivered, but she did as he said and climbed into the backseat ahead of Ruth and Sarah, who continued to giggle for no apparent reason. From what Isabella could see in the streetlight, the car featured ripped cloth seat covers stained with food.

She inhaled the lingering scent of burnt motor oil mixed with the other girls' *schtinkich* of pool hall. She likely smelled the same way. She would have to make sure to be first in line to wash clothes on laundry day. "I don't understand. No one knows you have a car?"

"Nope. No one knows. We pooled our money and bought it off a guy before he left for college in January. It was headed for the junkyard." Jacob turned the key. The motor coughed and wheezed as the car bucked and shimmied forward. The junkyard might have been a good place for it. "It doesn't go very far or very fast, but it gets the job done."

"What are you going to do with it when you get baptized?"

As they surely would be. Jacob was the son of the deacon.

"Sell it to someone else." Ruth said it like any person with smarts would know the answer to that question. "Get our money back."

"Where do you keep it then?"

"In that old shed way out back on Andrew Glick's farm."

"Used to be Andrew's." Milo swiveled in his seat, a huge grin on his face. "Now it's Will's farm. He'd have a cow if he knew."

Will's farm. Isabella slid down in the seat as far as she could go. Gott, *let him be a typical Plain man, early to bed and early to rise.*

☙⚬

Work had never felt better. Will stretched and yawned. The mingled aroma of overripe tomatoes, dust, and homemade candles filled his nose. He liked the smell; it smelled homey. But the store was missing a few key ingredients—like a cookstove and a bed. Time to head home.

Keeping up with the books had taken more time than he expected. Leroy had been meticulous in his record keeping, but business had been brisk since his convalescence began. Keeping up with the inventory, dealing with the customers, making sure he had enough change—the responsibilities were many.

He slid a soft rag over the double rocking chair. It was a centerpiece near the door. Every day *Englischers* came in and looked it over. Touched it. Sat in it, but so far no one had plopped down their hard-earned cash. It was a chunk of money but worth every cent.

Truth be told, he would be sad to see it go. He sank onto the seat and allowed himself a quick rock. He tried not to imagine himself sitting here, his *fraa* at his side. A *bopli*. It was a silly game to play. Not one a grown man played. *Gott's* timing. *Gott's* will. *Gott's* provision.

Will's stomach rumbled. Time to stop dillydallying and head home, feed his livestock and himself. Working long hours kept the evenings short. He could eat over the kitchen sink and fall into bed without giving any more thought to his *onkel's* direction regarding a *fraa*. Which reminded him. He'd forgotten to put birdseed in the feeder out front. Leroy would have his hide if he didn't feed the birds who were making their spring sojourn up north.

Leroy and Phineas liked to watch them perch on the feeder shaped like a little apartment complex high up on a pole. Truth be told, so did Will. He'd like to fly away with them some days. What a fantastical notion. He shook his head, stood, and gave the chair one last gentle push. It rocked with nary a squeak. Mordecai did good work.

Unbidden, unwanted, Isabella Shrock's sweet, heart-shaped face shimmered in his mind's eye. She had been nice to him at the hospital even after he was abrupt with her earlier in the day here at the store. She'd seen his hurt and responded with kindness. Not because he'd made a good impression. Still, they'd had that odd moment over a bag of rags, no less. Her gaze had gone right through him, warming him to his very marrow. She had seen him. She hadn't gone off with Maisie the way he'd thought she had, either. She'd shown good judgment in that. Her impression of him surely was worse than his mistaken first impression of her.

He grabbed the bag of birdseed from the floor next to the door and strode out into the yard. A mockingbird perched atop the apartment-style bird feeder meant for visiting purple martins sang its melodious song, matching Will's melancholy frame of mind. Finding a *fraa* was not something a person did on demand. No matter how much Will respected Leroy and wanted to please him, he couldn't simply turn off the feelings of the last two years. The hurt. The rejection. The dissipation of hope. The bird took flight, wings making hardly a noise in the night air, leaving Will with his uncomfortable thoughts.

Maybe it was easier to hang on to those familiar friends who kept him company late at night than it would be to pick up his flashlight and head out in the buggy one night after dark. A girl like Isabella deserved a man who held her and only her in his heart. Not a bunch of old painful memories.

The complaining cough of an engine sadly in need of repair broke the quiet evening. They didn't get much car traffic on this road after dark. Curious, Will turned. Headlights flashed in his eyes. He raised his hand to shield them. A huge boat of a four-door car, an ancient Oldsmobile with more rust than paint holding it together, sputtered along the dirt road. It carried a full load. At least five folks.

His hand dropped along with his mouth. Jacob King, son of deacon Mordecai King, drove that car. Milo Plank, whose father recently drew the lot for minister, sat scrunched down in the passenger seat, as if trying to hide his rotund body.

Will hugged the bag of seed to his chest and forced his mouth shut. It wouldn't be the first time a Plain teenager scratched that itch during *rumspringa*. They all talked about it—the boys anyway. He and Jesse had done more than talk about it. Under the watchful eye of an indulgent used-car salesman, they'd walked the used-car lot on Washington Street in Beeville. They touched the shiny chrome, slid across leather seats, and manhandled the steering wheel as if doing sixty on the highway. They dreamed that dream—until reality set in.

Now Jesse not only drove a shiny, blue minivan, he owned it. An *Englisch* man needed to be able to fit a car seat in the backseat and a stroller in the cargo area.

Swallowing the bitter bile in his throat, Will forced himself to lift his hand in a simple wave. An acknowledgment that he saw and he understood. The person in the backseat came into focus. Her face bleak with misery, Isabella Shrock stared out the window at him.

So she didn't hang out with *Englischers*, but that didn't keep her from joyriding with these boys. They'd probably been to a kegger in some *Englisch* farm pasture where the boys smoked cigarettes and drank beer from red plastic cups. The girls took off their *kapps* and tried out blobs of mascara and lipstick that ended up smearing around their lips.

The car slammed to a stop. The back passenger door opened. Not Isabella's, a blessing in Will's mind, but the other side. Ruth hopped out and scurried to the tall weeds bending in a moist late-spring breeze. A second later Isabella opened her door and bolted round the car. While Ruth doubled over vomiting, Isabella seemed to be patting her shoulder and holding back the strings of her *kapp*. She handed the other girl a handkerchief. Ruth wiped at her mouth with her sleeve and straightened. The two girls raced back to the car.

Will should simply turn around and go back into the store, but he couldn't look away. Not at Ruth, but at Isabella, who hadn't looked in his direction once. She huddled in her seat, hunched down as if she wanted to disappear.

As well she should. A person would be painted with the same color as the company she chose to keep.

Not that he cared. Not an iota. Yet he continued to stand there, staring as the car engine idled on the dirt road, smoke spewing from the tailpipe, filling the air with the nasty *schtinkich* of burning oil and gasoline.

Isabella was new to Bee County. She had choices to make, as did the others in their *rumspringa*. How that turned out would depend on her and on them. They had to find their own way of their own free will.

Sometimes a person needed a nudge in the right direction.

Sometimes a person didn't know which way to turn until someone older and wiser helped out. As Leroy had done for him.

Will's chest ached. His heart skipped a beat, seeking a rhythm he hadn't experienced in years. He stared at the deep-black sky decorated with pinpoint stars that seemed to spell out a message.

Don't be a coward. Take up this burden.

Gott, I'm too old and tired for this.

Nee, Leroy is old and tired. You are the new generation.

I'm not gut *enough.*

The weak, the sinful, the uncertain—they are most often the ones called.

Called. Called like Jesse was called? How egotistical. Still, Will bowed his head. He fit the bill when it came to weak, sinful, and uncertain. He wasn't arrogant enough to think of himself as worthy of any calling from *Gott.* He was certain of only one thing: *Gott* would prevail.

He leaned the bag against the pole and strode across the yard, one hand lifted, palm up. "Stop. Jacob, wait."

Jacob stuck his head out the window, his expression chagrined. "I know, I know, but I didn't think anyone would be out—"

"You didn't think anyone would see. I figured as much." Will planted himself closest to the backseat where he could see Isabella's face. Even in the dusky moonlight, its red hue was evident. "Have you been drinking alcohol?"

"*Nee.* I know better. I wouldn't put the others in danger."

The shame mixed with a silly grin on Milo's face told Will what he needed to know about that one. Ruth's display on the side of the road told her story. Sarah wouldn't meet his gaze. That left Isabella.

"We'll leave for another day the question of whether any of you know better." Will tugged open the back door. "Anyone who would rather get home in a way more suited to a Plain person should get out."

The occupants in the car were quiet. The engine rumbled, died away, then rumbled again. Isabella slid out, a plume of dust rising around her sneakers. "I wouldn't mind a ride home."

He nodded. "Anyone else?"

Silence. It didn't surprise him. If they'd been drinking, they wouldn't want a ride home with him. "Fine. Get yourselves home in one piece."

He pivoted and marched toward the store, then took one quick second to scoop up the bag on his way. Isabella's quick breathing told him she followed. "I need to lock up the store and I'll be ready to hitch up the horse."

"Why are you doing this?"

He glanced back. The girl had dark circles under her eyes. She looked wane and ill at ease. He cleared his throat. "Concern."

"For me?"

He turned to face her. "Following the crowd can get a person into a lot of trouble."

"I don't follow the crowd." Isabella smoothed her apron. The smell of beer and vomit wafted from it. "I needed a ride. That's all."

"You didn't have a good time among the *Englischers*?" Will was acutely aware that he sounded like his *daed* when he intended to make a point about a chore done poorly or left half done. He wasn't that old, barely a few years older than she was. He still remembered the excitement of trying something forbidden. Once Leroy had caught him smoking behind the barn. He still shuddered at the memory. "One could hope for a lesson learned."

"One could hope."

She sounded so penitent. She was a good woman, no doubt. He forced himself to break his gaze. "Come inside. I need to turn out the lamp and get the key. Then I'll get you home."

"Will." She scrambled to keep up. He slowed. "It's hard."

"What's hard?"

"Being new and trying to figure out what to do, where to fit in." She ducked her head. Her *kapp* had slipped back, revealing chestnut hair. It looked soft and shiny in the moonlight.

"You would think we would have a built-in community, but when folks grow up together, they tend to have their close friends already. Making room for others can be hard, I reckon." He tore his gaze from her pretty, troubled face and her shiny, soft hair and opened the door, letting her enter first. "I'm sorry."

"You have nothing to be sorry about. I made work for you in the store and then you see me gallivanting around in a car late at night. I'm the one who's ashamed."

He dumped the bag in its spot by the door and snagged the key from the nail over the counter. "This is the time in your life for such things."

"Did you do them? Did you ride in a car or buy a car?"

"I considered it." He couldn't help himself, he smiled. Those were good days. Days when Jesse had been more of a brother than a cousin. Days that seemed to last forever and then be gone in the blink of an eye. "In fact, Jesse and I spent more than our fair share of time rattling around the used-car lots pretending we could afford to buy one. We drove the salesmen crazy with our questions and our fingerprints all over their clean cars."

"But you never actually bought one?"

"Couldn't afford it, which was for the best." He pointed to the rocking chair. "You look tired. Have a seat." He intended no sarcasm in his words, but her face turned pink. "I just meant I have to do a couple of things, then we'll go. The truth is I don't mind Jacob and the others hiding that Olds on my property. It's as if I get a little taste of what it would've been like."

She sank onto the rocking chair, her slight body barely enough to make it rock. "You know?"

"Of course I know." He turned the knob on the propane lamp behind the counter. The darkness gave him a reprieve from knowing she watched his every move. "I live alone. It's very quiet in the country late at night. There's no being stealthy when an engine belches and groans and moans like that one."

"Why are you here so late at night?"

The question caught him unaware. "It's my job. I like to do it well."

"And that means being here late at night when there's nary a customer."

"There are books to keep. I want to make sure everyone who contributes merchandise for the store gets their due from sales."

"No one thinks you would cheat them, surely."

"*Nee*, but I want to make sure there are no mistakes."

"You're a conscientious sort. I'm sure people appreciate that. Leroy wouldn't have left you in charge if he didn't think you would do a good job."

Her voice was soft, her tone encouraging. It felt like a salve that could heal a wounded heart. "Anyone who can do math can do the job." He put his hand on the doorknob. "Let's go."

"Then that leaves me out." She smiled as she stood. She was so short her head barely reached his shoulder. "I don't miss that part of school at all."

"I liked math." He locked the door behind them and headed to the buggy parked in front of the junkyard with its collection of buggy parts and farm equipment. "I'm not a big fan of writing, though."

Why were they talking about school? Because he would talk about anything that caught her fancy to fill these moments. He hadn't been alone with a woman since Leila. Isabella was different. Quieter, softer. He focused on hitching Jake to the buggy, aware with every fiber of his being that she waited and watched, hands clasped in front of her.

He wiped his hands on his pants and held one out to her, to help her into the buggy. She could get herself in, no doubt, but the idea of touching her hand—he couldn't help himself. Her fingers were warm and soft. He squeezed. She squeezed back, her gaze on his face, her lips parted as if she sought to take a breath.

He forced himself to keep talking. "I don't think *Englisch* folks can understand why we do things the way we do."

"I won't be spending time with those *Englisch* folks again." Her voice quivered. "That's a promise."

Why would she feel the need to make the promise to him? They hardly knew each other. He picked up the reins and took a long breath, gathering his thoughts. It wasn't the light conversation of two people just beginning to court. To court.

Would she consider this ride the beginning of a courtship? Not likely. It was just him giving her a ride home so her parents and Mordecai, the deacon, wouldn't hear a car belching and fuming its way up the drive to the house.

"Not all *Englisch* teenagers are the same, just as all Plain folks aren't equal. We all err. *Gott* forgives. I only want what's best for each one of the younger folks in the district."

"You say that like you're so much older."

"I guess I feel that way sometimes because of the experiences I've had. I'm not a lot older, but maybe wiser." That sounded prideful. Those experiences had broken his heart. He didn't wish that on anyone.

"You're afraid for them."

"Afraid is a strong word. I know *Gott* watches over them and He has a plan for them."

"Yet you worry."

"It's sinful, I know."

"Maybe so, but it also shows you have a good heart."

"The consequences of a wrong path taken are—"

"I know."

Night sounds filled their silence. Crickets made a racket and frogs croaked in response. A mosquito buzzed his face. Will swiped at it. Jake nickered, no doubt anxious for the barn and rest.

"I—"

"I—"

"You first." He kept his gaze on the road illuminated by the battery-operated lights. At least she couldn't see how red his face was. "What were you going to say?"

"I shouldn't have gone with Maisie. I understand that. That's all I'm saying. It's not going to happen again."

"You don't have to tell me that."

"I broke a jar in the store and you had to clean it up. Then you see me running around in a car. What you must think of me."

"Do you care what I think?" The question was out before he could assess the position in which it put her. "You don't have to answer that, either."

"I want to answer it." Her voice was barely a whisper. "I'm not good at this. I'm a quiet person. Men don't much appreciate that."

"Because it's easier if the girl does the talking, then they don't have to do it. They're lazy."

She laughed, a sound as sweet as the honey he stirred into his *kaffi* every morning. "I want to fit in here. I never did in McKenzie."

He couldn't imagine how a sweet girl like her didn't fit in. He wouldn't embarrass her by asking. "Why did your family move here?"

"*Daed* had a heart attack. He couldn't work the land the way he used to do. We didn't have family there anymore. Abigail is like a sister to my *mudder*. They missed each other so much. She invited us to come, saying this district needed new blood. Families keep leaving so there was a farm here for the taking and Mordecai offered to help. It was a new start for all of us."

"I'm glad you came." The words surprised him. Will hadn't felt glad of anything in such a long time. Would she feel the same way? He couldn't make out her expression in the dark. She ducked her head. He had to bend close to hear her whispered response. "Me too."

He halted the buggy in front of Mordecai's house. In the quiet, awkwardness descended again. He hadn't done this for a long time. "Well, here we are."

"*Danki* for the ride." She moved as if to hop down.

"Wait." He hurled himself from the buggy and strode around to her side. "I'll help you down."

The words sounded stupid in his ears. She'd been getting down from buggies her whole life. Still, when he looked up at her, she smiled. Her face was heart shaped and small. She had dimples. He held out his hand. She took it. He helped her down, but her gaze remained on his face. For a second, a mere wisp of a second, he considered kissing her rosebud lips.

Nee, nee. *Hold your horses.*

A man didn't do such a thing. Not a man who knew how to treat a woman. He cleared his throat and let go of her hand. "Good night, Isabella."

She nodded and slipped past him. "*Danki* for the ride."

He climbed into the buggy and turned it around, headed for the road. For once it didn't seem empty. It seemed full of life. Full of possibility. He began to whistle. He hadn't whistled in years.

CHAPTER 6

I sabella grabbed the porch railing with one hand and leaned over to tug off her sneaker. Bare feet were quieter. She breathed in the fresh night air, dizzy with the fragrance of honey-suckle that wound its way around the railing. Or with the sudden turn in her life. She'd started out the evening thinking she was going on an adventure with an *Englisch* girl, but the real adventure had come at the end of the evening in a buggy ride with a man whose touch sent goose bumps up her spine.

"Who was that?"

Isabella jumped, dropped her sneaker, and slapped her hand against her chest. "*Daed?*" She peered into the dark corner of the porch that had seemed empty only a second before. "What are you doing out here in the dark?"

He leaned forward, his weight making the old lawn chair groan. "You answer my question, I'll answer yours."

Isabella scooped up her shoe and moved onto the porch. Weary, she plopped down at his feet and sat cross-legged like she had as a child when he told stories in front of the fireplace on cold winter nights. "You should be resting."

"I've rested so much it's making me sick. It's hard to sleep at night when you don't do a thing to get a body tired during the day." He grunted and leaned back in his chair. "Who was that?"

"Will Glick."

"Friend of yours?"

His neutral tone didn't fool Isabella. Her father had a heart of butter and honey, but he protected his *kinner* with a ferocity that amazed her. Especially when some days he didn't seem to have the strength to pull himself from his bed and teeter to the kitchen table.

"I think he might be."

"You think."

"How does a person know?"

"Did he try something untoward?"

"*Nee, daed.*" She smacked his knee with a playful swipe. His feet were bare, a fact that made him seem unaccountably delicate. She swallowed a lump in her throat. Gott, *please don't take him yet. I'm not ready, even if he is.* "He's a good person. He runs the store for Leroy."

"I've been sitting out here a while and I didn't see him come fetch you." *Daed* sniffed, his face wrinkled in a frown. "Did he take you to one of those *Englisch* to-dos where they drink beer and smoke? You smell funny."

"*Nee.* He sort of rescued me."

"Why did you need rescuing?"

"I did something stupid and he came along and gave me a ride home."

"Are you going to keep doing stupid things?"

"*Nee*. I learned my lesson."

"That's good because you're too big now for me to take you out to the woodshed and turn you over my knee."

"Too heavy."

"You have put on some weight."

"*Daed!*"

"Are you happy we came here?"

The question surprised Isabella. It wasn't often that the head of a Plain home asked the *kinner* what they thought or what they wanted. They would do and go where they were told. "I am."

"*Gut.* I know *Gott* will provide for you and see you through, but it's nice if you're happy along the way."

A strange thing for a Plain man to say. Isabella puzzled her way through his words. It was as if they ran parallel to her own. "You sound like you're ready to go somewhere."

"A person never knows when *Gott* will call him home."

"True, but you're fine. You're not going anywhere anytime soon."

"You may be right, but that doesn't mean a man can't hope for happiness for his oldest daughter. Even if she is wayward."

She smacked his knee again. "I'm not wayward."

"You left the house with someone earlier tonight and then came home with someone else. What is that if not wayward?"

The image of Ray at the pool hall loomed in her mind, immediately obliterated by Will's face. "It's a blessing."

Gott's hand on her head. That kind of blessing.

"Give your *daed* a smack on the cheek and go to bed, *dochder*." He cocked his head to one side as if to make room for her kiss. "Then get on up to bed. Don't think you'll be sleeping in tomorrow just because you've been out gallivanting half the night."

She rose, planted a kiss on his rough cheek, and did as she was told, lingering for a second with her hand on his shoulder. *Gott, put Your hand on his heart, make it strong. Make him strong.*

CHAPTER 7

No rest for the weary. Especially when it was their fault. Isabella squeezed her bowl of potato salad onto the picnic table between pickled beets and a platter of cheese-spread sandwiches made with huge slabs of sourdough bread. The end-of-school picnic was in full swing. Only two had graduated from the tiny one-room school. Sally and Luke. It might be a small school, but Susan and Rebekah took their charge seriously.

Thrilled to be out of school until August, the rest of the *kinner* were screaming with laughter over a game of volleyball that involved both teachers, Mordecai, and Phineas. Both men could spike the ball over the ratty net without their feet leaving the ground. The *kinner* found this funny, for some reason, even though it meant they invariably lost each match. Susan and Rebekah had teamed up to try to match the men. It was a battle that made for good entertainment on a fine spring day.

At least it would if she weren't so tired. Trying to ignore the headache that pulsed at her temples, Isabella picked up a Styrofoam plate and slapped a cheese-spread sandwich on it.

Between the smoke she'd inhaled in the pool hall and the late hour of the previous evening, she felt as if she were coming down with the flu. Not to mention the hours of wakefulness that followed as she tried to turn off the images that kept racing through her mind—Ray with his beer breath and clammy hands, the girls with their slurred words and bare heads, the car smelling of burnt oil and gasoline, and Will's whispered admission that he was glad she'd moved to Beeville. His hand on hers, helping her out of the buggy. The way he'd looked at her. No man had ever looked at her like that.

Goose bumps prickled up her arm despite the humidity-drenched heat. His hand had been so warm, his grip so strong. She swallowed against warmth that rose across the back of her neck and swirled around her cheeks.

She would ask Rebekah about it. Rebekah would know what it all meant.

"Are you hogging the food table?" Jacob bounded up the steps to the porch, an empty plate in one hand, a glass in the other. "Potato salad! That wasn't here before."

"I just set it out." Cheeks still burning, Isabella dropped her gaze and grabbed the ladle in the barbecue beans. She dumped more than she would ever eat on her plate. Juice ran into the sandwich. "We didn't want the mayonnaise to go bad."

Jacob sent a furtive glance toward the grown-ups seated in lawn chairs scattered across the yard. "So I guess you got home safe and sound."

"I did."

"Will preach to you?"

"*Nee.*" Nor had he shown up for the picnic, a fact that

surprised and dismayed her. "He was only concerned that I get home safe. That's all."

"He's a good man, but sometimes he acts like an old fogy. He's only a couple of years older than you and me. He's forgotten what this time is about."

"*Nee*, he hasn't. In fact, he knows. He knows what you've been hiding in his shed."

Jacob stopped, serving spoon hovering over a bowl of cabbage slaw. "He knows about the car." His voice dropped to a whisper. "Being in his shed?"

She nodded, not at all certain she should've blurted out this information. Spilled milk. "He knows and he understands, but I reckon it's time to grow up, don't you?"

His forehead furrowed, Jacob dug into the slaw and dumped a heaping spoonful on his paper plate. "I reckon you're right." He grinned, the spitting image of Mordecai, with his broad shoulders and thick, shaggy black hair peeking from under his straw hat. "It's been fun while it lasted."

"Fun is good and all, but there are more important things."

He nodded. "Like fishing. We're thinking of going to Choke Canyon Lake Monday. Want to come?"

He was incorrigible. Some men simply took longer to grow up than others. He seemed a mere child compared to Will. Will had a full-time job at the store and he took care of his farm. She liked that he was industrious. She liked that he could carry on a conversation about important things. And he had strong hands. "Monday is laundry day. *Mudder* will expect me to help."

"Surely she'll let you off for one day. You're new here and you haven't seen the lake." Jacob shook his fork at her. Slaw juice dripped on the table. "If we catch something we'll give it to you to take home and feed the family. Nothing like a catfish fry."

"I have five brothers and sisters." That statement spoke for itself when it came to laundry. "Maybe some other time."

"*Ach*, I get it. I'm too late."

"What?" Isabella wished for a trap door in the porch so she could fall through it and disappear from his sight. "I have no idea what you're talking about."

"One buggy ride with Will and you're in *lieb*."

"That is—"

"I know, private." He winked and sauntered past her. "Don't worry, I'll live."

"I was going to say ridiculous."

"What's ridiculous?" *Mudder* stomped up the steps, her empty plate in her hand. Rebekah came after her, wiping at her scarlet, sweaty face with a huge white hankie. "Why do you look so red?"

"I was playing volleyball earlier and got sunburned." Isabella added pickled okra to her plate. "The fried chicken was really good. Do you want some more?"

"You look guilty. What were you talking about?"

"You do look guilty. Spill the beans!" Rebekah grabbed a plastic tumbler filled with lemonade and gulped down a long drink. She wiped at her mouth with her sleeve. "In fact, you're glowing. What happened?"

"Nothing. Not a thing." Isabella squeezed past Rebekah, but *Mudder* blocked her exit from the porch. "Jacob was talking about going fishing on Monday. I said no because there is so much laundry to do on Mondays."

Mudder squinted against the sun. "There's laundry but a girl your age also might want to be thinking of other things, like the future."

First *Daed* and now *Mudder*. What had gotten into them? For *Mudder* to think she should ignore laundry day for fishing, this was a serious ailment. Maybe she had a fever. "I am thinking of the future, just not with Jacob."

Rebekah grinned. "I know who. I'm thinking it's—"

"Mind your own business, Rebekah Lantz!"

"Who? Tell me who?" *Mudder* sounded like a twelve-year-old who wanted to know what she was getting for Christmas. "I won't tell your *daed*."

"There's nothing to tell. I'm taking *Daed* a piece of pie. He didn't eat much. Maybe he'll be tempted by sweets."

"He needs more protein, not sweets. That's what the *Englisch* doctor said." Her mother picked up a paper plate and manhandled two drumsticks onto it. "Take these too."

Isabella accepted the plate. *Mudder* looked so worried. After all these years she still loved *Daed* like it was the first day after the wedding ceremony. Isabella leaned into her and planted a kiss on her cheek.

"What was that for?" Her mother looked startled and pleased. She grabbed a napkin and wiped up the slaw juice, her gaze averted. "Your *daed* and I know this move was hard for you. Sometimes it's hard to make new friends in a place where young folks have known each other since they were little."

She had Rebekah. And now Will, it seemed. "*Nee*. It's been fine."

"You don't miss your friends? Laura? Joanne? The *kinner* you grew up with?"

Truth be told, Laura and Joanne were best friends—with each other. They'd let Isabella tag along out of kindness because she had been so shy. "Sometimes a new start is good."

Mudder picked up a spoon and stirred the baked beans. The aroma of barbecue sauce wafted in the air. "As long as you get off on the right foot."

"I think I am. The singing was fun."

"Even if she can't carry a tune in a bucket." Rebekah chortled and threw herself into a lawn chair next to the table. "I made sure she met all the eligible boys."

"*Gut.* That's *gut.*"

Isabella added a peanut butter cookie to *Daed's* pie plate. For herself. "Did you always know *Daed* was the one for you?"

Mudder turned, her eyebrows raised. "Why do you ask?"

"I don't understand how you know."

"Me neither, but you do." *Mudder* picked up a brownie, contemplated it for a second, then returned it to the serving plate. "I thought your *daed* was a big dufus. I turned him down more than once, but he kept coming back for more."

Isabella giggled. "A dufus? You married a dufus?"

"*Jah*, but he's my dufus and I love him." *Mudder's* face turned red, whether from exertion or embarrassment, Isabella couldn't say. They'd never talked of such things before. Being the oldest of six *kinner* meant Isabella had the greatest burden on her shoulders to help with cooking, baking, cleaning, and gardening. Neither she nor her mother had much energy left for exchanging confidences. "Baptism classes will begin soon."

Nothing would be more important to her family than Isabella's commitment to the church. "Don't worry about that.

I'm ready. What I don't know is how they can help me choose the right *mann*."

"Follow *Gott* and He will lead you to the *mann* He intends for you."

Isabella sighed and clomped down the stairs, *Daed*'s plate in her hand.

From *Mudder*'s lips to *Gott*'s ears.

CHAPTER 8

I sabella didn't know where to look first. Her ticket clutched in her hand, she followed the others through the turnstile into the San Antonio Zoo. She'd only been to a zoo once before as a little girl in Tennessee, a visit she barely remembered. According to Mordecai, organizer of this impromptu field trip—and all such trips, apparently—this zoo had nine thousand animals and seven hundred and fifty species spread over fifty-six acres. It boggled the mind.

Despite the soupy humidity of a May day, the air felt cool against her skin as she traipsed along the stone walkway trying to avoid the clusters of folks stopped to look at maps and sip tall drinks that looked cool and frosty. She swallowed against a parched throat. It was enough that Mordecai had paid for her entry fee. They would have a picnic in the nearby park later. No need to spend more money here on sodas and snacks.

"Now don't get lost." Mordecai handed her a brochure with a map. "We'll meet back here at the entrance. No rush, though.

Mr. Cramer is going fishing in the river at Brackenridge Park while he waits for us. He's in no hurry."

Isabella nodded. She breathed and forced herself not to look back at the ticket booth. The second van had gotten stuck in a traffic jam involving a car accident according to Mr. Cramer who'd been talking on his cell phone to Mr. Martinez, the other driver. The others—which included Will—were probably just getting to the parking lot. Mordecai didn't want to wait. With the cost of the tickets, they needed to spend as much time enjoying the exhibits as possible.

She'd seen Will getting into the other van, but it had been too late to switch without everyone noticing. They hadn't seen each other since church on Sunday and then only long enough to say hello over the sandwiches she was serving. This would be the perfect opportunity. If the van ever showed up.

She hoped she knew why he'd come to the zoo, but she didn't want to presume too much from one buggy ride. One very nice buggy ride. Most of the men had stayed back. They had too much to do. Apparently Will had left Simon in charge of the store. This came as a great surprise to Sarah and Ruth, who were discussing it in the seat in front of her, along with a steady stream of other topics that didn't include her. Will spent every day, all day, at the store since Leroy handed him the reins. Until this.

Which was neither here nor there. Isabella was still alone at the zoo. Rebekah hadn't come, saying she'd been three times before and a person who'd seen one monkey had seen them all. *Mudder* had stayed home with Amanda and Molly, who were taking turns giving each other the flu. *Daed* was supervising her brothers, who were doing the planting but not very well according to *Daed*.

She hadn't thought ahead to how they would break off and go their own ways once at the zoo. Leaving her as the third wheel, just as she'd been with her friends in Tennessee. The tagalong. If only Rebekah had come.

Ruth and Sarah were already several yards ahead. She started their direction. Ruth looked back, shrugged, and kept walking. She whispered something to Sarah, who glanced back, frowned, and turned away. Neither slowed nor stopped. In front of them Jacob and Milo were clowning in front of the grizzly bear exhibit. Isabella hesitated. The girls had been cool toward her since that night at the pool hall. Surely they couldn't be holding that against her. Plastering a smile on her face, she kept walking.

"Isabella, want to see the Komodo dragon?" Jacob waved the zoo map in his big hand. "We saw him last time. His name is Bubba."

Milo snickered. "First we go to the reptile house. They have all kinds of snakes and creepy-crawly things."

"I'm not a fan of snakes." Isabella squeezed in next to the girls. They still didn't look at her. "I'd like to see the elephants, though, and the hippos, and the giraffes."

"There's only one elephant. Lucky, and she's old." Jacob studied the map. "Come on. Bubba is worth meeting."

"We'll go. Isabella should stay here and wait for the others from the other van." Ruth jerked her head toward the walkway. "We'll go to the reptile house and then to see Bubba since you're so excited about it, Jacob."

If she waited around, she'd run into Will. "I don't know—"

"Come on, be a good sport." Sarah tugged on Ruth's sleeve. "Last one to the reptile house has to buy everyone *raspas*."

Raspas, which Isabella had learned only on the trip over, were shaved ice with flavored syrup. They sounded *wunderbarr* in this heat. "I'll wait. That's okay."

Jacob walked backward, frowning. "Are you sure?"

"It's fine." She didn't want to give Jacob the wrong idea, anyway. And there was no doubt from the look on Ruth's face, that she didn't want him looking at Isabella at all, either. "You go on."

"You're welcome to come."

"Go on."

Still frowning, he whirled and strode away. "You can always change your mind."

Somehow it didn't seem he was talking about the reptile house.

Isabella could wander about on her own. She was a big girl. She threw back her shoulders and headed in the opposite direction. This would be an adventure. Her adventure. She would tell Amanda and Molly all about it tonight after their soup and crackers. They had been so sad not to be able to come. She would treat them with story upon story of what she'd seen.

The air was thick with humidity and smells, both good and bad, sweet mountain laurel and animal dung mingled. The sun peeked through overhead branches of trees laden with blooms, making patchwork on the paved stones beneath her feet. Sounds that might be screams or high-pitched laughter—she couldn't be sure which—pierced the air. Monkeys. The sign said they were common squirrel monkeys. Not so common in her neck of the woods. They scampered across branches high overhead, their grimaces somewhere between a smile and pain.

They were so ugly they were cute. She grinned to herself.

"What are you doing all alone?"

Isabella bowed her head and breathed. In a place with nine-thousand animals on fifty-six acres, he'd still managed to run into her. "Waiting for you." Heat burned her cheeks to a crisp. "I mean waiting for everyone, the others, the ones in the second van."

"Good. I was looking for you." Will smiled as if he had no idea the level of her mortification. "Can I show you something?"

He'd been looking for her, and he wanted to show her something. The heat melted away.

Isabella took a breath and summoned her best smile. "That would be nice. As long as it doesn't involve snakes or the reptile house."

"This way." He pointed in the opposite direction of the reptile house. They walked side by side, no doubt in Isabella's mind that he shortened his stride to match hers. "So you don't like reptiles?"

Or feeling unwanted by the others. "Not much."

"Me neither. Too much slithering for me."

They passed the pelicans and the pink cranes. Then white storks. Still, he didn't slow down. She saw signs for the hippos and the crocodiles, but Will didn't swerve that direction. He finally stopped at a wooden sign that read Lory Landing. High-pitched screeching of a kind very different from the monkeys greeted them. That and the laughter of folks who were inside the exhibit. "What is a Lory Landing?"

"Wait." Grinning, he stopped and tugged some bills from the inside of his straw hat. "Stay here. We need nectar from the Lory Café."

They needed nectar. Who knew? He seemed so taken with

the idea, Isabella stayed put until he returned with two small, clear plastic cups filled with a clear liquid. He handed one to her. "Now we're ready."

They tromped up the wooden steps and into a covered patio with netting and green canopies overhead. No wonder there was so much noise. The brightest colored birds Isabella had ever seen roosted in the trees and on the canopy and even on the shoulders, heads, and arms of the other visitors. Before she could say a word, a parakeet with a flaming-scarlet breast, royal-blue face, orange beak, and lime-green back swooped within inches of her face. "Oh my." She ducked. "Are we supposed to be in here?"

"*Jah*, this is good." Will held up his arm. The bird landed with grace on his wrist and proceeded to dunk his beak in the cup Will extended to him. "They're called lorikeets. They're a kind of parrot. They're from the Australian rainforest. They're very friendly."

Indeed they were. A second bird descended on Will's hat. Isabella laughed. Will's chortle could barely be heard over the raucous squawking of the birds and the delighted banter of the visitors around them. Birds dipped and swooped from tree branch to tree branch, seemingly in search of the best roosting spot for another sip of nectar.

"You've been here before then? Or did Mordecai tell you all about it too?"

"I always visit Lory Landing. It's my favorite exhibit." Will hunched over. The bird on his head took the opportunity to take a skip and hop over to Isabella's *kapp*. "They like people and they like each other. They usually travel in pairs. They're also great acrobats. Look."

He pointed with his free hand to a pair of birds upside down on the netting above them. The birds tumbled together and landed upright on the wooden banister that enclosed the exhibit. "I think they like to show off."

"By no means are they Plain birds." Isabella giggled at the thought. "They're so brightly colored. They stand out in every crowd."

"But they're all brightly colored so none stands out in their crowd."

A different perspective. Will had given this some thought. "That's true. And *Gott* surely gave them those beautiful colors."

A bird clothed entirely in royal-blue feathers except for a few strands of red on its back landed on her shoulder. Its claws dug into her skin under her dress. With a squawk it pecked at her cheek. "Ouch, that hurts!" She shoved the cup of nectar closer to him. "Try this. You'll like it better."

"I think one just pooped on my hat." Grinning, Will shook his head. "Maybe I don't like this as much as I remembered."

Isabella laughed at his chagrined expression. "I think I like it a lot."

"I'm glad then." He tossed the empty nectar cup into the trash bin. "It's worth it to hear you laugh. I like the way it sounds."

"I like your laugh too."

His grin died. He ducked his head, the fair skin of his cheeks reddening. The sound of the birds filled the space. For a second it seemed they were alone. Isabella searched for words and found none.

"I meant to come see you again after the buggy ride."

"But you didn't."

"I suppose I'm afraid." His gaze came up and met hers. He didn't look afraid. He looked like a man determined to make up for lost time. "When I heard about this trip, I thought I should come."

"You should come?"

"Because you were coming."

Delight tickled Isabella's very soul. She battled the urge to squeeze his big, callused hand. If she moved too quickly, she would scare him away. Like these birds. He'd made a huge admission, especially for a Plain man not used to discussing his feelings with anyone, least of all a woman. "You have nothing to fear from me."

He edged closer. His fingers took the cup from her hand. "That is good to know."

"It's not only scary for you."

The lorikeet took off. Will's gaze followed its flight. "I understand that."

"Do you?"

"I'm finding my way back."

"*Gut.*"

"You'll wait?"

"I'm not going anywhere." A bird, this one almost entirely a deep, vibrant green, landed on her arm and worked its way toward her cup, all the while chattering. "See, even this bird knows he has nothing to fear from me."

"You know Leroy is stepping down. Things are changing." His voice had grown sandpaper rough. His gaze bounced from her face, over her shoulder, and then back. "I have a lot of responsibility at the store. I have a farm to run."

"I know."

"I have to figure some things out. I had settled into a way of thinking that didn't—"

"Didn't include someone like me?"

"Anyone at all. I'm out of practice with all this. Can you wait to see how I manage?"

"I said I would."

His Adam's apple bobbed. "So you did."

A second bird landed on Will's shoulder. The look of delight on his face made him seem as young as little Molly. Isabella caught a glimpse of the Will who had loved to fish and hunt and play in the mud with his cousin Jesse. Before time and angst built walls around his heart. Her own heart ached for him. The two birds chattered back and forth. A second later they took off in a simultaneous flight that ended in the trees above.

They nuzzled close, there in the branches. She longed to do the same with Will. To offer him a comfort he couldn't refuse, wouldn't want to refuse. "Just don't make me wait forever."

A lump the size of a watermelon in his throat, Will stared at his hands. He would not embarrass himself or the others by shedding a tear. *Gott's* will be done.

The first lot for the new bishop had been drawn under Leroy's solemn direction. The former bishop, a hand-carved oak cane in one hand, had stood before the community looking weak, his skin pale, hands shaking, but his voice still had the power to spellbind as he reminded the church members how serious this rite was for the future of their district. Jeremiah Hostetler would serve as the new bishop, which meant Mordecai remained as deacon. That left the position of minister open.

Some of the women cried quietly, handkerchiefs clutched to their faces. Men huddled in whispered conversation. Even the children were unusually subdued, their crayons and their pretzel snacks forgotten.

Now each member would come forward to give Jeremiah his or her nomination for the open position. Jeremiah stood in the kitchen doorway, Mordecai seated at the table behind him.

He nodded to the first row. The men filed past him, one by one, whispering a name in his ear. He turned to Mordecai who scribbled the name onto a piece of yellow paper, his handwriting spidery and indistinct.

When it came Will's turn, he didn't hesitate. Phineas King surely would not want the job, but no man in the district had a better, deeper understanding of what it meant to do God's will. No one saw or cared about his scars on his face. He was a humble, obedient servant. He would speak God's Word from the heart. Jeremiah nodded, his expression unfathomable.

Will returned to his seat, glad to sit. His legs trembled and his hands quivered with the knowledge that any man in the room might end up in the kitchen drawing that lot. Gott, *have mercy on that man. On me.*

With such a small group of church members it didn't take long. Not long enough in Will's estimation. Postpone the inevitable or get it over with?

Jeremiah returned to the front of the room, Mordecai at his side. "We've heard your nominations. It is time to draw the lot." He cleared his throat. "The man chosen by *Gott* will speak His Word, leading this church with His sermons. *Gott* be with him and with you."

He strode back to the kitchen. He didn't look at the piece of paper in his hand. "Phineas King."

Deborah gasped. Her hands fluttered in the air, then landed back in her lap. Tears trickled down her cheeks. His expression stoic, Phineas squeezed past his brothers and stalked to the kitchen. He looked neither left nor right.

"Adam King."

Another good choice. A good solid member of the district who abided by the *Ordnung* and saw to it that his family did the same.

"Will Glick."

Time stopped. Oxygen seeped from his lungs. Will found himself unable to draw another breath. The ringing in his ears made it impossible for him to know with certainty that his name had been called.

Simon's elbow jabbed Will's arm in a painful one-two punch. "Go on. It's your name."

His cousin's loud whisper carried across the room. Hazel tittered. Abigail hushed her.

Will forced himself to stand. He wended his way past the other men in his row, unable to look at them. His throat was so dry he couldn't swallow, yet sweat made the palms of his hands slick. He wiped at his face with the back of his sleeve. *Please,* Gott, *don't let me heave.*

Not the strangest prayer *Gott* had heard. Or so Will hoped.

Mordecai smiled and patted Will's back as he passed him and entered the kitchen. The small gesture steadied Will. He breathed and studied the row of *Ausbands* arranged on Leroy and Naomi's pine table. One of the hymnals held the slip of paper that would determine how the one chosen by lot would spend a portion of his remaining days. The designation would be for life or for as long as the man was able to perform his duties.

He planted his feet and let his arms hang loosely at his side. Phineas and Adam did the same. Phineas looked sick to his stomach. Adam's face, still sunburned from a day fishing at Choke Canyon Lake, turned a deeper scarlet. The district had spoken.

One of them would join Jeremiah and Mordecai in leading the community. Either of the other two men would do a good job. Will would be happy to let them. They were thoughtful men of good character. Better men than he.

Jeremiah entered the room. If he felt the heavy yoke of his new duties, it didn't show. "Let us pray."

Will knelt next to his brethren and closed his eyes. *I'm not worthy, Lord, but I know through You all things are possible. I accept Your will in this and in all things. Make me worthy.*

The clearing of a throat told him the time had come. He opened his eyes. Jeremiah stood. The others did the same. "Now."

Phineas went first, picking up a hymnal. Adam followed. Will took the last one and held it against his chest. He felt light-headed. His heart thudded against his ribs. *Thy will be done.*

Jeremiah began with Phineas. He shuffled through the pages, then laid the book on the table. Phineas's sigh of relief was audible. Will squeezed his eyes shut again, then forced them open.

Adam's hymnal held nothing as well. Jeremiah stopped in front of Will and held out his hands. Ignoring the tremor in his muscles, Will laid the *Ausband* in the new bishop's hands. He flipped through the pages. His gaze lifted. He smiled and handed Will a piece of paper.

On it were written the words, "The lot is cast into the lap; but its every decision is from the Lord. Proverbs 16:33."

Will swallowed and met Jeremiah's gaze. The man nodded, his expression full of understanding and assurance. He gently closed the hymnal and laid it on the table. "Come. We'll share the good news with our church family."

Steady. Will forced his unwilling feet to move. Seconds later he stood before a community he'd known his entire life. Every face turned toward them, filled with expectation. Jeremiah made the announcement without preamble. A murmur rippled across the room. Smiles followed. A smattering of clapping. People began to stand and move forward. Phineas slapped Will's back and slipped away, Adam behind him.

Leroy, leaning heavily on his cane, held out his free hand. Will grasped it and looked into the face of a man he respected like no other. "You'll do fine."

"Don't you find it strange?"

Leroy did him the honor of not pretending he didn't understand. "*Gott*'s will is just that, His will."

"It's His will that I take the task that Jesse wanted so desperately that he chose to leave rather than wait on *Gott*'s will?"

"This isn't the time for that discussion." Leroy stood straighter, his face alight with a glow that could only be described as contentment. "Suffice it to say, *Gott*'s will was done here today. He chose you. You're the one He wants. Don't let Him down."

"I'll do my best."

"And remember what I said about the other thing."

Will ducked his head, feeling like a boy who misbehaved in school. "I haven't."

"Having a *fraa* is that much more important now. She will help you, give you support and strength. And she'll cook for you and do your laundry. You'll need that with all your additional duties."

Ever the practical man. "It takes time—"

"Don't argue with an old man."

"*Nee.*"

Leroy turned and shuffled away, Naomi at his side, one hand out as if to catch him should he fall.

His throat tight, Will watched them go. Would Jesse see it the same way as his *daed*? If he had waited, he might be standing in Will's shoes now. But Leroy was right. Jesse still wouldn't have been satisfied. He wanted more. It didn't matter. *Gott* had given Will this task to do. He would do it. With not only an obedient heart, but a glad heart.

He had the store. He had this new vocation.

Gott was good.

Will turned to make his way through the tight knot of friends and family, their faces smiling, offering pats on the back and handshakes.

In his path stood Isabella, her face alight with a smile. "*Gott* is good."

He nodded. "Indeed."

She looked as if she wanted to say more. Her little sister Amanda tugged at her arm. "I'm hungry, *schweschder*, I'm hungry."

Isabella shrugged and smiled.

Will nodded.

The crowd swallowed her up.

Leroy was right. Will could fill up his life to the brim and it would still be empty without a woman with whom he could share it. In order for his heart to have room for that person, he had to do something first.

He waded through well-wishers, trying to find her. All the gray dresses were the same. She was small and not easily found in a crowd. Not easily found, period.

There. She handed a chunk of bread slathered in butter to Amanda. "Use a napkin, child, don't get butter on your dress." She leaned down and handed a napkin to the girl and brushed a curl back under her small *kapp*. "The grease won't come out and you know how *Mudder* hates that."

"Yum. Thank you, *schweschder*." The girl planted a greasy kiss on Isabella's cheek. The two could be twins if it weren't for the age difference. "Can I go outside and play?"

"For a few minutes. I'm sure we'll be going soon. Chores to do."

"Chores to do." Amanda sang as she skipped away, her bread clutched in one chubby hand. "Lots of chores, chores, chores."

Will leaned against the door, smiling. Isabella laid a butter knife in the tub of dishwater and turned. Her expression changed. Uncertain, maybe a little happy to see him standing there, but more uncertain. "Are you hungry too?"

He shook his head. "I couldn't eat a thing."

"Are you nervous about being minister?"

"I am." He straightened. "I might be in shock."

"You'll do fine."

"How do you know? You hardly know me at all."

"Whose fault is that?" She must've heard the tartness in her tone. Scarlet galloped across her fair neck and enveloped her cheeks. "I mean—"

"I think that's exactly what you meant." He glanced back. The noise level in the front room told him everyone was still discussing and rehashing the events of the afternoon. "The zoo was nice."

"It was."

She wouldn't make it easy. He didn't deserve that. He could've gone to her house any night after their return and asked her to take a ride with him. But he wasn't ready. He'd made that clear, hadn't he? He had to clear a path that would allow them to go forward together. "I told you it would take some time. Now, there's this new duty."

"I know what you said." She picked up a dish towel, then dropped it back on the cabinet. "With this new duty, and the store and the farm, you'll need someone to help you, to share the burden.

"Are you offering?"

"I would never be so presumptuous." Red flamed across her cheeks again. She frowned, making her dimples disappear. He'd done that to her. "It's up to you."

"I wanted to come see you." Desperately. "But I couldn't."

"You didn't know where I live?"

"*Nee,* I couldn't because I have unfinished business."

"You still have feelings for another?"

"Not exactly."

She turned and stuck both hands in the tub. Water sloshed over the sides. Will moved closer. "Isabella?"

She glanced back for a second, then went back to the dishes. "I said I would wait. I'm waiting."

"I will come for you."

"Uh-huh."

"I mean it."

"There's no guarantee I'll be here forever."

"Where will you be?"

"A person never knows."

He sighed. "I still have to figure some things out."

"I hope you are able to do that." The words sounded very formal coming from a girl up to her elbows in dirty dishwater. "I really do."

Her plaintive tone was like a hunting knife twisted in his chest. "Me too."

"Chores, chores, chores," she murmured the words in a sing-song voice. "Chores, chores, chores."

As if she no longer thought of him. The rigid set of her shoulders told him differently.

She cared. He caught himself whistling again as he strode through the house, down the steps, to his buggy. Until he thought of the lot and what he had to do next. The whistle died on his tongue.

CHAPTER 10

F or an *Englisch* church, it was fairly plain. Will wiped his dusty boots on a welcome mat just inside the heavy double doors. His tread sounded loud in his ears as he strode through the hallway, peeking in open doors. Classrooms. For Sunday school, he supposed. It was a weekday, but surely Jesse would be here. Unless he was still taking classes. Or working with Matthew Plank, restoring a house. He was a jack-of-all-trades these days. Will didn't want to track his cousin down. He wanted this over. The church first. The last place he would look would be Jesse's home—the one he shared with Leila.

"Will? What are you doing here?" And there he was. Jesse in his khaki shorts and white T-shirt. He stood in the doorway, an enormous box filled with bags of rice and beans in his hands. "I mean, it's good to see you."

"Why do you have rice and beans?" Will couldn't explain why that question came first of all the things he wanted to ask Jesse. Was he happy? Was Leila happy? How did it feel to be her *mann*? Did he miss his family? Did he miss Will? "Do *Englisch* ministers have to cook too?"

Jesse laughed. Will closed his eyes and opened them. His memories of growing up overflowed with that deep chortle. "It's Food Bank day." Jesse jerked his head toward the door. His surprise at Will's presence had disappeared. "Come on in. Nobody around here bites—unless you take their piece of cake."

Will followed him into the sanctuary. He removed his hat and took a long look. He'd never been in an *Englisch* church before. This one held no fancy stained-glass windows or ornate furniture. Not even wooden pews. Instead it held rows of brown metal chairs with padded seats. Across the front the congregation members had set up several folding tables. Half-a-dozen people worked as they chatted in amiable tones, filling up paper sacks with jars of peanut butter, boxes of macaroni and cheese, cans of tuna, canned vegetables, and boxes of cereal. Jesse added his box of goodies at the far end where a young woman dressed in an AC/DC T-shirt and yoga pants immediately began to divvy up the contents.

"We do this every second Monday of the month. Folks will start arriving in about twenty minutes." Jesse turned to Will. "But I guess you had something you wanted to talk about."

A sudden lump in his throat made Will want to groan. He swallowed and nodded.

"Let's sit in the back."

Will didn't want to sit. He wanted to run, but he was no coward. He followed Jesse to the last row of chairs and slid into the one on the end of the row. Jesse took the one across from him. "How are you?"

"*Gut.* Good."

Jesse nodded. He ducked his head and studied the floor. "And my *daed*?"

"Better every day. As ornery as ever."

"I imagine. My poor *mudder*."

"She counts herself blessed."

"I know."

Will searched for words. Jesse waited. One of the workers said something. The others laughed. Someone broke into song. "Jesus Loves the Little Children." Everyone joined in until they all laughed again.

What was so funny?

His eyes bright with moisture, Jesse looked up at him. "I've always wanted to tell you I'm sorry. I know how I hurt you. I wish there had been another way, some other way."

"Don't be sorry. *Gott*'s will was done."

"Is that what you came here to tell me?"

Will turned his hat in his hand, the straw rough under his fingers. "I drew the lot."

"The lot?" Jesse's breath caught, sharp, in the air. He leaned back in his chair. "*Daed* stepped down?"

So word had not gotten back to Jesse. Will met his cousin's gaze head-on. Jesse should know. "He and Naomi moved into the *dawdy haus*. Jeremiah drew the lot for bishop."

Jesse nodded, but something like pain etched lines around his mouth and eyes. He looked so much like Leroy at that moment. "Which left open the minister's spot."

"*Jah.*"

Myriad emotions flitted across Jesse's face. Sadness, pain,

understanding, acceptance. His Adam's apple bobbed. "You're a good Plain man. You'll serve the community well."

"It should have been you. It could have been you, if you'd been patient."

"God's plan was already in place. You know that. If He intended for you to be the minister for our—your—district, nothing would change that." Jesse's voice turned sandpaper rough. He cleared his throat. "Besides, it still wouldn't allow me to do what I do best."

"What is that?"

"Win the lost and make disciples."

As usual Jesse spoke a language Will couldn't decipher. "What about preaching?"

"Another way of doing the same thing while still feeding the believers."

Will laid his hat in the next chair. He gripped his knees with both hands to keep them from shaking. "I don't know if I can do it." He whispered the words, aware that he sat in God's house. An *Englisch* house, but a place where the body of Christ worshipped, nevertheless. "How do you do it?"

"Preach the Word?"

"*Jah.*"

"I pray and I pray and I pray." Jesse's voice lost some of its rough edge. He smiled, a kind of contentment filled with happiness shining in his face. "I ask Him to put the words on my heart that each member of the congregation needs to hear. I surrender myself to Him knowing it's not about me. It's about them. I pray that He speaks to them through me, filling their needs, strengthening their faith."

Will forced himself to breathe and nodded. "Have you ever stood in front of folks and found not a word would come out?"

"Me?" Jesse laughed, that same belly laugh of their youth. "You know I'm never at a loss for words. You'll do fine, cousin, I promise. God picked you. He'll give you the words."

"It should be you."

"No." He slapped a hand on Will's knee. "God doesn't make mistakes. He chose you and He'll be with you every step of the way."

Will stared at the thick brown carpet under his work boots. He didn't dare look at Jesse. His cousin would see the unshed tears, the fear, the anguish, the uncertainty.

A hand squeezed his shoulder. He forced his head up. Jesse stood over him. "Would you like me to pray with you?"

Will closed his eyes and nodded. He swiped at his nose, wishing he had a bandana.

"Kneel with me."

Will dropped to his knees in the aisle. Jesse did the same. For a few minutes the sounds of sporadic chatter, the crackling of sacks being opened, and the thumping of cans against the tables at the other end of the sanctuary filled the silence. Then Jesse's voice, deep and gruff and so like Leroy's, warmed Will's heart. Jesse prayed with a fervor and a confidence that boggled Will's mind.

"Lord, I pray for my cousin Will. Give him the words, give him the assurance that You will be with him always. Let him feel Your presence. Guide him. Direct him. Comfort him in the dark hours of the night when he lies awake worrying and wondering at his own human weakness. And Lord, I pray You will send him a woman, a soul mate, someone who will share in this life journey with him, someone who will support him and give him the kind of human comfort a man needs in order for his life to be whole and complete. In Christ's mighty, mighty name, I pray."

The words ended, but Will remained on his knees, letting them wash over him, wave upon wave. The knots in his shoulders relaxed. The ache in his temples subsided. He didn't want to let go of this moment in which God's presence was palpable. The irony of it was not lost on him. He felt as close to God in Jesse's world as he did in his own. Indeed, God would find him where he was. He'd shown Will that over and over again.

And he'd already brought Will the soul mate he needed for this journey.

Jesse couldn't know that. Will already had found that woman.

Of course, she didn't know either. Time to tell her.

He rose to his feet. "*Danki.*"

Jesse nodded. Together they walked down the aisle. "You're welcome here anytime. And at our home. Leila would be happy to see you."

No stabbing pain followed those words. Their worlds had come together for this brief moment, but it wouldn't be a regular occurrence. It couldn't be. Will shook his head, but he managed a smile. "That can't happen."

"She misses her family. She misses all of you."

"She made her choice." He worked to keep his voice matter-of-fact. "I don't hold that against her. Or you. Not anymore. I want you to know that. Tell her that for me, would you?"

Jesse gave a jerky nod. "We're forgiven, then?"

"You are."

The painful ache that had been in his heart for so long disappeared, replaced by an empty spot waiting to be filled by another. "Godspeed."

Jesse held out his hand. Will took it. He found himself pulled into a quick, hard hug, the kind men gave men that ended with a slap on the back. Jesse whirled and strode away. Surely as confounded by emotion as Will felt.

Wiping at his nose with the back of his sleeve, he stopped at the door and looked back. Jesse had slipped into the assembly line. He tossed a can of corn into a bag and slid it over. He looked up, smiled, and nodded. Will smiled and nodded back. He slapped his hat on his head and went home.

CHAPTER 11

Light flickered on the wall, a strange zigzag. Isabella sat up in bed, sure she was dreaming. Amanda mumbled in her sleep and rolled over closer to Molly. The light zigged and zagged again. Rubbing her eyes, Isabella tossed back the sheet and slid her bare feet to the floor. Surely Maisie hadn't decided to pay her another visit. After her early departure from the pool hall, Isabella hadn't heard a peep from the *Englisch* girl. Jacob knew better than to show up in the Olds. Fine and dandy with her on both counts.

She pushed her damp hair from her face and padded to the window. Her nightgown stuck to her chest in the humid heat that had not abated after the sun went down. The light smacked her in the eyes. "Hey." She stuck her hand to her face to shade her eyes. "Who is that?"

"It's me. Will. Come out."

She jerked back from the window. A strange feeling like the flu welled in her stomach. She inhaled and blew out air. *In and out.* No more waiting. It was Will.

Only Will.

Finally. He'd finally come.

Hallelujah.

Isabella stuck her head out, careful to keep her nightgown-clad body out of the flashlight's beam. "Give me a minute."

She slid into her dress and swept her hair up in a bun with trembling fingers. The pins kept falling to the floor. She knelt and tripped over her skirt.

Breathe. In and out.

Shoes in her hands, she slipped from the bedroom and tip-toed down the hallway to the front room and the door. Her hand felt slick on the knob.

In and out.

Will stood ramrod straight next to the buggy. He'd turned off the flashlight. Her eyes adjusted to the night lit by a half-moon and stars whose brilliance was unfettered by clouds on a clear, hot May night. Still, she couldn't read his expression.

He took a step toward her. "Would you mind going for a ride with me?"

"I wouldn't mind." Her voice sounded like someone else's in her ears. High and quivering. "If you're offering."

"I am." He held out his hand. "It's a perfect night for it."

She took his hand and he helped her into the buggy. Seconds later they were on the road, the *clip-clop* of the horse's hooves the only sound in the night air. He would have to speak. She had no words.

He chuckled.

"What's so funny?"

"I had so much to say before I got to your house. Now my mind is blank."

"I'm no help. I'm new at this."

"I figured as much."

"What does that mean?"

"Nothing bad." He glanced her direction and then away. "Only that you look so nervous, I'm afraid you'll fly off the buggy into the ditch if I say the wrong thing. You still have an innocence about you."

His voice faded away. He cleared his throat. "That's a good thing, in case you're wondering."

"Can a person still be innocent who's been to a pool hall?"

"It takes a little more than that to spoil a girl's innocence."

"I'm not a girl."

"How old are you?"

"How old are you?"

He laughed outright then. "Twenty-two."

Her shoulders relaxed. She breathed. "*Ach*, older than rain."

He shook his head. "Too old?"

"Too old for what?"

He pulled the buggy onto the road that led to the store. "I've done this before, is what I'm trying to say. I don't know if that's fair to you, but I think I might get it right this time. I've had practice."

"Practice is a good thing in some cases." Isabella clasped her hands in her lap, her fingers interlaced, to keep from touching his. She wanted to wipe the concern, the shame, from his face. "Sometimes that's what it takes to get it right. Sometimes I think *Gott* is teaching us what we need to know so we can, finally, get it right."

"I sure took my time."

"Some take more time than others, I reckon."

"You're so sweet and I wasn't very nice to you the first time we met."

Heat blazed through her. It wasn't the humid air of a south Texas night. Nobody had ever called her sweet before. She squeezed her hands tighter yet. "You've more than made up for that since. I had a really nice time at the zoo."

"Me too." He cleared his throat. "Still, I'm sorry I didn't make a better first impression."

"You definitely made an impression."

He halted the buggy in front of the Combination Store.

"What are we doing here?"

"Here's where I feel most at home." He said the words simply as if they explained everything. He hopped from the buggy and jogged around to her side. "Come inside with me?"

She'd felt at home with him in the store the first night. The time he'd saved her from herself. This was a good place for a meeting of their worlds, a meeting of their minds. Without answering, Isabella hopped down and followed him in.

He lit a kerosene lantern on the counter, blew out the match, and let it drop to the counter. The smell of phosphorus and kerosene mingled, pungent in her nose. Will turned, his body backlit by the lantern's light. "I like it here."

Isabella studied the contours of his face, half hidden in shadows. "I like it too."

He strode away, disappearing into the dark of the first aisle, leaving her standing by the door, hands clasped in front of her. A scraping sound broke the silence. He reappeared pushing the double rocking chair. He parked it in front of the counter. "Have a seat."

Not knowing what else to do, she gathered the skirt of her dress around her and sat. Will sank onto the seat next to her. He was so close she could smell his scent of soap and wood. The rocker squeaked under their combined weight. His fair skin reddened. "Would you like a glass of water? I have some in the back."

"*Nee*." He was as nervous as she was. The knowledge gave Isabella courage. She leaned back and pushed off with her legs. The rocker rocked. It was a calming motion that reminded her of cuddling her little sisters after their births on nights one year apart. It reminded her of the day she'd brought the baked goods and sat in this chair, daydreaming about a moment very similar to this one. "What are we doing here?"

He tapped the floor with his work boot. The gentle rocking continued. "I wanted to ask you something."

"And it had to be asked here?"

"*Jah*, it did." He slid his hat from his head and plopped it in his lap. His hair was the color of wheat, thick and straight. She wanted to brush it from his forehead. "That first day you came into the store, you remember that day?"

"How could I not? I broke a quart jar of beets on the floor and you were mad at me."

"I wasn't mad."

"*Jah*, you were."

"Not at you. I was mad at life. I was mad . . . at *Gott*."

Isabella smoothed her fingers across the coarse cotton of her apron, the words ringing in her ears. Could a person admit such a thing and still live? "Mad at *Gott*?" she whispered as if He wouldn't hear her if she spoke softly. "Why? Because of Jesse and Leila?"

"I blamed everything on Him because I didn't understand His plan for me."

"And now you do?"

"I do. I had it all wrong then, but not anymore."

"What do you understand?"

"That I needed to wait. For you. I needed time to get ready for you. *Gott* knew you were coming. He only wanted me to be patient. To wait upon Him."

Her knuckles went white. Her fingers hurt. Isabella forced herself to loosen them. "I've waited too. Waited to get here. I never thought what I longed for, what I needed, what my heart cried out for, would be in Texas. A person can't even begin to wrap her mind around such a thing."

"I'd say *Gott* is gut. He's shown me the path I'm to take with the store and being chosen as minister." He slid closer, much closer. His long, thin fingers touched her hand. "Look at me." She raised her head and met his gaze. He smiled. "He is *gut* because He brought you to me."

Isabella turned her hand over. His fingers entwined with hers. "And you to me."

"I'm not an easy person to know."

"Nor am I."

"I'm a few years older, a little scared, a little worse for wear around the edges, as you pointed out earlier."

"In years, but you're a man so you don't act so old."

His laugh wrapped around her like a warm summer night full of promise. "Are you saying all men are childish?" His voice was close to her ear. Somehow he'd moved yet closer without her realizing it. "Am I childish?"

She ducked her head. "It's what *Mudder* says. She says boys take longer to grow up so girls have to pick up the slack when it comes to taking care of things."

His fingers touched her chin, forcing her to look at him. He leaned in. His lips touched hers. They were warm and soft and tasted of peppermint. Her breath seeped away. She wanted to lean into his touch but found she couldn't move. Their lips parted. "Is this all right with you?"

Isabella swallowed and nodded. Her first kiss had come and gone before she could grasp the memory and hold on to it.

He leaned down again. This time, to her delight, his kiss lasted. The tension that held her captive melted. She slid her arms around his neck and found herself pressed against his chest. The solid beat of his heart caused the jitter of her own to slow. She breathed, every bone and muscle in her body in sync with Will's.

"You're the one," he whispered, wonder in his voice. "You've always been the one. I just didn't know it."

"You had to grow up first."

"Funny woman."

"That's me. Funny."

"You'll be my *fraa* then?"

She eased back so she could see his face and planted her hands on either side of his head. The hope in his eyes made her stretch up and plant a kiss on each cheek and yet another on his forehead. "I have to be baptized in the fall."

"I'll wait."

Just as she had waited. Joy would come in the waiting. "More buggy rides will be needed."

"Many more, I imagine. A man like me apparently needs much practice."

A man with a good heart and a sense of humor in the face of all he'd suffered and learned. "Then *jah*, I will be your *fraa* if you will be my *mann*."

His response came in another kiss, still sweeter and deeper and fiercer than the last. Sweeter than honey.

The rocking chair kept rocking. It might be the first piece of furniture in their someday home. A place where they could rock their someday *boplin*. Isabella snuggled closer and prayed those days would come along right when *Gott* intended.

Gott's will and *Gott*'s Will were one.

DISCUSSION QUESTIONS

1. Will is stuck. He can't move forward in his life because he hasn't dealt with his hurt and anger over Leila Lantz choosing another man. Is there anything in your life that keeps you from living fully in the present? What do you need to do to move forward?

2. Isabella is a quiet, shy girl. It's made it hard for her to make friends, even in a small, friendly community such as the Beeville District. Have you ever gone out of your way to include someone who is quiet or reserved in your circle of friends? Is it possible you've missed out on a friendship because you thought someone was "stuck-up" rather than reserved?

3. Isabella tags along with Maisie to the pool hall because she feels she is missing out on an adventure and Maisie includes her in her group of friends. Have you ever felt pressure to go along for the ride in order to feel included or part of the "in-crowd" even though you knew the activity was wrong or not right for you? How did it end?

4. Leroy tells Will that he's hanging on to an old anger with both hands because it is impossible for him to embrace new love in his life. Is there someone you need to forgive in order to enjoy love to its fullest? How do you do it?

5. Will thought he would love Leila forever. Then she married his cousin and he met Isabella. Do you believe there is only one love in this world for you, or do you believe in second chances? Why?

ABOUT THE AUTHOR

 Kelly Irvin is the author of *The Beekeeper's Son*, the critically acclaimed first novel in the Amish of Bee County series. Kelly is also the author of the Bliss Creek Amish series and the New Hope Amish series. She has also penned two romantic suspense novels, *A Deadly Wilderness* and *No Child of Mine*. The Kansas native is a graduate of the University of Kansas School of Journalism. She has been writing nonfiction professionally for thirty years, including ten years as a newspaper reporter, mostly in Texas-Mexico border towns. She has worked in public relations for the City of San Antonio for twenty years. Kelly has been married to photographer Tim Irvin for twenty-seven years. They have two young adult children, two cats, and a tank full of fish. In her spare time, she likes to write short stories and read books by her favorite authors.

Twitter: @Kelly_S_Irvin
Facebook: Kelly.Irvin.Author

Love in Store

VANNETTA CHAPMAN

For Jodi Hughes

GLOSSARY

daddi—grandfather

danki—thank you

dat—dad, father

Englischer—non-Amish person

fra—wife

Gotte's wille—God's will

gudemariye—good morning

gut—good

kapp—prayer covering

kinner—children

mamm—mom

mammi—grandmother

nein—no

rumspringa—running around; time before an Amish young person has officially joined the church, provides a bridge between childhood and adulthood.

schweschder—sister

willkumm—welcome

wunderbaar—wonderful

ya—yes

youngie—teenaged to young adult

"Whatever you do, work at it with all your heart, as working for the Lord . . ."
—Colossians 3:23

"How pleasant and good it is when brothers are peaceable, when their doings are in agreement."
—Amish proverb

PROLOGUE

NAPPANEE, INDIANA
MARCH

D avid Stoltzfus didn't wake planning to save a child's life. He'd worked the first half of his shift at the Old Amish Mill and then walked over to the market building. In the back, past the Plain merchandise and the canned goods, was a bakery where he liked to sit and enjoy his lunch. The first bite of his sandwich tasted delicious. He was about to take a second when he heard a woman scream in alarm. Looking up, he saw her standing next to a child that was probably not yet a year old.

"Cough, Cami. Cough!" the older woman said.

The little girl's face was turning blue. David didn't hesitate. He hurried to the child's side, scooped her up, and held her face-down over his forearm. Holding her jaw with his left hand to support her head, he used the heel of his right hand to slap the area between her shoulder blades. With the third slap a grape popped out and rolled across the floor. The child pulled in a deep breath, pinking up immediately. David breathed a prayer of relief and handed the little thing back to her grandmother.

"I was cutting them in half." Tears coursed down the woman's cheeks as she clutched the child to her chest. "I turned around for a minute and I guess . . . I guess she managed to grab one off my plate."

Stella Schwartz had hurried from the register to the woman's side. "Would you like us to call an ambulance?"

"No. No, I think she's all right now."

"Let me bring you another hot tea—to calm your nerves. And perhaps a bottle of juice for your granddaughter?"

The woman nodded and then suddenly seemed to realize that David was still standing there. "How can I thank you?"

"Not necessary. Glad I could help. You have a *gut* afternoon." David went back to his sandwich, but the rest of lunch was not to be the peaceful half hour he had envisioned. The manager of the Mill must have been called. He checked on the woman and child, and then he thanked David and Stella for their help.

"Quick thinking and calm in a crisis," Bobo McPherson said. "We need more employees like that."

David only nodded as he gathered up his trash. But his mind wasn't on the child as he made his way out of the restaurant. Instead David was thinking of Stella, the gracious way she had helped the grandmother, the tender way she had looked at the child, the look of pure gratitude she had shared with David before returning to her work and her normal, somewhat dour, disposition. Stella was an enigma to David, as most women were. He'd been fortunate to have one woman by his side for most of his adult life. He still felt Beverly's love like a blanket that comforted him. He supposed he always would.

But what was Stella's story?

His daughter had told him that Stella had never married. Why?

And why the perpetual bad attitude? If David hadn't seen her with the child, he never would have believed she could be tender and compassionate. But he had seen her, and it wasn't a sight he would soon forget.

CHAPTER 1

APRIL

Life took more turns than a country road. David Stoltzfus was currently navigating one of those turns, and he marveled that he could still feel peaceful about it. Then again, his parents had been an example of faith in daily living, not even worrying through the long Wisconsin winters. Yes, he'd had good people to bring him up in the faith, and faith was what would see him through this current crisis.

He nearly laughed to think what his *mamm* and *dat* would say about his living in Indiana. They'd already passed before his daughter had married and moved. Though David loved the area where he'd been born and raised, he also found these first few weeks in Nappanee, Indiana to be a pleasant change. Anywhere family resided was a wonderful place to be, in his opinion.

David walked toward the icehouse on the northern side of the property of the Old Amish Mill complex, known to locals as simply the Mill. The property had close to forty buildings, including a large gift shop, market, café, and theater. The majority of the buildings were historic in nature—either from the original farmstead or restored buildings that had been moved to the site. He whistled as he walked past each one. Why wouldn't he whistle? It was a fine spring day—the temperature in the forties but projected to rise to a balmy fifty-six. He had a job that he enjoyed, and he was now living with his daughter. He was grateful for the chance to help Rebecca during her time of trouble.

Yes, life was good. He thanked the Lord each night that in spite of their troubles, they were able to enjoy the small blessings of life.

"*Gudemariye*, David." Peter Yoder raised a hand in greeting. He worked in the maple-sugar camp, and their buildings were adjacent to one another.

Peter was a few years older than David, surely in his early sixties. David had recently turned fifty-two. Though they'd only known each other a few weeks they were fast becoming friends. In fact, Peter was the one who had mentioned the job opening at the Mill to Rebecca. The community had certainly rallied around Rebecca since the death of her husband. It had been a tragedy for sure and for certain, but now David was there to help her with the three children and provide a little extra income.

"It's a fine morning indeed," David said. "Reminds me of when we'd rise early to work in the fields."

"Only now our job is to escort *Englischers*, teaching them our ways."

David and Peter stood with their backs against the wall of what they called the sugar building and studied the fields that stretched to the north of the property. The sugar building was an old wooden structure that had been moved to the area many years ago. For the entire month of March, a sweet aroma would seep from its walls, as sap water was boiled down into maple syrup.

"Do you miss it?" David asked. "The farming?"

David could see, off in the distance, one of the younger employees farming five acres of the north pasture. Though the Mill was a tourist attraction, it was also a working farm.

"*Ya*. For certain I do, especially as I'm driving past the fields in the morning, watching the *youngies* out there driving the horses and plow."

"It's a satisfying thing indeed to work the land."

"My mind and heart misses it." Peter cast David a sideways look, his eyes crinkling as he smiled. "But my back and knees? Not so much. It is *gut* that we pass such work to our sons."

"Indeed. I'm thankful for this job. The extra money helps Rebecca."

"How is she?"

"Some days better than others."

"Young Jacob's life was complete, but I know firsthand that grief is a hard thing. We will continue to pray for her and the *kinner*."

David nodded. He'd learned, in the few weeks he'd been in Nappanee, that the community was a close one and went to great lengths to support one another through seasons of trouble. By the time David had moved to Rebecca's, the spring planting was already underway, the barn had been repaired, and the livestock were being cared for—all by church members or family of Jacob's.

"How do you like the icehouse?" Peter asked.

"*Gut* enough. I don't mind showing the young children or even the old *Englischers* how we harvest the ice and store it. Such a simple thing, but they seem astonished when they learn the process."

"They're amazed because it's done with the work of our hands and the sweat of our brows, not by pushing some button."

Peter was getting wound up for one of his lectures against modern conveniences. He had that look in his eye and shake to his head. David needed to escape.

"Suppose I should be moseying over. I still need to check the rooms before the first tour group comes through."

"Pleasant day to you."

David walked across the dirt lane to the icehouse—what he was already thinking of as *his* house. Donning the coat he kept on a hook inside the door, he walked over to the cubby built into the south wall. It was where he kept his things. He stored his lunch and glanced over his supplies. Only the most basic of tools were required to care for the icehouse. There were work gloves and a clipboard, along with several sizes of ice picks and mallets to use in demonstrations. There was also an assortment of hooks to show the youngsters how to pick up the blocks of ice. Though only twelve by eighteen inches and twelve inches thick, each block weighed eighty pounds—always a surprise to the children who thought they could pick one up.

The clipboard contained an updated schedule of tours. Since it was a Friday, they would have three groups. Saturdays were even busier and he could only imagine what the summer crowds would be like. He'd only worked at the Mill for two weeks.

At the moment his job was to oversee the icehouse and the several hundred blocks of ice in it, which wasn't a difficult task. He enjoyed explaining to visitors how the ice had been harvested from area lakes and ponds, even the small pond the icehouse was positioned near. *Englischers* were always surprised that the ice didn't melt, even during the warm summer days, but the building had been constructed with that purpose in mind, and it was well built.

So he was flabbergasted when he began his morning inspection and found water standing throughout the building. Some of it had frozen and the place had become a virtual ice rink. He carefully made his way to the faucet at the back of the building, filled a mop bucket with hot water, and began cleaning up the mess. Water or ice on the floor might cause a visitor to slip. The Mill would be responsible, and David would probably lose his job. Fortunately the rooms were small and the cleaning only took a few moments.

When he was done, David checked to see if he needed to add any sawdust around the hundreds of blocks of ice, but there were only a few small gaps. He preferred to let one of their guests take care of it. There were always volunteers, and they seemed to enjoy helping—usually pausing so that someone could take a picture on their cell phones.

David had reached the back of the icehouse and was turning again to the front when he spied something red out of his peripheral vision. Moving back toward the corner, he stepped to the left and then the right trying to make sense of what he was seeing.

There was a rubber chicken—no doubt at all that it was not real—lying across one of the blocks of ice. A red substance had

315

been dripped around the chicken, and an ice pick had been stuck into the chicken's neck. Why would someone leave such a thing? And who would do it?

Then he remembered—the day was April 1. Someone was pulling an April Fools' joke. The Amish didn't usually participate in Fools' Day pranks and jokes, but the *youngie* might and the *Englisch* certainly did. David grunted as he moved to where his tools were kept and retrieved a large ice pick, a mallet, and a bucket. He hurried to the scene of the mock killing and placed the chicken and small pick in the bucket. Then he set about chipping away the ice that had been stained. Lastly, he retrieved his mop and cleaned up the mess on the floor.

The chicken was a joke, for sure and certain. But the partially frozen water on the floor? Someone must have come in the evening before, for it to be frozen already. Had they dropped a bucket of water and not taken the time to clean up? Why would they need a bucket of water? Why would they even be in the icehouse to begin with?

By the time he had finished cleaning up the mess, a double tap came over his walkie-talkie. That would mean Stella Schwartz had begun her tour. She would be at the icehouse in roughly an hour. He had enough time to go next door and chat a little more with Peter Yoder. The two men lived in opposite directions, so they only saw each other at church meetings or between tour groups. Peter drove his own buggy to work—he lived to the east off Highway 6.

David lived to the west, and he rode to work with several other Mill employees. They hired an *Englischer* with a large van to transport them each morning and evening. He could have driven Rebecca's buggy, but she only had the one and he didn't like leaving her with no means of transportation. Riding with the *Englischer* was no problem and cost only twenty dollars a week, far less than the cost of another horse and buggy.

Earlier, David had stepped out of the van in the parking lot and then walked straight toward the icehouse. He hadn't seen anyone near the building, but perhaps Peter had. David didn't plan to reprimand the person, but he did want to remind him or her that a child could have found the pick and gotten hurt, or an older person could have slipped on the red juice. It hadn't been paint, because it washed off too easily. Jell-O, maybe.

Looking out across the property, David saw Stella and her group enter the Meeting House. He'd be back well before she made it to the icehouse. One thing was for certain, he did not want to start off his day irritating Stella Schwartz.

The woman had a sharp tongue and a bitter spirit.

And yet, something about Stella intrigued him. He couldn't help thinking that there was more to her. What, he wasn't sure, but he was interested in finding out. Time would tell whether that was foolish or wise.

CHAPTER 2

Stella Schwartz led her group of twelve guests past the Round Barn Theater and into the Meeting House. As she did, she happened to look up and see David Stoltzfus dash from the icehouse over to the sugar camp.

"Why can't he stay at his assigned post?"

Ethel Miller's eyes widened. In Stella's opinion the girl was impossibly young and terribly naïve. But then no one had asked Stella if she wanted seventeen-year-old Ethel as an apprentice. And what was the point anyway? The girl was already seeing one of the boys who worked on the grounds crew. By the time Stella trained her, she would be married and gone.

"Maybe he wanted to say hello to Peter."

"Work is not the time to socialize." Stella made a sound like *humph*, then wished she could take it back. She sounded like her mother who had died in her eighties. She didn't want to sound eighty or any age other than the fifty years she was.

She would have liked to remind young Ethel to pull her *kapp* forward—too much of her blond hair was showing. It was all about fashion and style with the young girls, but Stella thought they would do well to mind the ways of their elders.

She couldn't reprimand Ethel though, because her guests had all walked into the Meeting House and taken a seat on the long wooden benches. It was time to acquaint them with the history of the Amish in general and this facility in particular.

"*Gudemariye* and welcome to the Old Amish Mill. We are pleased that you have chosen to spend your morning with us. The Amish Mill encompasses seventy-two acres and is listed in the National Register of Historic Places. As she proceeded to tell them how Amish settlers had first come to the Nappanee area in 1839, she released some of the tension from her muscles and forgot about the sharp edges of her life.

Her regrets slipped away.

Her anger quieted.

For a moment, she gave rest to the bitterness in her soul and instead focused on the young and old in front of her.

They were a varied lot—from small ones who could barely toddle to an older gentleman who was using a cane. They had respectfully silenced their cell phones, and perhaps that helped to brighten her mood. The small group was friendly and attentive, and Stella relaxed in the knowledge that she was being useful. She was teaching others about the history of the area, important aspects of the past and the present. Something they hopefully would tell others about. Maybe they'd even learn to apply some of what they saw while on the grounds to their everyday, mostly urban, lives.

After she'd handed out maps and told them the tour would take nearly two hours, she nodded to Ethel. The girl was already in the small sound room at the back, and she pushed the button to start the film. The lights dimmed and the ten minute documentary began. Although Stella didn't abide television or picture shows, she thought the film was well done, and the guests seemed to enjoy it.

When it was over, they moved smoothly through the first forty minutes of the tour—seeing the orchard, which was just beginning to bloom, the blacksmith shop, and the sorghum press. When they reached the maple-sugar camp, Stella thought to ask Peter why David had been dashing over to see him.

She decided it was none of her business.

As long as he did his job, she had no interest in what David did.

She had been repeating that very thing to herself all week, but that hadn't stopped David Stoltzfus from popping up in her path when he had no business being there. Nearly every day he stopped into the bakery where she worked in the afternoons. He always purchased a small item—a pack of gum or sometimes a soda. She couldn't imagine why he wasted his money on such things.

Her mind flashed back to the little girl David had saved. He had scooped her up and patted her on the back like it was something he did daily. Perhaps he had some medical training. Or maybe he had learned to do so after someone in his community choked. She knew he was from Wisconsin, but other than that he was a mystery—a mystery that she had no intention of unraveling.

Guiding her group across the dirt lane to the front of the wooden icehouse, she refused to meet David's eyes. He had an unnerving way of smiling at her. Best to appear occupied with other things.

"*Willkumm,*" he said robustly. David wasn't one to keep his voice down. He spoke as if he were preaching at the front of a church gathering. "I'm pleased that you have stopped by to visit my humble icehouse."

"It's not as if it belongs to him," Stella grumbled under her breath.

Ethel nearly giggled at that, which made no sense.

"Today I will explain to you how the building was constructed, how we cut and store the ice, and why it lasts all year long."

"We push a button and ice comes out of our refrigerator," a small *Englisch* girl said.

"Ah, *ya,* and is that so?"

David was playing stupid. Another child had said the same thing earlier in the week.

"Our ice does not come out of a machine, but from the ponds and lakes. For some Amish communities, like those in Wisconsin where I am from, it even comes from the rivers. Let's walk around to the back porch which stretches out over the pond, and I will show you what I mean."

David tugged on his beard, no doubt reminding the small ones of Santa Claus. The little girl who had mentioned her refrigerator reached up and snagged his hand as if it was the most natural thing in the world.

In that moment, Stella felt a pain in her chest that was akin to a physical ache. She'd grown accustomed to it long ago, yet such moments still had the power to steal her breath. She mourned for the children she never had, the bareness of her womb, and she wondered—once again—what was the point of her life?

Ethel's walkie-talkie squeaked, pulling Stella back to the present. The voice of their manager, Bobo McPherson, came over the device. Stella closed her eyes and tried to find a bit of patience from deep inside. There was much about Mr. McPherson that rubbed her the wrong way.

They both stepped away from the group while David continued with his demonstration.

"Hi, Ethel. This is Bobo."

Stella resisted the urge to roll her eyes. Bobo was not a proper name, and in her opinion Mr. McPherson would do better to remain on a more formal basis with his employees.

"Good morning," Ethel said.

"It is. However, we had an employee call in sick at the restaurant. Could you possibly abandon Stella and go lend a hand?"

"Abandon me?"

Stella glanced at Ethel, shoulders raised in a questioning pose.

"Fine. I can escort a group of twelve, including an infant and an old cripple, all by myself." Stella did her best to put a sarcastic tone in her reply, but Ethel didn't appear to notice.

"Ethel, I've asked David to fill in your spot," Mr. McPherson continued. "Peter will cover both the sugar camp and the icehouse. It'll only be for this tour and the next, then we'll have things all straightened out."

Ethel responded with something inane like she'd be happy to, and Stella stared left then right, hoping a different solution would pop out of the shrubs. Instead all she saw was Peter Yoder, making his way across to where they stood.

With a sinking feeling, Stella realized that her Friday had taken an abrupt turn for the worse. She'd be spending hours in the company of the one man she'd rather not be around—David Stoltzfus.

CHAPTER 3

Stella survived the morning tours.

During the afternoon hours she worked quietly in the market, lost in her own thoughts and speaking very little to the other workers. She couldn't put her finger on what it was about David Stoltzfus that bothered her so much. He was polite, did his job well, and was personable with the guests.

She thought suddenly of the old tomcat her sister insisted on feeding. The pitiful thing had part of one ear missing, continually showed up needing bandaging, and yet he lay in the sun content as a newborn kitten.

That was it.

David's contentment.

"Can you tell me if these potholders are actually made by Amish women?" The customer was holding eight in her hands.

Stella wondered who needed eight potholders, but she didn't comment on that. "*Ya*, they are made by a woman in my church, and they're hand stitched and hand quilted."

She rung up the woman's purchase and then returned to dusting shelves.

David's contented attitude was more than she could fathom, and it caused her soul to bristle. Why wasn't he railing against the injustices of life? She knew little about him, but of course she had attended Jacob's funeral. It was the first time she'd laid eyes on David, and even then—though he'd been properly somber—there was a peace about him that defied explanation.

His daughter was a widow!

His grandchildren fatherless!

Yet he stood next to them at the graveside, back straight and shoulders square as if he didn't feel the burden that had been passed to him.

"If you dust those shelves any harder you're going to take off part of the paint." Joan Neeley was Stella's age and had worked in the market nearly as long.

"Seems I just did this job yesterday."

"And we'll do it again tomorrow."

Joan hurried over to the register to check out another customer, and Stella continued the never-ending task of keeping the market clean. Her thoughts though, they returned to David Stoltzfus.

A real tragedy what had happened to David's son-in-law.

Her life was nowhere near as tragic, and yet she didn't feel the need to placidly accept it. *Nein*, when something was wrong, then it should be treated as wrong. Hadn't Job argued with God? Didn't they all have the right to struggle against the curves and turns their lives took? Acceptance and peace were all good and well when spoken by a preacher, but in Stella's opinion it went against human nature.

David Stoltzfus went against human nature.

She spent the rest of her shift ringing up orders for the customers who purchased fresh bread, pies, and cookies. Then she walked to the barn. Eli Strong had already fetched her horse and hitched it to the buggy. Eli was a good lad though not particularly bright. She had to check and make sure the harness was fastened correctly.

Satisfied that her buggy wouldn't come unhitched and kill her on the way home, she climbed up, nodded to Eli, and set out to the west down Highway 6.

She'd traveled less than a half mile when she spotted David walking along the side of the road.

What was the old fool doing now?

Rebecca's farm was a good four miles from the Mill. Against her better judgment, she pulled over to the side of the road and stopped. There was no need to get out of the buggy. David walked up alongside her window within a few minutes.

"Afternoon, Stella."

"What are you doing?"

"Ah, well, I'm walking home from work."

"You ride in the van."

"Most days I do." David smiled and the folds around his eyes crinkled.

"Then why are you walking?"

"Didn't quite finish my work in time. They left without me."

"How late were you?"

"Doesn't matter. Sandy has to pick up her daughter from gymnastics by five, so she can't wait. It was my fault, not hers."

There he went again, looking on the sunny side. It was enough to make Stella want to clap her hands over her ears or drive off without him. Of course, she did neither.

"Better climb in. Four miles is too far to walk for folks our age, especially after a full day at work."

David shrugged at that, but he did walk around the buggy and climb in.

She prayed they would ride in silence, but that was not to be.

"I enjoyed working with you this morning, Stella. You do a *gut* job leading the tour groups."

Stella didn't respond to that compliment, though she could feel her ears warming. No doubt they were also pinking up like a spring rose. Fortunately her *kapp* covered her ears, so David wouldn't see.

"Mr. McPherson would do well to have more standby employees for when there's an emergency. Ethel shouldn't be pulled in to whatever spot he needs filled. She has a regular spot—with me."

"Yet change is *gut* for us. Don't you agree? I certainly enjoy working in the icehouse, but it was nice to have a morning out on the property."

Stella made the *humph* sound. It was getting to be a habit. She needed to find a better way to express herself.

"I've only been here a little while—"

"Less than a month." Stella sniffed.

"But I can see that Bobo is a fair and competent manager. At least he seems that way to me."

Stella didn't respond to that. She wouldn't be baited by David into gossiping. Instead she focused on her driving and hoped that he would take the hint and ride in silence.

He didn't.

Instead he talked about the interesting people they had met in their groups that morning, pointed out flowers that were blooming on the side of the road, and regaled her with stories of his grandchildren.

His daughter, Rebecca, had a boy who was just starting school and twin girls who were still in diapers.

"Emma puts everything in her mouth, but Sophie holds anything she picks up next to her ear. They look completely alike, other than a tiny birthmark on the back of Sophie's neck, but in many ways they're different. It's an amazing thing, twins. Never had any in our family, but my wife's family—they had plenty. I guess that's why Rebecca had a set."

Stella could almost smell the baby powder. She wished she could tell David to stop talking, but she wasn't sure he was capable. He'd already moved on to describing the older boy to her.

"Teacher says he's *wunderbaar* with numbers. It's his reading that is poor. Any idea what would cause that?"

She realized with a start that David was waiting for her to respond.

When she didn't answer, David said, "I told Rebecca not to worry, but I suppose it's natural for a *mamm* to do so. Still, it seems to me that children will learn most things in time and it's best not to make too big a fuss."

"Glasses."

"Pardon?"

"The boy might need glasses."

David stroked his beard. Finally he asked, "Then how does he complete the math lessons so well?"

"Math is usually written a bit larger, at least in our school books. There's more white space on the page too. Reading on the other hand—the page is cluttered with print."

Now David was studying her. It made her decidedly nervous.

"Ask him to read to you tonight. See if he squints or tries to bring the page closer."

"I hadn't even thought of that," David admitted. "*Danki*, Stella. I'll watch young Adam, and I'll let you know if that seems to be the problem."

Stella had endured quite enough of David Stoltzfus's cheery conversation for one day. With a sigh of relief, she saw the corner of her sister's property.

"I'm afraid you'll have to walk the rest of the way. My *schweschder* doesn't like me to take the buggy farther than work and back."

"No problem at all. I appreciate the lift. Rebecca's is only a short piece from here." David wished her good night, waiting until she glanced his way before nodding and then moving out of the buggy.

Overall she was happy with the afternoon. She'd done her good deed by giving David a ride and now she was rid of him. Hopefully tomorrow everyone would show up for their assigned duties, and she wouldn't be bothered with his constant presence.

She ate a quiet dinner with Carolyn. They spoke of the inconsequential aspects of their day. Carolyn described the progress of their vegetables in the garden, how the baby birds situated in the barn eaves had begun to fly, and some silly thing the old tomcat had done. Carolyn started to mention a letter from her daughter, then changed the subject.

"You might as well tell me. What did it say?"

"It's nothing . . . nothing I want to talk about just yet."

"You're the one who brought it up, so you must want to talk about it." Stella waited, but Carolyn only changed the subject again.

It was later as Stella washed the dishes that she allowed her mind to comb back over the conversation with David in the buggy. Washing dishes always soothed her. It was a quiet task and easily done. Carolyn always cooked and Stella always washed up. But this evening she took longer than usual. She'd find herself holding a plate and wondering if she had washed it or not. When she was finally finished, she draped the towel over the dish drainer and glanced a final time out the window—westward toward Rebecca's farm. As she gazed at the last rays of light spreading out across the sky, she couldn't help wondering if David was sitting beside young Adam Hotstettler as he did his homework and whether or not the young boy was squinting at the text.

CHAPTER 4

David wanted to go see Stella the next day and tell her about his grandson, but he had no time. The Old Amish Mill was closed on Mondays, except for the inn, which was always open. Most Amish employees worked Tuesday through Saturday. He knew Stella would be leading groups and working in the market, but he'd once again been pulled away from the icehouse. Actually, Bobo McPherson had come to visit him before the workday had begun. They'd stood on the back porch, looking out over the pond.

"I read your report about the prank yesterday." McPherson was probably in his midthirties. He was most certainly not Amish. His black hair curled at his neck and sometimes flopped into his eyes. And his clothing was somewhat casual—always blue jeans though he wore a crisply ironed cotton button-up shirt with them.

"Certainly I didn't want to get anyone in trouble," David said. "It was harmless enough as pranks go, but it worried me that someone might slip on the ice that had formed on the floor."

"Yes, well. What you couldn't have known is yours was the third report I've received in the last week."

"Did they all involve rubber chickens and red Jell-O?"

McPherson smiled and leaned against the porch railing. "No. As a matter of fact, your report was unique in that aspect." He hesitated. "Someone switched out the Girls and Boys signs outside the bathrooms at the old schoolhouse last week. They also removed all the brooms from the broom shop and placed them on the porch of the Walnut Street House."

David ran his fingers through his beard. "Sounds like a teenager. Silly things, but nothing that would really hurt anyone."

"I agree. However, it doesn't present the Mill in the best light when visitors walk into a broom house with no brooms."

"Or step into the wrong bathroom."

"Exactly."

McPherson hadn't stopped by simply to chat, so David asked, "What can I do to help?"

"You're new here, so I think you could be objective. You don't have any ties or connections to any of the workers."

"Amish workers?"

"Or *Englisch*. You have no history at all here." Bobo had been studying the pond, but now he turned his attention to David. "You're also quick to respond to a situation appropriately. I saw that when you saved the girl from choking."

"Anyone would have done that."

"Some would have, I suppose. Some wouldn't have known what to do, and some might have stood there in a state of panic. A hesitation of even a minute might have cost that child her life."

David didn't respond. The thought was sobering, and he

once again thanked God that he had learned the technique in the first-aid class back in his old community.

"What I'm saying is that I'd like to make you my grounds inspector. Your job will be to walk the property, become familiar with the employees, of course help where you're needed but also report back to me at the end of each day."

David had rather liked his simple job at the icehouse, but he could tell that McPherson was worried. David would hate to see tourism fall off at the Old Amish Mill. He might lose his job just when the income he was giving to Rebecca was needed the most. The crops had been planted by Jacob's brothers, but she was also missing the income from Jacob's side business of fixing broken farm tools. No, now would not be a good time for him to be unemployed. So, he looked at McPherson and said, "Sure, I'd be happy to help."

"Great. You'll start today. Now let's map out a strategy for catching our mischievous culprit."

"Have you alerted the police?"

McPherson hesitated and then said, "Not yet. All police reports make it into our local paper. I don't want the bad publicity."

"But you will, if the situation grows worse?"

"Yes, of course. But my hope is that we can stop whoever is doing this before it reaches that stage."

❧

David spent the rest of the day walking the property and becoming familiar with areas he hadn't been in. The site had many historic buildings, plus the inn, which was actually more recently constructed but designed to blend in with the structures around it.

McPherson already had a decent plan—that David would check each building at least once a day, look for anything that might be out of the ordinary, and try to win the trust of the other employees. David only dissented in one respect.

"The term *inspector* makes it sound as if I'm checking up on them."

"You are."

"*Ya*, for certain. But perhaps they would take me into their confidence if they thought I was only there to help—which I will be so it's not dishonest."

"You don't like the job title."

David had glanced out toward the road. Stella was walking toward them with the first group of the day. It seemed as if he'd been talking to McPherson for hours, but in fact it had only been thirty minutes. As he watched Stella, he remembered what she'd said the day before—that there should be more employees who could fill in when needed.

"I could be your handyman. That sounds less intimidating, and actually you could use someone who can fill in the gaps, work in any position." He turned his attention from Stella to McPherson and waited.

"Handyman?"

"*Ya.*"

"Sounds like I can pay a handyman less than an inspector." Bobo thrust out his hand.

David shook it, and the deal was sealed.

So he'd spent the day walking the Mill property, talking to

employees, and giving them his walkie-talkie channel. "If there's anything you need, call me."

No one did, until an hour before his day was to end.

Then there was a crackle on his walkie-talkie, and Frank Black's voice came over the line. "I'm at the mint distillery. You stopped by earlier today."

"*Ya*, I remember. How are things going, Frank?"

"Not so good, but before I call the police, I thought I'd call you."

"That bad?" David was already reversing course and heading toward the mint distillery, which happened to be across the pond from the icehouse.

"Bad enough."

"I'll be there in five minutes."

He saw Frank before he had skirted the pond.

David had noticed that approximately half the employees at the Mill were Amish—the other half were *Englisch*. He supposed this worked well, especially for filling Sunday shifts—though no doubt some of the *Englisch* wouldn't have wanted to work on the Sabbath either. From what he'd been able to gather, they alternated Sundays when they worked, and McPherson also closed some of the less frequented buildings in the Mill. This way there were enough employees to go around, but no one had to work who strictly did not want to. Again, it reminded David that McPherson was a fair and compassionate employer.

Frank Black was older than David, in fact—he probably could have been David's dad. The whiteness of his hair and lines around his eyes attested to his age. From their earlier visit, David had learned that Frank worked full time into his sixties and then took a part-time job at the Mill over ten years ago. At the moment he was standing outside the mint distillery, and he'd put a Closed sign on the front door. The building wasn't part of the tour, but guests were able to walk the property and stop in if they were interested.

"Thanks for coming so fast."

"It's no problem at all."

"There are fumes coming from the distillery."

"Fumes?"

"Yes, and they are not natural fumes."

David studied the building and sniffed the air, trying to detect anything unusual. His wife had claimed he wouldn't be able to smell a skunk if it walked into the house and sat under their sofa. That might have been an exaggeration. Rebecca had burned the oatmeal just that morning, and he'd certainly smelled that.

"You're certain?"

"Worked in Indiana's largest mint distillery for over twenty years. Yeah, I'm certain."

"All right. Well, let's go in and see what we can find."

CHAPTER 5

A s soon as they walked into the main room, David's eyes began to water and shortly after that he felt rather light-headed. He waved to Frank that they should leave. Once outside, he pulled in several deep breaths of air.

"See what I mean?" Frank asked.

"*Ya.* Any idea what's causing it?"

"None." Frank fiddled with his glasses—behind them his blue eyes looked worried. "It's not a natural by-product of the distilling. I'd only just turned the machine on. Plus it's never happened before."

"Did you have a chance to look around?"

"No. By the time I recognized that something was wrong, the fumes were so strong that I had to leave."

At that moment Jimmy Cotton turned a corner round the pond and headed toward them on his riding lawn mower. Jimmy was an *Englisch* teenager who mowed the areas bordering the dirt path, as well as the walking areas around the pond and through the cultivated fields. He mainly worked after school and on Saturday.

David held up his hand, and Jimmy stopped.

The boy was all arms and legs with a good deal of acne thrown in. David didn't envy him that time of life, though he could have told him it wouldn't last. He had good years ahead of him.

Jimmy shut down the motor and pulled out the earbuds that he always wore. Perhaps it helped to shut out the noise of the mower, though the raucous music David heard coming through the small device sounded worse than a mower to him.

"Hi, Jimmy. Could I borrow your—" He put his hand over his nose and mouth to indicate that he wanted the mask Jimmy was wearing.

"This? We're not supposed to use each other's."

"*Ya*, that makes sense, but there's a problem in the mint distillery. I need to cover my mouth and nose . . ."

Jimmy wasn't listening. He'd hopped off the mower, pulled up the seat, and was digging through the items in the storage compartment. Finally he pulled out a package of face masks and handed a clean one to David.

"*Danki*."

"No problem." Without another word, Jimmy replaced his earbuds, started the mower, and drove away.

"Want me to go in?" Frank asked.

For a moment, David almost said yes. But then he remembered Frank was closing in on his eightieth birthday. While he might know what to look for, the dangers seemed too great.

"I'll just take a look around and then come back and describe it to you."

"Should we call the police or Bobo?"

"Not yet."

McPherson had been quite adamant that he did not want the police involved if it could be helped. Obviously if someone was hurt, they would need to file a report. Otherwise, he wanted David to handle things on his own and report back to him.

"Let me take a look first."

David placed the mask firmly over his mouth and nose and then walked into the distillery. He really had no idea what he was looking for. His eyes once again began to water, but he didn't feel light-headed as he had before. Walking through the main room, he saw nothing out of the ordinary. Then he moved to the room where the actual still was located.

He didn't know a lot about the process, though there were a few distilleries back in Wisconsin. He'd never been involved in harvesting or distilling any of the plants, and he had never tried to grow mint as a crop. His wife had a few spearmint plants here and there in her garden—claimed they helped keep insects away. That thought made him smile. Always Beverly's sweet memory seemed to hover around the edges of his life, comforting him when he needed it most.

He was certainly out of his comfort zone now.

But looking at the machinery, it seemed simple enough to him. Water was added to the bottom chamber of the still and fresh herbs were placed in the middle chamber. Glass tubing collected the steam. The end of the tube emptied the oil extracted into a jar. David didn't know all of this instinctively. Someone had put a flow chart on the wall, no doubt for the guests to read.

So what had gone wrong?

If it happened as soon as Frank turned the still on, then

the problem must be in the bottom chamber. There hadn't been enough time for any amount of oil to collect in the jar. He knelt next to the bottom chamber, pulled a handkerchief from his pocket, and dipped it in the liquid. By that point, tears were pouring from his eyes. He knew if he waited much longer, he'd be walking out unable to see a thing. He reached over, shut off the machine, and then hurried outside yanking off the mask as he pulled in a deep breath of the clean April air.

Frank waited while David flushed his eyes from an old hand pump located next to the building.

"Worse than peeling onions," David muttered.

"I thought Amish women did all the cooking." Frank's mouth twitched into a smile as he handed David a clean rag to blot his eyes.

"Often that's true, but during canning season? Any person not busy was fair game. My Beverly could be very persuasive on that point." David reached into his pocket and pulled out the handkerchief he had dipped into the bottom compartment of the still. "What does that smell like to you?"

David took a strong sniff, then held the cloth at arm's length, staring at it incredulously. "Vinegar. No doubt about it."

"I thought so. When you're close to the bottom chamber, the odor is quite strong."

"But I put water in that chamber not an hour ago."

"Explain to me your process."

"Each day after the last of the tourists come through, I fill the pail up with water. Then I do a test run for the next day's visitors. Once I see that everything is working as it should, I shut it down."

"But today everything wasn't working as it should."

"No. No, it wasn't."

"Someone substituted vinegar for your water. It must have happened sometime between when you filled the pail and when you started your test batch."

Frank adjusted his glasses, a look of worry on his face.

"What is it? What are you remembering?"

"I don't think I filled the chamber. I ushered the last visitor out, then hurried over to the barn for a bottle of water. There's a small refrigerator there where we keep drinks and such. My throat was dry from talking, and Bobo doesn't mind if I take a short break when needed."

"I'm sure he doesn't."

"When I returned, I went to put the water into the chamber, but it was already full." Frank shook his head. "I thought I must have done it before I left, but now I'm wondering . . ."

"Maybe someone did it for you. Only they used vinegar instead of water."

Frank glanced left and then right. "But why would anyone do that?"

"Couldn't say. Is there a lock on the door?"

"Yes. I don't use it unless I'm leaving for the day."

"Until you hear back from me, start using it whenever you're gone."

"All right. Thanks, David."

"No problem. I'm glad you called me."

David turned and headed toward the Mill's offices. His reports to McPherson were always verbal, as the man didn't want any records of what was going on—*not yet*, he had said.

His mind cataloged the events of the last few days. What was bothering him was not what *had* happened, but what *might* happen next. It seemed that their prankster had been working solely on the northwest side of the property, but he was now out of buildings. If he wanted to attempt new destruction, he'd have to move toward the center of the property.

And that could spell trouble for their guests.

CHAPTER 6

S tella couldn't remember a Sunday morning when she had felt so unsettled. It had all started when David Stoltzfus greeted her with a wide smile and a rousing "*Gudemariye.*" She'd nodded uncertainly and turned to hurry away, but not before she heard David telling his daughter, "Stella is *wunderbaar* with the tour groups. You should see her!"

What had gotten into the man?

Everyone knew that she led the tour groups and no one thought she did a *wunderbaar* job. At least no one had told her that before. David was new to the community. Maybe he didn't realize that she was the black sheep.

That thought popped into her mind before she could pull it back. Black sheep. Was that how she saw herself? It didn't help that the Scripture they read was Isaiah 53:6, "We all, like sheep, have gone astray," and then the sermon focused on hearing God's voice, for "He is the good shepherd."

It was David's fault that she was distracted throughout the entire service.

Did she see herself as a black sheep?

Because she couldn't have children?

They rose to sing. Stella's voice joined those around her. She tried to focus on the words, the tune, the rhythm of the praise to God. But still her mind wandered.

Certainly she wasn't the first woman with a barren womb, though perhaps most women didn't receive the news as young as she had. When she was seventeen and still showed no signs of having her monthly time, her mother had taken her to the doctor. He'd confirmed what Stella had already suspected—she was different. She would never be able to conceive children.

Though she'd barely begun seeing boys, she immediately stopped. What was the point? No Amish boy would want a barren wife. Perhaps *Englischers* could overlook such a thing. Over the years she'd noticed *Englisch* couples who had simply decided not to have children, but among the Amish, having a home full of children was very important. Who would be willing to marry her? *Nein.* She could not put someone else through such tragedy and disgrace. Or so she had thought then.

She sat as the singing ended, though she couldn't remember if they'd sung all the verses. Her sister looked at her curiously, but Stella simply shook her head and stared down at her open Bible.

Later, she'd received some attention from widowed men in the community, but she'd become set in her ways by that point—and perhaps hardened by some perceived rejections. Looking back, she'd never given anyone the chance to reject her.

She'd accepted her fate and decided she was to spend her life alone.

Had she been wrong?

Had she refused to listen to the voice of the Shepherd?

She brushed such foolish thoughts aside as they stood for the final singing. The next hour was spent helping to serve the food, and then suddenly she found herself sitting among the women, eating and listening to the chatter.

Tidbits were shared about their children, their grandchildren, even their nieces and nephews. Yes, the Amish life certainly centered on children. With a start she realized that Rebecca Hotstettler was talking to her, or about her.

"Ya, we never realized that Adam wasn't able to see. It was Stella who suggested *Dat* watch him read."

All eyes turned to Stella. She'd just popped a large bite of ham into her mouth and she had to chew around it and swallow before she could answer.

Finally it was Helen Miller, Ethel's mom, who said, "How curious that you would think of it, Stella."

"Yes, well . . ." She stared at her hands and then looked up, surprised to see several women smiling at her. "The guests at the Mill, sometimes the little ones will wear glasses. I saw one last week who couldn't have been three years old, sporting a bright pink pair that was fastened around her head with an elastic strap."

"You don't say?" This from her sister, Carolyn.

"Ya, surprised me too. Now and again I'll see one of the older guests peer at our pamphlets and then say they'd forgotten their glasses. I guess my mind put the two things together."

"I'm glad that you did." Rebecca wiped the mouth of one of the twin girls—was it Sophie or Emma? David had said that Sophie had a small birthmark on the back of her neck. Stella had an urge to ask to hold the child and check. She didn't of course. She rarely held children and probably wouldn't know how to do so properly.

The conversation had turned to happenings at the local schoolhouse, and Stella's mind drifted to other things. She finished her meal, then hurried over to lend a hand with the cleanup. She helped every week, since she had no family to tend other than her sister who was perfectly able to take care of herself. Carolyn was ten years older than Stella. Some days it seemed as if it had always been only the two of them at the old farmstead.

"If you're done wiping that already clean table I thought we might take a walk."

Stella looked up into David's blue eyes. He was holding one of the twins in each arm and had a diaper bag slung over his shoulder. She found herself at a complete loss for how to answer the man. All her usual sharp retorts simply deserted her. "Pardon?"

"The table—" David nodded at the makeshift table, a board that had been set across two sawhorses. "Looks clean."

"*Ya*. I suppose it is." She flicked the dishcloth across the plyboard one last time and tried to regain her composure.

"Would you care for a walk?" He juggled his twin granddaughters, who stared at her with wide blue eyes. "I thought I'd give Rebecca a bit of a break, but it doesn't seem to work unless I leave her immediate area. Otherwise she's wiping their faces, checking their diapers—"

"Being a mother hen."

"Exactly."

Before Stella could think of a reason to say no, David had thrust Emma into her arms. Certainly it was Emma as there was no birthmark below the hem of her *kapp*, and she could see Sophie's strawberry mark from where she stood.

"There's an old blanket stuffed in the diaper bag. I thought we could set the girls down under the shade of the maple tree— should be safe from the breeze there, too, since the barn will block the northern wind."

Stella nodded, completely distracted by the heavenly weight in her arms.

As they walked, she focused on holding the baby correctly. What she wanted to do was smell little Emma's neck, take off her socks and examine her toes, hold her close to her bosom. But she hadn't taken complete leave of her senses, so she chattered with David about the service and the food and then they were standing under the tree.

"Can you hold both while I—"

"Certainly." The two girls stared at each other and then at their grandpa. Sophie waved a pudgy hand at David while Emma proceeded to chew on Stella's *kapp* strings.

David spread the blanket on the ground and then turned to take Sophie. "All right. That should do it. Down you go, baby girl."

Stella sat on the blanket and placed Emma beside her sister. The girls lay on their backs, staring up at the new green leaves of the trees. Emma reached for her foot and attempted to pull it toward her mouth. David gave them each a toy from the bag he was carrying. Emma immediately tried to chew hers; whereas, Sophie pressed hers against her ear.

"I told you," David said, smiling. "It's as if Emma is exploring the world through taste—"

"And Sophie through sound."

"Exactly." David leaned back on his elbows.

Though Stella had spent a lot of time arguing with David Stoltzfus in her mind, she hadn't actually allowed herself to study him much. Now, with him preoccupied with the grandbabies, she did. His blue eyes were the color of the sky—clear and serene, if eyes could reflect such things. His beard was mostly gray, owing to his age, which he had told her was fifty-two, but his hair looked like that of a younger man. There was still more brown than gray. He was a few feet taller than Stella, probably topping her five-foot-six height by a good three inches. And although he wasn't thin, neither had he gained the large belly that many older men did.

There was a scar above his lip, and somehow it kept him from being too good-looking. It made him seem like a normal guy. She wondered how he'd come by it, but then felt foolish. She had no business asking David about his scars.

Out of the blue, David said, "Rebecca tells me you've never married."

"*Nein.*"

"It's a shame."

"I . . . I couldn't have children," she said, and then she wondered what had caused her to share such a thing.

"You would have made a *gut fra.*"

Stella shrugged and retrieved the rattle that Emma had tossed to the side. Perhaps it was because she was holding the little child's toy, or it could have been the way the sun was slanting through the leaves, but suddenly she wanted to know about David. She wanted to know his past, his joys, and his heartaches.

"Tell me about your *fra.*"

"Beverly?" The smile on David's face widened until his eyes were nearly closed. "We met when I first moved to Wisconsin, a lad of nineteen. Our family is originally from the Ohio area, but I set out looking for something different."

Stella nodded as if she understood.

"I suppose I found it, as Beverly was about as different as you could imagine. She had red hair for one—"

"That explains Rebecca's strawberry blonde."

"It does. Our boys—all five of them—"

"You had five boys?"

"*Ya.* A big group around the table, especially as they grew older and started to bring friends to dinner. Each of them, even Rebecca, had the reddish tint, which they inherited from their mother. Not a common sight in an Amish community."

Emma began to fuss, so Stella reached forward and picked up the babe. Such a simple thing to do, but she couldn't fathom that it came natural to her. She had helped with her nieces and nephews, but that had been years ago.

"Beverly was a *gut* wife, and I loved her dearly."

"What happened?"

"Cancer . . . of the ovaries. It's been five years now."

"I'm sorry."

"So am I. When one dies we say their life is complete, and I suppose hers was. She was happy and content, even through the final months." David leaned forward and caught Emma's foot causing her to laugh. "I think it helped that she was surrounded by her family—all of our *kinner* were home when she died. Their love comforted her, like a quilt on a cold winter's day."

Stella didn't respond. She could picture it—a redheaded

Amish woman, burrowed under a quilt and surrounded on all sides by her children.

"Your family has experienced its share of tragedy."

"I suppose, but then haven't we all?" David ran his hand over the top of Sophie's head. "I would never wish for my *doschder* to walk this road of single parenthood. But her husband's untimely death has brought me closer to these two."

"I'm surprised she didn't move back to Wisconsin."

David laughed at that. "Rebecca never was fond of the outhouses we still use."

"Understandable."

"It is. But more than that, I think she has come to see this community here in Nappanee as her home. She'd rather not take the twins away from Jacob's family, who have been a real help to her."

"And yet you felt the need to move here and help."

"I wanted to be with her during this time."

"How long will you stay?" The question popped out of her mouth before she could snatch it back.

"As long as I'm needed, I suppose."

Stella realized that was no answer at all. It could be a month or until the children were grown and married.

David was watching something over Stella's shoulder. He stood and said, "Rebecca's trying to get my attention. I suppose it's time to get these two gals home for their naps."

As they carried the babies and blanket and diaper bag back toward the main group, Stella thought of what a strange day it had turned out to be. She'd started the day feeling out of sorts, but now her mood was curiously relaxed—even after passing an hour with David Stoltzfus. Truly surprising, but then life had taken more curious turns. She supposed that the two of them could go back to being adversaries when they returned to work on Tuesday.

CHAPTER 7

Since the Old Mill was closed on Mondays, Stella spent the day at home helping Carolyn with the laundry and cleaning.

As they hung their clothes and sheets on the line, Carolyn said, "I noticed you enjoying some time with David."

"He needed help with the twins."

"I'm not criticizing you, Stella. It was *gut* to see you relaxing."

Stella sniffed. By the time she'd returned home from church, she'd come to her senses. No doubt folks were talking about what a fool she was—sitting alone with David on a blanket! Of course the twins had been there, but still, she wasn't sure it was entirely appropriate. What had caused her to say yes? She wouldn't fall for his smooth charm or blue eyes again. No, she'd be on her guard and keep a good, healthy distance from the man in the future.

But as she hung laundry, changed their bed linens, and scrubbed the bathroom, her mind kept returning to the feel of Emma in her arms, Sophie's sweet smile, and how David was completely smitten with his granddaughters. Even the young boy . . . what was his name? Adam. Even Adam had come up to her as she was leaving and given her a plate of cookies that his *mamm* had kept in her buggy.

"I go to the eye doctor next week," he said.

"Is that so?"

"*Ya. Daddi* says it will help me to read."

"I imagine it will."

"Have you ever worn glasses?"

"*Nein.*"

The boy frowned and stared at the ground.

"But my nephew does. He lives over in Goshen, and he's worn them for many years now."

"Can he still play ball?"

"Well he's a *dat* now and not quite as good with a bat and ball as he once was . . . but yes, he does still play with the *youngie*."

Adam's expression changed to one of relief. He thanked her and ran off toward his mother. She'd replayed the conversation in her mind several times and found herself praying that the boy's vision was easily corrected.

As she carried the mop to the back porch, she noticed Carolyn sitting at the kitchen table, the day's mail spread out before her.

"A letter from one of the girls?"

"*Ya.*" Carolyn regularly received letters from her children. The two girls wrote the most—they had married and moved to Pennsylvania. One son had purchased a farm in Goshen, and four other sons were in Ohio. Her family had spread out like so many leaves in the wind. Usually she shared the letters, but today she quickly folded the page and stuffed it under the pile of circulars. "Rebecca's cookies are *gut*—oatmeal and chocolate chip."

Stella poured a glass of milk and sat down across from Carolyn. "Are you looking forward to work tomorrow?"

"I suppose."

Carolyn leaned forward. "You don't have to continue to work, Stella. Not if you don't want to."

"I'm not shirking my responsibility."

"But it's not needed—not strictly speaking. We'd get by fine with what we make off the fields. The King boy—"

"He's past thirty, Carolyn."

"Yes, well, he tells me the yield will be *gut* this year. If you don't want to work you shouldn't."

Stella felt prickly again. It felt good, like putting on a pair of shoes that were worn out and comfortable. "And what of next year? If I quit my job and then we need income—"

"The Lord provides." Carolyn reached for another cookie. "As He has since we've been here alone."

How had that happened? Not so long ago the house had been filled with the sounds of her parents, Carolyn's husband, and their seven children. Carolyn's husband died of a heart attack—late one fall afternoon they'd found him in the fields, lying among the tall stalks of corn, his expression one of utter peace. Their parents had passed within a few months of each other. Now they were alone. So much for Amish families remaining close.

That was an uncharitable thought and she knew it. The children had been faithful to send money and they visited as often as possible.

It wasn't their fault that they had a widowed mother and an old-maid aunt living back at the farmstead.

Some days it seemed to Stella that she had been a burden to

others all of her life. She sighed and pushed away from the table. "The last of the laundry should be dry. I'll fetch it."

"Before you go . . ." It wasn't like her sister to hesitate when she had something to say. The oldest child in their family, Carolyn seemed more like a mother to Stella than a sister in many ways. They had four brothers between them—all now living in Ohio. How had their family become so scattered?

"I had heard there was some trouble at the Mill."

Stella felt her spine stiffen. "It's not like you to listen to gossip—"

"Honestly, Stella. You can be so sensitive sometimes." Carolyn broke her cookie in quarters and popped a piece in her mouth. "No one was gossiping. One of the women mentioned a chicken in the icehouse."

"A childish prank."

"And the switching of the restroom signs."

"I didn't see it myself."

"Also some nonsense with the brooms?"

Stella sighed. "I don't know. Maybe someone has spring fever. Maybe one of our boys is indulging their *rumspringa*."

"You think it's an Amish person?"

"Or maybe . . ." Stella clasped her hands and stared down at them. "Maybe it was an *Englischer* who doesn't like the horse droppings on the road or waiting behind a buggy driver."

"I know there have been some complaints, but nothing recently."

"No, it's been a while since the proposition to diaper our horses came before the city council."

"And it failed as it should. Our city leaders might not be Amish, but they seem to have a reasonable head on their shoulders." She finished her cookie and then asked, "So you have no idea?"

"I only lead the tours, Carolyn. I don't run the Mill."

"You're bright though, and you listen and pay attention. I'd think if anyone knew, you would."

Stella shrugged. She'd received more compliments in the last week than she'd been given in the last ten years. Or was she just now noticing them?

"*Danki,*" she said belatedly.

"Did you know about David's new job?"

"New job?" Stella's heart kicked into a faster rhythm. Was David leaving the Mill? Wouldn't he have mentioned it the day before?

Carolyn proceeded to tell her how he had joked about his "handyman" title and that he would be working in various positions as needed.

Stella didn't know what to make of that, so she repeated that she hadn't heard a thing and headed outside to retrieve the laundry.

She glanced back when she reached the door. Carolyn had pulled the letter out from the stack of mail and was once again lost in its contents.

What was in the letter that was of such interest to her?

And why would Bobo McPherson have given David a new job? He hadn't been at the Mill long enough to warrant a promotion. And anyway, handyman didn't sound like much of a promotion.

No, she suspected something else was going on. David's job had changed at the same time that the incidents were increasing.

That couldn't be a coincidence. So had McPherson asked David to spy on the other employees? And had he said yes?

The thought bothered her. She'd finally let her guard down. If she were honest with herself, she was beginning to like and trust David Stoltzfus. Now she didn't know what to do with this new information.

Of course it was none of her business—but then again in a small community, what affected one affected another. With that thought in mind, she determined that the next day she would begin her own private search for an explanation for the strange happenings occurring at the Mill.

CHAPTER 8

David was surprised when he looked up and saw Stella hurrying toward him. The day had turned cool for April and a light rain was falling.

He stepped onto the porch of the Oak Street House and waited for her. There was no doubt she was walking in his direction, unless she'd felt a sudden need to take a tour of the one-room schoolhouse, which was directly across from him. He couldn't think of a thing she'd want to see there or in the Oak Street House, which was a representation of one of the local homes from the 1800s.

"David, I wasn't sure I'd find you. Seems I was destined to lag ten minutes behind wherever you were—"

He was actually pleased that she was looking for him. Perhaps she had softened toward him after their walk on Sunday—though on Tuesday she'd refused to even return his greeting.

"*Ya*, they've had me quite busy today. A squirrel loose in the soda fountain shop, molasses spilled in the blacksmith shop . . ."

He pulled off his hat and scratched his head. That last one still made no sense to him.

"Word is that you have a new job title."

"Oh, that." David wondered how much McPherson would want him to share, but then this was Stella. Surely she needed to know what was going on. She led morning tours all over the property. Besides, nothing would remain a secret for long with so many employees. It was probably best she heard the details from him. "It's true, though I'm not sure how much help I am. Trouble seems to pop up in a different corner of the property faster than I can clean up after it."

"Trouble? What kind of trouble?"

They were standing near the porch rail, but now the light rain had turned to a downpour, and they stepped back at the same moment, their shoulders brushing up against one another. Stella took two steps away and repeated, "What kind of trouble?"

He told her about the previous incidents, and McPherson's idea that he might be able to fend off real trouble.

"He wants you to spy on employees?"

"*Nein.* That's not it at all. It's only that he thought I could see things more objectively. Honestly, none of what has happened makes any sense to me. It's all very random. My guess would still be the *youngie.*"

"Amish?"

"Or *Englisch.* I couldn't say."

Stella folded her arms across her chest. "I'm glad I asked. It seems to me that you need the insight of someone who has lived here awhile, someone who could make connections you couldn't possibly know about. I might be able to help."

"Help is one thing I can always use."

"I'll keep my eyes open on my tours."

"And during your shifts in the bakery. Perhaps our culprit has a sweet tooth."

Stella gave him a reproving look. He wasn't surprised that she was taking the situation seriously. He tended toward a more casual outlook. Other than the vinegar in the distillery, it didn't seem to him that anyone was causing any real harm. There were certainly plenty of worse things that could have happened.

As if to prove his line of reasoning wrong, the day took a drastic turn. At that very moment, shouts and cries rang out from across the lane.

He and Stella both stepped forward and saw young Ethel Miller standing inside the schoolhouse with her face pressed against a pane of glass in one of the schoolroom windows. She was hollering and waving her arms, apparently trying to get their attention.

Without another word, they both began running through the rain. Stella ran up onto the front porch of the schoolhouse. David hurried to the side window where Ethel continued to holler. He ignored the rain that was falling in sheets, soaking him through to the bone.

"What's wrong?" he shouted.

"The doors. They're stuck! We can't get out."

"Front door?"

"Won't budge."

"How about the back?"

Ethel shook her head. Now that he was closer, he could see the guests behind her. Some stood in groups, looking perplexed.

Others were trying to open some of the windows, but the humidity had caused the old wooden casings to swell.

He hurried back to the front porch. Stella was rattling the door. "It seems to be stuck."

"Not stuck, jammed." David knelt in front of the lock. "Look. Someone has locked the mechanism and then broken off a piece of metal inside of it. We'll need a locksmith."

"How are we going to get them out?"

David shrugged. "I'll check the back."

What he found there caused his blood to boil. Someone had taken a rope and tied one end to the doorknob, the other end to an old water pump that was beside the porch but toward the front of the house. The result was a tension in the rope that couldn't be lessened without disconnecting the rope. No wonder they couldn't open the door. David pulled out his pocketknife. It took several moments to saw through the rope, which was new and stiff. By the time Stella had joined him at the back door, the rope had surrendered to his knife's blade.

The door opened easily, and he stepped inside.

Ethel hurried over to speak with them. "I don't know what happened. We came in and everything was fine."

"This is not acceptable." One of the male guests stepped forward and interrupted them. "My name is Ethan Avery, and you can be sure I will be contacting the city and possibly the police about this."

Two more families approached him, and from the corner of his eye, David saw an older woman walking in through the back door.

"I was in the outhouse. What happened?"

"We were locked inside, if you can you imagine that." This from an *Englisch* grandmother who wore a T-shirt that said *I'm a grandma. What's your superpower?*

"It's nothing to worry about, Mrs. Benson." Stella hurried over to the older woman with long gray hair pulled back with a simple band.

David noticed she was a small thing, rather like a bird. He also noticed the thin scar along her neck. His *aenti* back in Wisconsin had one of those from when her thyroid was removed.

"I didn't know you were visiting us today," Stella said.

"Is that a crime? I suppose I can visit any day I want."

"Yes, of course you can."

"Why would anyone do such a thing?" Mr. Avery was still standing directly in front of David, as if to block his exit. He pulled out his cell phone and began to tap away. "And why would you allow it?"

"I can't say as we're allowing it." David worked to keep his tone pleasant.

"Hoodlums probably. You can't win against people like that." This from Mrs. Benson. "I only went to visit the outhouse— which you have remodeled nicely, I might add. Still, I could have been locked out from the group, and you all could have been locked inside for hours. The world is a dangerous place."

Stella attempted to reason with the guests, but David stepped to the front of the room and held up his hands. "We're sorry for any inconvenience and hope that you have enjoyed your time here at the Mill."

"We were locked inside a one-room schoolhouse. I wouldn't call that enjoyable, and I still want to know how such a thing could have possibly happened." Mr. Avery finished tapping on his phone and stuck it back into his pocket.

David began to answer, though he had no idea what to say, when he looked outside and saw that the motorized trolleys had arrived. They were only used during the rain or when they had a handicapped guest who needed transportation assistance. "Your ride is here and will take you back to the shop and bakery, and I'm happy to inform you it's a covered vehicle—so you'll be able to remain dry. Be careful as you leave that you don't slip in the mud."

The rain had lightened, but everyone still seemed appreciative for the ride. No doubt they were ready for hot coffee and pie.

David pulled out his walkie-talkie and called maintenance. When he finished speaking with them, he was surprised to see that Stella was still there. He joined her at the window, watching the trolley make its way along the wet but still hard-packed dirt trail.

"These incidents—they're all connected," she said.

"Probably."

"Then we need to catch whoever is doing them. The Mill doesn't need this kind of publicity." She paused, tapping her fingertips against the windowsill, as if she needed to buy time. Finally she said, "Most people in Nappanee enjoy and support the Mill, but not everyone. We've had our fair share of battles over the years. I would hate to see this facility close over these sorts of incidents. More than half the employees are Amish. The jobs help our community."

"Why would we close?"

"The public's opinion is fickle and nothing stays the same in this life."

"The older woman you were speaking to—" David traced a finger across his throat, indicating her scar.

"Mrs. Benson."

"She seemed particularly upset. What's her connection to the Mill?"

"We used to see her a lot here on the property, but in the last few years, not as much. She's old and widowed. Perhaps she's bored."

"Idle hands—"

"Are the devil's playground. *Ya.* I heard that one too. But Mrs. Benson doesn't strike me as being capable of such things. No, I think it's being done by a person with a plan. Maybe someone wants to purchase the property to put up a new hotel. It seems I read about them wanting highway property. It could be that they offered to buy the place and the owners said no."

"Huh."

"Or maybe someone would like to build a golf course."

"Golfing?"

"There was a developer a few years back, he offered one of our farmers three million dollars for his eighty-acre property, but the farmer—who was Amish—turned him down. The developer did not accept losing gracefully."

David ran his thumbs under his suspenders. "I haven't thought about it to that extent. We didn't have much tourism in our Wisconsin community."

"Well it's big business here. Amish are big business whether we like it or not. Sometimes that's okay and we can live in harmony. But sometimes there is dissension between Amish and *Englisch.* Whenever that has happened—we always back off."

"Because we want to remain separate."

"Ya."

They were both silent for a few moments. When Stella turned and looked up at him, David felt something stir in his heart. There was a certain quality about Stella, a strength which might be disguised as bitterness. He thought that beneath the exterior shell was a beautiful and caring woman.

"I want to help," she said. "I care about this place and I want to help you catch whoever is doing this."

And so they became partners in solving the crimes at the Old Amish Mill.

CHAPTER 9

S tella met with David each day at lunch. He would share with her any odd events that had happened in the previous twenty-four hours, and they would try to discern any connection between them. It became the favorite part of her day, the hour that she looked forward to most.

The day after the schoolhouse incident the lights went out suddenly in the gift shop. Guests and employees were plunged into darkness until the breaker box could be located. They couldn't determine what had caused the breaker to flip.

"It might have been an accident," David said.

"Doubtful since we haven't had this many accidents in ten years." She felt as if a clock were ticking somewhere, ticking down to a terrible event that she couldn't imagine.

Things were quiet for the next three days. Though Stella remained worried, David began to think perhaps they'd imagined a conspiracy when there had been none.

"Perhaps it has simply been a run of bad luck," he said as they sat on a picnic bench sharing cheese and sausage and crackers.

She didn't answer him then. She was thinking how her life had changed since David came to work at the Mill. She found herself humming as she went about her tasks, and she was certainly less irritated by young Ethel. She had even sewn a spring dress to replace one of the old worn ones she should have cut up for quilt squares years ago.

She began to hope that perhaps her life had found some peaceful, natural pattern and maybe the problems at the Mill would disappear.

But the following week dispelled any possibilities of that.

The animals were let out of the hog house.

Bees were stirred up and chased one man across the property. Some of the bees had to be moved to a different hive as the first had been bludgeoned with a bat. They'd had to call in a beekeeper to relocate the queen.

The wooden hand pump, which connected the open well with the milk house, was broken in two. The basement of the house was flooded and one guest slipped on the steps, spraining an ankle.

"Perhaps it's time to file a report with the police," she suggested.

David stared down into his cup of coffee. "That's McPherson's decision. I don't know that we need more folks traipsing around watching us work though. There are city officials here nearly every day now. You can't walk ten minutes without tripping over someone with a city badge and a clipboard."

David's mood was sour, which was unusual. She wanted to reach out and touch his shoulder, to comfort him somehow, but she didn't.

Instead she said, "We simply need to look over all of your reports one more time."

"Sure. You're right." He looked at her and smiled, and all was right with her world in spite of the mysterious happenings.

"I'll bring them tomorrow, to lunch. Maybe you can spot something I haven't been able to see."

That luncheon was destined not to happen though. They had barely sat down to eat the next day when David's walkie-talkie suddenly squawked and a grim voice came over the line. "David, I'm at the back of the wetlands." Sixty-five acres had been set aside for a Federal Wetlands Reserve. Several times a week, Joe Briar led a group of bird watchers along a trail through the area.

"We have a fire here. I've contacted the fire department. I need you to get the trolleys over here so we can evacuate these folks. Do it fast."

David began to run toward the maintenance building where the trolleys were kept. Already Stella could hear the sirens of the fire engines coming down the road. She stood there, helpless, and watched David jump on one of the trolleys and begin to drive it toward the fire. It wasn't natural to run toward a fire— that was something you ran away from. Why did he have to be the hero? Why couldn't he have sent someone else?

Though they'd had rain recently, the grasses were high on that portion of the property. She'd once seen a grass fire, and it had burned incredibly fast. Already David was a mere dot in the distance as folks began to come out of the building to see what the sirens were about.

A part of Stella's heart ached even as her pulse raced.

Why had she let herself care about this man?

What if something happened to him?

What if she was once again plunged into the loneliness and bitterness that had defined her life before?

Stella hurried to the bakery, assured customers that the fire was on the other side of the pond and they were safe. She filled orders and made change and wiped down shelves. She did her job, and as she worked she allowed doubt and fear to seep in and control her outlook.

She'd made up her mind by the time she walked to her buggy. Employees were abuzz with news of the fire, which had been put out by the local fire department. No one was hurt, but Ethel had heard one of the city officials tell McPherson that if another incident occurred, the place would be shut down. They cited all sorts of city ordinances as well as a few OSHA regulations. Stella didn't even know what OSHA was until someone pointed out the poster in their workroom. Occupational Safety and Health Administration. She wondered if OSHA would help them find new jobs.

Another nail of fear slammed into her thoughts.

Another part of her heart turned back toward expecting little from life but trouble and heartache.

It was then David caught up with her, as she was about to climb into her sister's buggy—her *sister's*. She'd never even owned her own horse. Her entire life had been possible solely because of the charity of others.

David had soot smudged across his face. Dirt marked his sleeves and pants. She could make out a small blister on the back of his right hand. And still he smiled.

That smile sealed their fate.

She understood in that moment how different they truly were.

"I wanted to catch up with you. Let you know everything is fine."

She nodded but didn't answer, didn't trust herself to speak.

"One more thing to add to our analysis of events, which I suppose we'll have to postpone until tomorrow."

"I can't—"

He stopped talking, cocked his head, and studied her.

"I'm busy at lunch tomorrow." She wasn't but she could be. It wasn't exactly a lie.

"Oh. Maybe afterward then."

She shook her head. How could she explain to him what she'd been through the last four hours? He'd been fighting a fire and she'd dismantled her life, seeing what a fool she had been to think that she could start over.

"What's wrong, Stella?" David stepped closer.

Stella stepped back, bumping into the side of the buggy. "I have to stop seeing you."

"Seeing me?"

"The lunches . . . the shared rides home . . . the walks after church. It all has to stop."

"Stop?" He took off his hat now and ran his fingers through his hair.

She'd noticed it was something he did when he was stumped. The look on his face almost made her relent, but she closed her eyes and resolved to hold firm. "I have to go, David."

He reached for her arm, and she practically batted him away.

"If you have to go, okay. But tell me what's wrong. Tell me what's happened since I saw you four hours ago."

Tears stung her eyes, and when she tried to speak, words caught in her throat.

"I can see you're upset. Let me help."

"You can't help me. Don't you understand? I'm hopeless." When he tried to argue, she held up a hand. "I'm not one of your projects, David. I'm not a puzzle you can solve. I'm a woman, and though my life might not be good, it is my life. It's what I have, what I've always had, and I was foolish to think that things could change now."

"But they can change "

"They cannot!" Her voice rose in anger, and she fought to bring it back down. "You are an old fool, and I almost followed you down some reckless path. We're not *youngie*. We're old, David. Now I don't want to talk about it, and I don't want to see you again unless it's in passing. Please, just leave me alone."

Stella hopped into the buggy, released the brake, and called out to the mare. As she made her way across the property and out onto the two lane, she swiped at the tears running down her cheeks. Pain was something she was used to. It was hope that was difficult to bear.

She stared straight down the road and didn't give David even one backward glance.

CHAPTER 10

Aweek later David still had no idea why Stella wasn't speaking to him. He gave her space, as it seemed that was what she wanted. But he thought of her constantly. He wondered if he had said or done something to hurt her. He prayed that God would soften her heart.

On Friday he was once again late leaving work. They were all under increased pressure from city officials, and he had been called a dozen times to different buildings by disgruntled employees. Mostly people wanted assurance that they were following the city ordinances to the letter, and in the majority of cases they were.

But the officials that he and McPherson had spoken with weren't concerned with the intent of their laws. They were in full defense mode, and they were combing over the ordinances carefully, looking at anything that could possibly be perceived as noncompliance.

An Exit sign with a flickering bulb.

Emergency exit plans that had grown a bit faded or were not displayed as prominently as a fire chief might suggest.

A step that wasn't marked with caution tape.

Any of several dozen rules could sink them. The sad part was that David had been into other establishments that didn't do half of what they had done to ensure employee and guest safety. But the other establishments weren't the ones under the microscope. The Old Amish Mill was. If they had any hope of staying open, then they had to persevere through this difficult time and do so together.

He stopped to drop off his report for the day—they were now filing everything on triplicate paper forms so that they would have back-up evidence of all they'd done to comply with the city regulations.

He neatly wrote down the day's activities, then signed the sheets and put them in McPherson's mailbox. His own box was typically empty, as folks usually just called him on the walkie-talkie. But when he glanced over at it, he saw a single envelope with his name scrawled in black ink on the outside. Turning it over, he was surprised to see it was sealed.

He broke the seal, pulled out the paper, and then sank into a chair as he read the seven lines.

> I told you that you couldn't win.
> Go home, David. Go to New York.
> Immerse yourself in your plain and fancy life.
> Even Joseph Stein can't rebuild what has been destroyed.
> It is time for these acres to lie fallow.

It is time for a genuine jubilee.
It is time for the soil to rest.

He read the note again, but it made no sense. Perhaps Stella could make sense of it. Though she still remained angry at him, more like her old self than the woman who had been helping him these last few weeks, he felt a strong desire to show it to her and to ask her opinion.

He glanced out the window. Sunlight faded across the fields and darkness pushed its way over the land. The day had slipped away. He would be walking home again, and his route happened to go directly by Stella's farm.

He tucked the letter into his pants pocket and hurried out into the night. The miles fell away as he thought of the words written on the sheet of paper. Why address it to him instead of McPherson? The first line, "I told you that you couldn't win," made it sound as if he knew the person. Could he have met the person responsible for the recent destruction at the Old Amish Mill?

He turned down Stella's lane and nearly changed his mind. A single light shone from a back window. Perhaps she'd gone to bed early. Maybe she was sick. Should he be bothering her? She had said she didn't want to see him anymore except in passing.

But this was different.

Even as his mind struggled with the wisdom of visiting Stella, his feet hurried down the lane and up the steps of the front porch. He knocked softly on the door and waited. A lantern was lit in the front room, and then the door opened, but it was Carolyn who answered.

"David. Is something wrong?" She held up another small battery-powered lantern to get a better look at his face.

"Yes. Maybe. Is Stella here? I'd like to speak to her."

Carolyn glanced over her shoulder and then back at David. "She's here, but . . ." Carolyn pushed the screen door open and then stepped onto the porch.

She walked to the railing, set the lantern down, and stood facing out toward the night. Carolyn was in her sixties and her skin was wrinkled from years of being in the sun, of being a farmer's wife. There was a softness about her though. She seemed a gentle soul. David wondered about their life here—two women living alone. Were they content? Did they have other options?

When David joined her at the railing, she glanced up at him. Her arms were crossed but a smile played across her lips. David thought her expression was tinged with sadness, but he could have been imagining it.

"Stella's life has been difficult."

David didn't know how to respond to that, so he remained silent.

"She told you why she never married?"

He nodded, and then added, "Weeks ago. That first Sunday she sat with me and helped with the twins. Such a thing though—it doesn't matter at our age."

"Indeed. And yet after she learned that she couldn't have children, when she was only a young woman, she withdrew from life. Stella practically embraced being alone, and she cultivated a bitter attitude." Carolyn ran her hand back and forth across the porch railing. "Perhaps that was my fault. I was already married with a houseful of *kinner*. I must have been a daily reminder of what she'd never have."

"*Gotte's wille,*" David said softly, because he felt he should say something.

"I suppose. And yet a difficult path, especially for one so young. She lived with my parents—here. Then as they grew older, my husband and I moved here to help with the land. We'd been leasing a place on the other side of town."

Carolyn's voice had grown soft, and David knew she was remembering that other place, her husband, and the sound of small feet running through the house.

"For many years, this house was full of life and laughter and even some sadness. But we had each other to lean on. The last few years—well, they have been filled with loss. First my husband, then our parents. By then, my daughters and sons had married and moved to farms of their own. And so it's been just me and Stella."

David's mind and imagination easily captured the scenes that Carolyn was describing, but another part of him was thinking of the letter in his pocket. He needed to speak with Stella.

"I've enjoyed Stella's friendship," he said. "She's a special woman, and I do . . . I do care for her. I thought maybe she cared for me, but the last few days she has been—"

"Afraid. She has been afraid, David."

Any response stuck in his throat. He finally managed to ask, "Of what?"

"Of being left alone again. Of caring too much. Of seeing yet another life slip through her fingers." Carolyn's head bowed for a moment, perhaps in prayer. Finally she turned to him, patted his arm, and then asked, "Are you sure you want to come in?"

Her eyes sparkled with good humor, and David found himself smiling and following her into the house.

They walked through a sitting room that was immaculate, something he could see even though the lamp was set to low and cast shadows across the floor. He thought of his daughter's house, of the chaos and liveliness there. Of the laughter and tears and small arms clasped around his neck. Would Stella want to share that life with him? Would she be willing to trade this for that? The thought should have surprised him, but he knew in that moment that he had been considering it for weeks. He'd even gone as far as to speak with his daughter. She was keen on him pursuing the relationship. David had been on the verge of doing just that when Stella had broken off their friendship.

Maybe she'd been able to sense his growing feelings for her. She was a perceptive woman. Maybe his feelings had frightened her.

What did he actually have to offer her?

And how could he banish her fears?

Then they entered the kitchen, and Stella looked up from her needlework. Perhaps she hadn't heard his knock. Maybe she didn't realize her sister had stepped outside. For whatever reason, her expression was one of complete surprise and even joy at seeing him. Then her mind caught up with her heart, and it was as if a shade was quickly pulled down over her features.

David knew in that moment that if he was to win Stella's heart, it would not be easy. In fact, only God could cut through such deeply ingrained fear and heartache. Their road might be tough. But then, much of what was worth having was difficult to come by. Fortunately, David was a patient and persistent man.

CHAPTER 11

Stella carefully stored her needle into the pillowcase she was embroidering for her niece. She didn't look up at David again. She couldn't find the courage to meet his gaze.

Carolyn said, "I'll be in the sitting room if you need me."

And then Stella was left alone with the man who had filled her thoughts for days.

Her cheeks burned with embarrassment. "Why are you here?"

"Because I needed to see you." He hesitated and then motioned toward the chair across from her.

She nodded, though she still had trouble meeting his eyes. Instead she glanced around the kitchen, her sister's kitchen. Her eyes landed on the dish drain. It held two plates, two forks, and two knives. Suddenly she remembered something her mother had often said. "Mistakes are like knives—they serve you or cut you, depending on how you use them."

She remembered her mother—her kindness and wisdom. She thought of how much she cared for David, and how embarrassed she would be to apologize. But what was more important?

Her pride? Or her future? She knew what she should do, and she prayed God would give her the courage to say what needed to be said.

"I'm sorry. I'm sorry I spoke to you as I did. I was cruel and ungrateful, and I wish that I would learn to hold my tongue." She stopped, wondering if she'd said too much.

But David merely smiled, reached across the table, and covered her hands with his. "We're all allowed a bad day, Stella. I want us to be friends, to be more than friends if you want the truth."

Her eyes widened, but David only laughed. "And if you can not be honest with me when you're having a bad day, then who can you be honest with?"

She shook her head. "But that doesn't excuse—"

"You apologized, and I accept your apology. What more is there to say?"

She only stared at him, her heart tapping out a too-fast rhythm. Then David's face turned serious, and he pulled an envelope from his pocket.

"But tonight I came here for a different reason. There's something I want to show you."

She studied the outside of the envelope as well as the note. She read it twice, then a third time. Finally she pointed toward the first line.

I told you that you couldn't win.

"Perhaps this person has spoken to you before."

"Maybe. I can't remember. There's something in the back of my mind, but I can't put my finger on it."

"And this—" She tapped the second line.

Go home, David. Go to New York.

"It's curious since you're not from New York. Everyone knows you're from Wisconsin."

"Maybe not everyone."

"Our community isn't so large," she reminded him. "But look . . ." She turned the page around so that he could better see it and she was reading upside down.

"This next line—*plain and fancy life*—has to be speaking of the musical. The writer is speaking of the show that is performed in the Round Barn each evening."

"And Joseph Stein?"

"The author of the original book—*Plain and Fancy*."

"I haven't read it," David admitted.

"The show is a big success in *Englisch* circles."

"Is it now?"

"*Ya*. Auditions for the cast are actually held in New York City."

"Now you're pulling my beard."

"I'm not. The casting auditions have always been in New York. They bring in some of the best talent in the country."

"To perform at our little Round Barn?"

Stella laughed. "It's odd, I'll admit, but as we know, Amish tourism can bring big money to a community."

She tapped the words *New York* on the note. "Perhaps the play explains the reference."

David sat back and ran his fingers through his beard. "I haven't seen the play myself, but these last four lines—they don't seem to be referring to a play. They seem to speak of something else entirely."

Stella stood, murmured, "Wait here," and hurried from the

room. When she returned she was carrying a well-worn Bible. "It's in Leviticus. I'm sure of it, but I can't remember the chapter or verse."

"The year of jubilee."

"*Ya.* Exactly."

He moved next to her, his fingers following hers down the page until they both paused over the tenth verse of the twenty-fifth chapter. "Consecrate the fiftieth year and proclaim liberty throughout the land to all its inhabitants. It shall be a jubilee for you, each of you is to return to your family property and to your own clan."

Stella sank into the chair beside him. For a moment neither of them spoke, and then she asked, "Do you usually check your mailbox at night?"

"*Nein.* Most days, I do so first thing in the morning, but I was late turning in my report, and then as I put the report into McPherson's box I noticed the letter in mine."

"So whoever did this, whoever left it, didn't expect for you to find it until tomorrow morning."

They stared at one another, realization dawning in Stella's mind at the same time that David stood, nearly knocking over his chair.

"We have to get to the theater."

"We can take my buggy."

"I'll go and hitch it up."

Carolyn said she'd stay up until they returned and spend the time praying for their safety.

It was with her sister's words of comfort echoing in her mind that Stella climbed into the buggy beside David. Though it was Carolyn's buggy, David drove. And when they reached the end of the lane, she pointed in the opposite direction of the Mill.

"There's a phone shack only a quarter of a mile down the road."

David nodded in agreement, but when they'd reached it, he didn't call the police. It didn't seem they had enough to go on yet—only suspicions and weakly drawn conclusions. Instead he dialed McPherson's number, which he'd memorized the day he'd first taken on his new job as handyman.

"What did he say?" Stella asked as they hurried back to the buggy.

"He'll meet us at the theater. He knows someone on the police force, a friend of his. Said he'd ask this man to meet us there as well."

As the mare clip-clopped down the road, forcing them to slow down when Stella would have liked to run, she again remembered her sister's words. *I will pray until you return.*

She would do well to follow Carolyn's example. So she did. As David drove the buggy she prayed for their safety, for the well-being of the guests watching the play in the Round Barn Theater, even for the misguided person who was causing such trouble. Finally she prayed for David and Mr. McPherson and his officer friend and herself.

David pulled the buggy to a stop at the side of the theater. By the time Stella hopped out and shut the door, feeling remarkably younger than her fifty years, he had already wound the horse's lead around the hitching post.

"Wait here for McPherson."

"*Nein*. I'm going with you."

"Stella, I need you to wait here." David put his hands on her shoulders, and then he did something she did not at all expect. He leaned forward and brushed his lips against hers. When he spoke again his voice was husky and tender. "Wait for McPherson. Tell him I went inside to search for this person. I need you in my life, Stella. Promise me you won't go inside and confront this man."

She nodded mutely, the blood rushing to her ears and her heart hammering faster than the wings of a hummingbird in flight.

David squeezed her hands, and then he turned and walked into the theater.

CHAPTER 12

Within minutes Stella came to her senses. She'd let herself be swayed by a kiss! Why had she promised to stay outside? What good could she do out here?

She paced back and forth beside the buggy, and then McPherson pulled his car to a stop next to her. He was followed by a Nappanee officer who was in uniform but driving his personal vehicle. The two men hurried over to her.

"Where's David?"

"Inside. We think, that is to say, we're certain someone is going to interrupt the play, maybe even hurt some of the guests in the process. There was a letter, and—"

"I trust your and David's judgment." McPherson turned to the officer.

Stella could see his name tag now that he'd walked closer under the eaves of the building where there was soft lighting. Dark-skinned with a perfectly bald head, Officer Parris was approximately the same age as McPherson. He nodded at Stella in greeting, then said, "I suggest that we pull the fire alarm and get everyone out of the building."

"But what if . . . what if we're wrong?"

"If we find no danger, then the show can continue. But we err on the side of safety."

McPherson was already moving toward the front door when the sound of a small explosion boomed from inside, followed by gasps from the audience. All three of them ran into the building.

"What was that?" McPherson asked an usher.

"Fireworks, sir. Apparently they've been added to the play."

"No. They haven't."

McPherson opened the inner door to the theater and strode inside.

Parris stepped closer to Stella. "Go back to the front door. Hold it open and help usher people outside."

Then he walked over to the red fire alarm handle on the wall and pulled it down. Immediately the building was filled with a bright strobe light and a piercing siren. Stella clapped her hands over her ears and rushed to the front door.

By the time she pushed it open, people were already streaming out of the building. She was relieved to see they remained fairly orderly. The workers in the theater must have been trained to handle just such an emergency. Some helped the guests. Others were already standing a good distance away, waving flashlights and directing people to stand behind a fire lane. Stella was so focused on the scene across the parking lot that she almost missed the man carrying some sort of messenger bag.

Why would someone carry such a large tote bag to a play?

Why was he wearing a floppy waterproof hat when the weather had been clear?

She watched him clutch the bag to his chest.

As Stella watched, he looked left, then right, and then pivoted and moved back into the building, working his way against the throng of people. Stella glanced around, hoping she would see David or McPherson or Officer Parris. But there was no one—only a mob of guests and employees who were helping them outside.

She couldn't let this man walk away.

What if he was going back inside to finish what he'd started? If she didn't stop him now and he *was* the person bent on the destruction of the Mill, he'd just move on to his next plan, and it could be worse than this one. She thought of her promise to David, but if she stayed outside someone could be hurt. Wondering if she'd taken complete leave of her senses, she stepped away from the door and followed the man back insided.

He moved toward the south side of the building where the actors changed costumes and applied their makeup. There were no crowds here. She waited until she saw him go through the door that led to a staircase. Stella had been to the theater many times, sometimes filling in for someone who couldn't work their shift. The staircase led up into the rafters. It was where the stage crew worked on any lighting problems.

Giving him a head start so he wouldn't see her, she followed him through the door and then crept up the stairs. As she reached the top, she saw him drop the bag he was carrying onto the floor and then unzip it. It seemed to be filled with packages of fireworks. As she watched, he pulled out two, and proceeded to light them with a lighter from his pocket. He peered over the balcony to make sure no one was looking up at him, and then he dropped the lit fireworks onto a seat beside him where they began to smolder, small flames licking up. Quickly he pulled two more from his tote and began the same process again.

"Someone help! He's up here trying to light the place on fire," Stella screamed.

The arsonist turned to look at her, and Stella stumbled backward, unable to believe what she was seeing—the man they had been chasing wasn't a man at all. The arsonist was a woman, and someone that Stella knew. Regaining her balance, she rushed forward and attempted to knock the fireworks out of the seat and onto the floor. She was terrified the floor would catch fire, but certainly it wouldn't combust as quickly as fabric. She stomped on them, wondering if they would burn through the soles of her shoes.

At that moment, David burst through the door.

The arsonist attempted to run past him, but David was bigger and quicker. He blocked the exit, snatched the firecrackers away, and began to stomp on them. If he was surprised to see the arsonist was Mrs. Benson, he didn't show it.

"Watch her!" he called out as he took off his jacket and slapped it against the seat cushions, which had continued to smolder. "Don't let her leave."

Stella wasn't sure how she was supposed to stop her. The woman had fallen into a seat when David snatched the fireworks away, but now she had righted herself and was attempting to flee. Unsure what else to do, Stella began to scream and wave her arms. She must have looked positively crazy, for Mrs. Benson backed away and looked around furtively for another exit.

The area filled with the smell of singed upholstery and carpet. Unable to escape, Benson was attempting to light yet another firecracker, but now McPherson and Parris were rushing through the door. They quickly assessed the situation, strode over to the culprit, and snatched away the rest of the explosives.

As the older woman reached for her nefarious supplies, the hat fell off and gray hair straggled down around her face. She scowled and pursed her lips, accentuating the roadmap of wrinkles. Raising her chin in defiance, Stella could clearly see the scar on Mrs. Benson's neck as the red emergency lights continued to pulse.

"Get your hands off me. You're ruining everything. Stop. Just stop."

"You're under arrest for violation of the city fire code, among other things." Parris pulled a set of handcuffs from his pocket and slapped them on the older woman's thin wrists. "You have the right to remain silent when questioned. Anything you say or do may be used against you in a court of law. You have the right to consult an attorney . . ."

His voice faded as he marched her down the stairs.

Stella collapsed onto a stool.

"You were going to stay outside," David said, but the smile on his face told her he was proud of her actions.

"I promised I would, and I meant to. Then I saw him . . . I mean to say her . . ."

"The woman from the schoolhouse."

"*Ya.* Mrs. Benson."

"The woman with the scar?"

"The same. She used to be a regular around the Mill, but I hadn't seen much of her in the last few years."

"Until recently."

"Yes, she'd begun showing up again, like she did the day at the schoolhouse." Stella paused, shook her head, and said, "After Parris pulled the fire alarm, I saw her sneaking back into the building. Who goes into a building that might be on fire?"

"It's a good thing you followed her," McPherson said. "Parris and I found the firecrackers on the stage the ones that the guests thought were part of the show."

"Apparently they were meant to be a distraction." David shook his head in disbelief. "The real damage was going to be done up here."

"If she had succeeded in lighting more of them . . ." McPherson wiped at the sweat on his face. "This is a sixty-foot, self-supporting wood dome, and it's a historical treasure."

He glanced from Stella to David. "I don't know how to thank you."

"Keep the Mill open," David said.

Stella nodded in agreement. "That will be thanks enough."

CHAPTER 13

David drove Stella home that night, and even took Carolyn's buggy on to his daughter's house when Stella insisted. "You shouldn't be walking down the road this late in the evening. What if . . . what if something happened to you?"

He'd kissed her again, like he had outside the Round Barn Theater, and he'd taken the horse and buggy on home. He also made sure he returned it the next morning in plenty of time for her work shift. Driving her to the Mill was a pleasure, and David could imagine doing it every day. He realized anew that Stella had captivated his heart.

But he took things slowly.

The Mill had temporarily closed while the police processed the crime scene. Within forty-eight hours of the incident, the Mill reopened. The number of visitors had risen drastically in the days following Mrs. Benson's capture. Especially at the theater. No doubt the news stories had fanned the flames of curiosity.

David waited a week before asking Stella to share a lunch with him.

Ten days after that, he invited her to dinner at Rebecca's.

Within six weeks it was common to see them walking together after the church service.

Always he remembered Carolyn's words, her description of Stella's fear. "Of being left alone again. Of caring too much. Of seeing yet another life slip through her fingers."

He prayed that such fear would leave her heart and that she would be filled with God's peace. When he couldn't sleep, he pulled out his Bible and turned through its pages, searching for guidance. Often he found himself reading the first book of John, chapter four verse eighteen. "There is no fear in love. But perfect love drives out fear." He prayed that he could offer Stella the kind of love that would drive out a lifetime of fear. He prayed that she would lean on God's love, which was perfect.

And he continued to wait.

One night, while they were eating dinner with Carolyn, he shared the status of the case against Mrs. Benson. "As you know, the police have charged Gwyneth Benson with trespassing and intent to cause bodily harm."

"She's lived in this area all of her life," Carolyn said.

"I don't understand why she would do such a thing. What was she hoping to accomplish?" Stella stirred her bowl of stew, but didn't eat. Finally she placed her hands in her lap.

"She previously owned the southeastern portion of land, where the inn was built."

"That portion was purchased years ago," Carolyn said. "I don't remember the woman, but I do remember that we couldn't imagine what the Mill owners would do with so much land. We didn't envision the many buildings McPherson has added over the years."

"Her husband actually sold the land—something about back taxes that were owed. Over the years, she became convinced this was the reason for her financial problems. She has been a widow these past ten years, and apparently struggling both financially and emotionally."

"Why the reference to jubilee?" Stella asked.

"The fact that she left a note at all has convinced the district attorney that she isn't in her right mind. From what McPherson has told me, Mr. and Mrs. Benson moved here and purchased the land for a farm fifty years ago when she was a young woman of twenty-nine. The approaching anniversary was what made her decide to act now."

"What did she hope to accomplish, David?" Carolyn helped herself to another piece of cornbread.

"The closing of the Mill, I suppose. Somehow in her mind, she envisioned herself owning that land again."

"Will she go to jail?" Stella fiddled with her *kapp* strings.

"Due to her age and mental issues—which may be dementia of one sort or another—the prosecutor is recommending parole. Several of the local churches are reaching out to her, helping her with the home she's in—which has fallen into disrepair. They also are providing financial assistance to help her with groceries and utilities."

"But why did she focus on you? Why did she address the letter to you?"

David shrugged. "According to her statement to the police, she confused me with the man who had negotiated the original sale of the property. I suppose her dementia mixed everything up in her head. She thought if she could convince me to leave and reduce the flow of tourists, life would go back to the way it had been."

Silence followed for a few minutes, and then the conversation turned to crops and harvests and fall festivals, which were just around the corner. In one sense, it was hard for David to believe that he'd been in Nappanee for six months. In another sense, it felt as if he'd always lived there.

David continued to be patient, until he was certain that Stella was ready. He waited another month, which seemed to him like several months. Autumn arrived and the leaves began to fall. David waited until his heart wouldn't allow him to wait any longer.

And so it was that one evening, when the moon was high and the air held a pleasant coolness, that David asked Stella a very important question.

They were sitting on Rebecca's front porch, rocking Emma and Sophie, both girls wrapped in well-worn baby quilts.

The sun had set, leaving the sky softly colored with pink, purple, and gold. Behind him, in the house, David could hear Rebecca speaking with Adam as they washed dishes together.

"The glasses have helped?" Stella said.

"They have, and since two of the older boys in our district are now wearing them, he doesn't feel self-conscious about them."

"He'll have a *gut* school year."

"I think so."

Their rockers made a soft murmur against the wooden porch floor.

"All three of the children look forward to your visits. They've even taken to calling you *Mammi*."

Stella's smile widened. "Never a *mamm*, but now I'm a *mammi*. Sounds like a story from the Bible, even though it's not official."

"Let's make it official."

"What?"

"Marry me." David stopped rocking, moved Emma to his right arm and reached out with his left to claim Stella's hand. "Marry me, Stella. You know how I care for you, and Rebecca would be happy to have you here with us."

Stella slipped her hand out from under his, pretending that Sophie needed to be better covered. "Wouldn't she resent me? No one wants their mother replaced."

"You wouldn't be replacing Beverly." David paused. He'd learned it was best not to rush Stella, best to give her time.

Finally she asked, "Are you certain you want to marry again?"

David's laughter echoed through the night. "If you asked me that a year ago, even six months ago, I would have said no. I never planned to marry again, but then I also didn't plan to meet you. It seems that *Gotte* had different ideas for my future than I did."

"Six months ago, I never would have dreamed . . ." She stopped midsentence, shook her head, and stared down at the babe in her arms.

"For some widows, it would be the wrong thing to remarry," David admitted. "Some are quite content in their solitude."

"Like Carolyn."

"Yes, I suppose." David thought of the letters Carolyn had received from her daughter, asking her to move to Pennsylvania. She had not shared them with Stella, didn't want her sister to feel pressured to make any kind of change. He knew that Carolyn was content to be widowed, but she longed to be with her children and grandchildren. It was only her sense of duty to Stella that kept her at the old farmhouse.

"We may have strayed from the path I'd hoped this conversation would take." David stood and pulled his rocking chair around so that he was facing Stella. "I love you, Stella. And I would be honored if you would marry me."

When she looked up, David saw that his prayers had been answered. The expression of fear was gone, and in its place was one of joy.

Then she said "yes," and David shouted in celebration, waking both of the girls and causing them to fuss. Which was fine. The joys and trials of life made it rich, and he would be sharing them with the woman he loved.

When he'd come to work at the Mill, he never supposed that God would have a new life in store for him, but that was exactly what he'd received—a new life and a new love. He'd thought that stage of his life was over. Stella's smile assured him it wasn't. As to what would come next? He didn't have to worry about that. He'd learned that God held the future in the palm of His hand. All David had to do was prayerfully navigate each day.

DISCUSSION QUESTIONS

1. At the beginning of this story, Stella is a bitter person with a sharp tongue. As the story progresses, we learn more of her past and perhaps we understand how she came to be this way. Have you ever felt yourself fall prey to bitterness? If so, what things helped you to change back to the person God calls you to be?

2. At first the problems at the market are inconvenient, but not actually harmful. Soon they become more serious. We have things in our lives like that—habits and sins that seem to hurt no one, but soon become destructive. What does the Bible say about becoming a new creature?

3. David is willing to move to live with his daughter, to help her through a difficult time. He wants to care for her and support her as well as the grandchildren. In what ways can you support someone in your life?

4. The letter David receives refers to Leviticus 25:10. "Consecrate the fiftieth year and proclaim liberty throughout the land to all its inhabitants. It shall be a jubilee

for you; each of you is to return to your family property and to your own clan." Obviously the writer of the letter in this story has misconstrued its meaning. What could this verse possibly mean to us today?

5. David and Stella find that God has brought them together, though the path they've lived has curved and dipped and sometimes even reversed itself—in the end the path God laid out for them brought them to one another. Psalm 119:105 reminds us that "Your word is a lamp for my feet, a light on my path." Share three Bible verses that have helped you to follow God's path.

ACKNOWLEDGMENTS

This book is dedicated to my associate editor at HarperCollins Christian Publishers/Thomas Nelson, Jodi Hughes. Jodi is a real pleasure to work with. She answers my emails in a timely fashion, gives me good feedback, and maybe most importantly—laughs at my jokes. We also share a love of all things Miranda Lambert. Hugs to you, Jodi, and thank you for all you do to bring my fiction to readers.

Thanks also to my pre-readers: Kristy and Janet. You ladies were able to do this on a quick turnaround, and I appreciate that. I'd also like to thank my agent Steve Laube who guided me through the contractual aspects of this story and always provides judicious advice when I need it. A special thank you to the folks at Amish Acres who gave my husband and me our first real glimpse into Amish life. If you happen to be passing through northern Indiana, I encourage you to take a few hours to visit the Amish Acres facility in Nappanee.

And finally . . . *always giving thanks to God the Father for everything, in the name of our Lord Jesus Christ* (Ephesians 5:20).

Blessings,

Vannetta

ABOUT THE AUTHOR

PHOTO BY JASON IRWIN

Vannetta Chapman is author of the best-selling novel *A Simple Amish Christmas*. She has published over one hundred articles in Christian family magazines, receiving over two dozen awards from Romance Writers of America chapter groups. In 2012 she was awarded a Carol Award for *Falling to Pieces*. She discovered her love for the Amish while researching her grandfather's birthplace of Albion, Pennsylvania.

~⦿~

Visit Vannetta's website: www.vannettachapman.com
Twitter: @VannettaChapman
Facebook: VannettaChapmanBooks

SAUERBRATEN

Marinade:

- 1 roast
- 2 cups vinegar
- 1 tablespoon of salt
- $^1/_2$ teaspoon pepper
- 2 onions sliced
- 1 carrot sliced
- $^1/_2$ cup chopped celery
- 4 cloves
- 4 whole black peppers
- 2 bay leaves

S tanding time in marinade: 5–6 days, turn daily. Remove from marinade and throw marinade away. Sear meat with

3 tablespoons of shortening. Pour large can of beef broth over meat and simmer for 3 hours.

IN PAN, BLEND:

- · 5 tablespoons of melted butter
- · 5 tablespoons of flour
- · 1 tablespoon of sugar

Blend until smooth on low heat. Stir into simmering meat liquid. Continue simmering until tender.

*Note: Recommend serving potato dumplings by Panni with sauerbraten. They can be found in the international section at some grocery stores.

RECIPES FROM KATHLEEN FULLER'S
A Bid for Love

BUTTERSCOTCH PIE

For the Crust

· One 9-inch baked pastry pie crust

INGREDIENTS

· 2 tablespoons butter
· 1 cup firmly packed brown sugar
· $\frac{1}{2}$ cup hot water
· 2 large egg yolks
· 2 tablespoons all-purpose flour
· 2 cups evaporated milk
· 1 teaspoon salt
· 3 tablespoons cornstarch
· 1 teaspoon vanilla extract

- meringue (optional)
- whipped cream (optional)

To Prepare: Brown butter in a saucepan over low heat. Add brown sugar and hot water, being careful as it may spatter. In a separate bowl, blend egg yolks, flour, evaporated milk, salt, and cornstarch with a whisk or in a blender. Add milk mixture slowly and carefully to hot sugar mixture. Cook over medium heat until thick, stirring constantly. Remove from heat; add vanilla. Pour into crust and refrigerate until ready to serve.

For the garnish, top with meringue or whipped cream if desired.

*Recipe from *Me, Myself, and Pie* by Sherry Gore

Amish Caramel

- 2 c. white sugar
- 2 c. heavy cream
- 1 $^3/_4$ c. corn syrup
- 1 c. butter
- 1 tsp. vanilla

Boil together sugar, syrup, butter, and a little cream. While boiling, add rest of cream slowly. Don't allow to stop boiling. Boil until it forms a soft ball (236-240 degrees). Then add vanilla. Pour into a buttered pan. Cool. Cut into squares.

*Recipe from House and Hone, http://www.houseandhone.com/2011/12/hone-made-amish-caramel-yummy-treat.html

SIMON'S FAVORITE PEANUT BUTTER COOKIES

- 1 $\frac{1}{4}$ cups flour
- $\frac{3}{4}$ teaspoon baking soda
- $\frac{1}{4}$ teaspoon salt
- $\frac{1}{2}$ cup butter *or* margarine
- $\frac{1}{2}$ cup peanut butter
- $\frac{1}{2}$ cup granulated sugar
- $\frac{1}{2}$ cup packed brown sugar
- 1 egg
- $\frac{1}{2}$ teaspoon vanilla

Stir together flour, soda, and salt. In a mixer bowl beat butter for 30 seconds. Add peanut butter and sugars; beat till fluffy. Add egg and vanilla; beat well. Add dry ingredients to beaten mixture; beat until well combined. Shape dough into

1-inch balls; roll in granulated sugar, if desired. Place 2 inches apart on an ungreased cookie sheet; crisscross with the tines of a fork. Bake in a 375 degree oven about 10 minutes. Cool about 1 minute before removing to a wire rack. Makes 48.

Oatmeal Chocolate Chip cookies

- 1 $^1/_2$ cups chocolate chips
- 6 cups all-purpose flour
- 3 teaspoons baking powder
- 1 teaspoon salt
- 1 teaspoon ground nutmeg
- 1 teaspoon ground cinnamon
- 1 $^1/_2$ cups shortening
- 3 cups white sugar
- 2 cups quick cooking oats
- 3 teaspoons baking soda
- 1 cup buttermilk
- $^1/_2$ cup dark molasses
- 4 eggs

S ift flour, baking powder, salt, nutmeg, and cinnamon into a very large bowl. Cut in shortening using a pastry blender until mixture forms fine crumbs.

Add ground chocolate chips, sugar, and oats. Mix well. Dissolve baking soda in buttermilk in small bowl. Add molasses and 3 of the eggs, and beat with rotary beater until blended. Add to flour mixture, and mix well with spoon.

Drop by heaping tablespoons about 3 inches apart on greased baking sheets. Flatten each with floured bottom of a drinking glass. Beat 1 egg in a bowl until blended. Brush tops of cookies with egg. Bake at 375 degrees F (190 degrees C) for 8 to 10 minutes or until golden brown.